D A WALMSLEY

The Twelve

Chapter 1

From out of the darkness and into the yellow glow of a street light steps the figure of a man. The dim light mixes with a fine drizzle and hangs in the air, creating a haunting mist. The figure stops, looking around at the terraced houses that make up this long narrow street, then slips back into the shadows, only his footsteps betraying his presence.

He is not alone; another set of footsteps can now be heard, quicker, lighter, more urgent. A curtain twitches, exposing a yellow glint of light, followed by a stifled cry. The figure of a young man is standing at the gate, a gun in his hand.

Through the mist the first man approaches. He is taller, broader; he too carries a weapon. He nods and goes through the gate to the door, flicking a half smoked cigarette away before banging on the door with a black gloved hand.

"Stay here and shoot anything that tries to escape."

"OK Boss. Don't you just love nights like these?"

"I like it when people pay what they owe!"

"I like it when they don't!"

For the residents of Zaricus Street, the presence of Matthew Levi and Dave Milo means one thing; trouble. When they turn up, it's time to lock the door, turn off the lights and pray it's not you they are coming for. For the men, this is just another night, another call.

The light suddenly goes out, but it's too late. He bangs on the door again, this time louder. Still nothing, only the sound of a siren in the distance.

Matthew checks the door handle, to see if it's unlocked. It's surprising how many times he can go straight in. This time no such luck. He steps back and points his Jericho semi automatic at the lock.

"Please, let me boss." says Milo, who then raises his own huge Desert Eagle hand gun.

Matthew nods and stands back as Milo unloads two rounds at the door. The noise is so loud it sets off several car alarms but before the noise has faded Matthew's foot smashes open the door.

Stepping inside, he checks for the light switch, which should be to his left; it is. He flicks it... nothing happens. Great! He takes a small flash light from his coat pocket, very useful in this kind of work. The narrow beam of light scans the hallway.

"Come on Danny, I know you're in here."

There is no answer.

With Milo watching the entrance and the stairs, Matthew decides to check out the downstairs first and finds a light switch for the living room. This time, there is light.

The room is sparsely furnished, a portable TV sits in the corner and there's a well worn sofa and chair in the middle of the room. Children's toys are scattered about, nothing of value. He moves through to the kitchen where he hears some scratching followed by a whimper. He brings his flash light up to the gun. Another whimper. The torchlight shines across the room. In a dark corner two sets of eyes stare back at him.

One is a little girl, her back pressed against the wall. She is holding tight to what appears to be a small spaniel puppy. Shining the light in their faces, he slowly bends down to their level.

"Where's your daddy?"

The little girl doesn't answer.

"Come here. Why don't you show me where he's hiding?"

He reaches in to grab hold of her but as he does she bites his hand.

"Ow, you little bitch!"

He shines the torch into her eyes. She covers her face with her hands, letting go of the dog which runs into the living room.

"If you do that again I'll shoot you, understand?"

This time he pulls her out quickly and forcefully and drags her back though the living room. She squirms and wriggles, trying to escape.

"How long are we going to do this Danny?" he shouts from the bottom of the stairs.

"Remember the good old days, when you always paid me. Remember all the discounts I've given you? How many others would do that, eh Danny? None, that's how many. So why are you hiding? You've betrayed me Danny boy, and now I want my money."

He nods to Milo and they both start to slowly climb the stairs.

"I'm going to give you a choice; either you come out and give me my money or your little girl here gets a 9mm through her little skull, understand?"

A woman screams as Matthew and Milo make their way upstairs. They are halfway up when a light is snapped on and a small scruffy man steps forward at the top of the staircase. He has both his arms in the air and is shaking.

"Good choice Danny. Now get me my money."

"OK OK, please don't hurt her.... please."

The screaming is coming from the bathroom. "Don't hurt her, my baby, my baby," pleads the woman.

Matthew points his gun at Danny, and when he gets to the top of the stairs he releases the little girl. She runs to her sobbing mother, who along with another three children are huddled together in the bathroom. Milo follows and begins checking the rest of the upstairs.

"This is all I have, it's everything." Scrambling in his pockets Danny pulls out a rolled up wad of old notes. He shakes as he thrusts them at Matthew.

"I just need more t...time, honest."

Matthew brings his face close to Danny and shouts at him, "You've had plenty of time, and this is all you can manage?"

He presses the gun hard against Danny's head.

"Please no, please no, it's been a bad month, I'll get the rest, I promise I'll get the rest."

It's a promise Matthew has heard thousands of times before and one to which he has become immune. Looking around he knows Danny can't pay. Why do these people have so many children if they can't provide for them.

Matthew releases the pressure from the gun, and steps back. Danny sighs.

"Anything?" Matthew asks Milo.

"Nothing."

Matthew raises his gun again at Danny.

"Boss, come on, have a heart. It's my favourite part of the job."

"Fine, have your fun." Matthew heads back downstairs as three shots ring out.

At the door Matthew takes out his notebook and scribbles *Paid* next to Danny's name.

"Who's next?" asks Milo.

"I think we'll call it a night" says Matthew.

"Good, I've got something personal to take care of." Milo points his key remote towards a black BMW, which flashes its indicators in response.

For Dave Milo, being in the debt collecting business has been very rewarding. His brand new BMW is proof of that, but as with anything there can be downsides. Bullet holes and a smashed rear side-window are the reality of this very violent occupation. Matthew is always stressing, "Dead men don't pay up, but a frightened one pays on time." In most cases this is true, but a desperate man can be a dangerous man. The number of dead collectors testifies to that, not that it worries Dave. In fact he loves it; that feeling he gets when pulling the trigger of his Desert Eagle. The smell, the sound; the power that it gives.

The few cars on the roads keep well away from the 2.5 litres of BMW engine, giving the 192 horses under the bonnet a serious workout. Within minutes Dave gets across the city, the rows of terraced houses giving way to larger semis. Slowing down he checks to see if he's close, squinting to read the house numbers... no it's too dark. He drives on for a couple of hundred yards then parks.

With just a street name and vehicle type, getting the right house is a long shot. A blue Audi is not easy to pick out in the dark. He walks up the street checking all the cars; crosses over and walks back down. Just as he's about to leave, he

5

hears voices, one male, one female, a few doors away. His first reaction is to go for his gun, fearing he's been spotted. But then more out of curiosity he goes over to have a look, making sure not to be seen. A girl is standing at a half-open door saying goodbye. A guy inside tries to get her to stay longer. As Dave stares, it appears the man wins, the girl steps back inside and the door closes. Through the glass topped door with the hall light behind them the couple's silhouettes merge as they kiss each other.

"Lucky bastard" Dave whispers to himself.

As he turns to go, he notices a car parked on the drive behind a silver Ford Fiesta. It is a dark Blue Audi. He looks again at the couple. Is this the guy he's looking for? Should he call out and see if there's a response? But that would cost him the advantage. Then the couple separate and the outline of each of them is clearly seen. Yeah, it's him alright.

Dave's heartbeat quickens and adrenalin surges through his body. He checks that the clip in his 9mm is full, and then from a shoulder holster produces another piece, flicking off the safety as he moves onto the drive.

"Revenge is so sweet," he says, before pointing both weapons at the couple and opening fire with both guns simultaneously. The noise is so loud with each explosion and flash that to Dave it's like slow-motion. His ears pick up the smallest of noises: the glass smashing, the hall-light popping from a hit, the sound of the casings hitting the Fiesta next to him. He laughs as one after another the bullets smash through door and flesh. He's not concerned that the girl is innocent; she is mere collateral damage and he is enjoying this way too much to care about her. He only stops when both clips are empty. Now it's time to get the hell out of here.

Chapter 2

As the early morning mist begins to lift over the sea of Galilee and the dawn chorus starts to find its voice, for some it's the end to a long, hard night's work. One by one fishing trawlers, their lights blazing, return to the harbour.

The beeping sound of an articulated lorry with the words CATCH OF THE DAY written on its side reverses slowly along the quayside, its hydraulic brakes swooshing as it comes to a stop. The sounds of a busy harbour play like a symphony, the natural and man-made all interwoven: waves splashing against the wall, diesel engines rattling, seagulls singing, men shouting. Fishermen begin unloading their catch onto the quayside and several men place the fish into trays and pack them in ice. They are then loaded onto the lorry using a forklift truck. Within hours today's catch will be in the shops and supermarkets all across the country.

Above all the noise one voice stands out, a loud booming baritone shouting at the last of the trawlers pulling up alongside the quay, "COME ON, HURRY UP." Simon Peter, his stature as big and broad as his voice, is having a bad morning. This is because he had a bad night; the number of fish caught were well below his forecast. To anyone else it would still be a good night's work, but for Simon Peter who had predicted record results, things are about to get a whole lot worse.

On the boat pulling in alongside Simon Peter are two brothers, James and John. James, a younger version of Simon Peter, appears as fresh and alert as when he first set off, ten hours ago.

"How's he look?" asks John, peering out of the cab.

"Miserable." replies James.

"Yes, I bet we've beaten the big man." He starts to sing "*Oh what a night, the fish were biting La la la la la.*" He does a little dance.

On the quay those within earshot all laugh. Simon Peter swears under his breath.

"Sorry, what was that?" James shouts sarcastically.

"I said get them weighed before you start celebrating" snaps Simon Peter, who turns away and shouts at two workers to help unload, "come on don't just stand there."

As the men start to bring the fish ashore, Simon Peter looks over the amounts for himself and sighs.

Another fisherman steps from the trawler. He is Andrew, Simon Peter's younger brother who has been with James and John all night. He pats Simon Peter on the back before saying, "look on the bright side; more fish more profit, and hey you didn't have to spend all night listening to those two argue." He helps with a heavy crate being lowered from the boat to the ground. Last off the boat is John. He jumps down and studies the fish with James, double checking the numbers and weights. They don't want there to be a mistake and Simon Peter to wriggle out of his bet and not give them a day off.

"Oh I'm gonna enjoy that lie in," James says, trying to wind Simon Peter up.

"You haven't forgotten what you're doing later have you?"

says Simon Peter, a knowing smile poking out from his beard.

Quite clearly they have. Simon Peter continues, now unable to contain his delight. "Your father said I should remind you both about your community service, so don't go home just yet."

James and John both sigh. "I can't believe we've got that to do," moans John.

James turns to Andrew and asks "Hey Andy, any ideas how we can get out of the community thing we've to do?"

"Ha, is that today? Well, you could pay the fine instead" laughs Andrew.

Both give him a *please be serious look*. Andrew adds, "try to mention the lowest fresh-water lake in the world, and... don't forget the net."

"Oh cheers Andy, big help," says John.

As part of the drive to extol the virtues of Capernaum to a wider public, the Tourist Board runs tours of the local beauty spots, showing off the natural wonders of the region and its long history. There has been fishing on the Sea of Galilee for thousands of years and they thought it would be a good idea to demonstrate how fish used to be caught before they turned to the more modern trawling method. James and John were the only two they could get. The brothers are doing this as part of their community service after they damaged the newly built harbour wall when they rammed into it with their trawler.

"You don't know what you're doing."

"I do, just shut up."

"You're not even holding it right, let me have I go."

Surrounded by a group of people, James pulls back his arm and is about to throw the net into the sea. "Try bending your knees" John shouts to his brother. James stops mid throw and turns to John. "Will you shut up, I know what I'm doing, get on with the introduction."

"Err...hello, this is Lake Galilee, the world's lowest fresh-water lake 680ft below sea level. It is roughly 13 x 7 miles with an area of 90sq miles and has a maximum depth of 150ft. It is fed by the river Jordan, flowing from Mount Hermon in the north." John reads from a crumpled up piece of paper, points north " ...and to the Dead Sea in the south," he turns and points south. "Now James is gonna show you how they used to fish in the olden days before electricity and stuff."

James limbers up and does a few arm stretches before carefully picking up the prepared net. It is circular and has small weights set at regular intervals around its perimeter. The idea being by getting it to spread out and land flat on the water, the weights sink to the bottom and then an attached cord is pulled tight trapping any fish that have been covered. He swings his arms a few times and throws the net. It opens up perfectly, spinning as it does, a bit like when you skim a stone across the water; the trick is the quick flick at the end of the throw. The problem is that James has let go a little too early. Instead of landing in the sea it goes into the air and lands perfectly... over John, entangling him like a fly caught in a spider's web. Quickly James pulls the cord, turns to the crowd and with a big grin exclaims, "and that's how you catch a shrimp!"

The crowd thinking this is all part of the demonstration, laugh and applaud. James takes a bow, and moves towards John offering to help release him. The crowd, a foreign coach party, take photos of the brothers. James flexes his muscles at a couple of giggling teenage girls. John, red with embarrassment and struggling to escape the net, mumbles "you did that on purpose."

James laughs, saying "did you say something?" Then, seeing his brother's discomfort, adds "wow, how red are you?"

Within the crowd a couple of tour guides watch, big smiles across their faces as they think of the large tips they'll receive later if this continues.

John frees himself, throwing the net to the ground. James, loving the attention, and the excitement of performing, becomes a bit too over confident as he announces "my beetroot faced assistant here will now fold the net." He turns to John, "properly this time please," getting more laughs from the crowd. "Then I'll... "

"I'm not your assistant."

"What?"

John, angry and embarrassed, says again "I'm not your assistant, it's my turn."

James gives him a long stare, not wanting a scene, but not prepared to give up the spotlight. He puts on his *I'm older, do as I say voice*, "don't be silly, now pass me the net." John can't stand James when he does that; thinks he can push me around does he, just because he's a couple of years older? James stands waiting impatiently, "come on."

John, the anger building up, slowly bends down, picks up the net and hurls it as hard as he can towards James, the weights striking into his body and rocking him backwards making him stumble. John rushes towards James and dives forward, rugby tackling him. It sends them into the cold sea and they land with an almighty splash. The crowd a moment earlier laughing, now stare in disbelief, as the two young men punch and wrestle each other in the shallow waters of the lake. Arms flail and legs kick as John, then James try to get the upper hand.

It takes Officer Michaels all his strength to break up the two fishermen, but once John has looked in the Officer's eyes and realised who it is he calms down. He and James allow themselves to be escorted back to the office to face their father.

When they arrive at Zebedee and Sons Fishing Company, Officer Michaels knocks once and pushes both lads inside.

Their father who is talking on the phone waves them in. "Okay, yes I understand, thanks for doing it so quickly." He looks up to see his two sons standing there dripping wet, covered in cuts and bruises. He shakes his head.

"Look I'll have to go, okay mate, cheers," he puts the phone down.

"Please tell me this isn't as bad as it looks?"

Michael's been here on more than one occasion and has got to know Zebedee and the boys very well. "Well, they're lucky the tour guide didn't want any trouble." Turning to James and John, "try to control yourselves or next time I'll have no choice but to charge you both."

Zebedee thanks him, "go see Simon Peter, he'll fix you up with something as a thank you."

Michaels leaves the office and closes the door.

John breathes a heavy sigh and braces himself for what is to come next.

"I have been a fisherman all my life, as was my father. The last few years have been the best I have ever known, the business going from strength to strength. Yet God chastens me so I don't forget how blessed I have become."

"So, you would say we are a gift from God," says James.

"You know how hard it was when you two were children, when the country was in a seemingly endless recession."

Here we go, this again, John sighs. Every time something happens they have to listen to their father go on and on about the past.

"We used to be a proud country, a prosperous nation. Now we are broke and under the control of others."

John and James know the story backwards and feel annoyed that their generation has to suffer for the mistakes of others. Though their father is doing okay, even employing several fisherman and owning a growing fleet of trawlers, John has seen how his father has to grease palms and suck up to foreigners just to get fishing rights to the lake that their family has fished for generations.

Zebedee gets up from his seat and goes over to a photo of himself next to a fishing boat. "They were hard times, I had to work alone, in seas so rough that I thought this little boat would be my tomb. I would go days never seeing your mother."

"Lucky you," whispers James. John laughs.

... "and now you two are the ones trying to put me in an early grave." He raises his voice, "I don't know what to do with you both. I just don't. At this rate you're gonna bankrupt us all."

Blood trickles down from John's nose, he sniffs then wipes it with the back of his hand and shows it to James. "You've bust mi nose, I don't believe it."

James retaliates, "well you gave me a black eye, I can feel it swelling up already."

"Will you both shut up" Zebedee shouts.

Under his breath, James adds, "It's not my fault, he started it."

"I started it?" John responds. "You deliberately made me look stupid."

James counters in a much louder voice. "You don't need me to make you look stupid, you do that all by yourself."

Zebedee just shakes his head. Calmly he asks, "finished?" They both nod. "Good, because I'm not bothered who started it, I've just got off the phone with the boatyard," he pauses, before adding "you did three grands worth of damage."

"We're insured" James points out.

"Oh yes, insurance, thank you for reminding me James. As you say we are insured but thanks to you two we pay the highest premiums of any and I mean any, fishing business in the country. Did you hear that? - In the country! I've had a word with Simon Peter and the next time and I'm guessing there will be, it's coming out of your wages, OK?" Both lads nod. Zebedee just looks at them, shaking his head. His attention is drawn to James' footwear.

"Are those your brand new trainers? Who in their right mind goes fishing in brand new trainers. Where are your work boots?"

"I dunno, I can't find them."

John looks away trying to hide a smile, but James notices. "You hid them didn't you, I knew I put them by the door, you little..." James aims a punch at John who ducks and pushes him away. John grabs James' arm and they wrestle with each other before losing their balance and fall forward just missing their father's desk and hitting the hard wooden floor.

Zebedee exclaims "Oh for the love of God!"

Chapter 3

A few days later Matthew is sitting in his office. From a window he can see the hills on the other side of the lake. A shepherd leads his sheep as the setting sun turns the green hills into golden orange. Matthew has sat watching this scene many times, daydreaming about what the life of a shepherd would be like: peaceful, quiet, only you and your thirty-nine sheep and five goats for company. (He counts them regularly to make sure they're all there.) One of Matthews earliest memories as a child is of Uncle Eli bent over an old desk counting piles of money. It was in those seemingly innocent years that he swore one day he too would become that rich. Twenty five years later Matthew Levi sits at the same desk in his own office of Levi and Associates. Uncle Eli wouldn't recognise Capernaum now but he would have been proud of his nephew. Since Matthew took over, profits have grown year on year and as Capernaum grows so does the opportunity to extract more taxes in the form of Excise Duties. Not that Matthew gets to count much of it these days. Most is done through electronic transactions and the cash that is collected is counted by machines; it's not the same.

Raised voices interrupt his thoughts.

"The boss only asks for what he's entitled to, and this is

how you repay his kindness."

"Kindness, you call pointing a gun at us kindness?"

Two members of staff, checking the toll booths have brought a young couple into the office and reported to Dave Milo.

"This couple were attempting to drive through the nothing to declare lane. A spot check revealed they were importing two hundred white roses."

Milo pats them down for weapons, and takes his wallet and her handbag.

"The roses are for our wedding," pleads the man.

"Importing into Galilee is taxable, you know that."

"Even for personal use?"

"Especially for personal use."

Milo empties the wallet and bag onto a counter. The only thing of interest is an expired credit card. He slides it across a glass partition on the counter to a woman on the other side who swipes it along a card reader. After a few seconds she shakes her head.

"You can't pay. What a surprise."

Now Milo and the two security guards gather round the couple like a pack of animals. Milo strokes the cheek of the young woman, who flinches and pulls away. "So darling, tell me how you paid for the flowers?" asks Milo.

"Cash," replies the man.

Milo glares at him, "I'm not talking to you."

His focus returns to the woman, he looks her up and down and noticing her engagement ring, he grabs her hand. She immediately pulls it away.

"Not her ring, that was my mother's," says the man.

Milo punches the man in the stomach, knocking him to the

ground, only to be spat upon by the woman.

"You bitch," he raises his hand to hit her.

"That's enough." Matthew comes out of his office.

"These two..." Milo starts to explain.

"I heard."

Matthew helps the man get to his feet, "Let me congratulate you on winning the hand of this beautiful woman. I believe marriage is a wonderful thing, two people holding each other close." He takes hold of the woman and pulls her slender body close to his, "kissing," he leans forward and kisses her, first on her cheek and them gently on the lips. She knows who he is, everybody knows who he is, so she closes her eyes and doesn't resist, He presses firmer and surprisingly finds a more than willing recipient. It's the kind of kiss her fiancé has only dreamed of, a kiss that says more than I'm only doing this because I know what you are capable of.

"What the? hey, get off her." the man splutters.

Without stopping Matthew takes his gun from his belt and points it at the man. Milo and the other members of staff all laugh, and encourage their boss. "Go on boss, give her one for me."

Only now does the woman pull away, but Matthew's arm prevents her and he forces another kiss before relinquishing his grasp.

"Take half their flowers and let 'em go," he says to Milo, then to the couple, "If either of you can't pay me again you know the penalty. I will come looking for you and I will hurt you."

Behind the counter is the main office. Bullet proof windows let in the morning light and from here you can see along all the six lanes of toll booths, including the commercials only lane. When Matthew enters, his secretary shakes her head at him. He winks, checking his mouth for lipstick residue. A young man is at a desk feeding papers into a shredder.

"Great party last night boss," says James Alphaeus.

"As always. Hope you're not too hungover this morning."

"I can take it boss."

"Good to hear, and what did I tell you Alphie, I said those girls would take a shine to you."

Everyone took a shine to him, he was a good kid. If he worked hard like he himself had done, no reason why Alphie couldn't make it in this business one day.

Matthew's mind once again thinks of Uncle Eli. He knows why, for now he is the same age as Eli was when he died, stabbed in the back as he collected the tolls. "Grab a vest and we'll work the commercials for a bit," he tells Alphie.

A sign on the door reminds staff that bullet and stab proof vests must be worn outside at all times. Alphie sighs, "can I at least get one that fits, they're all too big?"

"Fine, order one later, but you must wear one now. Remember, one of the hazards of this occupation is people want to kill you."

The commercial lane splits into two. One is a weighbridge where lorries pay by their weight, regardless of what they carry. Matthew has found this speeds things up considerably and payment, once companies have set up an account, is done all electronically. The other lane is used for spot checks. As they go towards it, Alphie is still fiddling with his vest. Matthew recognises the man stepping down from a white transit van emblazoned with the words Chorazin Honda that has just pulled up. The driver avoids eye contact and goes to the back of the van. Alphie follows him and when the driver pauses to light a cigarette Alphie reaches for the door handle. Matthew puts an arm out, stopping his young apprentice.

"We never open any door or boot ourselves. Always make the owners do that, just in case."

The driver sighs and opens the door. The back of the van is full of air con units.

"You can close up and drive onto the weighbridge" says Matthew, knowing that they weigh a tonne, that's why the man has stopped here. He'd been hoping to pay per unit rather than weight. The driver swears under his breath.

Next to enter the weighbridge is a beat up, rusting 7.5 tonne lorry. But instead of slowing down, the driver accelerates towards the commercial lane barrier. There is a crunching of gears and the lorry swerves slightly from side to side, the driver trying to position it in the middle of the lane. Matthew and Alphie have to dive out of the way as it passes them and smashes through the barrier sending pieces of wood and metal in all directions. It immediately triggers sirens and flashing lights. A split second later...POP, POP...POP, POP. Spikes shoot up from the ground puncturing all four tyres. The driver, as if he was expecting that to happen, jumps out and makes a run for it. Matthew, who managed to stay on his feet, takes out his gun and starts shooting at the driver, but he's too far away. The driver gets in to a waiting car and with screeching tyres it speeds away. Milo and the other staff scramble out of the office door, guns in hand to fire at the car, then pepper the lorry full of bullets, though more out of anger than anything.

By now all the traffic has stopped and is starting to back up. This annoys Matthew, people hate paying to get into the city as it is, he doesn't want to add to their anger by them having to queue.

"Get it moved, quick," he says to two of the staff. "Milo, come on let's sweep the area."

The two men now high on adrenalin and guns raised, move through the stationary cars, scanning for anyone else intent on trouble.

"Come on, keep moving," Matthew yells to no car in-particular.

A driver at the front of one queue fumbles his cash, missing the big metallic bucket. Others behind hit their horns as the driver, who is now aware he's causing a hold up, desperately searches for more spare change. Matthew watches, making sure it isn't anything more sinister. The driver finally finds more change and the barrier springs up. Matthew shakes his head. Why are drivers of old cars such pricks?

When he and Milo are satisfied there is no more danger, they begin to head over to the lorry, which has been towed to a safe zone, away from the roads and buildings and is just about to be checked over. Alphie unbolts the back doors and pulls the handle down...

"NO," shout Matthew and Milo simultaneously.

Chapter 4

"People need to find a cause, something to believe in, otherwise life can have no real meaning, just a long slow walk to nothingville. We have a cause, we have a goal and that goal takes back our country."

The speaker, Caleb G Barnabas, gets a round of applause from the three hundred strong crowd. "We have let this go on far too long, happy to take the mighty Euro in exchange for our very sovereignty. We have helped line the pockets of those thieving collectors and vile leaders."

The crowd is getting excited, shouting and clapping as Caleb's voice gets louder and louder.

Standing in the wings at the side of the stage are Simon and Flatpack. They are the special guests and are waiting for Caleb to finish his speech, which has turned into more of a call to arms. A technician checks their handheld microphones and whispers some instructions.

"What did he say?" Simon asks.

"He said Caleb will introduce us when he's finished his speech and everything's all set upstairs on the desk."

"Good, but I still think we should have brought Big Mike, I don't trust just anybody to do my sound." Simon's complaining is drowned out by more cheering and clapping.

Caleb's on a roll now..."My message to Rome is leave us now or leave in a coffin. We don't want your stinking Euro, we don't want your high taxes and your corrupt leaders."

Simon and Flatpack join in the cheering.

"I've had enough, and I'll promise you this, I won't rest 'til every one of them has had a visit from an assassin's knife."

With those words still ringing round the auditorium, the lights suddenly go out, plunging the whole place into blackness.

"We're not on now are we? I thought there was more," Simon takes a deep breath and waits for the music to start. Suddenly doors burst open and there are flashes of light; dozens of police rush in.

"Armed police, everybody get down."

This causes people to panic, others scream aloud, some try to get out and scramble over seats.

From the stage Caleb shouts "Israel for ever!" as he is gunned down. The shots start the crowd stampeding blindly towards what they hope are the exits, but there is nowhere to go, they are surrounded.

At the first sound of trouble Simon had instinctively ducked down and grabbed for his knife. He had been on edge all night so it wasn't much of a surprise. At least two officers had rushed passed him but the fact that he was ignored meant they were probably after Caleb. The shots did surprise him and he ran in what he thought was the direction of the nearest exit but slammed into a wall and as he stumbled around he fell down the steps at the side of the stage.

"Simon, you there? You OK? " Flatpack shouts.

"Yeah, forgot about the steps."

Fumbling around in the darkness, Simon carefully makes

his way to where he thinks Flatpack is.

"Flatpack."

"Simon," shouts Flatpack from about two feet away, startling Simon who is not expecting him to be so close.

They both slowly make their way along a corridor, using the wall for guidance. They turn a corner and a voice shouts "freeze, don't move." Simon slips his knife up his sleeve, hoping it wasn't seen.

"Now, slowly move forward," the voice shouts.

Then Simon feels an arm grab him and he is dragged down the corridor. Still in complete darkness he can hear Flatpack struggling with someone behind him, then a thud.

"Bastards," Flatpack shouts.

As they near the exit, the red and blue flashing lights from the police cars begin to penetrate into the long corridor. When they finally reach the door Simon is released from the man's grip and is pushed out by the point of a rifle forced into his back. Now for the first time he can see his captors. With their black uniforms, body armour and helmets they look a fearsome sight. He looks around, desperate to escape but the police appear to be everywhere. They certainly have taken this meeting very seriously.

"Over there," his captor says, jabbing the gun once more into his back and ushering him towards a cordoned off area surrounded by more police, all holding rifles.

"You can't do this to me, I know my rights, this is assault," Flatpack yells.

Simon looks round to see his friend has blood running down his face and is still in the grip of an officer.

They are both herded into the cordon with all the others. A voice comes over a megaphone.

"Stay calm, if anyone tries to escape they will be shot."

More and more people are being led out of the venue and the cordon starts to grow. Everyone looks scared, some are visibly shaking. Simon stands on tiptoe to see what's happening, "it looks like they are being taken to a tent and I bet they are being searched."

From the tent comes shouting and officers rush over. The voices are muffled but from the reaction of the police they've found a weapon.

"You still packing?" Flatpack asks Simon.

"Shit yeah Steve, you?"

"Still got both, we can *not* get searched."

"Tell me something I don't know!"

"We could plant them on someone else," Flatpack whispers.

"Yeah, or drop them on the ground," Simon replies.

Another group goes, and everyone moves forwards a few feet. A young man stares at Flatpack and glances across at Simon. He nods at them. The last thing they want to happen is that they get recognised, and the lad won't stop looking.

"Will you stop staring."

The lad is surprised and answers.

"What, me?"

"Yes, you!"

Simon whispers " You okay Steve? it's only a kid."

Flatpack, getting more and more agitated and fidgeting, ignores Simon, instead turns round and shouts at a woman behind him.

"Stop, shoving, bitch."

The woman, starts to shake and her eyes fill up with tears.

Simon grabs Flatpack, by the arm, "mate, calm down."

Flatpack pulls away, "get off me. Will everyone stop

pushing!"

An officer tells him to be quiet, and someone in the crowd near to Simon shouts to the officer "he's claustrophobic."

Simon asks "are you really?"

Flatpack doesn't hear the question, he's starting to panic. He pushes and shoves everybody and anyone around him, including Simon. All this has caught the attention of a senior officer, who allows the cordon to be extended giving everybody more room. Simon fears if Flatpack doesn't calm down they'll take him out to one side and they will be sure to search him. If they find his guns when he's this unstable anything could happen, what should he do? Help him hide in the crowd, maybe push a bit further back to buy some more time. Should he attempt to go with him and risk getting searched? If he drops them, will someone pick them up, stress can make people do stupid things. All the questions race around his head, each one has the same outcome, they're in the shit! Oh, why did they have to come to this meeting? Caleb has this reputation for threatening violence, why get dragged into it. Better to operate in secret, in the relative safety of Capernaum.

Suddenly a single gunshot is heard from inside the venue followed by a volley of return fire. At once all the police radios come to life, "Man down, man down."

Simon watches as half the officers run back into the venue. When word gets back that an officer has been shot dead by someone hiding inside, a few people cheer. This gives others the confidence to join in.

"Israel, Israel," they shout.

When an officer strikes one of those chanting with his rifle, others try to fight back. Officers guarding the cordon rush over. The distraction couldn't have been planned any better. Simon, Flatpack and half a dozen others all take the opportunity to duck under the cordon and make a run for it.

"Behind that," points Flatpack to a police car.

The car is twenty feet away. They run as fast as they can, diving behind it. Flatpack gets his gun out ready to return any fire.

"Steve, what the?... put that away, they'll kill us for sure if they see that."

Flatpack nods and puts it back inside his belt. "Now where?"

"The wall."

With the car park surrounded by a five foot high stone wall and police moving about, they are not safe yet, but they are away from the lights; the night has come to their advantage. Simon, keeping as low as he can, runs over to the wall. He knows that if they get spotted they will be shot at. This makes him run as fast as he can, praying they won't be seen. He scrambles over the wall, landing on his backside. It hurts, but it's nothing to the relief he's feeling. A second later Flatpack follows him over, landing on his feet. Shots ring out - others may not have been so lucky.

"Let's get out of here."

When they'd arrived there was nowhere to park so Flatpack had to leave the car down a side street, and he'd moaned about it all evening, but he's not complaining now!

"The car is on the other side of the theatre. Let's take a long way round to it, and get away from this place."

They run as fast as they can, until neither can run any further.

"Wow, that hurts," says Flatpack, holding his chest and

breathing heavily.

They rest awhile, the sounds of sirens are distant now. After half an hour they walk back towards the car, constantly checking for police. Neither says a word. Simon thinks how lucky they just were. One wrong move and he could have easily ended up...he tries to put it out of his mind, no, today just wasn't our day to die. He then thinks about Flatpack, all the years he's known him, he never knew he was claustrophobic, I guess it never came up. They carry on walking in silence, until Simon can't keep it in any longer.

"What happened to you back there?"

Flatpack doesn't speak.

"Shit, you really freaked out, I seriously thought you'd lost it."

There is silence for several seconds before Flatpack answers, "I don't know what happened, I've never felt like that before, must have been the lights or something."

When they finally get back to Flatpack's black Jaguar all is quiet. They get in and head back to Capernaum. What had started out as a gig, albeit an independence rally, had turned into a whole lot more. What has happened to their country, their Israel?

Simon finally fell asleep at around four am. The whole night kept replaying in his head, over and over; he couldn't let it go. He realised he needed some help and a bottle of his favourite drink. Hennessey Cognac finally sent him into unconsciousness.

He was woken at quarter past seven by what sounded like a fire alarm. Actually it was only his phone. Oh shut up, please shut up. It keeps ringing. He reaches across to the bedside table and answers.

"Go away!" He shouts at the caller, and throws the phone across the room.

A few minutes later it starts ringing again. Simon puts his pillow over his throbbing head in the vain hope of blocking out the sound.

The longer he lies awake, the stronger the urge to pee, and that means he will have to get up. He feels so rough that it crosses his mind just to do it there and then and let his cleaning lady sort out the mess, but that would mean lying in it, not such a good idea. He goes to his en-suite bathroom and while he's there he takes some painkillers. He's just crawling back into bed when once again the phone starts to ring. "Damn it." With his half open eyes he goes to the corner of the room where he threw it. He bends down and picks it up.

"This better be important."

"I think it is," Flatpack answers.

"Oh, it's you Steve, what's up?"

"Yesterday, that's what up, look I've had some ideas, I'll be round in about an hour."

"Eh, No."

"You okay?"

"I had a bit to drink when I got back, I finished off a bottle of Hennessey."

Flatpack laughs, "I'll let you sleep it off, I'll be round later."

"Yeah, good."

Simon goes back to bed.

When he wakes it's late in the afternoon, and after a shower and some toast he feels a lot better. His apartment, while still in the Neziah estate, is on the better side of the valley, away from the rougher centre, but close enough for its tenants to still feel one of the people. It's a dream of the young in Neziah to move on to the hills. It says you have made it, that even the poor can become somebody. Simon sees himself as a role model to the youngsters and if that means encouraging them to stand up and fight the Government, so what! The fact that most of his record sales tend to come from rebellious middle-class teenagers makes him laugh, and to some extent pleased. At least they can afford it, and maybe they might believe the message. The Government thinks so, or why would they do last night's raid. He gets himself a coffee and sits on his brown leather suite. From the living room window he has views of the lake and the hills on the other side of the valley; as the evening sun streams in, he closes his eyes.

Not for the first time today he is interrupted, this time it's the door bell. He lets Flatpack in and goes back to sit in the sunshine.

"Have you had the news on?" Flatpack asks.

Simon shakes his head.

"Well, I think you might want to see it."

Simon looks round for the remote and then turns on the large TV. Flatpack gets impatient as Simon, not in any rush, flicks through the channels.

"Give it here," he grabs the remote and puts the news channel on.

There is a live feed outside the theatre in Jericho. A woman reporter is interviewing an elderly man who lives opposite. He is telling her what he saw and heard, which doesn't appear to be much. He saw police cars and vans, that's it. Along the bottom of the screen the ticker scrolls along with the latest updates. Simon watches as the ticker reveals the words: two men were..., his heart misses a beat, and his brain finishes the sentence ...seen running away. He can picture the photofits with help from the people in the crowd, his face will be all over the country and he braces himself for the inevitable. ...shot dead, police confirm. He lets out the biggest sigh, and is visibly shaken.

"Oh shit, I thought...Oh shit."

"That's exactly how I felt the first time I saw it," Flatpack laughs.

"You could have just told me, I nearly had a heart attack!"

They both sit and watch the report. It explains how the police had a tip-off that Caleb G Barnabas would be speaking at the rally organised by the Independence League of Israel (ILI). It says that Caleb was wanted by the police for the murder of a foreign politician working for the Union and that he was considered a threat to national security. The most interesting thing though is what it doesn't say. It doesn't mention anything about the police storming the building, or the way they treated those inside, and the use of several police is some way off the fifty or sixty that were actually there.

"Looks like they were really only after Caleb," Flatpack points out.

"So you're saying we were just in the wrong place at the wrong time,"

"Yeah, bad luck, that's all."

Simon gets angry "bad luck, Steve get real, back luck would be if we'd gone to the theatre to see Snow White and the Seven Dwarfs, that would have been bad luck."

Flatpack smiles "Hey, that's good, mind if I use it in something?"

"Sure, all your best lines come from me anyway."

On the TV they are showing a picture of the politician that Caleb killed. Flatpack points to it.

"You see, that was Caleb's problem, he was too high profile, the Government had no choice but to react. I'll tell you something else... how come you haven't offered me a drink?"

"You know where the kitchen is, get one yourself!"

Flatpack does, and while he's in the kitchen decides he's hungry and looks in the fridge. Butter, beer and milk.

"Flatpack comes back in with a bottle of Goldstar lager."

"That'd better not be the last one."

"What are you moaning about, I thought you had a hang-over?"

"Had! I had one."

"In that case," says Flatpack "let's go down the Angels."

From the apartment to the Angels it would only be a short walk downhill, but they take Flatpacks car anyway, which he drives while drinking his beer. Simon notices it takes longer for Flatpack to reverse into the space than it would have taken him to walk there and back. It might have been to do with the fact that he did it while holding the bottle, but more likely he's only just got his new Jag and is extra careful.

Inside the club they go to their favourite table, and both order burger, fries, and more bottles of Goldstar.

Toothless is in there and wanders over.

"*Thup guyths*"

"You heard about Jericho? Simon asks.

"*Yeth, you guyths okay?*"

"Fine."

"*Tuth on Caleb. Thucking polieth.*"

From out of his pocket Simon takes out a large roll of notes and peels off a tenner, handing it to Toothless.

"Get a round in for you and your mates."

"*Cheerth Thimon.*"

Simon peels off another note and sits staring at it. He hates these things, he hates everything they stand for. He hates the colours, the fact that they look like toy money. Worst of all is the picture; a building in Rome. The Government had promised to have pictures of Israel on them, but like everything else these people promise, it never happens.

"We need to do something," says Flatpack.

"Like what?"

"I don't know, something that people can see, a statement."

Simon takes out his cigarette lighter and holds the note above it. Flatpack stops him.

"I don't think so, you can buy beers with that."

Simon leans back and looks up at the ceiling, trying to think of something.

"We could go looking for a collector," suggests Flatpack.

"That's not a statement, that's a typical Monday," laughs Simon, who has a better idea.

"But we could go and smash up their office."

"Not bad, that'll get noticed. It's the collectors so the police won't do anything. I like it."

Flatpack gets on his phone and calls up some reinforcements.

Simon waves Toothless over.

"You and your mates up for a bit of revenge later?"

Simon knows it was a silly question really, the chance to do some damage with him and Flatpack.

"*Oh yeth.*" was the expected reply.

Flatpack comes off the phone.

"Midnight."

Toothless goes over to tell his mates that tonight they mix with the big boys.

Midnight arrives and Simon and Flatpack haven't left their table all night and they're a little worse for wear. They've been joined by Hannah, Flatpack's girlfriend and her friend, who is sitting on Simon's knee. Another half a dozen lads hanging round next to the door signal when a van pulls up.

They all make their way out to the van as its side door slides open revealing two boxes. The first is full of torches, hats, scarves, and children's masks. The second is full of crowbars and baseball bats. A figure dressed all in black starts to hand them out. Once everybody has got what they want, Simon and Flatpack jump in the back of the van, others get into their cars. They shout and cheer as each car tries to burn more rubber than the others.

"Good turnout," says Simon.

"The targets are the toll booths. The idea is to do as much damage as we can, put the booths out of action. Break into the offices, torch any documents and smash up what we can. There isn't any one working at this time of night, only CCTV. So masks on at all times. We have eleven minutes, that is the time it will take for the police to respond once the alarms have been triggered. Plenty of time when you consider they would be at a bank raid in under four," says Flatpack.

The van parks just before the booths and well away from any cameras. A Ford Focus pulls up behind it and five guys get out. Counting up, Simon thinks that there are plenty here to cause some serious damage.

They run along the sides of the roads, keeping in the shadows until they get to the booths, and split into two groups, one attacking the toll booths and one the offices. The front of the offices are heavily protected by steel shutters and the windows are made from bulletproof extra thick glass.

"This won't take a second," says one lad, as he reveals a shotgun from under his trench coat. He blasts the door twice, the sound echoing around the area. One of the guys pushes it with his shoulder to try and open it.

"Give it another go, you're almost there."

Flatpack takes out one of his guns, a Desert Eagle .50 and with two hands blows a hole right though the lock, the recoil knocking him backwards.

"After you ladies" he laughs.

The deafening noise of the alarms immediately sound. High in a corner is one camera. Simon, wearing a child's Spiderman mask looks directly into it, giving the bird before smashing it with his baseball bat. One lad writes on the wall using black spray paint. Another does the same on the outside. They all have a go at destroying a large wooden desk. They smash whatever they can find. Some have gathered together as many paper documents as possible and set fire to them. The alarms make it impossible to hear anything, even the sirens from the police, so after the eleven minutes each man stops what he's doing and leaves as quickly as possible. Once outside they all run back to their vehicles. Sounds fill the air from all the alarms, and as the sirens get closer, the lads slip away into the night.

Chapter 5

Simon Peter wakes up and for a second doesn't know where he is. A yawn has trouble escaping as his tongue has stuck itself to the roof of his mouth. It feels as dry as the Judean desert. He reaches over for Ruth, only to find that she isn't next to him. He sits up, the double bed small in comparison to his six foot frame. He looks around the room, oh that's right, he's in Jerusalem. It was certainly a long night. How many bottles of wine did they get through? He braces himself for the pounding to start. Huh, it doesn't, no headache! It has been years since he's come to the city and visited some of the clients the fishing business supplies. Every one of them had opened a bottle. How can you say no? He had thought about just sticking to beer, but didn't want to appear a typical unsophisticated working class lad from up north, and the wine they all chose did accompany the fish perfectly. Normally Zebedee or Andrew are the ones to schmooze the clients and his brother was all set to do this trip alone, but Simon Peter had other ideas; there was no way he was going to miss out on this one, oh no.

He gets up and showers before heading downstairs. As he enters the kitchen, Andrew is already up, sitting at the table, nursing his head and sipping a drink. Simon Peter opens the fridge door, aargh it's empty...of course it is, this place isn't used that much. Zebedee has a second home in the city, an investment property bought cheap in the recession. The plan was to sell when the economy recovered but his family like it so much they've kept hold of it.

"There's no milk, if you're thinking about having a drink," says Andrew.

"Ughh, I don't know how you can drink black coffee?"

"Easy, it means I don't have to remember to buy milk."

Simon Peter's stomach rumbles as he looks through the empty cupboards; he really needs to eat something.

"No point hanging around here, come on," he says, eager to get going.

Zebedee's house is in the suburbs of Jerusalem, a ten minute taxi ride from the old city. Like most others its appearance is just a white box with a flat roof. The neighbourhood is good and well kept, but it is easy to get lost as the houses look all the same and the roads are not very well signposted. They had driven down in Andrew's truck. Knowing the state of his own, Simon Peter is quite happy to let him. As they drive along, he can't help looking up at the majesty of the old city on the hill, its yellow stone setting it apart from the modern new white buildings surrounding it. Andrew heads towards the main road, but instead of going north back home to Capernaum they have other plans. The first being to get something to eat and drink, then on to Bethabara, a place the sat-nav has apparently never heard of. The info Andrew had from the latest emails and texts aren't much help either; they just say Bethabara.

Andrew has an idea where it might be and thinks it's worth a shot as it'll only be twenty odd miles away, should only take half an hour.

Simon Peter is starting to get excited. He has been looking forward to this ever since Zebedee mentioned a trip south was on the cards. Ruth wasn't too pleased but she has her mother staying, so she'll be fine.

An hour and a twenty minutes later, much of which was spent trying to negotiate their way through the grid lock that's Jerusalem's rush hour, Andrew finally sees a road sign up ahead. Bethany (Bethabara) 2 miles.

"See, there we are, not far now!" exclaims Andrew, pleased with himself.

"There had better be shops, I'm starving."

It looks like they're not the only ones making the journey. Cars line both sides of the road leading into the town and predictably the traffic comes to a halt. Not again - all they've done this morning is queue in traffic. When several people pass them on foot Simon Peter thinks it's time to park up and walk, so when the cars slowly move forward again he points to a side street.

"Why don't we park up, this is ridiculous."

Andrew agrees and turns off, finding a space to park his truck.

Simon Peter has no problems leaving his overnight bag showing on the back seat, but Andrew having brought his Laptop decides it's best if he takes it with him.

"Good, if you're taking that you can fit in some books I want signing," says Simon Peter handing Andrew his copies of *A Voice Shouting in the Wilderness* and his favourite, *Brood of Vipers*. Andrew pops them in the bag alongside his laptop.

Not knowing where they're going they just follow the crowds, until Andrew spots a bakery.

"Oh at last," says Simon Peter.

In the shop, there's a dozen people queuing. Two women are serving behind the counter; both look fed up.

Finally it's his turn, "passing trade's good this morning," he remarks.

"Eh, oh yeah, I see what you mean, very good."

"Can I have a couple of those large pasties, two iced buns and a large white coffee please." While the assistant gets his order he turns to Andrew.

"You having anything?"

"Oh, I thought...a pasty and a black coffee, thanks."

The woman hears and nods.

"Don't suppose you know where I can find..." Before he finishes his sentence the woman says, "Oh so you are one of them too are ya?"

"One of what?"

The question seems to baffle her and she ignores it "Er...That'll be eight seventy four."

Simon Peter takes a sip of the hot coffee, finally his mouth can re-hydrate. Before they've even left the shop he takes a bite out of a pasty.

"Oh that's good," he announces to those in the queue.

Once outside they rejoin the throng, all going in the same direction. As they all go though a village and down a slope towards the river, he polishes off the whole lot. Mmm, just what he needed.

On the banks of the river Jordan, he and Andrew join thousands of others. Some of them, going by all the accents, have travelled hundreds of miles to be here.

Standing waist high in the river, with unkempt hair and a long beard is the preacher the press have dubbed John the

Baptist. His message is simple. "The Kingdom of God is near, so turn from your sins and turn to God." He then baptises people by dipping them in the river, making them clean before God.

They find a good spot on the grassy slope where Andrew finishes his breakfast, and Simon Peter sips his coffee. They watch as one after another go down to the river to be baptised. Every so often John stops and addresses the crowd, after which more people go forward.

"A lot of them are going be late for work this morning," a man beside them remarks. Andrew laughs, agreeing with him.

"Come far?" the man asks.

"From Galilee," says Simon Peter.

"Wow! Really, good for you."

"Well, we were in the city on business, so we thought we'd try and see him."

Simon Peter and Andrew had heard about John from a TV documentary entitled A Voice Shouting in the Wilderness, named after John's first book. The wilderness being the desert country around Jericho. It showed John living a very simple life, going around the small towns and villages in the area with his message of repentance and baptism. It wasn't until his second book, Brood of Vipers, attacking the holier than thou approach of the religious authorities, that his popularity took off. In this image obsessed world more interested with looks than substance, to some John is a laughing stock. But to others his words ring true and crowds flock to hear him speak and be baptised. This had struck a chord with the brothers.

Again John stops baptising, and turns his attention to the crowd. "I baptise with water those who turn from their sins, but someone is coming soon who is far greater than I am. So much greater that I am not even worthy to be his servant. He will baptise with the Holy Spirit and with fire."

"Wow, did you hear that, S P?"

"I wonder who it is?"

More people get up and go forward to be baptised and Simon Peter feels the urge to get up and go down to the river himself. He resists, it's not really his thing, but his hands start to shake and he gets all nervous. He fights it - no not me, not in front of all these people.

Feeling uncomfortable he gets up.

"I can't just sit here, maybe I'll just nip down and get my books signed."

He stands up and the next minute he's in the water and John, the actual John the Baptist, is lowering him down into the river. He is under the water for a second and when he is lifted up he makes quite a splash with his arms and it takes two of Johns' assistants to help him. As he is led back to the bank of the river he's sure he doesn't feel any real difference - only he can't stop smiling. He is given a towel and is handed his wallet and phone. It happened all too quickly. He looks back to where he'd been sitting, unable to see Andrew. That's because his brother is right behind him coming out of the water.

As the sun is shining, they decide to sit back down and dry off a little before going home. He's got a change of clothes in the truck but the truth is, he doesn't want to leave. John has a few close friends who help him, one of them sits down next to Andrew. He asks him where they're from, and does he have any questions?

"Yeah, who is this man John talked about?"

"He was here a minute ago, on the grass over there." He points to the place where Simon Peter and Andrew had been sitting.

Chapter 6

Capernaum Police Station, the once white exterior now weathered and grey, isn't as imposing these days. Today it's half hidden in between larger office blocks and apartments. Inside it's still got the same big wooden counter and light blue walls from when it was new, though they are now old and worn. The musty smell takes Matthew back to the first time he ever walked through the doors. It was two years after his parents had died, so he would have been thirteen. Old Eli had brought him here saying, "so, you enjoy the money; well, you also need to know the risks." Sixteen years later this is still the worst part of a collectors life.

It's busier these days. Three officers are behind the counter now, instead of one. He joins the queue and waits for his turn, listening to the utter trivial things people are here for. One woman is worried about her lost cat: a man wants to know what they are going to do about all the litter in his neighbourhood and an old woman in front of him wants something done about her noisy neighbours. An officer tries to look concerned and gives her a form to fill out.

"Next" he shouts, before recognising Matthew, "I know why you're here...." Matthew nods.

"I'll get someone to take you downstairs."

"Thanks. Is Hebdon around?" asks Matthew.

The old woman interrupts, "Excuse me, I haven't finished. What are you going to do about...?" Matthew turns, looking her straight in the eye and shouts "go away." She looks at the officer who ignores her and phones officer Hebdon.

Officer Tim Hebdon comes out of his office and waves Matthew through. They walk along a corridor and down two flights of stairs, the same walk he did all those years ago.

"Isn't it time they built a new station?"

"Tell me about it," replies Hebdon, with a sigh of resignation. "Y'know they've got a new one in Chorazin."

Matthew nods, "I do, intimately."

The basement feels damp and cold. A fluorescent light flickers over a sign indicating Morgue. Hebdon tells Matthew to wait while he goes to a desk and explains to another officer the situation.

"Got your ID?" asks Hebdon, beckoning him over.

Matthew knows the drill and produces his driving licence and his official collectors licence.

"Any ID for the deceased?"

Matthew takes out two brown envelopes from his jacket pocket. He puts one on the desk and slides it over to Hebdon, who empties the paperwork out and hands it to the other officer who flicks through it. "That's fine, come this way," says the officer.

All three enter the morgue, but Matthew hangs back, standing in the entrance a second. He covers his nose and mouth with his hand, the pungent odour filling his nostrils. He knows the smell is a mixture of spices from traditional Jewish burials and the more modern embalming fluid. On a steel table is a body covered with a white sheet. The officer uncovers the head.

"Thanks, that will be all," says Hebdon, hinting that the officer should leave.

When your occupation is violence, you'd think you would become accustomed to death, but Matthew hates it. He's not yet seen a peaceful corpse. He'd said to old Eli all those years ago, "it looked like his soul had been sucked out." Old Eli was a wise man; bringing his young impressionable nephew down here had helped keep Matthew alive.

"That's him, that's Dave Milo. Where?"

"An alley at the side of Angels nightclub."

"Never heard of it."

"That's because it's in the The Estate. What was he doing down there?"

"Nothing official."

Hebdon covers up the body.

"Oh, this is for you." Matthew hands over the other envelope.

"Much appreciated, " says Hebdon peeking inside to see how generous Matthew has been this time.

"What about his belongings?" asks Matthew.

"We didn't find anything, no weapon, wallet, keys, not even spare change."

"You've not found his car then?"

"You know The Estate. We don't have enough officers to cover half the city, let alone that place. I'm surprised someone even called us about your man."

Matthew takes a business card out of his jacket pocket and hands it to Hebdon.

"Do you know this guy?"

Hebdon looks at the card. On it is the name and number of

Adam P Samuels, Funeral Director.

"All too well."

"He'll arrange collection."

Both men shake hands and Matthew makes his way upstairs, getting out his mobile and dialling the office.

"Hey it's me, get hold of Samuels and tell him to ring me, I'm going over to Dave's place."

It takes Matthew only half an hour to drive to the small town of Nain, the other side of Mount Tabor and south-west of Capernaum. He'd been to the town a few times but never to Dave's apartment. Collectors, along with other government officials and many from the police force, live in their own community. Anyone helping the Union are seen as traitors and hated by society.

Dave had stayed put in Nain, never getting round to moving. Matthew always told his people that south Capernaum was the safest place to live, they have protection and safety in numbers.

Collectors are either born into the job, or drawn into it. Dave was the latter and when Matthew hired him, under next of kin Dave had left a blank. This means that under the law, Matthew must act as executor in the event of Dave's death. The government includes a special clause in licences for the tax and debt businesses, as it was regularly having to sort out the mess of so many dead collectors. Matthew has an insurance policy just to cover the funeral costs of his employees, should they leave no next of kin.

The apartment on Cedar road is just off the main street. Matthew pulls up in front of the white two storey building and gets out of the car. A residents parking area, enough for four cars is to the left and there is a large Cyprus tree to the right. Matthew wonders why the road isn't named after *that* tree as there haven't been cedars around Galilee for generations. He also isn't expecting to be the first here. He takes out his gun, holding it low down to avoid arousing suspicion. In the building there are four apartments, two up, two down. Matthew goes to number seven. He tries the handle. To his surprise it's locked, maybe nobody has been after all. He looks around, the road is quiet, there's no one about, "Okay, Dave, lets see what sort of security you have."

Matthew steps back a few feet and then as hard as he can, lays into it with his shoulder. There is a crack of plastic, but the door stays intact. He tries again and this time one side comes away from the wall, leaving him enough room to squeeze in. In front of him are stairs leading to the first-floor apartment. Going up them two at a time Matthew stops when he reaches the top, his feet crunching on broken glass.

Someone has been here. The place is trashed; every cupboard, every drawer has been emptied onto the floor. Matthew rubs his shoulder, puts his gun away and goes into the living room. A black leather suite has been slashed with a knife, a chrome finished cabinet is in pieces. That's it, they've taken everything of value. He looks through the rest of the apartment; it's the same. What's left is smashed up or of little worth. Matthew rummages through the papers on the bedroom floor, looking for anything that may be important. He picks up an official looking letter with an insurance company's name on it. The address is here in Nain, let's see what this is for?

He rings the number at the top of the letter.

A woman answers, "Good Morning, Nain Insurance, how may I help you?"

"Hello. I'm ringing on behalf of a Mr D.R. Milo account number DRM995483, could you tell me what kind of policy he has with you?"

"One moment please."

There is silence for a few minutes until a man's voice speaks. "Hello, I'm the manager, how may I help? Matthew repeats the question again.

"Hello, is that a Mr Milo?"

"No, this is his employer."

"Well, I'm sorry, I'm not allowed to give out customer information."

Matthew rings off, not even bothering to say thank you and goodbye.

The address for Nain insurance is along the main road, so Matthew decides to walk there and talk to the manager in person.

The office has several staff either tapping away on computers or talking on phones. There's an empty chair behind the nearest desk. Matthew suspects it belongs to a receptionist as nobody even looks up at him. He decides to find the manager himself and goes towards an office at the back of the room. A young man with a headset on looks up. "Excuse me sir, you can't go in there."

"Wanna bet?"

The young man tries to stop him but he is connected to the phone and is pulled back by the lead. Matthew opens the door and enters. A man in his late thirties or early forties is sitting behind a desk. He almost jumps out of his seat when this strange man bursts in on him.

"Wha... What are you doing in he... here, wh... who are you?"

"We spoke on the phone a few minutes ago, about a Mr

Milo."

Matthew slaps down his government licence and Dave's employment contract, causing the man to jump again.

"Now, I do have the right to the information, Mr?..."

"Johnson."

"Mr Johnson, if you will tell me about the policy my DEAD employee had with you."

With his hands shaking the man looks it up on the computer.

"The policy is a home contents, plus he had just renewed his car with us."

"Contents, good. I need someone to come round and assess the place, it's been completely trashed."

Mr Johnson has seen the gun on Matthew's belt and can't stop staring at it.

"Are you listening?"

"Oh, sorry, I'll send someone round in the next couple of days. We're very busy just now. If you leave a contact number someone will be in touch."

Matthew isn't going to be fobbed off like this.

"What! A few days. I want it done now."

"I don't have anyone available," Mr Johnson splutters.

"You can do it?" says Matthew, pointing at him.

"No, I... I'm..."

"Get what you need and come with me."

Johnson stands up, and with as much authority his five foot something frame can muster, reaches for the phone saying. "I'm calling the police, I think you should leave."

Matthew, his nostrils still filled with the smell of death from the morgue, is not in the mood. He knocks the phone off the desk before Johnson can pick it up.

"You want to play it like this, fine," Matthew grabs hold of

Johnson's arm. Johnson tries to pull away, but Matthew's grip is too tight. When Johnson has the nerve to throw a punch, Matthew shoves him against a wall, and then squeezes Johnson's throat, whispering. "You are so lucky I'm here and not Dave Milo. He would have put a bullet in your skull by now."

This time, Matthew doesn't grab an arm but gets hold of Johnson's thinning hair, "Why would you make it so hard for yourself? Why? This time, you won't put up a struggle will you?"

"No... No... aargh."

Matthew drags Johnson by the hair, out of the office and passed his employees, who stare with open mouths. Pointing to the young man with his spare hand Matthew says "You, go get some assessment forms and whatever else your boss will need for a home insurance claim and follow me, NOW. And nobody be so stupid as to call the police."

Matthew marches out of the building with a bent double Johnson being dragged behind him. The young man starts to collect what he needs and runs after Matthew.

"Please let go, you've made your point."

"I could, but then if you tried to run away I would be forced to shoot you, so I'm actually doing you a favour."

Just before they arrive at Dave's place, the young man catches them up.

"This is the place," Matthew gestures towards the building. As they get up to the door he lets go of Johnson's hair, who pulls away feeling his head very gently. The young man gives his boss a form on a clipboard and a pen. Johnson snatches them, giving his young employee a glare.

"You don't have to include the door, I did that." Matthew

informs them.

All three men then walk through the property, room by room, going over what is damaged or has been stolen.

Matthew's phone rings. It's Adam Samuels, the undertaker.

"*Hi, your secretary has explained the urgency. I've already been on to the police and got a priest. The body is being collected as we speak and will be taken to the plot. I'm guessing there won't be a funeral.*"

"No, just the usual, can you get it done today?

"*Well if there's no one going to attend, then of course, no problem... Oh there was just one thing, for speed I promised the priest and the gravediggers an extra two hundred, is that OK?*"

"Of course, just add it to the bill." As Matthew puts his phone away the young man asks.

"Will it be a big funeral?"

Matthew shakes his head, "what's your name kid?"

"Timothy, er... Tim."

"Well Tim, apart from being violent bastards, we collectors are also superstitious. We don't go to funerals because we think it's bad luck, like we may be next. Hey when you're dead you're dead, no one gets another go, right, no one! Who cares if a few people gather round crying."

Matthew pauses for a moment, thinking of the last and only funeral he's ever been to, that of his parents. Before old Eli died, he made Matthew promise he wouldn't attend, "Just let me be, kid. Just let me be."

"No Tim, tonight I'll just have a drink and be glad it wasn't me."

Chapter 7

"Kill, kill, kill" chant the packed crowd as two rappers strut around the stage encouraging their audience to respond and wave their arms in the air. With the lines *my knife in your back* and *your death is my glory* their message is clear. Wearing large gold chains round their necks and very baggy clothes, like millions of others around the world, you'd be forgiven for thinking this is just a gimmick. Violence sells as they say and maybe for many of the kids who buy the CDs and T-shirts that's *all* it is - the latest cool.

But let's be in no doubt, this is more than slogans, these are threats, and many have been on the receiving end. Steve aka Flatpack and Simon the Zealot, are just two of the death rappers who back up their lyrics with real action. Even their names, while on the face of it seem harmless, have darker meanings. Flatpack is a slang term for a cheap coffin and Zealot is taken from Simon's weapon of choice, the brand name of the knife he carries.

"We want our country back, we want our country back," chants Simon.

At the same time, Flatpack raps "It's time we get these foreign dogs outta our, b-lov-ed land. We will not rest, nor will we sleep, til we have our own country, BACK! The day will come, when we will see, blood, of every Union oppressor and Jewish traitor and Israel WILL BE FREE."

"*We want our country back, we want our country back.*" The crowd join in.

Flatpack usually works solo, preferring to have the stage all to himself. Simon, while still having a decent following in Capernaum, his home town, is usually the support act. Tonight though, Flatpack was *his* guest, these *his* people.

When they come off stage it takes half an hour just to get to the door. Everyone wants an autograph or a photo. Simon gets the number of a brunette he wants to meet later. Later is in the Angels Club where he has a private table and can chill without being interrupted by fans.

"Did you notice we had unwanted visitors?" Flatpack says as they enter the Club.

Simon hadn't. When he's on stage, with the lights shining on him, everything becomes a blur.

At the bar a group of young attractive girls are talking and sipping cocktails. Flatpack has a word in the ear of a friend who goes over to them.

The lads are shown to their booth and order the usual drinks.

"So did you get a good look at those men?" Simon asks.

"What? No. my eyes aren't that good, but shit, they won't dare mess with us, right!"

Three girls are shown to their booth and slide in next to them. This is the best way to relax Simon thinks, as one of the girls leans over and kisses him. A waiter brings Simon his Hennessey cognac and Flatpack a whisky. Flatpack, his arms round the two other girls, orders them champagne and points to two mates standing near the dance floor, chatting up some twins. "Get them whatever they want." The waiter nods.

This is a far cry from how Simon thought his life would go. He was shy as a child and would never have thought he'd be on stage in front of hundreds of people. His mother had wanted him to study and go to university. She hated living in the Neziah district of Capernaum. A run down estate famous only for its violence and high crime rate. Growing up without a father had been tough for both of them. His mum worked long hours in a factory just to feed them. He knew she hated it, but she got up everyday and never once complained. One day while travelling south between Capernaum and Magdala she hadn't enough money to pay the toll. If only she'd lied, given them a false name and address they wouldn't have kept calling. Even after she'd paid it all back – including the interest, they kept harassing her. No, mum would never have lied, she was too honest. She'd never had a day off sick until that incident. But the cancer spread quickly and Simon has no doubt what caused it. Even up to her death she urged him to study, make something of himself. If he'd studied hard the best he could have hoped for would have been a job in an office. As the girl nibbles on his ear, he wonders if by now he'd have been married and stuck at home with a wife and kids. He can't help thinking back to that one incident that changed him forever.

A few coins that's all it took to alter his path. If his mum had had enough money to pay the toll, he might have been that office worker and his mum still alive today.

"Hey cheer up, you look like shit." Flatpack brings him back from the memories.

"Oh, was just thinking about mum."

"This guy," Flatpack tells the girls "This guy here, is a legend. Stuck a knife in a collector who was harassing his mum, yeah, stuck it in, twisted it nice and good."

"My hero," says the girl.

A friend comes over to the table and leans over and says something in Flatpack's ear. Simon can't quite hear what is being said, but it seems serious as Flatpack's demeanour changes and he pushes the girls out of the way and beckons Simon to follow him.

"What is it?" Simon asks as he tries to catch up.

"An unwanted visitor."

Their friend points to the back door where another man is waiting for them.

"He has a gun! What should we do? " asks the man.

"I only came out for a smoke, and saw him - I don't think he saw me though."

Simon carefully pushes open the door slightly and looks out.

"Car headlights, I can't see anything for the headlights." With the continuous thud of bass from the music inside seeping through the walls and the noise from the car engine, it appears their presence has gone unnoticed. Simon again peers out down the alley; this time Flatpack does the same. Between them and the light two men are in what looks like a very one sided fight, with one guy on the floor being kicked almost to unconsciousness.

Flatpack whispers "When I arrived I noticed a black BMW, ring any bells?"

Simon nods, "same car that was seen speeding away from Adam's."

"Right, word is he's a collector, a real psycho, kills for fun."

Simon bends down, taking his knife from his ankle holster. He hesitates, maybe this isn't the time, better play safe.

Instead he reaches for the gun on his belt. Flatpack pats his back.

"Right, we need to put a stop to this. Everybody, after three just start firing at the bastard, but watch out for the kid on the ground. Aim high.

Another kick lands into the ribs of the young man curled up on the ground, before the assailant presses his gun hard into the man's forehead and laughs.

"NOW!" Flatpack yells.

A hail of bullets hit the man and also knock out the car headlights. plunging the alley into darkness.

They stop firing. "Think we got' im?" asks one of the men.

"Oh yeah," says Flatpack.

They move slowly down the alley, trying to see in the dark. There is movement and then a voice *"Ith's me, don't thoot."*

"Toothless?" Simon asks.

"Yeth, I think, you got' im."

"Come to us, slowly," says Flatpack.

A battered and bloodied Toothless approaches them and he is ushered inside the club.

"Am I tho glad to thee you."

Simon and Flatpack go to look at the mess they've just made.

They hear the last gasps of a desperate man. When they get to him, he has managed to pull out his phone. He has been hit several times but unbelievably is still alive – just.

"Matt, aargh, oh shit, Matt," with each word taking all of his strength he is trying to call for help. "Aargh, I didn't see them, I didn't see…"

Flatpack stands over him, raises his gun and finishes him off.

Chapter 8

"Can you hear music?"

"No!"

"Listen."

"Oh yeah."

It's dawn and two men are fishing over the side of Capernaum harbour wall, well away from the hustle and bustle of the commercial businesses operating on the opposite side.

"It sounds like it's coming from out there," one of them says, pointing out towards the middle of the lake.

A morning fog has descended on Lake Galilee and although it's now starting to lift around the shore, the centre of the lake is still covered in a thick dense blanket.

"I can also hear an engine, oh, it'll be from a trawler."

The engine noise grows louder and they hear voices.

'The time is six fifteen and you're listening to Capernaum 106, with me, Sparky In The Morning. A big hello to James and John fishing out on the lake. The weather centre says the fog will lift, but not until mid-morning. The guys say that the fish love Sparky In The Morning so much they jump into the boat. Nice one guys, you'll be receiving Sparky In The Morning mugs and baseball caps.'

"We got a mention, we got a mention. I can't believe it, that is so cool, and we're getting free stuff...yes!"

"What do you mean we? I texted in, so I'm getting the stuff."

"Eh, no way, you can't do that, my name was mentioned as well. James, come on."

"Ha, ha, ha, you're so easy to wind up."

James and John are on their way back to the harbour from a long night's work.

At night the lake is one of the best sights. Above are thousands of stars twinkling. The hills surrounding the lake are scattered with orange dots from the street lamps; it's an awesome sight. When it's bad weather, it can be a rough place to work and when there's fog there is an eerie feeling of being all alone. So closed in that even after a few hours some fishermen can become weary and disorientated.

The boys cope with the long hours and hard going any way they can. James had wanted to text something about Simon Peter being a slave driver, but John had wisely talked him out of it, as they were thirty minutes late and didn't want Simon Peter to be any angrier.

They had set their course for home but had got distracted when they were mentioned on the radio, so hadn't noticed that their position was nearer the harbour than they thought. They burst through the fog, with their lights blazing and engine at full power, still arguing.

John looks up to see they have come out of the fog and are very close to the harbour, unfortunately aiming straight for the wall.

"Quick, turn left."

James turns hard left.

"This is gonna be close."

The loud scraping noise of boat hull sliding along the entrance makes everyone in the harbour stop and stare. But the lads are going way too fast for a trawler in a harbour. John kills the speed but the momentum has them heading for two other trawlers unloading at the quayside. Everyone watching braces themselves for a crash. James turns hard left again, steering the boat into a gap between the two trawlers with inches to spare. The buoys on the side gently bounce off the quay as the boat comes to a calm rest, in perfect position. James and John give each other a high five and pump their fists.

"Yes! come on. Nice control."

The sudden stop creates a wave that travels through the harbour, lifting up boats as it passes underneath them. The two men on the wall watch as it starts to get near them. They start running, but they can't escape it and the wave hits the wall sending water high into the air and drenching them. James and John are oblivious to this, they're congratulating each other and are still excited at getting a mention on the radio.

Zebedee, having seen and heard them make their entrance, strolls over. He studies the trawler, looking for damage, shakes his head and tuts.

John jumps down from the boat on to the quay. "Relax Dad, it's only a scratch."

"You'd better have good numbers, or were you too busy trying to get on the radio?"

"You heard?"

Zebedee nods.

John calls out to James, "Hey, Dad heard the radio."

James laughs.

"You know it was me who thought of the line about the fish jumping into the boat."

"Thought it might have been."

John stands next to his dad and they watch as James and two other employees unload the catch.

Zebedee turns to John and looks at him; John's deep in thought. They stand in silence for a moment.

"James wanted to say hello to all you losers on the shore, and slag off S P, but it makes more sense to be nice if you want to get a mention, you know, kiss up a bit."

From out of nowhere Simon Peters voice booms "Don't just stand there John, get to work." Again Zebedee shakes his head. "You'd better help unload, the fish might have jumped in but they'll need help getting out."

* * *

Simon Peter looks out of the first floor window overlooking the harbour, keeping an eye on James and John.

"Relax, Zeb's down there, everything will get sorted."

"Yeah, but what about the boat, maybe I should go down and have a look at it."

Andrew comes over to the window and looks out.

"Zeb doesn't seem worried, so it should be alright. Look on the bright side, it didn't sink this time." He then goes and sits back down to finish off checking his own paperwork before putting it on Zebedee's desk.

"I knew something would happen, what did I say, if they don't concentrate?" says Simon Peter.

Even with all his years of experience he had come pretty

close to the harbour wall himself on many a foggy morning, though it must be said, never actually hitting it. So after he'd finished unloading and sorting out his paperwork he had come upstairs to watch out for James and John. If the brothers weren't one hundred percent... He had stood watching and waiting, knowing something would happen. Call it intuition, or the fact that their boat's powerful: they're late so they'll be going too fast, they'll be excited at having their names read out on Capernaum 106 and they both have terrible concentration. Less like intuition, more like an inevitability.

"So, come on, you must have found out something by now, who is he?"

"It's only been a day," Andrew smiles.

Simon Peter knows his brother too well, he knows that as soon as Andrew got home he would have been on the internet, finding out as much as he could about this man Johnny B talked about.

"OK, but S P, don't get too excited. After we left, something happened. It was on the news in Jerusalem last night. I rang one of Johnny B's followers to confirm it.

"And what happened?" Simon Peter doesn't do the news so has no idea what his brother is on about.

"I don't know if it's true or not, but what I heard is Johnny B refused to baptise this guy because, he John was unworthy. This guy insisted and as he was coming up out of the water a voice spoke and some say there were doves, others a cloud of some sort. That's all I know, I'm not sure I believe it?"

"Why didn't you tell me this earlier? This is unbelievable."

"It's only rumours."

Another loud crash outside rattles the windows and Simon Peter's attention turns back to the harbour.

"James?" asks Andrew.

"Of course, he's taken over the crane." Simon Peter puts his hand up to the glass to bang it, but sees Zeb is making James give the crane back to its operator.

Simon Peter knew that one day Zeb's sons would join the family business, but he was a little relieved when they went to college after high school, although he suspected the teachers had something to do with both lads leaving their respective courses early and being encouraged to take up the family business. While Zebedee rarely goes out in the boats any more, preferring to run the business from the comfort of the office, Simon Peter fishes. That's what he's always done; that's all he knows. The days and nights can be long and it's back breaking stuff but he wouldn't swap it for anything. There have been times when the weather has been bad, storms raging, the sea at its most violent. Zebedee will remind him he doesn't have to do it, there's a safer, warmer place he could work from. As a business partner he has employees to do the leg work, so why should he risk himself? Zebedee just doesn't get it, because that's when Simon Peter is most alive, when it's him against the elements, that's when he's happiest, that's who he is. He could never sit in an office all day pouring over tax returns. He's a fisherman and fishermen catch fish.

He watches as John is again just standing there, hands in pockets. What's he doing? He can't resist opening the window. "John, get back to work." Simon Peter believes their parents are too soft, they let them do what they want, so he likes to keep them busy. Nothing wrong with a bit of verbals now and again to let them know who's boss.

Zebedee comes into the office and heads over to the window. Pointing down at a couple of crates he says. "See those down there, they're for Zak's restaurant in Jerusalem."

"Only two crates, I was hoping for more," says Andrew.

"They are just testing us, soon it will be more, you'll see," Zebedee tells him.

"We have the best quality in the country, 'course they'll order more," says Simon Peter before a yawn slips out. He's tired, it's been a long night.

Simon Peter likes his routine which means when he gets home after a night's work he has breakfast with his family, before Ruth takes six year old Naomi to school. Four year old Jacob goes to a nursery where Ruth helps out. This gives Simon Peter time to unwind and then sleep. He usually goes to bed mid-morning and gets up around six. This gives him time with the kids before they go to bed and some time alone with Ruth before he goes to work for ten; then the cycle begins again. Ruth hates him working nights and they've had many an argument over it. Simon Peter suspects Ruth has expressed her concerns to Salomé, Zebedee's wife and mother of James and John. That's why Zebedee keeps suggesting he needn't work nights. If there's one thing he hates it's being told what to do, no matter how well-meaning the intention.

Two sets of work boots thud up the wooden steps that lead to the office and James and John burst in.

"We've finished," James announces.

"I'm starving, can we go now Dad?" John asks.

Zebedee nods.

"Hey, if you've damaged the boat, you'll pay for it!" says Simon Peter.

"It'll be fine, they got lucky this time." Zebedee says to him.

The lads smile at Simon Peter and John asks. "You gonna

come S P? Andy? We're going to the café for breakfast."

"Yeah, why not?" says Andrew standing up. "You can tell me about the radio."

"Not me," Simon Peter shakes his head, trying to conceal another yawn.

"S P looks too tired, he's getting old," James says to John.

"Hey I'm not..." he yawns. It's big and slow. "I should be getting home, back to the kids."

"Pity, I was going to treat us all," says Andrew.

"Oh well, In that case, I'm in," says Simon Peter

James and John laugh and leave with the same bounding enthusiasm that carries them through life, which at times does annoy Simon Peter, but which he also can't help admiring.

All four make their way down the stairs, passing the big six foot high metal bin brimming over with old packing boxes and cardboard. On it someone has written *Simon Peter's Lunch box* in black paint.

It's a few minutes walk to the Lakeside Café on the other side of the harbour, a popular place for the fishermen. As they approach, the owner, a Greek named Nicholas, is putting tables and chairs out.

"Morning Nick," they all say before going inside. James and John head straight to a table near the back and pore over the menu. Simon Peter and Andrew go over to a mate sitting by himself drinking coffee.

Philip has known the lads a long time as their parents were friends. He works just round the corner from the harbour in an office, which he hates.

"Alright Phil, what are you doing here this early?"

"The boss wants us in at half seven this morning, thought I'd grab a coffee first. You guys just finished?"

"Yeah."

James turns round looking for Andrew and notices Philip.

"Hey, it's Philip" James says poking John who still hasn't made his mind up what to order. John waves and carries on studying the menu.

"We got a mention on the radio this morning." James says to Philip, loud enough for the other diners to hear.

Philip laughs, "Nice one, you want to ask if celebrities get discounts."

John looks up. "Discounts, really?"

James and John look towards the food counter where a middle-aged woman is serving. She overhears, "no chance," she says with a smile.

"It's OK, Andrew's paying anyway!" says James.

"So how did your trip go?" Philip asks Andrew and Simon Peter.

"You mean you don't know. We got baptised, by none other than John the Baptist," says Simon Peter.

"No...really."

"Yeah, by the man himself, full on, in the Jordan," says Andrew.

"Shit.."

"I forgot to get my books signed though," says Simon Peter.

"But that's all you've talked about for the last week."

"Yeah, well, I wasn't going to actually ask him when he was in the middle of the Jordan was I?"

"That's exactly what we thought you'd do, " says James.

"So how was it?" asks Philip.

"Unbelievable, there were thousands and it took ages, but well worth it. You've read the books right, heard him on telly, everyone wanted to see him. But hearing him speak close up, that's something else," says Andrew.

Philip sighs, "If I could get time off work I'd love to go."

Andrew leans over, "He said something else, that there will be another coming soon." He pauses, thinking for a few seconds before adding in a whisper. "He will be *The One*."

Philip raises his eyebrows and leans back in his chair. Andrew carries on "He was there, I mean I never saw him, but John said HE was there."

Chapter 9

"S P wake up."

Bang! Bang!

"Simon...Peter."

"Ruth, can you get that," shouts Simon Peter from the bedroom.

He sits up and looks at the clock. 10.15, he's only been in bed an hour.

"S P get yourself up."

He recognises his brother's voice. Oh great what have James and John done now. Couldn't this wait until later? He gets out of bed, his body still aching from the long night's work.

"It's your brother," shouts Ruth, before telling him off for waking her mother who isn't feeling so well.

"I'm getting up, give me a second."

He descends the stairs with heavy legs, still half asleep.

"This better be important."

"It is, come on get dressed. It's him, I've met the one Johnny B talked about," Andrew can't hide his excitement.

Still half asleep Simon Peter asks, "him, who?"

"I've met the Christ, the Messiah. HIM! I mean Jesus, he's called Jesus. "

"Good for you."

He turns his aching body and starts to go back to bed. Half way up the stairs he stops, I'm so tired I must have misheard. Did he just say...? He can't mean? He turns and looks at his brother, who has the widest grin he has ever seen.

"If you want to meet him, he's at the café," says Andrew.

"I'll be two seconds."

He runs upstairs and quickly pulls on some jeans and a T-shirt. His aches and pains are disappearing as excitement and adrenalin kick in. Could this be true, could he be meeting the one who is going to save Israel?

"You planning to go barefoot,?" asks Andrew as Simon Peter dashes downstairs.

He takes the nearest pair to the door - his work boots.

He and Ruth live a stones throw away from the harbour, only a few hundred yards from the café. They can get there by going along the shore. They run, his work boots sinking into the sand and pebbles.

When they get to the cafe there are dozens of people and Andrew leads the way to a group sitting at a table.

"Ah, the fishermen."

"This is... my brother, Simon Peter," says Andrew, stopping to take a breath before adding, "S P this is Jesus, the man I was telling you about."

"Well, it's good to meet you," says Jesus and they shake hands. Simon Peter is surprised. Jesus' hand is as calloused as his own, his grip is firm. This is a good sign.

"Mind if I call you Peter, it means a rock."

"Does it? that's great." He looks around at all the others watching and he feels ten feet tall.

They sit down. Nick is hovering nearby.

Andrew beckons him, "coffees for both of us, please Nick."

"Right Andrew. We also have some of your favourite pie left, S P."

"Oh that'll be great Nick."

"Okay S P, or should I say Peter? Much prefer that, too many Simons, very common."

Peter could have sat and listened to this guy Jesus all day. The man knows his scriptures alright, better than any Rabbi he has ever heard. Even Nick the café owner was happy, but that may be because Jesus drew a large crowd that needed to be fed and watered. They'd been listening for hours and Peter had started to drift off a couple of times. It was really tough having to leave but at least he'd outlasted Andrew, who'd slipped away an hour ago. Now he too must say his goodbyes; after all, he has to be up in five hours.

As he walks home, he smiles to himself. Today was an amazing day, plus in a couple of days he gets a day off to go to a wedding. A whole day without James and John, bliss.

* * *

Ruth drops Peter off at the bus stop and kisses him goodbye.

"Don't embarrass yourself."

"Then come with us, your mother will be fine."

"Simon Peter, she is sick, you know I can't leave her. Anyway who is there to sit the kids? And don't say James and John, remember what happened the last time they babysat?"

He'd been looking forward to the wedding for ages and so had Ruth.

"It won't be the same without you," he says as she hands him the card and present he'd left on the back seat of the truck.

There are a few others waiting and no one that he recognises. He nods to them as he fiddles with his shirt and tie. Oh he hates ties, why did Ruth make him wear one. Once the truck is out of sight he takes it off and shoves it in his trouser pocket.

Andrew is next to arrive, he must have been doing a bit of last-minute shopping as he has a toaster under one arm and a roll of wrapping paper and tape in the other.

"A toaster, really?" asks Peter.

"Everyone likes toast, anyway what did you get?"

"Oh, you know?" He hasn't a clue, Ruth sorted it all out.

"Andy," yells a lad who has just got off a bus opposite and is quickly running across the road. He is carrying a poorly wrapped present and dodging the traffic. "Alright big man," he says to Peter.

"Nathaniel," says Peter.

"Where's the missus?" Asks Nathaniel.

"At home, the mother-in-law's sick."

"And the other two?"

"Not invited."

"What, everybody in Capernaum has been invited."

"I know, they aren't happy either, especially as they've heard its a free bar."

"Free bar! Sweet."

"So, how's it feel going back to your home town?" asks Andrew.

"A bit weird, haven't been to Cana in years, well, no need now mum and dad live in Chorazin. Be good to see the old place though."

"Wonder if Philip thinks the same? I don't know, would you attend your ex's wedding?"

"Hey, you'll never guess who I met yesterday? This Jesus

guy, that's who," says Nathaniel.

"You too, I heard Philip went to the synagogue and saw him."

"Yeah, it was after that. I met Phil for a pint in the town centre and as we were walking home we see this Jesus guy coming towards us. When Jesus sees me he says. *Here is a real Israelite, there's nothing false about you.* I'm like how do you know me man? and he says, *I saw you when you were in The Old Fig Tree.*"

"Since when do you go in there?"

"There's a quiet corner I like, no one bothers me. The thing is, I've never seen this Jesus guy in there before. So I just blurt out so you are the Son of God, you are the King of Israel."

"What!"

"I know, it just came out, but get this; he said we will see heaven open up and God's angels going up and coming down on the Son of Man. I swear, that's what he said." Nathaniel raises his eyebrows and shrugs his shoulders.

"I hear you've been given a new name," he says.

"Yeah, Jesus calls me Peter, not Simon Peter, 'cos Peter means rock."

"Now James and John have started calling him Rocky," laughs Andrew.

Several more people turn up, most of whom are friends of the family and when the minibus arrives and everybody gets on the driver is keen to get under way.

"Are we all here?" asks the driver.

"Just waiting for one more, five minutes." Andrew says as he sits down and starts wrapping his present.

The driver taps his fingers on the steering wheel. Nathaniel looks at his watch, "well Philip was told if he wasn't on time they wouldn't wait."

Andrew is just about to tell the driver he can go when he sees Philip running up to the bus.

"He's here," Andrew says to the driver.

Philip jumps on the step, pats the driver, and lets out a big sigh. He sits down next to Nathaniel and looking around acknowledges Andrew and Peter. The driver closes the door and sets off.

"Didn't think you were going to come," Nathaniel says, surprised.

"No, neither did I, but you know..."

There is silence on the bus only for a few seconds before Peter has to know, "So, why did you and Naomi split up?" he asks in a loud voice.

Philip gives him an angry stare and gets Andrew to swap seats so he can explain to Peter that it was years ago, when her family moved to Jerusalem, but they had stayed in touch and he's met her fiancé at her last birthday party and he's alright.

The small town of Cana, is only fifteen miles north west of Capernaum and it takes little time to get there. At the hotel the driver has trouble getting up the drive, so many guests are arriving at the same time. Cars circle the car park looking for a space. Another minibus is unloading passengers at the door, whilst behind them another turns into the drive.

"Do you think this is why we weren't invited to the ceremony?" an old lady asks her husband.

"At least they get plenty of presents," the husband replies, holding their gift-wrapped parcel.

As they are getting off the bus Peter asks "are we going to tip the driver?" He is given some glares from the other passengers – that clearly didn't go down well.

"You can't complain, I've heard the drinks will be free all night," he says defiantly.

"A few Shekels each should cover," says the old man. "Euros now," his wife reminds him.

"Bloody Euros" he mutters.

By city standards the hotel is small with only twenty or so rooms, but it is renowned for its quality and luxury. Andrew sees a side room with a table where they place their gifts. Before they can enter the reception, the wedding guests must wash their hands. This tradition goes back centuries, where ritual washing was part of everyday life. Though many of them have been forgotten, this particular one was mainly done before eating. As Peter waits in line he thinks this is a nice touch. On the floor is a large stone jar, very expensive looking, probably an antique. As he waits he looks at it. It must hold twenty or thirty gallons. The thing is massive, mind you it needs to be because every person gets clean water scooped from it and poured into a white bowl by an attendant. When it's his turn he nods in appreciation to the young man as he pours the water. He is given a white towel and the bowl is emptied ready for the next person. Now they are clean they can meet the new bride and groom, who are standing at the other side of the doorway. Then they are each given a glass of champagne by the brides father.

The room is packed and some double doors at one end of the room have been opened onto the patio, giving extra space.

"Seen anybody we know?" asks Andrew.

"Not yet, but it's hard to tell, there are so many people," says Peter.

Nathaniel comes over.

"Philip got a kiss from Naomi, you should see how red he's gone."

Philip takes his glass of champagne and looks around for the others. As he walks over they laugh. One of his cheeks is still bright red, the same colour as the tiled floor.

Peter finds this very amusing, "I'm not surprised it didn't work out with you two, you've had an allergic reaction to her." He laughs aloud. The people nearby turn to look and Philip, in his embarrassment goes even redder but this time on both cheeks. He downs the champagne in one go.

"I'm just going to get a drink and be in a corner somewhere."

"If you see my parents, let me know," says Nathaniel before Philip disappears through the mass of people.

"Peter," says Nathaniel.

"What, what did I say?"

"Philip's still, you know..." Nathaniel tries to make him understand.

Peter looks surprised. "Really, he's still... Naomi....why? It's not like she's been blessed with looks is it, he can do a lot better than that."

Both Andrew and Nathaniel stare at Peter in disbelief.

"You can't say that! You're at her wedding for goodness sake," says Andrew.

"Anyway, look who's talking," Nathaniel adds.

Andrew spots the groom's father whom they do a lot of business with and waves. He is talking to Zebedee and his wife Salomé, James and John's Mother.

"Watch S P will you," Andrew says to Nathaniel and goes over to say his congratulations.

"Oh, well, seeing as it's a free bar and the missus isn't here,

I may as well enjoy myself," says Peter.

He drains his glass of champagne and heads over to the bar. It's a crush just to get near, and the staff are run off their feet. He wonders what he fancies, he's not really the champagne type, or wine for that matter, though it was good the other night.

"A large glass of red please," he booms at the bar staff.

It appeared to be someone else's turn but the bar staff serve him first. He sips the wine, umm it's not bad, "Actually make that two, it will save me coming back for a bit. Oh and don't be shy with the amount, right up to the top this time."

When he manages to get back to the others, he notices Philip sitting nearby looking wistfully out at the veranda as a middle-aged woman sitting next to him asks if he's alright.

"I will be after a few more of these," Philip says waving his empty glass and heading once again to the bar.

"Really, Peter, you've got yourself two drinks?"

"Hey, if you want to queue every-time, that's your call. Me, I'm just being practical."

"His wife's not here, he's not always like this," Nathaniel says to the woman.

"No, he'd be looking for the buffet, hey S P," says Andrew, who has just come back over.

"Buffet, where? I really should eat if I'm drinking you know."

Philip returns from the bar holding a bottle of blue WKD."

"If you want red wine, tough, it looks like Rocky over here has finished it all off.

"Hey."

"We know each other," Philip tells the woman.

Peter smiles as the woman introduces herself as Mary, a

relative of the bride. Then she asks where they are all from.

"Capernaum," Peter says with pride.

"Oh Capernaum, my son has just moved there, you might have met him."

"I doubt it, it's a big place, what's his name?"

"Jesus, I'm sure you'd all get on."

They all look at each other. No, it can't be, can it?

"He wouldn't be from Nazareth would he?" asks Peter.

"That's right, I knew you'd have met him." Mary looks round the room, "he's around here somewhere."

When she can't see him Nathaniel suggests he may be getting a drink.

"He'd better be quick, if they've run out of red wine already I don't hold out much hope for the white. Hope he likes this stuff," Philip waves the bottle and puts out his tongue, which has turned blue.

Mary gets up and goes to the middle of the room. The lads all watch, trying to see where she goes. "There, in the middle, hey it *is* him," says Andrew.

They can see Jesus shaking his head as Mary talks to him. There are too many people and they lose track of them.

Peter clears his throat, all three know what's coming... if he was in charge...

..."If I was in charge this would never have happened, I would have made sure there was more than enough. They knew how many people had been invited, if they all drink x amount of glasses each, spread over y amount of hours, now add into the equation z that people drink more of one than the other.... take... into...account...p..."

"Well you're not, but Jesus is here. Why don't we see if we can find him?" Andrew suggests.

There are more people than ever crammed in and they can't see him so they go out into the reception area. Nothing! Andrew points out a waiter struggling to move the stone jar.

"Need a hand with that?"

"Please, it's really heavy, even though it's now empty."

"What are you doing that for anyway?" Nathaniel asks.

"Someone needs it in the kitchen."

Andrew grabs hold and helps carry the jar as Philip holds the door open and they enter the kitchen. Peter and Nathaniel follow them in.

To the lads surprise they find Jesus and Mary there.

"Just there will be fine" says Jesus.

Peter is a little put out as Jesus doesn't seem to recognise him. Jesus seems preoccupied and orders a waiter to fill the jar up with water from a stainless steel sink using a retractable hose. Peter notices that another waiter is also filling up a second stone jar with water. He counts six jars altogether, including the one that's just been brought in.

"That's it, fill it right up to the brim." Jesus tells the waiter.

Mary turns to the lads and gives a knowing smile.

When all six jars have been filled, Jesus tells the waiters to draw some water out and fill one of the glass carafés they have got out. A waiter dips what looks like a large ladle into the jar and fills up a carafe, but as the water pours into the carafé it's turned a deep red.

A waiter smells it. "Impossible!" he says, and offers the others a chance to smell also.

"Take it to the bridegroom, for his approval," Jesus tells them.

The waiters look at the bar manager for confirmation. Jesus hands a glass to the bar manager, who pours some of the liquid. He drinks it in one.

"Well, what is it?" asks Peter.

"It's amazing!" Says the bar manager and pours himself another glass. He now hurries the waiters to refill more carafés and take them to the bridegroom and to the bride's father. Quickly the waiters fill up more of the carafés and make sure everybody has a drink who wants one.

They all watch from the doorway of the kitchen as one of the uncles of the bride stands up on to a raised step and taps his glass to get some quiet. The whole place slowly falls silent as the man is a retired naval officer and very respected. When it gets as quiet as it can be with so many people, he begins.

"Firstly I'd like to thank everybody for attending this great occasion."

He turns to his brother.

"To my brother and to the bridegroom and his family. I have been a guest at many great banquets in my time and dined with some of the richest men and women in Israel. On each occasion they serve their best wine first, then, when I'm nice and drunk, er.." he pauses for effect and some laugh, as does Peter. The man continues, "when the guests have had plenty, they serve the ordinary wine. But you, he turns and looks at both families, you have kept the best wine, and I mean the very best I have ever tasted, until now." He steps down to applause.

Jesus and Mary have left the kitchen, having followed the waiters into the main room. The lads in the doorway watching, go back into the kitchen. Two more waiters are busy filling up more carafés. Peter takes a glass and dips it into one of the jars. He smells it, like he knows what he's doing, then takes a drink.

"What's it like?" asks Nathaniel before he too tries some.

"That is the best wine I have ever tasted, " Peter tells him.

Andrew and Nathaniel both take some, "Wow, that is so good," they both say.

Philip, still holding his WKD, pours it down the sink and grabs a glass.

Chapter 10

His footsteps are slow and heavy as he makes his way down for breakfast. Every thud of his bare feet on the wood takes him further from his bed as a half-asleep Jude comes down the stairs. He opens the door to the kitchen to find his parents and their two dogs are already up. As soon as he slumps down at the table his mother starts to fuss over him.

"Happy birthday, Oh I can't believe my baby is twenty-one, here are your presents, here are some cards, I think this one's from your Auntie Mary, you can tell by the handwriting and the cat she always draws on the envelope. I've made you egg on toast and a cup of tea, but I can make you coffee. I can't believe it's twenty one years ago today. You know I was in labour twenty one hours, Oh and you're twenty-one, isn't that a coincidence. Do you want one slice of toast or two?"

His breakfast is put on the table in front of him and he starts to pick at it.

"Mum, I'm fine," he murmurs, still not fully awake.

"Happy birthday son, you got in late last night," says his dad from behind the newspaper.

"Uhh."

While they wait for their son to come round, his mum Beth, starts to load the dishwasher and his father carries on reading the paper. Jude has never been a morning person. He eats half of his breakfast and pushes the rest away, and while drinking his tea starts to open the birthday cards. Also on the table are a few presents and when all the cards are open and he is more awake he picks a parcel up. It is quite large and he can tell it must be clothes. Beth stops him, and gives him a smaller box.

"Why not open this one first? It's from me and your dad."

His father closes the Financial Times and stands up. Jude studies the box and wonders if it could be a watch, only the box is too big for that. It's also very light, maybe there's a cheque inside.

"The only way you're going to find out, is by opening it," his dad says, getting a little impatient.

Jude tears off the paper and opens the box. Inside is a key.

"You bought me a car?" His bed now holds little attraction.

"Well, there is something parked outside!"

Quickly he dashes outside.

"No way, it's...it's," he's too excited to speak.

Parked on the graveled driveway is a V-Rod Harley Davison bike, its silver alloy frame glinting in the morning sun. And with a swooping exhaust, scooped saddle and a top speed of one hundred and forty miles an hour, it looks worth every euro of the twenty thousand his father must have paid for it.

Jude gets on it, puts the key in the ignition and starts it up. The deep throaty roar of the V-twin 1250cc engine kicks into life.

"How did you know I wanted one?"

"You always want the best, right? Like father like son."

"It's unbelievable," beams Jude as he revs the engine, sending an echo reverberating around the hills and valleys of Upper Hebron.

His father looks at his watch.

"If you're going to open the rest of the presents you'd better hurry up. Just because it's your birthday doesn't mean you can be late for work."

Jude gets off the bike, and all three go back into the white limestone, six bedroom family home in Kerioth, a small village a few miles north east of Hebron. It's a very exclusive area, with only a few houses scattered along its narrow winding lanes.

His father sets off before Jude, in his burgundy Aston Martin, but Jude knows he can't be too late. It may be his birthday, but he is also the boss's son and that comes with a pressure. He has a lot to live up to.

The ride to work just may be the best commute he's ever done. The sound of the engine, the power as he pulls back the throttle and the looks he gets, makes this his best birthday present yet. He pulls into the private car park behind the offices of Iscariot Insurance Ltd in the centre of Hebron and parks next to his dad's Aston Martin, revving the engine before turning it off. His father stands by the entrance of the five storey building.

"Well, what do you think?" asks his dad.

Jude takes off his helmet.

"Awesome, the best ride ever, you have got to have a go."

"No, it's fine, I much prefer sticking to four wheels. Just do me a favour, don't let your mum know how fast it can go!"

They go inside, riding up the elevator together before going to their own offices. Jude had hoped his dad might give him the day off, so he could spend it with his girlfriend Sarah, but he was never going to ask. His parents had kept hinting that he was getting an expensive birthday present. His older sister had been given a car for her twenty-first and that's what he'd expected, as he knows his mum has never liked his passion for bikes. Mind you, he has come off his Suzuki Bandit a few times. The last time he had broken his collar bone. His mum and Sarah had both pleaded with him to trade it in and go to four wheels like his dad. Maybe that's why he loves bikes so much - the fact that his dad doesn't ride them! It shows the persuasive power of the man if he can talk round his mother. That's one thing Jude has inherited, his dad's gift of the gab. Between them they could sell ice cream to the Eskimos. He gets a cup of tea from a drinks dispenser in the kitchen area, and goes into his office, closing the door behind him. He loves his father and respects him, but he has always been Simon's son, only not quite as good as the real thing. He desperately wants to be his own man, have his own dreams and ambitions, only he hasn't figured them out yet. He is twenty-one, has his own office in a very successful company, works hard but he knows that the rest of the staff think he's only there because of his dad. He turns on his computer and as it starts up, he sips his tea and daydreams about the bike. It definitely gets people's attention. It handled the winding roads alright too, better than he first thought it would, not as good as his Bandit but then they are different beasts. What he really needs is a long straight road to really let it rip, like one of the coast roads.

Iscariot Insurance own the whole five-story building. The firm has the top three floors and rents out the bottom two. The latter are now vacant as the tenants have moved on. Jude has been given the responsibility of overseeing refurbishments and finding some new tenants. This is a big deal, and probably the first time he's felt his dad trusted him with something important. He is determined to do the best he can and that means hopefully charging more than before. This is a sought-after location, and already has interest even before it is finished. He'd been on to some commercial letting agents to gauge their mood as to the maximum possible rent he could charge. They were pretty much all the same, so he had gone with a company in a building opposite who had a good reputation. They had promised that on their books they had several companies looking for just such a property.

Once his computer is up and ready he checks his emails. There is one from the letting agents, saying that they are arranging viewings to start from Wednesday. That's cutting it fine.

Sarah has also sent an email wishing him a happy birthday and looking forward to seeing him later. He is a little surprised she hasn't phoned. He checks his mobile to find two missed calls, both around the time he was out looking at his new bike.

Before starting some work he'd better give her a call.

"Hey babe, it's me."

They talk for ten minutes, mainly about his bike. She doesn't like riding on the back, finding it much too scary, and had hoped he might had been given a car.

The office intercom on his phone rings, it's the receptionist.

"Have to go babe, it's work."

"There are two gentlemen here to see you," the receptionist tells him.

He wasn't expecting any visitors, "Do you know what they're here for?"

"They're here about the vacant offices."

Jude goes out to meet them. Gentlemen is not the word he would have used to describe them. One is short and muscular, with tattoos on his hands and neck. The other is taller, slightly older and has a menacing stare. Both are wearing expensive suits.

"Hi, I'm Jude Iscariot, how can I help you?"

The tall man repeats that they are interested in the vacant offices below and asks to speak to his boss. Jude explains that he has been put in charge of the offices and it is being dealt with by a lettings company, adding that they are not quite ready for viewings.

"We've already had a look round," the small man informs Jude.

"Really?" Jude says, surprised.

"Yeah, one of your carpet fitters let us in."

"How did you know it's available?"

"We hear things, now do you have an office kid, where we can talk in private?"

Jude's stomach starts to churn, he has an uneasy feeling about this. He shows them into his office and offers them a drink.

"The receptionist has already offered us one," says the small man.

"So what kind of business do you have?" He knows the answer. As soon as he saw them he knew.

"Customs and Excise, but I'm guessing you knew that," says the tall man.

Jude nods, "The problem is, the council has regulations on what type of businesses can or cannot operate in this part of the district."

He searches his desk for the relevant paperwork. Jude is not known for neatness, his whole desk is one large pile of folders, reports and bike magazines.

"I'm sure I have a copy here somewhere."

The receptionist comes in with the drinks. After she leaves the tall man gives his friend a nod, who then takes his drink and leaves the room, closing the door behind him. The man takes out a gun, and puts it down on the desk. Jude knows all about collectors, what they are capable of and what they can get away with. It's common knowledge that they carry nine millimetre Jericho's. Jude stares at it with a mixture of fear and curiosity.

"Now kid, are you going to help me or am I going to have to be a little more persuasive?"

"There's nothing I can do," Jude says apologising.

"Wrong answer, you can always do something."

The man picks up his gun, stands up and moves towards Jude, who starts to back away. The man's hand reaches out and grabs Jude's throat, squeezing it in a vice like grip. He is slightly smaller than Jude but his strength scares him. The man forces the Jericho hard into Jude's temple.

The searing pain makes him want to shout out but he is unable to because of the hand around his throat. He starts to struggle for breath, the pressure on his windpipe not letting up, the pain makes thought impossible and just as he starts to pass out, the man lets go and releases his grip. Jude falls to the floor, gasping for air. As if nothing had just happened the man picks up a bike magazine from the desk and flicks through it.

"So you're into bikes, I don't much care for them myself, but I did notice you arrived on a Harley this morning, very nice and expensive. You wouldn't want anything to happen to it now would you?

Jude's throat is burning but he manages to groan out "up

yours!"

"The rich kid's got some fight in him, I'm impressed."

With that he kicks Jude in the stomach. Jude groans. Next the man knocks the computer onto the floor, smashing it up with his foot, laughing. "Didn't really want to rent your offices kid, they were too small for what we need, I just don't like little rich kids."

He goes and opens the office door.

Pointing his Jericho he says, "Oh and I don't like being lied to, this area doesn't have any regulations about tenant businesses."

Jude stares up at him as the man says "kid, consider yourself lucky, usually when I've finished with someone, even the Miracle Man couldn't help them."

When staff see the men leaving, both holding guns, the receptionist rushes into Jude's office, as a secretary goes to get his dad.

"Are you alright? What happened? Shall we call the police?" Jude is bombarded with questions. He struggles to talk, but insists he's okay and doesn't want the police involved. Anyway what would they do - this stuff goes on all the time.

He is slowly helped up onto his chair, as a secretary picks up the bits of computer scattered over the floor.

His dad comes rushing in, "Jude, what the hell happened?"

"Check the bike." Jude croaks.

"What?"

"Check it's OK."

Simon points to a young man, standing by the door. "Paul, go and check his bike, and my car."

A bump is starting to appear on Jude's temple and the mark from the gun is clearly visible.

"I'm getting you to the hospital," his father says.

Jude shakes his head, "I'll be fine, really."

His dad helps Jude into his own office where there is a comfortable leather suite, then he calls a doctor friend.

Jude starts to get his voice back slowly and manages to tell his dad all that has happened, including the part where he lied to the men, claiming they couldn't have an office in the building because of some regulations.

The young man comes into the office to report on the bike, "it has been pushed over and there's a few scratches, it took two of us to lift it up," adding "your car is untouched."

Jude had thought they would trash it completely so he was actually quite pleased. One thing did puzzle Jude, what had the man meant when he said "even the Miracle Man couldn't help them."

The doctor arrives and checks Jude over. Although his throat is fine, when the doc gently presses his rib cage and Jude flinches, he is sent for an x-ray just to be safe. While Jude is at the hospital his dad will arrange for the Harley to be taken to the garage to have the damage fixed.

* * *

Arriving back from the hospital he winces as his mother carefully helps him on to a lounger in the conservatory. No broken ribs, that's a relief. Looking out at the hills of Judea with the warmth of the morning sun on his face, he realises he got his day off after all. Unfortunately his head feels like it wants to explode and every time he moves, or even breathes too hard, it's like he's being stabbed. This is very similar to the last time he came off his bike, but there are some major differences, his mother and Sarah. While his mum looked after him before and helped him recover there was always the implication of *you'll learn.* Sarah was pretty much the same. This time he is the victim, so nothing is too much trouble. Every time he winces it's "Oh my poor baby, what can I get you?" Sarah has gone to get him his favourite magazines and some chocolate, whilst his mum makes sure he's as comfortable as possible. Once the painkillers kick in he might start to enjoy this.

Sarah returns with a bag full of goodies for him. She enters the conservatory and puts her soft manicured hand gently on his head and bends down to give him a kiss. They first met at high school and the moment he saw this blonde haired beauty, wearing a short skirt to show off those amazing legs, he could think of nothing else. He made up his mind right then and there that this was the girl for him, but it took more than his good looks and charm to get Sarah. She wanted to see the real Jude, the person nobody else saw. So when he realised she wanted a kind, thoughtful, honest and considerate boyfriend that's what he became, to her anyway.

To Jude she was the best thing to have, any other girl would have been second best. Right from an early age his father kept telling him and his sister they could have anything they set their hearts on. Nothing was out of reach, they just had to grab it. His sister has done just that by marrying a very successful stockbroker and now has everything she ever wanted: money, big house and nannies to look after the kids.

Sarah sits down next to him and starts to show him what she's bought: choc's, crisps, two bike mags Street Bike Monthly and Super Bikes, The Life newspaper and a very big get well card. In it she's written a love poem expressing her innermost thoughts.

"So you didn't get me any bottled water like I asked?"

"I can go back out and get some if you want?"

"Oh would you, that's great babe."

He picks up the paper, the front page story is about the Temple in Jerusalem. He is just about to throw it down when to his amazement he notices the words Miracle Man. The paper goes into details of the man's actions, and quoted what he'd said, that if they tore down the Temple he would rebuild it in three days. There's more about this same man turning water into wine at a wedding up in Galilee. They report that there are claims that this man can heal the sick, cure cancer and fix broken bones just by placing his hands on people. There are eye witness accounts claiming that he can talk to evil spirits and cast them out, whatever that means.

So that's what the collector had meant by Miracle Man. Later when I can move around a bit more I might go on the Internet and see if there's anything else about this guy. Maybe he could heal my ribs?

Simon gave Jude the rest of the week off, but on Monday morning he is expecting him to be at his desk, no excuses. Jude had overheard his parents talking about how well he dealt with the incident. His dad thought something as traumatic as having a gun pressed into ones skull would send some people into counselling for months. It wasn't all positive though, both his parents noticed a change in him.

Jude is completely unaware of his fathers presence until his music stops.

"Oh, Shi...t Dad, what are you doing here?" He jumps putting pressure on the ribs and grimaces.

"You shouldn't have this thing so loud, it's got to be bad

89

for your ears. Anyway pal, it's my house."

"So what do you want?" Jude asks.

"Nothing, just had to be here for a delivery."

"Oh," Jude turns back to the computer. Simon comes over to see what his son is looking at.

"What's all this then?"

"Research."

"On what?"

"Nothing."

"Right, on nothing, that means it's something. Come on, let your old man have a look."

Jude sighs and shows his dad.

On the screen is a family tree. Simon studies it.

"I don't recall any Josephs on my side of the family and I'm sure there's none on your mothers." He picks up some papers Jude has printed out about the Miracle Man.

"Jesus, Joseph, Mary. You've found out who this man is then?"

"Yeah."

"Well, what have you found out?"

"That people say he's from Nazareth, but he was actually born in Bethlehem at the same time that Herod heard a new king had been born. He disappeared for a while, but it looks like it's the same man who turned up in Nazareth."

He searches around his desk, but can't find what he wants.

"The ancient prophesies say the Messiah will come from Bethlehem, right?"

Simon nods in agreement.

"And they say he also comes from David's line, right?"

Again his dad agrees.

"This guy hits all the buttons," he points to the screen,

scrolling up the family tree.

"Right back to David, and I've read that some say right back to Abraham himself."

"Just be cautious son, others have said that they've found *The One* only to be ultimately disappointed. Many have come and gone. When I was young, there was a man we all thought was *The One*. I can't even remember his name now."

Over the weekend Jude's bike is returned and he has recovered enough to go out on it. The bruising has started to come out and on Monday he will have to go back to work, only he doesn't want to. The more he has read about this Jesus, the more he convinces himself he is the real deal. The whole country is talking about him, every TV programme is examining him in detail. John the Baptist certainly thinks he's *The One*, mind you a lot of people think John is also *The One*.

Jude knows that one day he has to stand apart from his father. To make a name for himself. If he wants to get close to this Jesus it's going to be tough,as he's already been to Jerusalem and there's no doubt all the who's who of the Capital will be positioning themselves round him trying to gain favour. Jude doesn't want to miss out. If this guy's for real, the whole country will see amazing things happen and he wants to be there, right at the centre. He hasn't gotten this excited about something for a long time and he has started to realise, while reading all the reports, that this is what he wants to do. He believes he has the personality, charm and talent to convince this Jesus guy that he is worth having around.

The latest information Jude has is that Jesus has gone back to Capernaum in Galilee. So that's where he must go, bruised ribs and all.

Later, when he tells his parents his plans, they are cautious, but supportive. They know he is ambitious, that's how they've brought him up. His dad even offers to look after him financially while he checks this guy out. His mother wants nothing but the best for him and if he's happy then she is. The reality is, Jude knows they both think he will be back home within a couple of weeks, that he'll soon get fed up with being surrounded by strangers and living out of a holdall.

To Jude this isn't a trip or a holiday. To him this is real, he's never failed at anything so why would he come back and carry on as if nothing has happened. The difficulty will be telling Sarah. They've arranged to go out on the Sunday night, when he'll tell her his plans. Even though he'd been talking about this Jesus for the last couple of days he's never told her what he was really thinking.

Sarah picks him up in her Fiesta and they go to see a film just like most Sunday nights. Afterwards they go to the bar next door, where Jude is going to tell her. He wished he had done it earlier because he couldn't concentrate on the film, and he knew she could tell something was bothering him.

He gets a Sarah a coke and he has a pint of Goldstar.

"Don't go," Sarah tells him. Jude is taken aback, how does she know?

"What do you mean?"

"I know you Jude, more than you realise. I don't want you to leave."

He'd been rehearsing his goodbyes for days and now she's caught him out, what should he say?

"It's only for a while, babe, you know, I thought you might come with me." Smooth, now that is thinking on your feet...

Actually, she should, why not?

"I can't just leave."

"Why not, it could be fun?"

"Jude...this is not just a holiday to you is it. This is real."

He sighs, she's right, he's not going to have fun. Actually he hopes to have *some* fun, but this is serious, this is his destiny.

They kiss and hold each other tight.

"If you need anything just ring, and ride carefully. Is that thing on tight enough?" His mum fusses as Jude puts the holdall over his shoulders and fastens it around his waist.

"I've put enough clothes in for a couple of weeks, after that you will need to do some washing."

The weight pulls on his ribs and he winces. As he starts up the bike, a tear rolls down his mum's cheek and she wipes it away. His father gives him an envelope.

"Just a bit of something to see you alright."

"Cheers Dad."

Jude puts the envelope into the inside pocket of his leather jacket and zips it up. Then he puts on his helmet, waves goodbye and rides off.

Chapter 11

"OK Spiderman, if you're so brave, why do you hide your face?"

Matthew is sitting at a monitor watching the CCTV recording of the night his business was raided. He studies closely the actions and mannerisms of the intruders. Coming so soon after the shooting of Caleb Barnabas, Matthew knows they are sending a message, not just to him but to the Government. Picking on collectors is just an easy way to put your point across. The police responded quickly enough but they aren't going to pursue it any further. No, if these people were really angry and wanting to be taken seriously they would have to do something big. This didn't even make the local news.

The death threats, written on the walls, disturbing at first sight, are nothing new in this business. This is the fourth time Matthew's offices have been vandalised, though it is the first time since he upgraded the security system and he is not happy. The damage, though superficial, did destroy some computers. They also set fire to a stack of paperwork, but the sprinkler system soon put it out. Anyway, everything is backed up or duplicated if it's on paper. It was the damage to the toll barriers that cost him the most. Until he turned up cars were going through for free. That's a few thousand he won't get back. Well if they think they can frighten him, they're way off. Being hated is a way of life, you get used to it, the money makes it all worthwhile. The average person around Matthew's age earns twenty to thirty thousand euros per year. He can clear that in a week.

He is surprised they got in so easily, so this time he's had more expensive blast-proof doors and windows installed.

Within hours he'd got in enough staff to temporarily fix the barriers, but the loss of Dave means he's a man short.

His CCTV cameras all record onto a hard drive which is hidden in the basement. There are seven cameras in total, some clearly visible, hence Spiderman staring straight into the lens and defiantly giving a one fingered salute. He pauses the recording, someone's mask has slipped and the idiots have put the light on. He zooms in on the face. He looks familiar, but just can't place him.

"Are you busy?" A secretary comes to his office door.

"Depends."

"The desk has arrived, they're just unloading it now."

Two carpenters bring it in and set the desk down in its place and thank one of the security guards for helping.

When he first saw the damage he thought nothing could be done, the top had been hacked and it had numerous gouges and scratches. Now, it looks like new. He examines it, looking closely where the damage had been and softly gliding his hand over the wood. Amazing! He can't tell it was ever touched. As he looks around it he becomes aware that the carpenters might be able to see his gun so he fastens his jacket.

"When you stop admiring that, you need to think about a replacement for Dave Milo," says his secretary.

"Someone quit?" asks one of the carpenters. Matthew just

shakes his head, but the secretary is only too happy to say what happened. Matthew is uncomfortable. Strange, but he doesn't want these men to know what really goes on.

"Ever considered a career change," one of the men suggests.

"Not until recently," says Matthew immediately, which comes as somewhat of a surprise to him. Where did that come from and why would he tell a stranger?

"Simonson," he says aloud, confusing his staff and the carpenters, "that's the guy on the CCTV, bet we have his address on file."

When the carpenters leave, Matthew goes back into his office. An IT company has installed a whole new network, the latest and most expensive on the market. They reinstalled all his files from the back up and talked about a cloud or something. The screen he was watching the CCTV on has gone blank. He presses a few buttons but nothing happens.

" Aargh, I hate computers, someone get me Alphie?" he shouts.

When James Alpheaus comes in, Matthew still hasn't worked out how to get the screen back. The young man takes one look, presses a button and...the screen pops back on.

"There," he says avoiding Matthew's gaze and heading back towards the door.

"Where are you going? Sit! You might as well help me."
Alphie sits in Matthew's chair.

"I want you to find a file called Mug Shots.

Alphie finds and opens the file and they begin looking through personnel files Matthew has collected over the years.

"Stop! Matthew sees the familiar face. That's him."

"Nathan Simonson, thirty-six, no dependants, current

address 1105 Shemar St. Capernaum," says Alphie.

"Wonder if it's still a valid address?"

"We can find out." Alphie goes onto a Government database and brings up all the Simonsons in Capernaum "yeah, he's still living there."

"I'll pay him a visit later. Well done Alphie."

Matthew has a few things to do before then and on his way out the secretary calls out.

"Don't forget we're short staffed."

Replacing Dave Milo will not be easy. Dave may have been a little gun happy, but he got results. Even other collectors would take him along when they had a particularly difficult problem. A few years ago it would have been Matt himself who was in demand. Now he is seen as the boss, the old pro, which considering he is only twenty-nine says a lot about the business. Tomorrow he'll ring round the other offices and borrow someone for a while. You can't just put an ad in the Galilee Gazette. Most collectors were born into the business, so you have to ask around, ring other collecting companies. If there's no one available you have to bring in someone from the outside. The money will tempt many to the profession, but finding someone who can be tough and violent when needed but also calm and knows when to back off won't be easy. Milo was too violent and attracted trouble. Matthew would like to recruit someone like James Alphaeus. He can be smooth and chatty most of the time, but tough when it's called for, and apparently he knows his way around computers. Matthew has interviewed young men in the past and the only thing they are interested in is when do they get a gun? They'd be dead in a week.

* * *

One of the inconveniences of being in an occupation that is hated by a large majority of the population, is that some businesses refuse to be associated with a collector; his Mercedes being a prime example. The showroom in Galilee refused to deal with him. This meant he had to use a dealer in Jerusalem and then only because he paid cash and didn't let on what he did for a living. The same happened when he wanted to buy a watch, not just any watch, but an Audemars Piguet Royal Oak. It is brushed steel and Swiss made with a 22 carat gold weight on the inside. Like a lot of things he got it on the black market, from a friend of a friend. Which is fine, he doesn't mind that, only he damaged it one evening on a call that turned violent and as it cost ten grand it had to be repaired by a skilled hand. The man he found was recommended by a fellow collector and has a shop in a back street of Chorazin and now it is ready to be picked up.

The shop is down a narrow street, so he has to park his Merc on the main road and walk. The dark street feels closed in and menacing. He puts his hand on his Jericho - the feel of the weapon giving him some reassurance. As he enters the shop, a bell tinkles and an elderly man appears from a back room. He looks at Matthew, studying him.

"Ah yes, the Audemars Piguet."

"That's right."

The man then disappears into the back room and when he reappears he has the watch. He goes through what needed doing, a new face, strap and repairs to the winding mechanism - all delicate work and not cheap. Matthew takes out his wallet in readiness for the bill.

"So you're from Capernaum are you, I hear that the Miracle Man lives there, you ever seen him?" The man is trying to make small talk. Matt doesn't reply but shrugs.

"You know some people have spotted him right here in Chorazin."

"Really," Matts says, just wanting to pay and leave.

"My son's seen him...." Matt stops listening, it's not the man's fault he wants to talk, he probably spends most of his days cooped up by himself in this little shop, with only the odd customer to chat to. He nods when he feels it's appropriate and looks around the shop, which is more of a repair workshop. There are very few watches on display and those that are for sale have a cheapness about them.

"....and then he heals a woman, right there on the street, amazing! I'd love to see him."

Matt's attention turns back to the man. "Very good." Finally he is told the cost, five hundred euros. He pays the man, adding an extra fifty for his discretion.

As the evening begins to draw in Matthew thinks it's a good time to try and catch this Simonson at home. He reads the printout Alphie gave him. 'Nathan Simonson, thirty-six, no dependants, current address 1105 Shemar St, Capernaum.

He parks a few streets away, in a road he knows is safe and in the shadows walks the rest of the way. 1109,1107, he pauses taking out his Jericho and holding it by his side, he knocks on the door which to his surprise opens immediately.

"Oh, about time, I was beginning to think you'd got lost...Oh, you're not..."

Nathan Simonson takes one look at Matthew, spots the gun, turns and runs. Matthew recognising Nathan straight away, fires off a couple of rounds. Nathan has dived into another room and is now scrambling as fast as he can through the house. Matthew chases after him. Nathan goes out of a back door and is quicker as Matthew knocks into a hall table slowing him down. When Matthew gets to the door Nathan is pulling himself over a six-foot high wall that surrounds a small yard. Matthew has another shot, he misses again and Nathan disappears over the wall. Damn it. Matthew hates this bit of the job, if he had hit him straight away he wouldn't have to do this. He carefully climbs over the limestone wall, trying not to get his suit dirty. Jumping down into an alley at the back of the houses, he sees Nathan is getting away. He's heading into the centre of Capernaum. If he gets there first Matthew could lose him, it's busy this time of night with drinkers. Even running as fast as he can Matthew can't catch up. This guys done this before, he thinks as he loses him in the crowds.

He stops running, conscious that he is holding his gun and slips it back into his belt. He stands there in the busy street looking around for any hint of where Nathan might have gone. As he walks through the crowd he knows that it could be very easy for someone to recognise him and stick a knife in his back. He puts his head down and whilst struggling to catch his breath, he takes out his phone.

"Alphie, Simonson got away. Get across to 1105 Shemar as quickly as possible and either take anything of value or smash it up a bit. Let him know he's a dead man walking. If he comes home shoot him!"

Before Matthew heads back, one particular bar catches his attention. It is so busy people are standing by the door trying to see inside. A sign next to the door says LIVE JAZZ TONIGHT only there isn't any music playing. If Nathan wanted to hide in a crowd that would be a good place. Matthew tries to push his way in, but the bar is crammed full. He leans on the wall underneath an open window and while he decides what to do next he lights up a cigarette. Someone starts to talk, but they are drowned out by feedback from a microphone.

"That's better, thanks Phil. Can everybody hear me now? Right where was I...Oh yes, cheers Pete.

"A collector..."

Boos ring out from the crowd.

Matthews heart jumps, has someone spotted him? He looks cautiously around but everybody's attention is taken by the speaker inside.

"...and a Pharisee went up to the Temple to pray."

More boos.

"The Pharisee stood and was praying this to himself: *God, I thank you that I am not like other people: the swindlers, adulterers, or even like this tax collector. I fast twice a week; I give ten percent of all that I get to the Temple.* The tax collector, standing some distance away was even unwilling to lift his eyes to heaven, but was beating his chest, saying *God be merciful to me, a sinner!...* I tell you, this man went to his house justified rather than the other; for everyone who exalts himself will be humbled, but he who humbles himself will be exalted."

A tear rolls down Matthew's face and he quickly wipes it away. Shit, where did that come from? He wonders who the speaker is, a Rabbi? If he is, do his bosses know he is teaching in an unclean city centre bar? This must be the first time he's ever heard anyone preach. He knows the stories of the scriptures, but that's just what they are - stories. The religious authorities don't much care for his type - never have, and he has never set foot in a synagogue. He finishes his cigarette and stubs it out on the wall, temporarily forgetting why he was there in the first place. His mobile phone ringing reminds him. It's Alphie, he's just arriving at the house and has big Joe with him. They have the van so they are going to get as much as they can. Back to reality – no mercy and heaven for him today!

* * *

Back at the office Alphie and big Joe have unloaded the van. They have taken the usual items, TV, DVD player, stereo, fridge and washing machine. For some reason they have also taken Nathan's ironing board. Matthew has a quick look over the stuff, they'll get a couple of hundred for the lot. He takes from me, I take from him. Nathan's name and picture will be circulated to all the other collecting companies with a warning that he is a known trouble maker.

As the last of the evening shift head off home, Matthew goes to his office. He'll have a look at the accounts and today's takings. As he does he can't help his mind wandering to the bar. That voice, those words, he could swear he's heard him before. That teacher was very believable. He laughs, one minute he was trying to do some GBH, the next it couldn't have been further from his mind. He had overheard someone say the voice came from the Miracle Man himself, but he's never read that the man was a great teacher, maybe that doesn't sell newspapers.

Alphie and big Joe knock on Matt's door and come in.

"Right boss we're off," says Alphie.

Matt waves back, and carries on with his paperwork. A few minutes later and another knock. "What have you forgotten?"

Expecting it to be Alphie, he is surprised when the voice that answers back is someone else's.

"I haven't forgotten anything Matthew."

He looks up to find it's one of the carpenters who repaired his desk. It appears he's brought some muscle with him, two very big, broad, tough looking guys. Matt's first move is for his gun.

"How did you get in? What do you want?"

"Relax Matthew," the man comes over to the desk, while the other two men stay near the door.

"Look, if it's about your bill, my secretary deals with all that."

"No, it's not about that."

Matthew feels uncomfortable, he slides his gun into a drawer, it's the same feeling he had earlier with this man.

"I was just passing and saw you were still working."

Matt is now confused, his office isn't visible from the toll booths. How could he be seen?

"I know you were listening to me when I spoke in the bar earlier. I saw you leaning on the wall outside."

Any number of people could have spotted him, that's no help. He starts to get annoyed when...it clicks, something deep inside recognises the voice. Is he the teacher from the bar...therefore this man, the one who repaired his desk, *is* the Miracle Man...No shit!

"I'll be teaching down at the lakeside tomorrow evening, why don't you come. You'll be safe, it's OK."

"You DO know what I do, right?"

"Of course I do!"

Tomorrow seems an age away. Matthew wants to hear more from him now, he doesn't want to let the opportunity slip.

"Have you eaten? Why don't you and your friends come to my place, it's not too late."

"Great idea, we'll follow you."

Jesus goes over to tell his friends, who don't appear too keen. Matthew isn't concerned, he has a meal to organise.

During the journey home he phones just about everybody he can think of and for those that aren't answering, he sends them a text. When he arrives home there are already a dozen people waiting, all eager to meet this Miracle Man.

It's amazing what can happen in such a short space of time, for within an hour of arriving home Matt's house is packed. It seems that every collector in the area is here, along with their wives, girlfriends and most of his neighbours. This is the first time any of them have ever heard a preacher and they are gripped by Jesus' teachings. They hang on his every word, but there just happens to be a downside. It seems some religious leaders have followed and are watching from the bottom of Matt's driveway. The men heard where he was and have arrived to witness him not only enter a collector's house but enjoy eating and drinking with them.

From the door Matthew can hear them complaining.

"Shameless, disgusting, why does your leader party with these people?" they ask Jesus' friends and followers, who appear uncomfortable, hanging back trying to keep a low profile.

"These are the kind of people I have come to save, where else would I go if not here?" Jesus has heard their complaints and come outside to answer them. A huge collector with a scar across his face has followed Jesus outside. Thinking he's helping, he offers to make the religious leaders disappear. Jesus assures him it won't be necessary and as they rejoin the others he beckons to his followers to join him inside. "Come on inside, there's some people I want you to meet."

Chapter 12

Simon and Flatpack are in The Angels, playing pool and keeping their eye on the TV above the bar.

Flatpack paces the floor. "Do you want to be associated with them? I know I don't. Just when this guy is starting to get interesting and I was thinking he might be worth getting behind." He takes a shot and continues pacing, "the next time we see him we should ask him if he condones what they do and how they get so rich...hey are you listening to me? Simon?"

"Yeah, yeah, I'm pissed too, its just that..." he pauses and pots a couple of balls. "It's all you've talked about for the last week."

Since the news that the Miracle Man had been spotted hanging out with collectors, anger and disappointment had engulfed Simon and his friends. Simon and Flatpack have heard The Teacher speak many times and on one occasion had sat and talked to him right here in this very bar. No other followers in the way, no hangers-on, just the three of them. It was awesome. It reminded Simon of the first time he'd met Caleb, who had a magnetism, a presence that he and Flatpack were instantly drawn to. That was a good day. Simon remembers getting completely wasted that evening and even though Caleb had left with *his* girl, he had been impressed and followed him. But compared to Jesus, Caleb was nobody. This Jesus was different, the things he did, the stuff he said, that feeling you got from being around him. Seeing him hanging out with collectors is almost too hard to take.

"A friend of a collector is an enemy of mine," Flatpack shouts as a picture of Jesus appears on the TV.

"Shh, listen. Hey, someone turn it up," Simon tells the bar staff.

A news anchor is announcing breaking news.

"Reports are coming in to us that Jesus The Teacher has gone away to an unknown location where he is putting together a team to help launch his official bid for the Messiah-ship of Israel. I must stress that these are unconfirmed reports. We are joined by our senior religious correspondent, Benjamin Cohen and we have a live link to the Capital with Joshua Lindman, a member of the Sanhedrin, the religious counsel. Good evening Gentlemen."

The camera flicks first to Benjamin Cohen, a well-built man sitting next to the news anchor in the studio, then to Joshua Lindman, who is wearing the traditional white cloak of the counsel and is sitting in front of a picture of the Temple.

Both acknowledge the anchor.

"Let me start with you if I may Councillor Lindman? Are you expecting a call from Jesus asking you to join him?"

Lindman laughs, "No, I'm not expecting a call. Though I have met this carpenter from Nazareth and while I openly admit I have heard him preach once in the Temple and believe him to be an excellent teacher, I think Messiah is taking it a bit too far."

The anchor turns to the correspondent. "So what do you think this is all about?"

"Well, from what I understand, Jesus is putting together an inner circle, a team so to speak, who can help him achieve his goal."

"And that goal would be...?" the anchor presses.

"Oh, to be the leader of a free Israel, the God appointed Messiah. What else?

"And how does one go about that?"

"Any aspiring Messiah would need to win the hearts and minds of the nation and of the Sanhedrin."

"Never going to happen, never!" shouts Lindman.

"So, who do you think Jesus will choose? Do you have any inside information?" asks the anchor.

"Well, we know that Nicodemus, our honourable council member has recently met Jesus. Joseph Arimathea is another name that has been closely linked. Then there is the cost of such a campaign, so expect some big names from the City. There should be people with political experience, people with good connections to the government. If I had to speculate I'd say Jesus would need the High Priest Caiaphas on board if he is to be successful.

"Never happen, blasphemy," Lindman interrupts, "never!"

The anchor finally allows Joshua Lindman to respond.

"The thought of the High Priest joining this carpenter is blasphemy, I've never heard such nonsense. Plus I know Joseph Arimathea personally and he has never met this man."

"What about Nicodemus?" asks the anchor.

"Naive, very naive. He needs to be more careful who he speaks to in public."

"Thank you Councillor Lindman. So, in your summing up, Mr Cohen, when do you think there will be an announcement and where would this occur, if at all?"

"If the reports are correct, then perhaps in a few days. Expect some big names, experienced power brokers. At the moment Jesus could command say a few thousand followers, but he would need hundreds of thousands if he is to be successful. To get to that stage he would be required to perform more than a few miracles, he would need a good experienced team around him. As to the location, what better place than on the steps of the Temple here in Jerusalem, surrounded by his chosen ones.

"I'd turn him down." Flatpack tells the whole bar.

"What?" asks Simon.

"I wouldn't want to be associated with someone who hangs out with scum, a friend of coll..." Simon interrupts "He's not gonna ask you anyway."

"But if he did, there's no way I would join, it's just not right," Flatpack finishes.

Though Simon feels the same as Flatpack, he is as much disappointed as angry. He is in no mood to hang around here all night listening to Flatpack going over the same things again and again, so he heads off home.

When he arrives home his answer machine is flashing. He listens to the message while he turns on his TV and gets himself a beer from the fridge. A familiar voice requests his company at an unfamiliar address, very strange. Simon plays the recording back and immediately leaves his apartment, TV still on, beer untouched.

Chapter 13

A silver sports car swerves in and out of the evening traffic with all the grace and control of a blind lemming. Taking one corner too fast it clips the wing mirrors of several cars parked on the opposite side of the road.

"Wow... that was close," says John.

He has avoided the short cut through a residential area unlike James, who is now either in the lead or has crashed, he hopes it's the latter. It may be shorter but I must have been going way faster. Ahead is a junction to the main road, John grips the wheel and goes straight across without looking or giving way. I must be in the lead, there's no way James is beating me.

As dusk turns to night, headlights from the oncoming traffic dazzle. John has to concentrate extra hard, all the time keeping an eye out for any police that might be around. Suddenly he has to stamp on the brakes when a car pulls out of a side street right in front of him. It seems like an age before he can get up some decent speed again. That has cost him valuable time. He overtakes the offending car, shouting at its driver as he passes, "Idiot."

Bright lights appear in his rear-view mirror and he sees the flashing headlights from a car behind. No, it couldn't be James, no way. If it's not, it's a police car; he hesitates, briefly lifting his foot off the accelerator giving the car behind a chance to pull alongside. "Aargh," it is James.

Now both cars are side by side, but his brother doesn't have quite enough speed to pass him. A pedestrian just about to cross the road, has to dive out of the way; other cars are forced to pull over. In the distance are a set of traffic lights. Seeing they are at green, John pushes his foot even harder to the floor in the hope of squeezing the last amount of power out of his engine. The lights change to red and other cars start crossing well before they both arrive. John slows down watching James all the time, not letting him pull in front. James seems to have other ideas and has stayed alongside. What's he up to? He's blocking traffic.

At the other side of the road a queue of traffic has formed. Both wind their windows down.

"You're an idiot, there's only room for one car," John shouts, pointing to the single lane at the other side of the lights.

"And I'll beat you to it," James responds, adding "I've not even hit top gear yet."

"That's because you can't find it."

With engines revving and eyes firmly fixed on the lights it seems an age before they change. Both cars inch forward, "not yet, not yet...NOW go, go" John shouts out loud. James never really had a chance and has to brake almost straight away, giving John a slight lead. Now John has another decision to make, does he take the short cut this time? He sees a lot of traffic ahead and a lorry pulling out. He goes for it, throwing the car sharp right, down a side street, just missing an oncoming car.

He looks back. James has kept on, bet he never saw the traffic.

"Yes, oh yes, I'm going to win."

He spoke too soon. His rear-view mirror is filled with red and blue flashing lights and there's the sound of a siren, "Oh no, not again."

John puts the ticket in his wallet with the others and sets off slowly. When the police car is out of sight he phones James to find out where he is, expecting his brother to be gloating.

"Don't tell me you're there already," says James.

"Er... yeah." John can't believe his brother isn't already there, I'm still in this, better not let James know. "I'm there, I mean here! So you don't have to rush."

"Oh, liar, this means the race is still race on! Same rules, remember, first to the door-step wins," James reminds him.

Their destination is 34 Sychar Court Road and both arrive at the same time from opposite directions. They drive as fast as they can whist trying to see the house numbers. John recognises Peter's truck parked outside a house. He pulls in behind it, but has too much speed and can't stop in time. He bumps into the back of the truck. Fortunately, Peter has forgotten to put his handbrake on, so the impact is absorbed slightly. Unfortunately, the truck rolls into the space James is heading straight for. There is the all too familiar sound of crushed metal on metal as James, unable to stop in time, hits the front of the truck. Both lads leave their cars, headlights blazing, doors open as they scramble up to the house. There is nothing to separate them as they both stretch our their arms and... the door opens - the brothers fall into the house, right at the feet of a woman, who lets out a scream.

"I won, I got here first," says John.

"No you didn't, I did," argues James.

John starts to get up, but he is pulled down and James stands up first.

"Hi, I'm James, this loser is John. We were told to meet here."

"I'm Esther, come in." she says staring at the wreckage that is Peter's truck. "What have you done? I'd better tell Simon Peter."

John jumps up. "No, No, you don't need to tell him," he pleads.

"It's just a scratch, it'll be fine. Let's keep this between ourselves," James adds.

Chapter 14

"I'm telling you, it was on TV and in all the papers."

"What!"

"It's true, you can ask anyone."

"You're just messing with me."

"No seriously, and this was none of that cheap stuff either, this was like the best vintage ever."

"From ordinary water...into wine, no tricks?"

"No tricks."

"Shit."

As Matthew and Alphie walk along the dark road, Alphie takes out his phone and taps the screen a few times. "The correct address is 34, I told you we parked too far away," he grumbles.

"So I thought it said 84, alright." Matthew answers.

"You should get one of these," Alphie says, waving his phone in Matthews' face.

"I have, I make calls on it. If I need to make notes I use paper and pencil," Matthew replies, pushing it away.

Matthew keeps checking for danger and has noticed a car has slowed down as it approaches them from behind.

"Go home collectors," a voice shouts.

Matthew notices the glint of a gun barrel.

"Get down," he shouts, grabbing Alphie and pulling him behind a parked car.

BANG, BANG, BANG!

Matthew takes out his own gun, firing off a couple of rounds but the car speeds away. He checks up and down the street before standing up.

"Oh, just look at my jeans!" Alphie has knelt in some mud. He gets up more concerned with his appearance than anything.

"That was close!" says Matthew.

Alphie ignores him. "It's not coming off, you didn't need to grab me like that."

"Maybe next time I should just leave you. Come on we're nearly there anyway."

"My knee is wet."

"OK, I get it."

When they arrive at 34 Sychar Court Road, Esther opens the door. "Ah, good evening, this way, everyone else has arrived."

"Everyone else?" Matthew is surprised, he thought this was a private meeting.

"Yes. There's tea and coffee on the table. One person's asked for food so I'll be bringing some in shortly, anything else you just let me know."

"Any paper towels?" Alphie points to his knee.

"On the table." She stays at the door and Matthew and Alphie enter the room. Alphie heads straight for the table. "Oh good, there they are."

"No, No, No, What the shit are you doing here?"

Matthew recognises the voice, it's the one from the car. He scans all the faces staring back at him, trying to find the speaker. A man sitting near the table whips out a knife and grabs Alphie from behind, putting it to his throat. Matthew pulls out his gun and points it at them. Alphie, taken by surprise, attempts to reach his weapon.

"Don't you dare," Simon presses the knife hard into Alphie's throat and uses him as a shield.

"Let him go Zealot," Matthew, his adrenalin pumping, recognises Simon.

Simon shouts "I should have killed you earlier."

Matthew notices that Simon, whilst fighting the struggling Alphie, is trying to reach for his own gun. Matthew shakes his head. "Oh no you don't."

Alphie starts to panic, "Help me Matt."

Matthew knows he can't take his eyes off the Zealot for a second, but he needs to know if there are any others here he needs to watch out for. "Nobody else move," he warns.

From behind a chair a voice can be heard. "We're all gonna die. We're all gonna die."

"Just shut up, shut up," Simon shouts.

Blood rolls down the young collector's neck as Simon presses the knife in harder. Alphie lets out a cry, "he's gonna kill me, he's gonna do it, isn't he Matt?"

"Not if I kill him first," Matthew tries to reassure his young collector and inches away from the door, looking for a better angle. He weighs up the situation, he's been in similar positions before; tense stand-offs. This is different. From a selfish perspective, there's no gun being pointed at him. One shot could end all this. The right shot can save Alphie and kill the Zealot.

"Someone grab my gun, you all hate collectors as much as me. Let's finish this.

"You know who I am, then you'll also know what I'll do to

anyone who tries."

"Ignore him, he hasn't the balls."

Alphie tries reaching for Simon's gun.

"Don't be stupid," Simon presses the blade even harder.

It feels like an age, as Matthew and Simon stare each other down, neither making another move. Their eyes burn with concentration. No one else in the room is daring to move and Matthew can feel their fear. Alphie has stopped struggling, his face has started to turn white.

"Let him go and I promise I won't shoot you. I'll even let you walk out of here alive."

"You put down your gun first, or I swear I'll finish him."

Without warning a big guy stands up, one Matthew recognises as Jesus' muscle.

"I have had enough of this."

"What are you doing, you're going to get us all killed." says another.

"This is not why we're here."

"Stay out of this big guy," says Simon.

"You put your gun down, just lower it or something."

"The Zealot's right, you'd better stay out of this," warns Matthew.

Alphie, turning whiter, struggles, only for the knife to be pressed harder into his throat.

"My name is Simon Peter, but Jesus calls me Peter so, that's what everyone can call me."

"We call him Rocky," someone says.

As The Zealot reaches and tries once more for his gun, Peter moves towards them and unbelievably stands between Matthew and Simon.

"What are you doing, you'll get yourself killed," shouts a

voice.

Matthew and Simon, move around but Peter turns his back to Matthew. He is so big Matthew's view is completely blocked.

After another couple of well-built lads also stand in the way, Matthew lowers his gun. This better not be a trick?

Simon lets go of Alphie, who falls on the floor.

"You OK Alphie?" asks Matthew, wanting to get to him.

"Jesus is here!"

"How do you know?

"I can hear his voice."

"He's probably calling the police."

Peter bends over Alphie, now lying at the feet of Simon.

"John" Peter says, "you know first aid, come over here."

"Teacher, it's Alphie," says Matthew as Jesus enters.

Jesus goes over to Alphie and places a hand on his neck. When he takes his hand away not only has the bleeding stopped, there is not even a scar.

"I see you've met Simon," says Jesus.

"Unfortunately. Please tell me it's not always gonna be like this," says Alphie.

Jesus smiles, holds out a hand and helps Alphie to his feet and pats him on his back.

Matthew, his gun by his side keeps an eye on the Zealot. He watches him clean the blood off the knife blade with a paper towel and put it back in its sheath on his belt, next to his gun. Only then does Matthew feel comfortable enough to put away his own weapon.

"Everyone, please sit down," says Jesus.

Alphie grabs a paper towel before sitting down and dabs at his muddied jeans. In silence Jesus pours himself coffee.

He sips it, looking round the room. Matthew watches as Jesus looks each one of them in the eye. When it's Matthew's turn, after all that has just happened he is surprised to feel utter peace and it's like nothing he's ever experienced before. He can feel himself smiling back at Jesus, which in itself is strange, because he never smiles. Not in public anyway.

"I think now is a good time for introductions," says Jesus. "I believe this guy's already introduced himself," he stands next to Peter, "then there's Andrew."

"I'm James and this loser is my brother John."

"Hey," John, next to James, thumps him on the shoulder. James is just about to punch him back when Peter interrupts.

"Will you two, for once give it a rest." says Peter, shaking his head.

"He started it," mumbles John.

"I'll continue shall I James?" asks Jesus.

James nods.

"Next is Philip." Philip smiles at everybody.

"This is Nathaniel," Jesus says walking round the room. He stops in front of Matthew.

"We know who he is," says Simon, glaring at Matthew.

"Everyone knows who he is, but what's he doing here?" says James under his breath.

Matthew can feel their hatred and feels more vulnerable than ever.

"Teacher," he says, looking Jesus in the eye.

"Matthew," says Jesus before moving on. "Now we have Thomas, welcome Thomas.

This is James Alphaeus." Alphie smiles back at Jesus, rubbing his neck and smiling even more. Jesus now moves over to the other side of the room.

"Next is Simon or as some of you know him, the Zealot." It's now Matthew's turn to glare.

"Simon," says James. "John has all your albums."

"I have not, it's crap...I mean, no, not crap, er, it's not really my kinda thing, its a bit weird. No not weird..."

"While John continues digging a hole for himself, this big guy here is Jude Thaddeus. I hope you know what you're letting yourself in for?" Thaddy raises his eyebrows and laughs.

"And finally the man who's travelled the furthest to be here, Jude Iscariot. Hope everyone is making you welcome."

Jesus goes over to the door, "Well, thanks to Peter I believe Mary has prepared a few snacks for us, but before we eat I want you to remember one thing. You are all here tonight because I have chosen you. All of you.

James raises his hand. Jesus looks at him.

"Yes James, on purpose."

Chapter 15

Word soon spreads that Jesus has chosen a team and he is going to speak early in the morning. Not in Jerusalem as predicted, nor with the temple as his backdrop and the palace his destination, but in Galilee on a rocky hill north of Capernaum. Not surrounded by the brightest, richest and most powerful, but with a mixture of nobodies and wannabes, who can't even stay in the same room without trying to kill each other. The team had their names leaked to the media not long after the meeting had finished and when people woke up this morning it was to headlines: Galilean Nobodies screamed the Jerusalem post; A Damp Squid, went another, referring to the fishermen. Twelve reasons why Jesus isn't the Messiah, was what the Galilee Gazette went with.

When Jude got the call from Jesus, he imagined a well-oiled organisation, a team of go-getters much like himself. This guy Jesus has the power to heal people, preach like all the prophets combined. I should be with Kings and High Priests on the steps of the temple he thinks. Not trudging up a hill in the middle of nowhere. After all the negative press they had this morning, Jude is more than a little surprised to find so many people here. There must be thousands, with hundreds arriving all the time. The headlines haven't stopped the media turning up either, for they are here in great numbers. TV cameras, radio coverage and newspaper reporters from Egypt, Syria and even Rome - the heart of the Union have turned up to cover this breaking story.

Jude notices the two collectors standing some distance away, in a small group of men and women. They are being completely ignored by the rest. Just snide remarks and occasionally someone will aim spit in their direction.

It was bad enough turning up expecting to talk to Jesus one on one and finding others there. Worse still when he realised they were all idiots. But when two collectors showed up, it turned into a nightmare. Why them? Why? After all he'd gone through, leaving home, travelling to Galilee of all places, only to come face to face with two of the worst kind of scum in Israel.

Jesus appears from the crowd and sits on a rock at the top of the slope, just as the Priests in the Temple always sit down when delivering their sermons. The significance is not lost on the people, for Jesus has fast become the *go to guy* on all spiritual matters, much to the annoyance of the religious leaders. It's one thing claiming responsibility for the odd miracle, but taking their role as an authoritative elder is quite another. There is an air of expectation. What will he say? Is this the speech to rock the very foundations of Rome itself? How about another miracle? Members of the media rush to get their microphones in front of him.

"Where is my team, come on guys, sit here at the front, by me," Jesus says. He points to Matthew and Alphie and waves them over. The two men walk over in deathly silence.

When they're all sitting Jesus starts to speak.

"How many here are struggling with life?" Lots of nods

and agreeable groans.

"Or too ashamed to even step inside the Temple?" Some agree. Others nod.

"Are some of you grieving from the loss of a loved one? Well, now you can all dance for joy, for My Kingdom is for you. I say to the gentle and pushed aside, to the people who are hungry and thirsty, those of you who feel empty inside, to the peacemakers and those who are persecuted and hated, I say sing praises, for there is a special place for you in My Kingdom."

"Now, there are those who believe only in money, that we should do whatever it takes to get it. Those that force their will on others, think that might is right and retaliation is king. Those that spend, spend, spend. There'll be no singing and dancing for you, no, what awaits you is only death."

From the middle of the crowd two voices shout, "So you think all the sad and pathetic should be happy and all the successful, ambitious people are losers."

"Good luck selling this tripe mate, talk about losing before you've started."

Jesus ignores the hecklers.

"Now, what about the Ten Commandments, the most sacred of all the old teachings that Moses himself delivered to the people of Israel?"

All around there are whisperings, "he can't start changing these."

"So even if you break the smallest of the Commandments and teach another to do the same, you will be at the bottom of the pile in My Kingdom." He then goes on to say that not only is murder wrong but you shouldn't even hate, you commit adultery even if its just in your fantasies. If someone punches you, let him have another shot.

For some this is getting all too much and they start to wander off.

"You've heard the saying *love your neighbour and hate your enemy*, well I say you should love your enemies, because even collectors love their friends."

"This is rubbish," shouts someone and stands up to leave.

Others start to leave saying, "I'm off, I can't take much more of this."

"There is something for everybody... to feel inadequate about."

"Talk about making us all feel bad, I mean who can live up to all these rules anyway?"

"People don't want to be told they're doing it wrong, they need to be built up, you need to be all inclusive. This guy's just alienated ninety percent of the population."

"If that's his idea of the Kingdom he can keep it, it's just a bunch of losers. Who wants to be part of that?"

Those that call out and leave are in the minority. Most people hang onto every word, to such an extent that when Jesus has finished they don't want to leave. The camera crews start to pack up, journalists scramble to write their copy for the papers and once again Jesus is surrounded.

"Come on people, give the teacher some room," says Peter taking charge. He looks around for his brother, "help us out Andy."

As they walk down into Capernaum, the twelve surround Jesus like a team of bodyguards. By the time they are in the centre the crowd has thinned out and Jude hears that Esther is preparing a lunch for them. Not having taken his eyes off the two collectors the whole walk back he is glad to hear one of them can't stay. He can't quite work out the other collector, he's young and doesn't really look all that threatening. The others seem more accepting of him. Maybe it's out of sympathy, not that Jude has any, he'd wished the Zealot had slit his throat.

They arrive at Esther's to find around a dozen people gathered outside her door.

"Oh great, is it gonna be like this all the time" grumbles Thomas.

James looks around for Simon, "where's the Zealot, hey, Zealot, threaten 'em with your knife, that'll put the fear of..." But Jesus knows them and insists they come inside and share a meal. Inside, Esther, with the help of Jesus' mother Mary has prepared enough food for an army.

"Everyone just help themselves, there's plenty to go round," says Esther.

Peter's stomach rumbles so loudly that it could be mistaken for an approaching storm and the four fishermen are the first to the table, pushing and shoving each other. They are quickly followed by the rest of the group. There is chicken soup with matzo balls, salad and cottage cheese, yoghurt and fruit. For dessert there is a choice of chocolate cake, strawberry trifle and iced buns.

Jude hangs back, waiting a little. He watches as James goes straight for the chocolate cake, slices himself an enormous piece and devours it in two seconds leaving chocolate all around his mouth, "Umm, fantastic, nice cake Esther."

A small voice from the other group of people nervously tries to make himself heard, "er, excuse me, but shouldn't we say grace before we eat?"

Jesus, standing in the doorway, makes his way to the large

dining room, and without any fuss gives thanks for the meal and their hosts and gives a wink to Mary his mother, before squeezing in between Thaddy and Nathaniel and getting a bowl of soup.

Jude watches the young collector, who is the last to eat. He has never spoken a word and is staying close to Jesus, keeping a wary eye on the Zealot.

Jude takes his plate and sits next to one of the fishermen. John and a middle-aged woman sit in a chair opposite them.

"You must feel very privileged at being chosen to be a disciple?" says the woman.

John, his mouth full of matzo balls answers her, "A what?" he looks towards Jude for help, who shrugs.

"A disciple, that's what they will call you, you know it means learner or student."

John smiles and nods.

"I bet you made lots of notes this morning, I know I did, I've filled a whole notebook with what Jesus said about prayer and fasting."

John again smiles and nods. When she excuses herself and goes for a drink John shouts over to Peter. "Hey Rocky, were we supposed to make notes this morning?"

Peter shrugs his shoulders.

"And when did Jesus talk about prayer?"

Suddenly a woman screams from the hallway and everyone stops eating. Some rush to see what it's about. Esther is pushing Simon out of the house, "get out, get out, how dare you, how dare you." The Zealot, it would be the Zealot, now what's he done?" asks Peter.

"I don't care who you are she tells Simon, you can't smoke in my house." She pushes him outside and shuts the door leaving him to finish his cigarette on the step. Jude starts to laugh, more out of relief than anything, as Esther gets some deodorising spray to cover up the smell.

"I will not have anyone smoking in this house, nor will I tolerate swearing either."

"Oh great, we'll all be on the step in that case," says Jude.

John, still puzzled by what the woman said to him, gets Andrew and Nathaniel on one side. "Lads, that woman over there called me a disciple, she said it means student, is that right?"

"That's right," nods Nathaniel.

"I don't want to be a student, I hated college," moans John. "I mean, I thought we were chosen as Jesus' team, you know to help him and stuff."

"Johnny B's followers are called his disciples too," says Andrew.

"The word disciple means learner, so I guess we are expected to learn from Jesus" says Nathaniel. John doesn't seem convinced and wants to ask Jesus. He asks if anyone knows where he's gone? In the garden around the back is the reply, but he is not to be disturbed as he's gone to pray.

"I guess we wait here then!" suggests Peter, looking round at the food.

Chapter 16

The road around Mount Carmel is quiet this time of day, the tea time traffic having melted away. Andrew pushes his truck to the limit as it struggles to climb a steep stretch. They are passed by a car, that makes the mountain look flat. It sounds it's horn as it passes.

"How rude," says Ruth from the back seat.

"I think that was the Zealot," says Andrew as he changes down a gear. It struggles to engage and crunches before popping in.

"I think I need a new clutch."

"You need a new truck? I'm not sure we are going to make it?" says Peter from the passenger seat.

"Hey, it's newer than yours? And anyway we are having so much time off lately I don't think I can afford one."

Finally the road begins to drop down towards the Bay of Haifa and the City. Just beyond that is the port.

"See the boats, that's where we're heading," says Andrew.

A dozen yachts are berthed at the port, it being one of the few places on the coast big enough to moor the private yachts of Israel's mega rich.

When Jesus told the twelve about the invitation they'd received, their minds were on nothing else. He'd finished his teaching early so they could get ready.

Peter hasn't been to Haifa in years and never to the marina. Andrew seems to know where he is going, so for now he'll keep his mouth shut. As they enter Haifa, the buildings that looked small from the mountain road, now look large and imposing and when they come to a sign pointing towards the port Andrew hesitates and starts to turn in.

"No, it's not that one, go straight on and further round the bay, it's a private entrance," says Peter having bitten his lip long enough.

This time there isn't any doubt – before they even arrive at the entrance they see the large white luxury yachts all lit up.

Security guards stop the truck at the gate. Andrew gives them his name and is allowed to drive up to the biggest yacht.

"Now that is a boat." says Andrew.

Valets open Andrew's and Ruth's doors for them and they both step out. Peter doesn't wait for his to be opened, he jumps out straight away, staring up at the yacht. Oh, this is fantastic, imagine sailing one of these. I must get a chance to see the bridge.

Ruth, wearing her best dress takes Peter's arm as they walk up onto the yacht, tapping him whenever he touches his collar.

"Stop it," she whispers.

Once on board they are greeted by an attendant.

"Welcome, on behalf of the esteemed Counsellor, Mr Joseph Arimathea and his wife Bella." The attendant takes their names and walks them a few paces to the host and hostess.

Joseph welcomes them on board and introduces his wife. A waiter offers them a glass of champagne. The yacht is very impressive with a large ballroom that leads on to an open balcony. There is a band playing modern background music on one side of the room and there appears to be a good number of staff. Peter looks round while taking a sip of the bubbly, but he's not admiring the satin cherry tables, teak flooring or even the leather and marble furnishings, he's checking out who's here. He recognises a few business leaders, but no sign of Jesus. His tie feels like it's strangling him and he fiddles with it and downs the champagne in one go and looks round for a waiter.

"So now I understand why you let your brother drive," says Ruth, taking his glass and giving him hers. "I may see if they have something alcohol free."

Andrew joins them and points out the lads. They are all standing together in a group next to the bar. They go over and join them. Peter finishes the glass Ruth gave him and gets himself another from a passing waiter.

"Hey Andrew, I thought that truck of yours wasn't going to make it," says Simon.

"It was fine, I was just admiring the view."

Simon scowls as he looks over to the doorway, and Peter knows without even looking that Matthew must have arrived.

"Wow, look who he's brought?" says James.

Ruth squeezes Peter's arm and he too looks over. On Matthew's arm is who Peter can only assume is a model. She is tall, thin and wearing a long black dress. Her hair flows over her slender shoulders.

"Bet those are diamonds she's wearing?" comments Thaddy.

"Paid for by our tolls," says Jude.

As Matthew and his date start to come over Simon and Jude move away.

"So, that's The Collector you've been complaining about,"

says Ruth.

"That's him, as welcome as a shark in a swimming pool," Peter replies turning away, wanting to follow Simon and Jude.

Alphie has slipped in quietly to join the lads, and he waves Matthew over.

"This is Rebecca," Matthew says to them.

James and John push the others out of the way in an attempt to be the first one introduced.

"What *are* you wearing?" Matthew asks John.

Peter hadn't noticed, but John is the only man on the whole yacht not wearing a jacket and tie. In fact, he has on a short sleeved shirt.

"I left mi jacket in the car. When we pulled up and got out some guy got in and drove off! Mi jacket and tie were on the back seat."

The others laugh, Peter tuts and shakes his head.

"Why didn't you say something?" Matthew asks.

"I didn't get a chance, he'd driven off! Anyway, I don't like wearing a tie so why bother? They let me in didn't they. Hey, never mind about me, I didn't know we could bring dates, how come you brought a date?"

Matthew smiles, "would you turn this beauty away?"

"True."

"Hi I'm Ruth, Peter's wife, I've heard quite a lot about you," Ruth says to Matthew.

"That doesn't surprise me."

"And you look amazing," Ruth says to Rebecca.

Peter excuses himself, he needs another drink. He feels very uncomfortable, with the company and his collar. He fiddles with it again, it's way too tight. Ruth has told him to keep the top button fastened as he needs to look smart around all these people, but it's choking him. At the bar he undoes it and loosens his tie, oh the relief! Thomas wanders over and seeing he is ordering a Goldstar lager, asks for the same.

"Hey Pete, I'm gonna have a nosy around, you coming?"

"I wonder if they'll let us on the bridge?"

"I don't see why not, we are special guests."

Peter looks at Ruth talking to Matthew and Rebecca. She seems okay for a while. "Sure, why not."

They head to where they first came aboard.

"I think there might be some stairs around here," Thomas says.

"How about using that instead," Peter points to the lift doors.

"This things got a lift? no way!"

Peter presses the button to call the lift and the doors instantly slide open, revealing an elegant cherry wood lined interior with gold hand rails and a mirrored wall. Both step inside.

"So how much do you think one of these bad boys cost?" asks Thomas.

"I reckon around twenty-five to thirty million, maybe more."

Peter suggests they should start at the top and work their way down as he looks at the panel next to the door, before pressing a button labelled Sun Deck. It does feel a bit like snooping, but their curiosity far outweighs any sense of guilt. The size is incredible, the yacht has four decks, Lower, Main, Upper and Sun and it's room after room, all immaculate as the next. The Lower has most of the bedrooms and staff quarters and is the only floor not to have an outdoor deck area. It's here that a staff member asks them what they are doing and suggests they return to the main deck where the party is being held.

Stepping out of the lift Peter looks for Ruth. Oh great, she is still talking to Matthew and Rebecca. Not ready to go back he and Thomas explore the main deck. Opening one door, Thomas comes upon the dining room.

"Hey Pete, look at this."

A large table is set out with all kinds of food, from a seafood buffet to chicken and even grilled steak. If it had been the first place they'd seen, they wouldn't have gone any further.

Peter's stomach rumbles so loudly that Thomas is sure it could have been heard over the band in the other room.

"Look at all this food." says Thomas. "Do you think we can help ourselves?"

Peter is way ahead of him and is already loading up a plateful. Thomas does the same and then they both head back into the party.

John, standing with Philip and Nathaniel spots them, "Hey, where did you get that?"

"The dining room," Thomas points out.

John and Nathaniel both dash off to the dining room.

Peter takes his plate and goes over to Andrew to tell him about the buffet. The only one of the twelve to make any effort to talk to other guests has been his brother. He's a natural in this environment. The others just stick together looking very much like fish out of water.

"There's food!"

"Pete, what the hell. You can't just help yourself."

"The party is for us, why not." He then nudges Andrew. "Hey, I think that woman's daughter may have a crush on you."

"Oh no, not them as well," says Andrew as John and Nathaniel return and start demolishing large plates of what looks like chicken salad.

"Excuse me, everyone, may I have your attention?" Joseph has gone over to the band and borrowed a microphone. He taps it to make sure it's on.

Peter goes and takes a seat next to John.

"Thank you all for coming this evening, I have just been informed that the Buffet is now open, please help yourselves. Also in honour of my special guests I have arranged a short trip up the coast and in celebration of this joyous evening we will watch a magnificent firework display."

Some of the guests applaud. "Thank you, but before that I think it would be appropriate if we give thanks for the meal."

Peter and John look up in unison. Ruth puts her head in her hands and James laughs out loud and points. Jesus gives thanks to his Father for the good food and great company and follows the rest of the party to the dining room.

As guests stare, Peter doesn't feel embarrassed, why should he? It's been a long day, he fished half the night and slept only a few hours before heading to Esther's to meet with Jesus and the others. He hardly gets time to see Ruth and the kids anymore. Anyway, he saw Jesus stifling a yawn. It's been a long day for them all.

Thomas, who had been throwing down food and drink at an unequalled velocity has now stopped and is looking rather worried.

"Did you feel that, I'm sure I felt something?" he says to Peter.

"They must be setting off."

"Oh, I didn't know we would be going out to sea," moans

Thomas.

"What's wrong?" asks Thaddy.

"I get seasick."

"I thought your dad was a boat builder?"

"He is, and I've helped – on dry land! I'll be alright unless it starts to go up and down or side to side."

"These things have technology that stops them rolling about, you'll be fine. Unless it gets really rough, that is," says Peter.

Andrew, James and John come over.

"Come on Rocky," says James, "Joseph says we can visit the bridge."

The moment Peter heard that they were going on a yacht he'd hoped they might be able to see the bridge, he feels quite excited. Joseph accompanies them in the lift to the upper deck. Once there they stand quietly at the back as the Captain and two crew slowly manoeuvre the huge yacht off the side of the quay and out of the marina. The bridge is huge by the fishermen's standards and though there are many of the same instruments, they are the most up to date available. Once clear of the marina entrance Joseph introduces them to Captain Gerald McNeil, a retired British Navy Captain with forty years experience at sea. McNeil says hello and asks Joseph to look at a screen showing the weather charts. Peter tries to hear what they are saying.

"Peter, come here and have a look at these charts," says Joseph waving Peter over to look at the screen. "The Captain is a little concerned by the wind speeds."

Peter is only too happy to give his opinion. He studies the screen, oh this is so much better than the one on his boat.

"We'll be fine," he tells Joseph. McNeil raises his eyebrow.

Joseph pats Peter on the back, "good job" and heads back down to his guests. Now Andrew, James and John are studying the weather chart.

"Looks like there's a storm coming to me," John says.

"Yep, and just look at that wind speed, gonna be a bad one too," James adds.

Andrew, who never raises his voice with anyone let alone his brother, shouts "what on earth were you doing telling him we'll be fine. Did you actually look at those charts?"

Peter smirks, "It's well over a hundred miles away, and that's if it stays on the same heading, which I very much doubt."

"Anyway why is it your call, it's the Captain's decision," Andrew points out.

Andrew pushes Peter towards the lift and they all leave the bridge and head back down. "How cool would it be to have one of these," James wonders.

"Yeah, think of the girls we could pull," says John.

When they get down they find that most of the guests are outside on the deck. They can see Haifa with all its lights and buildings illuminated against the magnificent backdrop of Mount Carmel. Once the massive sprawl of the city has given way to singular and sporadic lights of coastline, the yacht begins to slow down.

Joseph announces that everyone should be ready to look out as the fireworks will start any minute. He gets on the phone to the organisers on the coast, says that the yacht is now in position and they can begin immediately.

Unfortunately, there is a delay, the fireworks don't start and after fifteen minutes of waiting the wind starts to blow harder and Peter has second thoughts about the weather charts. He and Andrew slip away and head back up to the bridge.

Peter knows the second he looks at McNeil's face, that all is not well.

"What's he doing here," Captain McNeil says to Andrew. Peter ignores him and studies the weather chart. The screen is showing an increase in wind speed and when combined with the low-pressure front, the window they have to get back to the safety of the marina is fast closing.

"If they don't start this blasted display soon..." warns McNeil.

Bang, Bang, the first sounds of the fireworks explode in the sky high above the yacht. Peter and Andrew dash back down to the others.

Thomas is trying to watch the display, but with the motion of the yacht he is finding it difficult to concentrate. "Oh I wish I hadn't eaten so much, Ohhh."

James and John are finding this hilarious, and continue to make fun of him until he can't take it any more and he dashes off to find a bathroom.

The band is playing a rousing soundtrack to the display, but before they get to their big finale a large wave hits the side of the yacht, knocking them and quite a lot of the guests and crew off their feet.

It seems that McNeil has had enough and the yacht turns around and begins to head back to the marina. Staff begin handing out life jackets and Joseph gets everyone inside and issues orders to his staff to clear away the buffet and anything breakable. This is a huge disappointment to Peter who had hoped to hit the dining room one last time before they got back to shore.

As another wave hits, the lights flicker, then go out, plunging the yacht into complete darkness. People start screaming.

Peter rushes to Ruth and puts his big arms around her. She puts her head on his chest.

"Everything will be alright," he says to her.

Even James and John look worried.

Rebecca, who has spent much of the night flirting her way round the room, is now firmly attached to Matthew. A flash of lightning streaks across the sky as if to announce the large wave that comes over the bow of the yacht. It knocks a crew member over as he is trying to close the doors to the deck and soaks everyone. They cry out as the freezing water hits them. As the storm increases, the yacht is thrown about violently, hurling marble tables and cedar chairs into the windows, sending huge shards of supposedly unbreakable glass everywhere.

Peter can no longer hear the sound of the engines, they are now helpless. In all his experience he can't remember a more violent and sudden storm as this.

Voices call out, checking on loved ones. Above the noise of the wind and waves Andrew shouts "has anyone seen Jesus?"

Just then another flash of lightning reveals a silhouette of a man standing outside on the deck. He has his arms outstretched and is completely unaffected by the wind and movement of the yacht. Suddenly the wind stops. Now Jesus' voice can be heard. He is telling the sea to be calm...and the sea obeys.

Chapter 17

Two bodyguards push through the crowds of pilgrims and visitors. They are in constant communication with the Temple control room via discreet earpieces and microphones. Their every movement is monitored by surveillance cameras.

"We're at the money tables." says one guard.

"Confirmed," crackles back in his ear.

The other guard hears and nods to his partner.

From between the two guards steps a bald man in his sixties. Men sitting working at tables, or booths as they are called, stop serving their customers and stand up. Each gets the same greeting, a firm hand shake, followed by the traditional kiss on the cheek.

"Shalom brother."

The men continue exchanging currencies into the Temple Shekel. Behind them a large computer screen shows the latest exchange rates, linked to the International Monetary Exchange. Josephus Annas likes to go down to the shop floor and inspect the booths and chat to some of his employees. It's not just the money tables he owns, he has the monopoly on the sale of animals for the sacrifices. This is where he's made most of his fortune. He has booths here and at the Mount of Olives, selling everything from sheep to doves and even pigeons. This is big business, for at Passover time alone two hundred and fifty thousand animals are slaughtered, most of which are supplied by Booths of Annas and Sons Ltd.

Jonathan Sethas his assistant, comes forward. "Sir, it's time you were moving on."

The guards once again take over, first letting the control room know that they're on the move. With swiftness and authority they push through the people, who move out of the way when they see the guards. They recognise Annas and so they should, for it wasn't that long ago that he was their High Priest. To many he still is, believing that the job of High Priest is for life.

At the next booth a queue has formed as pilgrims buy a sacrifice. A board above the booth has all the days prices. Annas stops, waiting and watching as people choose an animal, depending on how much they can afford. An old man purchases a dove and hands over his shekels. It would cost only a few cents anywhere else, but here he has to see the money changers and pay a premium for the dove. Well, he is buying it here after all. Another nice profit.

Annas followed the same path as his father who was a Sadducee and served on the Sanhedrin Council too but it wasn't until many years later that Annas got his opportunity to become the High Priest. From that time he built up his considerable fortune from the booths. The Temple took its fair share and the priests were very well taken care of but it was Annas who exploited every opportunity. Who was there to stop him? He was the High Priest, the most important and respected person in Israel. He was the chairman of the Sanhedrin and head of political relations with the Union. Historically, if anything were to happen to the King or Ruler of Israel, it was the High Priest who assumed the role of its leader, something Annas would have felt very comfortable with. He even managed to engineer a whispering campaign in Rome that suggested if the Union was to ever gain Israel's acceptance, a Jewish born Governor might be the solution, with his name being widely circulated.

Sadly for him nothing came of it. The greased palms hadn't worked on that occasion and when the Union installed Valerius Gratus, a tough ex military Commander, as the new Governor of Judea, Annas' days as High Priest were numbered. Gratus found Annas a threat to his own power and about a year after he had arrived in the province, stripped him of the High Priests' position. Gratus brought military justice Union style, with the death penalty installed and a clamp down on any independence protests.

Priests, as part of their duties, operate as guides and they can easily be recognised for they wear long white linen robes and have tubular hats. A guide, showing a large group of tourists around, spots Annas.

"Everybody, today God has blessed us, for here in our midst is our ex High Priest Josephus Annas."

The group all swarm around Annas and the guards struggle to keep them away. Annas smiles and even agrees to sign a few souvenir guide books. He is charm personified but when one woman tries to touch him his mood changes and the guards gently push her out of the way and take hold of their boss, quickly manoeuvring him away from the area.

"I know, I know, one day there could be someone with a grievance," says Annas.

They climb some stairs to the upper courts where he has an office. It is also where the control room is situated. Priests and teachers mill around, public are only allowed up here when lessons in the scriptures are being taught. Annas has two offices, one here and one at his residence. Here he can keep an eye on his businesses. Two men are sitting on benches that run the entire length of the corridor. Both stand up when Annas comes into view. He ignores them, walking straight passed and through a reception area where his assistant Jonathan works. There are two more doors, one to a private wash-room, the other to his office. Jonathan and two guards all follow him. "Will that be all sir?" asks one of the guards.

Annas stops at his office door, thinking for a second. Without turning round he says, "No, please wait outside and send in the other two."

His office is dark, the blinds on the windows closed, only a glimmer of the mid-morning sun shining through. He sits down on a soft brown leather chair and turns his back to the room facing the covered window and puts his hand to his face and thinks.

There is a quiet knock at the door, and Jonathan shows the two men in.

"Sir," one says.

Annas stays silent.

After a few awkward moments, the other man speaks up, "you wanted to see us sir".

"Do you like me?"

"Yes sir, of course sir," both men respond immediately.

"Really... You see, it doesn't appear that way. To me it looks like you want to embarrass me, you want people to laugh at me."

"No sir, not true sir."

Annas slowly turns his chair to face them and picks up a

report from his desk and throws it across the room towards the two men, scattering the papers.

"We can explain!"

"Can you! Can you explain why you weren't on that yacht, despite my specific instructions? Can you explain that while you were sitting in your car you missed the entire event? Were you even there when the yacht came back to the marina? Because the entire news media are reporting another miracle. Your report included a few dozen blurred photographs, three pages of drivel and concluded with *The evening passed without incident.* Did you think I wouldn't notice all the photos were of people arriving and none of them leaving? That you even had the audacity to submit that piece of garbage is beyond me."

He pauses, shaking his head.

"Answer me this, do you still... still, stand by that report?"

Neither man answers.

"Oh, what a surprise."

He shouts for his assistant, "Jonathan, get in here!"

Jonathan comes rushing in.

"Fetch the two guards waiting outside, what are their names again?

"Theo and Benjamin," Jonathan replies, then adds, "Sir you've also had several messages from Caiaphas while you were downstairs."

Jonathan goes to fetch Theo and Benjamin.

"Of course you two are no longer wanted here, now go wait in the other room while I talk to two *real* Temple guards," Annas says to the men.

Both sets of guards pass each other in the doorway to Annas' office. Annas waves Theo and Ben in and they shut the door.

"Escort those incompetents out of the Temple. You know what to do, after that."

They nod and smile.

He shouts for Jonathan again.

"I'm going to have to see Caiaphas in person, get me a new escort to the palace and let him know I'm on my way."

After his unfortunate and rather early departure as High Priest, Annas was in no mood to relinquish the power he had gained. Though he had been very astute in his business dealings and had the full confidence of the Sanhedrin, everything he had built was in danger of being passed on to someone else, and he was not about to let that happen. So when the Union decided that Israel should annually elect a new High Priest, he once again set about greasing the wheels and influencing the minds. He made sure the Sanhedrin gave him the responsibility of instructing and managing the new incumbent on the day to day duties of such an important position. For this act of sheer selflessness it would require that he remain in residence at the High Priests palace. It also meant he was able to keep total control of his Temple businesses. His plan worked even better than he had imagined, for the High Priest had become the main liaison between Israel and the Union and he was spending more time in meetings with the Governor, Gratus.

After his third High Priest, Gratus became fed up with having to deal with someone new every year. He was a military man, and had ordered routines. By the time he had got used to the foibles and weaknesses of one High Priest, another popped up and he had to start again. When he found his fourth High Priest just about bearable he put an end to the annual change.

That was several years earlier and Joseph Caiaphas had not

only seen out Gratus, but kept his job when the new Governor of Judea, Pontius Pilate was appointed. Annas survived the lot. Once Caiaphas, who just happened to be his son-in-law was appointed, his power base was secure. As was his wing in the palace.

The Palace is situated near the Temple and is a three storey high building with an inner courtyard at its centre. As is traditional in the wealthy areas of the city it is built facing inwards, away from the street. If the Temple in all its magnificence is the centre piece of Jerusalem, then the Palace is the heartbeat. This is where decisions are made and deals are done. The Sanhedrin often meet here in private, away from the intrusiveness of the media. Annas lives in one wing, Caiaphas has the other. They like nothing more than to put on lavish parties and entertain the country's finest minds and Union lackeys.

Annas' Rolls Royce slowly drives up the narrow street. Following is a black Ford with two temple security guards. Some of the streets in the old city weren't built for traffic and getting from the Temple to the Palace takes around twenty minutes; it would be quicker to walk. Traffic has been reduced around the Temple by making the area pedestrian only, with official cars being the only exceptions. With the narrow streets and large volume of people it's not an easy journey to make.

Security are expecting them and open the gates as they approach. Both cars turn into the palace. A bodyguard steps out as the Rolls is coming to a stop and quickly opens the door for Annas.

A footman is there to greet his boss. "Welcome Sir, you will find Caiaphas in the council chamber. Is there anything you require?"

"No, thank you, the chamber you say?"

The footman nods.

The council chamber is a large meeting room where the Sanhedrin gather. It can act like a judicial court when necessary, with a long table at one end where the High Priest and other senior members sit. The accused sit opposite, the Sadducee's would be to the side and any invited guests would watch from the back. It can fit in about thirty people when full, but couldn't manage the whole of the council's sixty-seven members.

Next door Caiaphas has his office, which is where he would normally be, but today about a dozen priests, several Pharisees and a few elders of the council have assembled. They are all asking the same question, "what is going on regarding this Galilean teacher?"

Annas walks through the palace and across the inner courtyard to the chambers, where he is immediately bombarded with questions.

"Have you heard what he's supposedly done now?"

"What are you going to do about him?"

"Why are you letting the papers print such lies?"

"Should we take him seriously?"

Annas raises his voice - "Gentlemen. I'm as concerned as all of you, I really am." He pauses, "personally I think this will all blow over and he'll be gone once his tricks have been revealed, these charlatans always come and go."

His answer doesn't remotely satisfy them and they have more questions. "This is the same man that went mad in the Temple, wrecking the booths and calling us thieves and cheats. Why wasn't he arrested?"

"It's bad enough that you refuse to do anything about the Baptist, now you are hiding from the Galilean too, we demand you do something about him."

Like the flick of a switch Annas' mood changes instantly. His body tenses, his face turns red and his eyes burn with anger. He shouts so loudly, it can be heard throughout the Palace.

"You demand... You come into the Palace of the High Priest and you demand! You useless pieces of excrement, demand!"

He screams at the top of his voice, "*IN MY HOUSE YOU BOW*" and pushes a priest to his knees before storming off in the direction of his office.

His son-in-law Caiaphas follows, closing the door behind him.

"They have genuine concerns," he says quietly.

Annas pours himself a whisky, offering one to Caiaphas who declines, instead preferring to make himself comfortable on a large leather chair.

"They are of course right. This Galilean has become a problem." Annas says pacing up and down.

"What can we do? The people are starting to love him, especially after the miracles."

Annas nods, "takings are also suffering. That temple stunt is still affecting business."

"We must do something."

Annas' pacing becomes more aggressive, he can't let the priests pressure him, but something does need to be done.

"The first thing we will do..." he says, "is nothing. If those Pharisees think this *teacher* as they call him, is breaking religious laws, let them catch him out. Get him to say something on camera we can use. No point just complaining.

Tell them, surely with all their supreme knowledge of the scriptures, they can outsmart one man."

Annas finishes off his drink. "Now, tell me you have spoken to Joseph this morning."

"I have, I asked him what happened on his yacht."

"And?"

"And, he was very guarded, but he did assure me he wasn't the one to notify the press. I thought we had some people on the inside?"

"So did I, but don't worry, that problem has now been rectified."

"We could do with more information on this team of his," suggests Caiaphas.

"Agreed. Also I'll order checks on some of the more prominent followers," says Annas.

Caiaphas stands up and heads for the door, "Oh, by the way, during my meeting with Pilate this morning he warned me of some news that's about to break. The Baptist has been arrested."

Annas smiles, "interesting, you'd better have your writers draft a statement, just in case we need to comment. Do we know why?"

Caiaphas comes closer to Annas, "well, it's not confirmed, but he's taken particular umbrage to Herod's latest marriage. You see it turns out that the new bride was married to his half-brother."

Caiaphas gets even closer and whispers into Annas' ear, "also she is the daughter of another half-brother of his." Annas' eyes light up. "She's therefore his niece."

Caiaphas steps back and heads to the door, adding as he leaves "on this occasion, I can quite agree with the Baptist."

Chapter 18

Jude slowly pushes open the heavy door to the Old Fig Tree and enters. The phone call from Jesus had been brief, a taxi would pick him up at 8.45. Jude hadn't dared ask why and no explanation was offered. He senses he's not alone.

"Hello," he calls.

There is an eeriness about the place with its old wooden beams and stale beer smell. It looks like it could do with a bit of a refurb. A noise spooks him, there is definitely someone here!

"Hello," he says again, slightly louder and if he is honest with a bit of a wobble.

"Johnny B's been arrested."

"What are you doing here?" asks Jude.

Philip is at the far end of the bar, watching the morning news on a TV and eating a bag of cheese and onion crisps. "The boss told me to meet him here. Why are you here?"

"He told me the same thing."

Philip leans over and picks up a bottle of orange from a table and takes a swig.

"You just helped yourself to them!"

"No, I left some money next to the till and it owes me eleven cents."

Jude sits down and watches the news, "I thought I would be the only one here."

"Me too."

One by one the rest of the twelve arrive. Simon and Nathaniel decide to make use of the pool table. Thaddy is next to arrive and then Alphie. When Thomas turns up he is really pleased to see everyone else there, "I was sure the boss was going to sack me."

Jude didn't see Matthew enter, he must have slipped in as there he is sitting alone in a corner. He has a letter in his hands which he just keeps staring at, apparently lost in his own thoughts. Last to arrive are the fishermen. They stroll in together, having been fishing for much of the night. James and John head straight for the pool table.

"I'll take on the winner," says James to Simon and Nat.

"Do you know the reason for all the secrecy?" Jude asks Peter, who shakes his head.

Once everyone has arrived Jesus comes out of a back room and locks the main door.

"Right everyone, gather round," says Jesus.

"Why didn't you tell me Jesus was already here?" says Jude.

"You didn't ask," replies Philip.

It is obvious to Jude that Jesus seems sad, melancholy even. Peter offers the explanation, "sad about John, huh boss?"

James isn't quite as clued in, "like you couldn't see it coming, the stuff he was saying about Herod's missus, I'm surprised he wasn't shot." Andrew gives his fellow fisherman a thump.

"What, we were all thinking it!"

Jesus asks them to sit down adding, "Matthew come and

join us."

Matthew moves closer to the others.

"These last few months have been good, haven't they?" There are various nods and general agreement.

"You've seen me do all kinds of amazing things, like healing the sick."

Peter can't help adding, "and calming that storm."

"That's right Pete."

Jesus continues, "you've all been hanging out with me, watching and learning from me," he pauses as a thought enters his mind. "Did you know that the Pharisees have been comparing you with John's followers? They've been saying that while John's followers like to fast and pray, all you lot do is eat and drink."

Jude looks at Peter, as does everyone else. "Hey, why's everyone looking at me?" They all laugh.

"Don't worry Pete, I defended you," Jesus says. Again they all laugh.

Jesus gets serious again, "phase two of your training starts today. This is where you get to do something."

John gets worried, "This is a test isn't it, oh no, I'm not good at tests."

"You'll be fine John," says Jesus.

"I don't know boss, he took seven goes to pass his driving test," James points out.

That explains a lot, thinks Jude.

Jesus begins to give them their orders and plan of action.

"There are still too many people who have not heard the good news I bring. So today you're to help me. I am sending you out in pairs and giving you the authority to heal the sick, to cast out evil spirits and to preach about the coming Kingdom.

This mission is for the lost sheep of Israel, and we will be just concentrating on Galilee at this time."

Twelve faces look back at Jesus, all with the same open-mouthed expressions.

"You mean, we're really gonna be able to heal people, no way!" says Philip.

"What?" says Thomas.

"This is gonna be sooo cool," adds James.

Finally something is happening. Jude and Simon had been getting rather frustrated just following Jesus and the crowds everywhere. This is more like it.

Jesus takes some papers from a folder. He hands them out, making sure everybody gets one. "Before you all get carried away, these are the rules I want you to follow."

On the paper is a list that the twelve must adhere to.

1. You either walk or rely on people's good generosity to get you from town to town.
2. No bag. You are not to take anything other than the clothes you are wearing.
3. No food. When you are hungry, find a good person, they will feed you.
4. No weapons. Please leave them behind.
5. No mobiles or other communication devices.
6. No money/credit cards. Personal ID only.
7. Don't charge people anything, you're not doing this for profit.
8. If the town or village doesn't welcome your message, leave immediately.

The smiles and excitement slowly drain away.

"Boss, this is impossible!" complains James.

"We have to speak in public, I can't do that," worries Thomas.

Jude stares at the list. This is mad, we can't take anything at all with us. He is only half listening when Nathaniel asks to team up with Peter, "How about me and you Pete."

"Yo Jude, me and you," says Simon. That's good, him and Simon could make a good team. Simon is sure to know people.

James and John team up, no surprise, then Philip teams with Andrew. Thaddy doesn't seem to like the choices that are left.

"No offence," he tells Alphie, Thomas, ...but they do take offence.

"You should have been quicker at asking someone!" shouts James, adding "you're just a bad loser." Thaddy doesn't like that and stands "come here and say that, if you dare?" James takes up the challenge and they both square up to each other and start pushing and shoving. James pushes too hard and Thaddy falls into Simon and Jude. "Hey give over", Jude pushes back. Within seconds eleven guys are all arguing and pushing each other. Peter is trying to stop them by pulling Thaddy and James apart, his big booming voice shouting "stop it, stop it" but he is making it worse.

All of a sudden Matthew stands on a chair and yells "Everyone stop and shut up."

They all stop, Jude notices Jesus helps Matthew down and pats his back. Teachers pet.

"I suppose you've learnt something from all this...none of them can read properly," Matthew says to Jesus. He points to a line near the bottom of the piece of paper.

"Why don't you all read this," he looks across at Jesus.

"Tell them what it says Matt."

Matthew reluctantly reads "...all teams will be assigned by Jesus on the morning of the training."

There is stunned silence.

Now the group begin to feel embarrassed and as they sheepishly come and stand close to Jesus, Peter is first to apologise, "sorry, boss."

One by one, with their heads down the others mumble sorry. Jude looks Jesus in the face "sorry boss."

With a tinge of disappointment in his voice Jesus starts to speak. "This has proved one thing, you're not exactly a team. There will be times when I'm gone that you'll need to work together, to trust each other. To help and be there for one another. For this reason I'm putting Simon and Matthew together."

There is a big intake of breath, but no one dare speak. Jude, you'll be with Alphie."

Jude daren't say anything, but Alphie, a collector, oh come on! He keeps his head down, avoiding any eye contact with Jesus or Alphie.

"Andrew you go with Philip. Then it's Peter and Thaddy, James and Nathaniel and that leaves you Thomas with you John. Right, are there any questions?"

After a few moments Peter asks, "Are there any particular places we should visit? Or can we just go anywhere. I've read the paper... now, and it doesn't say?"

"Good question Peter, you will need to sort that out between yourselves."

Peter asks if there is a map anywhere. Nathaniel says that there is an old one on a wall somewhere and after a few minutes of searching it is found and they all gather round it. Peter then divides up Galilee into six areas.

North above Capernaum to Chorazin and Hazor: The area in and around Beth Shearim to the east: Cana and surrounding towns and villages: Arbela area also eastward. Then two pairs going south: One following the main road through the mountains of Tabor and Moreh to Nain and on from there. Lastly, one heading towards Endor. This one confuses John, "Endor, isn't that a planet in Star Wars?"

Peter appears to have taken charge and no one argues. Jude is still annoyed he's been put with Alphie.

"Now starting with area 1, who wants to go north?" No one answers, "We'll have that then Thaddy."

Eventually each area is taken and Jesus hands out resealable plastic bags. "Put your mobiles, money, weapons etc in one of these, I'll put it in the safe."

Begrudgingly they all fill the bags.

"Don't forget to put in your backup weapons boys," Jesus tells Matthew and Simon. "I want both of you to return in one piece. Right, you can leave when you're ready. Just remember what I have shown and taught you. If you are stuck," Jesus looks over at John, "I've included a crib sheet to help you."

James whispers to John "I am going to heal more than you."

"No way," John goes off to hurry Thomas along.

One by one the pairs start to leave.

* * *

Before they set off **Jude** has one last cigarette. Not a bad way to quit really. He thinks it's a good idea to have a go at giving up, which shouldn't be too hard considering he'd only started when he went to work for his dad. As he stands outside the Old

Fig Tree enjoying his last Marlboro, **Alphie** is pacing up and down. He wants to get going and can't understand why Jude can't smoke and walk at the same time. In the distance there is a sound that is music to Jude's ears, and within seconds the roaring noise of half a dozen bikes, their engines screaming, come into view. They are a mix of new street bikes and old tourers. As they all pass, Jude waves, he knows most of the riders. They hang out at the Olive Grove, a café bar along Lakeside road to the south of Capernaum, which he frequents when he feels the need to talk about all things two-wheeled. The lead bike who had shot passed turns round and rides over, pulling up next to Jude. He and Jude give each other a two-handed handshake and then the rider takes his helmet off.

"Getting in an early session are you?" He points to the bar. Jude explains it was just a meeting point and in fact he is about to leave for Endor. The other bikes all pull up and Jude asks what they are up to today. Just out for a ride they tell him.

"We could drop you off in Endor," one of the bikers says.

Jude looks round at Alphie, "you got a helmet for this guy?"

The rider of a large gold tourer with side boxes on takes out a spare helmet and Jude passes it to Alphie.

"I've never been on a bike before," says Alphie a little apprehensively.

"Oh in that case, you need to ride with Mad Dan."

With a screech of tyres and a smell of burning rubber they all set off. Mad Dan with Alphie clinging on for his life. Jude laughs, if Mad Dan knew he had a collector riding with him this might turn into a one man assignment. He won't say anything, they might think he is one of them too. Alphie should be used to living on the edge, but he looks petrified. Jude signals to Alphie to let go and put his arms in the air.

Alphie ignores him and instead holds tighter. Wait 'til I tell everybody, the first thing Alphie did was put his arms round a biker. Jude tries to show him there is a handle behind his back. Alphie, puts an arm out, searches for it, but gives up when they hit a winding section of the road around Mount Tabor. The snow topped mountain, the sun on your back, nothing like it. Jude promises himself he'll come back later and do this road on a day off.

Mad Dan has already pulled up and Alphie is off the bike when Jude and the others arrive close to the outskirts of Endor.

"How was it?"

"Terrifying." Alphie says through the helmet.

"You won't be swapping your car then?"

"I don't think so."

"I had an idea when we were riding, about what we could do in Endor." That's what Jude loves about riding. He has all his best ideas when he is on a bike.

"This lot want to hear more about the boss. I keep trying to get them to hear him, but they never have time. Well I thought, why don't we ride into the centre of town." He explains his plan to Alphie, who is very impressed with it.

"Just one problem with it though. Do you know what we're supposed to say?" asks Alphie.

"We'll think of something, why don't you try thinking about it on the bike."

"No chance, all I can think about is not falling off."

Jude lets Alphie ride into Endor on the back of the gold tourer at a nice steady pace. He looks a lot more comfortable. They ride round the town looking for a good place to stop. It is market day and the town is busy. Jude chooses the town hall steps as the perfect spot. Just the type of place where Jesus would sit and talk.

The bikers gather round and Jude starts talking about Jesus. Soon shoppers stop to listen. Then it's Alphie's turn. Jude had to admit, he's impressed as the young collector talks about a new kind of adrenalin, an ever-flowing one.

* * *

Peter and Thaddy are the last out, they're heading north towards Chorazin. Peter had a brainwave, he borrowed a felt pen from the back room of the bar and tore off a piece of cardboard from a box of crisps. He then wrote Chorazin in big letters.

"This will help with the hitch-hiking" he proudly tells Thaddy, before saying goodbye to Jesus. "See you later boss."

"Er, Peter, don't you think you ought to tell your wife where you're going?" Thaddy asks him.

"Oh, I completely forgot Ruth and the kids."

"Don't worry, I will explain everything," Jesus reassures him.

Thaddy asks Jesus, if over the next few days, he'll be able to get a rest, once the twelve are out of his way.

"No, it's not time for me to rest just yet, I'll carry on as usual." He tells the lads that they can go out and not have all the attention of the media on them as he'll continue his work and this will protect them.

"Okay, so let's get cracking," says Peter, setting off once more... in the wrong direction.

"Er, Pete," Thaddy tries to catch him up, "Pete, where are you going? The best way to Chorazin is the other way, Pete."

Rather than go the short cut up onto the highway that

Thaddy would have taken they end up heading down into the centre of Capernaum. After half an hour of Peter waving his sign at every passing car without success, they get fed up and so they start to walk towards the highway. Thaddy mutters that he wanted to do that from the start.

"Now I can believe what James and John are always complaining about," he mutters.

Peter marches out in front. If a car doesn't stop soon, he'll walk all the way. An ambulance screams past, sirens blaring. Peter is tempted to stick out the sign in case they are heading their way. Ten minutes later they actually catch up with the ambulance. It has stopped outside a house and as they approach, two paramedics are bringing out a woman on a stretcher. She has an oxygen mask on and is hooked up to a heart monitor. Peter sees his opportunity and goes over.

"Can I help?"

The paramedics ignore him.

Peter is not going to let this opening pass him by, so just before the woman is lifted up, he asks her if she would like to be healed.

"I'm Peter, one of Jesus' team, you may have heard of him, love."

When the woman stretches out a hand, Peter takes that as a yes.

"Thaddy, get over here," what does it say we should do on that bit of paper. Thaddy takes the paper from his pocket and reads aloud. Jesus has included a few reminders for them, cue cards of a kind.

"In the name of Jesus...shouldn't you put your hands on her or something?" Peter shrugs and takes her outstretched hand.

"Where was I, oh yes... and the Father, be healed." The paramedics think this is a joke and start to load the woman into the ambulance. Peter starts to repeat the prayer but has to stop, "ouch, don't squeeze so tight woman."

One of the paramedics looks at the monitor, it has gone to normal. The woman starts to sit up and she takes the oxygen mask off.

"Thank you, thank you," she says over and over.

"I hope you're not on commission," Thaddy says to the paramedics.

To the amazement of Peter and Thaddy and the paramedics, the woman stands up.

"Oh, I feel so much better and, ohh I feel different, what can it be?" she looks down at her feet, "Oh yes, I don't have swollen ankles any more."

One of the paramedics has seen the sign Peter was holding and offers them a lift. First the woman insists they should all come into her home where she will get them all a well-earned drink. She also wants to know more about this Jesus person she has heard so much about on the TV. Peter notices that one of the paramedics has written on their call-out sheet *successfully treated at scene*. What a cheek! But when he thinks about it, well technically it is true, and who would believe it if they wrote *successfully treated at scene by a fisherman and an unemployed office trainee, neither of whom has any previous medical training.*

When the crew get another call-out to a nearby accident they ask if Thaddy and Peter would like to come along so that's what they do. Not so much ambulance chasers, rather ambulance riders, plus, Peter might get to turn on the siren!

* * *

James and Nathaniel are covering Arbela, and surrounding towns. It is only a few miles south of Capernaum. They didn't get off to the best start having only gone thirty feet out of the door when Jesus called them back. John, eager as ever to get one over on his brother, told Jesus that James had failed to hand in his mobile. So while James was emptying his pockets John and Thomas got away first. How did John know that he's tried to keep his phone? By the time they got out of the door a second time even Andy and Philip were in front, though not for long. As they set off running down the hill into the centre of town, they soon catch up and pass them.

As James runs passed them he shouts, "hey, Andy, you seen John?" He didn't hear a reply, though Philip did shout something back.

Nathaniel, not being as fit as James, was out of breath when they got into the town centre. As he's doubled over trying to regain the use of his lungs, a voice from a passing car calls out to them.

"Losers, losers."

They look around and see Thomas and John sitting in the back of a car. John has the window down and along with calling out is making the L sign on his forehead with his fingers.

"Losers, losers."

"I don't believe it, they've got a ride already," says James.

He urges Nathaniel to hurry up and while his partner is still recovering he taps on a parked car's window and asks if he could have a lift. The driver isn't all that pleased to be asked and points to a bus stop. James says that is no good, as he isn't allowed money. The driver doesn't hang around long enough to find out why. As James watches the car drive off, his attention is drawn to a row of bus stops around a hundred yards away. He is curious to know why there are so many people gathering round one particular bus. One person looks like the driver.

"Come on, let's see what's happening over by the bus stop," he tells a recovering Nathaniel.

As they get nearer to the bus, it becomes apparent that there is someone inside. James pushes through the group of mainly pensioners and students.

"What's happening?" he asks the driver.

"We were just setting off when this lad started to freak out," he points, "look."

The young boy of about thirteen is banging on the windows and shouting.

"This is the boy's mother," the driver introduces a woman standing next to him.

"His name is Steven," she says, "the doctors say he may be schizophrenic. He has taken his medication, and he is usually fine, but the moment he stepped on the bus he had one of his attacks. No-one can get near him when he's like this, so the driver kindly evacuated the bus and I've called his doctor."

"He could injure someone," the driver adds.

"I don't know if you recognize us, but we are members of Jesus the Miracle Man's team," Nathaniel says, loud enough for everyone to hear.

"Do you mind if we go in and help the lad?" asks James, winking at a young girl.

"If it's okay with you," says the driver to the boys mother. She nods, "be careful."

The driver opens the passenger door and James, followed by Nathaniel steps into the bus.

Steven is now sitting down half way up the bus. He is rocking backwards and forwards and has a spaced out look in his eyes, but the moment Nathaniel and James begin to move towards him he becomes agitated and his rocking gets faster, more violent.

"Get away, leave me alone Jesus, Jesus please leave, please leave".

"Is this a healing or do we cast out whatever's in him?" asks James.

"I'd go with a healing," says Nathaniel.

"I think he's possessed, I'm gonna go with a casting out." James counters.

"Oh, so you know what to do right?"

"No, not really. What does it say on that piece of paper?" asks James.

"I don't know, I didn't bring it with me."

"Right! neither did I."

"Well, what would Jesus do?"

"I don't know, but if I had my mobile, I could've asked him."

They stop a few seats away. Steven, still rocking and shouting avoids any eye contact with the lads. James can't decide what to say "Er."

"Do you want me to do it?"

"No, I've got it. You can do the next one."

"Alright Steven."

"Get away, Jesus."

"No, I'm not Jesus, I'm James. But I am from Jesus' team."

"Leave me alone Jesus."

"Er, I think I should pray, right?"

Nathaniel nods.

"OK, er God, it's James, I pray that whatever is wrong with Steven is healed. If it's an evil spirit, whoever you are, leave him alone you bastard... Amen."

Both James and Nathaniel watch and wait to see if anything happens. To their surprise Steven stops shouting and gradually stops rocking. He looks James and Nathaniel right in the eye and as if they are just fellow passengers, nods an acknowledgement and then looking all around and out of the window asks. "Where's the driver? And what's my mum doing outside?"

Nathaniel waves her in, and whispers to James "Don't think I've ever heard Jesus use those words before!"

Steven's mother runs the length of the bus to her son and puts her arms around him hugging him as tightly as she can, then smothers him in kisses.

Some of the other passengers also get on, as does the driver, who makes a point of coming over to Steven to see for himself the young lad's transformation. To James and Nathaniel's appreciation he offers them a free ride, but only if they tell everyone more about their boss.

* * *

I bet **Matthew** got a right kick out of telling us all what to do, **Simon** thought, as they set off on their mission. A kicking's just the thing he needs. Nice and simple, a warning that if he doesn't disappear he could expect a knife in his back. Yeah that's it. Trouble is, with this guy it's never that simple. He wouldn't take the hint, and now with Jesus encouraging him why would he? The thing that Simon hates most about

Matthew, more than anything, more than his job, more than the people he's hurt, more than the ruling Union scum, is the fact that Matthew's surname is Levi. Levi, such a strong Jewish name, and here he is, working for the enemy of Israel. When Jesus put them together, he never said a word. He waited until afterwards and then went up to Jesus and asked if he could be put with someone else. "See, no trouble boss, just keep him out of my way." Jesus looked disappointed and refused, saying he knew what he was doing. This could be the last straw, huh, how many times has he thought that lately? Many times, only for Jesus to say or do something to make him reconsider. Like he knew what he was thinking. This time, this time, it's like Jesus saying "go on then quit." There's no way a piece of shit collector is making me leave.

The two men walk along the same road, not saying a word but watching each other closely. Without communicating to each other they automatically head towards the intersection where several roads all merge together, including Cana road.

A small Peugeot pulls up with a man in the passenger seat and a woman driving. The man calls out. "Excuse me."

Matthew wanders over to the car, Simon stays where he is.

"Could you help us, we are trying to get to Cana, but we seem to be lost."

"I can, I'm wanting to head that way myself."

"Oh great, jump in the back. Is that your friend, does he need a ride as well?"

Simon doesn't, but when Matthew reluctantly slides over, he gets in. Does he really want to do this? No, they should have waited and got in a car with someone driving alone, so at least one of them could sit in the front.

They set off with Matthew pointing the way.

"It's tricky is this one, really you want to go straight on, but if you do you end up on the one way, heading back into Capernaum. So you need to get in the right hand lane and once you've passed these other turn offs, that's it, good, now you can go straight on. Whoever designed this system needs shooting."

Simon sits there, looking straight ahead and not saying a word, even when the woman asks him a question. After a few miles the woman says to Matthew, "you look familiar, have we met before?"

"I doubt it, but you might have seen me with Jesus, the teacher."

"No, that's not it, it's your voice, I know that voice."

The man then adds that his wife is a whiz at remembering voices.

As she's driving, the woman looks in her rear view mirror studying Matthew. Simon sees her go a deathly pale, yeah now she recognises him. For a second he thinks she'll just keep quiet, but her husband can tell something is wrong.

"We were, er, never, I mean, always going to pay," she finally blurts out.

"What?" asks her husband.

The car swerves slightly and Simon is sure they must have had trouble with Matthew before.

"This is a nice car, new is it?" asks Matthew.

"NO!" both answer. The woman's nerves are making her drive erratically.

Simon grits his teeth, trying not to explode, but even he can't believe what Matthew says next.

Matthew leans forward, "if you imported through my booths without declaring it's new, you do know I can legally impound it until you pay import duty on it".

"Get the cheque book out, get it out." screams the woman to her husband, who fumbles through his wife's purse.

"We'll pay you both, honest, we just thought it would be okay," the man says, his hand shaking as he tries to write.

"Both. You said both," blood vessels on Simon's temples are about to burst.

"You think I'm a collector," Simon's breaking point has now been passed.

"That's it, I'm going to kill you."

He lunges at Matthew with a punch, then in the small confines of the back seat just starts swinging his arms more in anger than anything. The woman starts to scream, this results in her panicking and losing control of the car. It weaves first left then right before skidding to a stop.

"I'm not a collector," screams Simon as he throws punch after punch. Matthew grabs hold of Simon trying to stop him. When the car stops Matthew fumbles for the door, opens it and with Simon's momentum they both fall out of the car.

Now in the middle of the road they have more space and trade blows. Cars are forced to stop as the Peugeot is blocking the carriageway. In the car Simon had the upper hand, but with more space the heavier built Matthew can get the leverage he needs.

"Is that the best you can do Zealot," taunts Matthew.

With all his strength Simon goes for him again.

A distant sound of sirens hint that someone has called the police and when they do arrive it takes four officers to prise them apart. They are thrown in the back of separate police cars and taken to Cana's police station, and placed into holding cells. Matthew is put with several others while Simon at least, gets one all to himself.

The officer pushes Matthew into a cell and slams the door. Simon can hear that Matthew seems to know those sharing his cell.

"Hey, Matt, haven't seen you in ages."

"Word is out that you are spending a lot of time with that preacher man."

"Oh yeah, it's unbelievable what this guy does and says."

"You know, we were thinking of checking him out."

"You should."

"Maybe this Preacher friend of yours could look at healing this bullet wound of mine."

Simon tries to work out what is going on in the cell next to him. He sits in silence, nursing his bruised hands and face, half listening and half thinking about what just went on. He lost it, he really did, if he'd had his knife there is no question in his mind, he would have killed Matthew. Now he has to listen to Matthew going on about how good it is to be with Jesus. He hears this other guy mention the wound and he shouts out, "Heal him, go on, that's why we're here isn't it Collector?"

"What?"

"Why don't you..."

"Yeah, I heard!"

Simon listens as Matthew heals a fellow collector and tells his cellmates all about Jesus. It isn't long before Simon's cell also starts filling up with people and although there isn't anyone who needs healing, he starts to talk about Jesus and the Kingdom. Even the officers listen as they can hear all that is said in the cells.

* * *

"Oh, that was so easy, I never thought we'd get a lift this quick."

After James' threat of doing better than him, **John** made sure that he and **Thomas** got away first. They sprinted down into the town centre and it only took a few minutes before they found someone willing to give them a lift.

"Hey, look over there," Thomas points at James and Nathaniel.

John winds down the window and shouts "Losers, losers."

"Quick, quick, do that sign with your fingers, you know."

John makes an L sign. He thinks that is so good, especially seeing the look on James' face.

The driver doesn't say much to the lads. After about twenty minutes, Thomas points out that the clock is wrong in this car.

"Mate, you're a bit slow. I make it ten fifteen. Yours says nine thirty, nine forty, nine fifty. Hey, I think there's something wrong with your clock."

"That's not a clock, that's the fare," says the driver.

"What!" They both say.

"Well, this is a taxi after all."

"I thought we'd hitch-hiked," Thomas says to John.

"We did, this guy must be trying it on," John replies. He leans towards the driver and says, "Mate, we don't have any money."

The driver slams on the brakes, stopping in the middle of the road. He starts shouting and swearing and threatening to call the police.

"Run, run," John shouts.

Both lads get out of the car and start running towards a field. They run through several crops until they are both completely exhausted. Checking to make sure the driver isn't following, they collapse to the ground.

"You stink at hitch-hiking," says Thomas in between gasps of air.

"I got us a free ride didn't I?"

"Yeah, but where to?"

They both look around, all they can see are hills and fields and in the distance is Mount Tabor.

John looks at his watch, then up at the sun. "I have no idea but I must be able to work it out."

He picks the spot he thinks is west and they set off.

After an hour, most of which is spent arguing as to what they'll do if they ever get to a town or village, they see in the distance, high on a hill, a town. "Right, now it's time to put our plan into action."

"This will never work," moans Thomas.

"Yes, it will."

They enter the town and head for the best and biggest houses.

"All we have to do is be nice and polite and tell them who we are and ask if they know anybody who might be ill or would like to hear about Jesus and that we will be in the town square all day."

"Wonder what town this is."

John shrugs, "does it matter?"

They open a gate and walk up the first drive they come to. "Stop," a voice shouts, "what are you selling?"

"Nothing, we just want to tell you about..."

"If you don't leave I'll set my dogs on you."

"He's bluffing," John carries on up the drive. Thomas is a little more hesitant. His caution is justified. Before John can even get to the door dogs start barking and come charging from around the back of the house.

"Run, run."

At the next house they end up having a shotgun pointed at them and at the third, well the lads have never heard such abuse, even compared to that taxi driver.

They don't give up. On the twenty-third door, someone is willing to listen. John thinks it's going really well until Thomas interrupts and talks about the miracles.

"Well, I missed the storm - I was sick then and the time he healed that blind man I hadn't got a good place and only saw the top of his head. You know he's thinning on top, yeah and he's only in his thirties. Then there was the guy with the broken leg, missed that one too. I see the before and even the after, just never the miracle itself."

The woman can't shut the door fast enough.

"Oh, that's just great, well done!" John moans. "Why oh why, did I have to be put with you?"

"Don't blame it all on me. Thomas gets defensive. "At least I talked to her face. What about the house when you just talked to that woman's breasts."

"You were the one who asked if they were real...in front of her husband."

They decide to leave this town and try somewhere else. On the way out they see a sign with the towns name: Nazareth.

"Oh great, we've just spent two hours in a place that even Jesus once got kicked out of," says John.

"Let's hope the next town is more welcoming or we're gonna have nowhere to sleep tonight," Thomas adds.

* * *

Andrew and Philip have chosen to go south. They walk down into the centre of Capernaum and discuss the best way to travel. James and Nathaniel both run passed them. James shouts out "have you seen John?"

"This is not a competition" Philip shouts back. Even so he and Andrew walk a bit faster.

"So what do you think we should do?" asks Philip.

Several options are analysed. Walking - way too far. Bus - no money. Taxi - same. Hitching a ride - road to Nain is a motorway. Then Philip has some inspiration. "Trucks, they go all the way along the motorway, got to be easier to get a ride on one of those big rigs."

Andrew agrees and he knows just the spot where they like to park up and get a cooked breakfast. It does involve a walk, which takes them half an hour, but when they arrive at the truck stop just outside Capernaum, the place is reverberating to the sound of engines. Philip suggests they look for a driver who is limping or has signs of a bad back. After several minutes of wandering around, they see a potential target. He is just roping up some sheets on his empty flat-bed trailer. The sign on the door of his cab says the company is based in Megiddo, which is south. He keeps stopping to rest and rub his back.

"Perfect candidate," reckons Philip.

"Excuse me mate," says Andrew. "You look like you could do with some help." The man stops, feeling his back as he stands up straight. He is grateful for any assistance they can give him. Andrew soon has the sheets roped down, it's not much different from the trawler. While he's doing it, Philip learns that the man, who is called Ben, has been suffering from back pain ever since he picked up his grandson last Passover.

"The kid weighs a ton and he's only eleven."

He asks them which truck is theirs and when they said that they didn't have one, but needed to go south, Ben was only too happy to give them a lift.

"Have you heard about this 'Jesus guy'?" Andrew asks as they get into the cab. "Yeah, maybe I could meet him and he could do something about my back."

As they travelled the forty odd miles south, Andrew and Philip tell Ben all about their boss and what they have been commissioned to do. They also attempt to release some of the power they have been given. Reading from the piece of paper they ask for healing for Ben's back. The pain immediately disappears, so much so that Ben pulls up, jumps down and goes round the truck tightening the ropes, bending and stretching. He was healed, no doubt about it!

"Wait 'til my wife hears about this, she won't believe me. In fact why don't you come and meet her, then she won't think I've gone crackers? And why don't you stay for dinner, she makes the best dumplings this side of heaven?"

Before Andrew and Philip can say anything Ben is on his mobile and arranging for an extra two more places at the table.

"I've met some young lads who are from that Miracle Man's team, no not that weird one," he turns to Andrew, "It's not that one from the desert who's been arrested is it."

Andrew shakes his head.

"No, don't be silly woman, you know the one who went mad in the Temple," turning to Andrew again "that's him right?"

173

Andrew nods.

"How do I know they're really them? Oh, I think I can show you some proof."

Ben drives straight to his house in the outskirts of Megiddo, a small town near the border with Samaria, rather than dropping the truck off at the yard. He is in a hurry to get to his wife. "I've been up since four this morning, so the truck can go back later" he tells them. As they turn into the street, to the surprise of all three men there is a crowd of about twenty people.

"Those dumplings must be good," says Philip.

Ben pulls up, gets down from the cab and runs up to a portly woman in the middle of the crowd. He puts his arms round her and with all his might lifts the woman in the air and twirls her round. She lets out a scream, "what about your back?"

Andrew and Philip get out of the truck and make their way over to the crowd. "I guess that's his wife," Philip laughs.

Ben has now put down his lady and waves the lads over. He introduces them to everyone.

"This is Andrew and Philip, two of the Miracle Man's actual team."

They become surrounded by people wanting to know all about their boss and all that they have seen him do. Ben's wife has made enough dumplings to feed everyone, so all the neighbours stay to eat with them. It seems that the whole town know about Ben's bad back, and when news gets around that two young men from Jesus' team have healed him, everyone wants to see for themselves, including Ben's boss and some of his co-workers. 'If you can heal him, what about me?' came the usual response.

So the lads begin to heal people, fuelled by the best

dumplings this side of heaven.

Chapter 19

"I hope that's for us," Thaddy says pointing to flags and banners as he and Peter walk up to the Old Fig Tree.

"There's a lot of cars, maybe they do a good lunch menu."

Peter pushes open the door and as soon as he steps inside he hears two familiar little voices.

"Daddy, Daddy."

Naomi and Jacob come running over to him and he scoops them up in his big arms and squeezes them tight. Oh, he has missed them.

"Where's Mummy? Ah, there she is." Ruth comes over and he kisses her.

Both Thaddy's parents have also turned up. His mother gives her son a hug, and points to his father over by the bar, who smiles and raises his glass.

"Where's Jesus?" Peter asks, before spotting him sitting next to two Pharisees.

What are they doing here, he wonders as he makes his way over, Naomi and Jacob still in his arms.

"Teacher, it was incredible. I can't believe all that we did."

Thaddy follows. "What are they doing here?" he asks.

"The High Priest sent them to spy on me while you were away." Jesus whispers in Thaddys ear.

"Bet they delighted in telling you about Johnny B."

"No Thaddy, they are truly saddened by it."

From outside and over the noise of the bar can be heard shouting.

"Oh yes! Oh yes! we're back."

A woman shrieks, "I know that voice, that's my James" and rushes to the door. James and Nathaniel enter the bar. James high fives as many people as he can. He sees his mother "Hi Mum, shit, look how many people are here."

She is just about to give him a hug but stops, slapping him instead, "watch that language."

"Oops, sorry Mum." He and Nathaniel push through the crowd, shaking as many hands as they can until they get to Jesus.

"Did you see us on the news? We got on telly," says James.

"Boss," Nathaniel says to Jesus shaking his hand over and over, "it was amazing."

"We did things that just blow the mind, things that, well, only you can do," says James.

It's only then that he notices Peter holding Naomi and Jacob. He looks at Jacob. "I was on the telly, did you see me?" Jacob shakes his head. "No, but I saw Daddy."

James looks at Peter "What?"

"Hey, you weren't the only ones to get noticed, it seems we all were, and yes even John."

"Oh great."

The next back is Simon, he is alone. He gets a warm welcome from a few friends who have turned up. One asks if he managed to kill that collector? He tells them he didn't, but adds "he won't be doing any more collecting." He then asks if they've heard from Flatpack. They warn him to keep his distance, "Flatpack thinks you're a traitor for even being near the Collector."

James sees Simon, "Hey Simon, where's Matthew? You didn't kill him did you?" Simon looks over and sticks up his middle finger.

James turns to the others "I think he has!" He pauses, adding, "Oh crap, now I owe John a tenner."

Peter doesn't believe for a second anything has happened to Matthew so he puts down his kids and goes outside. He sees Matthew leaning against a wall.

"You going to join us?"

"Any reason to?"

"To prove to people you're not dead, for a start."

As he pushes passed people looking for the teacher he forces a smile. People stare at him. Peter can see he's looking for his friends, maybe Rebecca. He daren't tell him there is no one here to welcome him back.

Jesus sees him and leaves Simon and his friends, "Matt."

Matthew sees him coming towards him, "Teacher."

Jesus shouts, "How's it feel to be an ex collector?"

There is a hush!

"I'm getting used to it."

"Well done, you and Simon did good, real good."

Matthew, slightly self-conscious, smiles again.

"Oh, by the way, you need to work on that smile," says Jesus.

Next to arrive are Andrew, Philip, Jude and Alphie. They are swamped by the crowd and struggle to push their way in. The volume in the bar increases as the lads exchange stories. They laugh and joke at each others adventures. Peter smiles at Jesus, these last few days have been amazing and by the look of it, for everybody. There is a difference, a confidence that wasn't there before, an understanding of their boss that the other followers can't comprehend. Maybe they *can* be the team the country expects.

The last pair to arrive are Thomas and John. Thomas' twin brother David has come to meet him. Peter knows the twins through their father, and while the brothers look alike there doesn't seem to be the same bond that even he and Andrew have or James and John have. Talking of John, the minute he walks through the door his mother is once again shrieking and fussing. She runs over to him and gives him a hug, "You've lost weight, look how thin you are."

"Mumm," John is embarrassed.

"I've baked some cookies, I knew you wouldn't eat properly."

"What kind?"

"What kind you say, your favourite, chocolate chip."

She hurries off to fetch him some as he and Thomas make their way to the others.

"You're the last," says James.

"Who cares, I bet we healed more than you and Nathaniel!"

"Ha, no chance!"

His mother is back with the cookies. John takes a couple.

"Mmm, I've missed your baking."

Simon's friends look uncomfortable and keep staring at Matthew. This in turn makes Peter edgy and he's relieved when they get up and go.

"*Later Thimon*," says one.

Things have definitely changed these last couple of days. Once they'd gone Simon comes over to join in the banter with the twelve. They are all filled with so much exuberance and passion that they are bursting with joy and happiness. It's infectious and it's not long before all the followers are laughing.

John empties a pocket. Pieces of paper, large and small fall onto the floor. Andrew helps John pick them up.

"Hey, these are all phone numbers!"

"Girls' phone numbers. It was unbelievable, even Thomas has some."

Thomas grins.

Without warning one of John the Baptist's followers, a young woman, erupts in a fit of emotion, shouting, "You're all insensitive, how can you laugh and joke." She starts to cry, and is comforted by an older couple. Through her tears she cries, "they carry on as if nothing has happened."

The place quietens down a little, as people think of The Baptist.

"What's she on about?" asks Thomas.

"Didn't you hear?" says Thaddy.

"Hear what?"

James butts in, "Johnny B is dead."

"How?" Thomas asks.

James gestures by sliding his hand across his throat.

"James," Ruth says sternly.

Peter shakes his head.

"That's what happened. Well, excuse *me* for telling the truth."

Peter, Jude and Simon are standing near to where the Pharisees are sitting. One tries to start a conversation, "we are only here to warn you that Herod has got it into his head that your teacher is the reincarnation of The Baptist.

"Everything you lot have supposedly been doing has made your teacher a target," says another.

"That's stupid," says Simon.

"People are asking who will be next? Your teacher's name immediately springs to mind."

Peter is just about to start arguing when Philip interrupts, handing out the plastic bags containing their possessions. "There's a de-briefing upstairs in five minutes," he says.

One by one the twelve make their way to a small function room on the first floor. Chairs and tables are scattered haphazardly and it looks as though it hasn't been used for a while. The moment they are alone the adrenalin of the last few days gives way to exhaustion and they slump onto the wooden chairs. When Simon comes in he flops down on the nearest seat to the door and lets out a great big sigh. "Ohhh, I'm knackered." He doesn't seem to care that he's next to Matthew.

The last of the twelve to come upstairs is James. He comes bouncing into the room. "Oh, look at you lot, you just can't take the pace any more, eh Pete?"

"How come you're not tired?" asks John.

James laughs and flexes his muscles. Just to prove it, he drops down and does twenty press ups. Jesus is the last in. He closes the door and tells James to sit down.

"Who wants to start?" Jesus says looking around.

"I tried to kill the Collector," says Simon.

"You, I don't believe it," says James. John smirks.

"But...we were thrown in the cells. I overheard Matthew talking to some fellow collectors. He even healed one of them. My hatred started to dissolve - it's difficult to want to kill someone when they're talking about *you* boss. If any of you say a word about this, I'll take my knife and cut off your..." he stops, looks Jesus in the eye, "sorry boss, old habits."

"Matthew, your turn."

Matthew takes out the letter he's kept. "See this, it's from the government, someone's reported that I have other commitments and that I have twenty four hours to choose between my business or as the letter puts it, my *new master*. I didn't realise it at the time but the other morning I gave up one form of power: the power to harm, destroy, intimidate and kill – for one to care, to heal, to bring hope and to restore. Before, I was torn between the two, now it's a no brainer."

"So, how come you both ended up in jail?" asks Nathaniel.

"Hey go steady on me, I'm unemployed, alright."

"So that's a no on the free toll passes then!" sighs John.

"By now the government will have taken the business. Funny, but the thing I'm gonna miss the most is the cedar desk you repaired boss."

Peter can't wait for his turn. He tells of his faith in the boss, that he's finally realising who Jesus is. He wants to say so much but has to make way for Thomas and John, who surprisingly did alright. Jude talks about the power that he felt inside himself. Andrew about the number of friends he has now made. Philip and Nathaniel both agreed that nothing prepares you for the sheer volume of people who want help.

"Hey, Matt," says Alphie. "I know you're not my boss anymore, but I want to say it anyway. I quit. Now you're not the only one out of work."

"We don't get paid for this do we boss, 'cos you know I too am currently in between jobs," says Thaddy.

"I can't believe that there are people who still don't think you are the real deal Jesus," says James. "I find it absurd that after all that has happened, they still think it's all a trick, some huge stunt." He stands up pacing the floor getting animated, "What are we going to do about it?" He is close to a window so peers out. "Oh no, look at all the people who have turned up."

There is a knock at the door and James is over to answer it in a flash. "What?" he says aggressively. A man explains that there are a lot of people asking for Jesus and it's getting difficult to keep them from coming upstairs.

"Are they wanting so see us, *the twelve* as well?" The man apologises and shakes his head, "just Jesus."

"Go downstairs to find out why not!" says James.

Jesus stops him and sends the man to arrange transport, quickly and quietly. The team aren't the only ones who are in need of some time out. The crowds have been getting larger and larger and ever since the twelve went on their mission Jesus hasn't managed to get much rest.

It only takes ten minutes before Peter's mobile rings, with news that the cars are in position, waiting in the back lane behind the bar. As stealthily as they can they go out down the back steps, through the fire escape and get into the cars. The next step of the plan is for Peter to organise a boat to take them across the lake. He makes a call to an old friend who owes him a favour and by the time they arrive at the harbour, his friend is there waiting with an old pleasure boat, one that is normally used for tourist trips around the lake.

Both men shake hands. Peter thanks him and introduces Jesus. "Any time," says the man.

"It's fuelled up so you don't have to worry about that, but there is just one stipulation. Please don't let James and John steer it."

"Oh, not a boat," says Thomas. I can get one of the drivers to take me round the lake and meet you over the other side?"

"You will be fine, we should stick together," says Jesus.

The old engine rattles into life and they all jump on board. If they think that they can just leave Capernaum without being noticed they are much mistaken. The crowd at the Fig Tree has soon realised that Jesus has left and in this technological age it's only a matter of time before his whereabouts are revealed. Within minutes the place is full of people wanting to see the country's No.1 celebrity. Hundreds arrive at the harbour only to see the boat heading across the lake.

"They're following us," Alphie points out.

"Some are even driving round the lake!" says Philip.

There's no need to stress yourselves, just rest up," Jesus tells them.

Peter is at the helm leisurely steering while the others lie down on the seats soaking up the spring sunshine. The water is flat calm, and even Thomas is managing to rest. They are heading towards Bethsaida. It's a place Peter knows well, he was born and grew up there. It is four miles from Capernaum by boat, a little longer if you are travelling by road.

When they are about five hundred yards from the shore Peter calls to Jesus, who is asleep, or is just resting his eyes, he can't tell. "Boss, you'd better take a look at this!"

All along the coast for what looks like miles, are people and traffic. Hundreds of cars, thousands of people.

"What shall I we I do? Shall I go somewhere else?"

Jesus stares out at the gathering crowd. "No, but let's head to the east, away from the town."

As they approach a solitary jetty, just big enough for the thirty foot boat, some people on the shore can be seen taking photo's. By now all the twelve are sitting up wide awake. James and John are standing in the bow. James waves to Peter to get closer, "keep going, keep going...stop." Peter cuts the engine and as Jesus and the team all step off the boat, Andrew makes sure it is tied up. Immediately Jesus is surrounded by hundreds upon hundreds of people wanting to be healed of one thing or another.

"You're not going to get a taxi in Capernaum today, they're all here," says Thaddy.

"Look, there's a school bus and even an ambulance," says Alphie.

"I would have made a lot of money today," Matthew whispers to Alphie.

Peter recognises some of his old neighbours. Now the residents of Bethsaida are coming, so much for a rest. Mothers are bringing along their children and shoving them at Jesus so he can bless them.

"Oh no, even Capernaum Radio has caught wind of it," says Thomas as a van pulls up.

The lads try to keep people at a distance but are overwhelmed by the numbers.

"This is what we trained for lads, come on," says Peter, knowing that after the last few days they can all help out. "Come on, those that want to be healed this side, blessings over there. Come on people, form an orderly queue," he shouts.

He is pushed aside.

"Jesus, Jesus," shout the crowd.

"Why doesn't he just heal them all at once, then they could all go home?" announces James.

After their dismal crowd management, and with their

attempts at healing ignored, the twelve withdraw to the grassy slopes of the hill that stretch up from the lake. They go up high enough to keep an eye on Jesus, in the middle of the crowd. Peter never takes his eye off him, and only speaks to confirm that Simon and Matthew have their guns with them, just in case anything were to happen.

"You know the Pharisees said that Herod might come after the boss! He wouldn't would he?" asks Jude.

"Not here, we're in Peraea now," says Andrew.

"Those tossers are just trying to scare you," Simon tells Jude.

The lads all sit quietly, looking out over the lake. Simon continues " I think we should take advantage of the situation. I mean, with the boss's power, and of course ours, Herod wouldn't stand a chance against us. Shit, forget him, we could even take Jerusalem."

"Oh great, the Zealot's trying to get us all killed," moans Thomas.

"Anyone brought any food, I'm starving," says Peter.

Eventually, it looks like Jesus has finished and he comes up the hill to join the twelve. He leads them further up the hillside, but they are followed by the crowd which, rather than dispersing, is steadily growing.

"There must be more here than Capernaum gets at home games," groans John.

"This is a good spot, plenty of space for everyone," Jesus says sitting down.

High on the green hillside overlooking the lake shimmering in the sun, he begins teaching about the kingdom of God, His kingdom. He tells them the choices they have to make and what they must do to receive it. Gripped by his words and amazed by his knowledge, no-one tries to leave. It's the twelve who are the first ones to want to.

"I'm starving," says Thaddy.

When Jesus pauses for a moment, Philip catches his attention and gently reminds him that they had missed lunch and now it's late in the afternoon. Jesus asks him what he thinks he should do about it. Philip, only happy to assist the boss in the decision making, suggests that Jesus sends the crowd away, back to their homes.

"If we're quick we can get to Bethsaida supermarket before it runs out of bread."

"That's a good idea Philip, why don't you go and buy food for everybody!" suggests Jesus.

"I didn't mean for everybody, I meant just for us! We couldn't afford to buy food for all these people, besides I doubt there would be enough food in the store anyway."

Jesus gives the twelve orders to see if they can find anyone in the crowd with food. They all spread out, asking as many people as they can. They come back empty handed, no one has found any. "Most of these people only thought they'd be out for a short while, those that had food have eaten it hours ago," says Nathaniel.

"The only thing I can find is this young boy's lunch. He has five small barley loaves and a couple of dried fish," Andrew says.

"Why aren't you in school?" Peter asks him.

"I wanted to see Jesus," he says.

"We can't split that! Right everybody, it's time to go," says Philip.

"Tell everybody to sit down and get into large groups," Jesus tells the twelve.

Peter's reminded of the time Jesus turned the water into wine, so when James and John start to complain he reassures them that the boss knows what he is doing.

Peter, involved at last starts to organise. "Right, come on people," he orders the team. "Don't just stand there looking confused John, move!"

"It's just like being at work," John mutters.

The twelve go round telling the crowd to sit down. People begin to ask what is happening?

"It's dinner time," says Peter.

When Nathaniel is asked the same question, he is less sure. "I'm just obeying the boss's orders." Eventually the twelve have put everybody into groups with spaces so they can move around easily. Jesus takes the bread, looks up high, gives thanks to God for it and passes it to Andrew, Philip and Nathaniel to give out. Peter stares intently at what is happening. The bread appears to come out of Jesus hands, like the scarves magic trick, the one where a big long line of scarves are pulled from the magicians' sleeve. Only this time it's real bread and it just keeps on coming. Each of the lads has been given the same.

"This is gonna take forever," says Matthew to Peter, "I have a quicker way, follow me."

Matthew goes to the nearest group and putting on his new smile asks if anyone has a bag he can borrow. He is refused, so he puts on his game face, his scowl.

"You'd better do as he says," warns Peter.

"Here, twelve bags," he hands them to the lads. "we can fill these up and we'll soon have this job done."

When everybody has bread, Jesus does the same with the fish. There is enough that people eat as much as they want.

Once the serving is over, the twelve get chance to eat. The bread may have been cheap barley bread, but it tastes so good and fresh, and the fish, just the right amount of saltiness and texture, perfect.

It's taken so long that when everybody has finished the light has started to fade. Soon it will be dark and once fed some people start to head home. Jesus tells the twelve to go round and collect up all the leftovers, he doesn't want to waste anything. While the twelve are doing this they overhear people in the crowd saying there must have been well over fifteen thousand people spread over the hillside if you include all the children as well. Peter overhears a few men saying they want to overthrow Herod.

Matthew must have felt the atmosphere change for Peter can see he has drawn his gun and is holding it at his side.

"The boss reckons it's time to go," says Philip to Peter. "I know a path where we can slip away from this lot."

Chapter 20

I can't believe they took the car. I paid cash, why did I put it through the books? It only saved a few thousand in deductibles. The first thing I'll do when I get back is look for a new one. Matthew throws a couple more shirts in his bag before scanning the room for anything he might have missed. No, that looks like everything. On his way downstairs he checks he's got his phone, wallet and gun. Stopping momentarily, he considers taking an extra clip of bullets. Shouldn't be necessary, I'll leave it this time. He looks at his watch, they should be here by now, so grabbing his keys from the kitchen worktop and locking up he goes and waits outside.

A few minutes later a blue minibus stops at the bottom of his driveway. Philip waves from the passenger seat. This is going to be an interesting trip. Wonder where we are going?

"Nice place," says Philip as Matthew slides open the side door and gets in.

"Good job it's paid for, otherwise I'd be screwed," his words sound selfish and he's relieved Jude or the Zealot aren't here.

"Just put your bag on the back seats," Andrew points to his and Philips already there.

"So where the hell are we going to this time?"

"No idea," says Philip as Andrew sets off.

Matthew walks to the back and throws his bag on top of the others, returning to sit nearer the front. The minibus looks new. Leaning forward he tries to see the mileage: 27k, not bad.

"The boss bought this, did he?" he asks.

"No, a follower of the boss, Mike. He's a car dealer. He's given it to us to use."

The name doesn't ring any bells. Well, there are so many people it's hard to know them all, though if this Mike is a car dealer, maybe I could get a good deal. I am in the market for one now after all.

Alphie is next to be picked up, followed by Jude and Thaddy. When they pick up Thomas, he's saying goodbye to his brother. Matthew can't tell the twins apart, even though everyone else swears they're not identical.

"Will we all fit in?" asks Thomas, climbing into the back and sitting on an empty seat.

"We should do, its a sixteen seater, so there's enough room for us and our luggage," says Philip, helping Andrew find the next pick up.

"I'd keep your heads down you two collectors, it's the Zealot next."

Matthew is sitting behind Andrew and Philip and Alphie joins him "You do realise some people will never accept us, we will always be the enemy," he pats his gun.

"You brought that with you. I didn't, I've left mine under my bed. I hope I never use one ever again."

"Good for you," says Andrew.

Matthew isn't so sure, it seems he will still have to look out for his young apprentice.

"So where are we heading Andy? asks Jude.

"No idea. Once we have everyone, Jesus has said he'll be at the synagogue. Then we'll find out," says Andrew, while having trouble with the gears.

"He's there. Stop." Philip has spotted Simon, at the bottom of his street, "you're in luck, we won't be going into the estate after all."

"I've been calling, why don't any of you answer?" Simon asks Jude as he goes to a single seat. "Stick that with the others," he passes his bag to Thomas.

"Right, James and John next."

"Better give them a call, hurry them up," suggests Andrew.

Philip rings Johns and James' mobiles, both without success, before getting an answer on the home phone.

"Hi, it's Phil, are the lads ready, we will be there in ten minutes... right, yes I get it, fine see you later."

"They're not ready are they?"

"Not a chance Jude, James is still in bed!"

"It's OK, we'll swing by Nathaniel's next, then Pete's. Anyone got any change?" says Andrew as he approaches the toll booths.

Matthew is not going to enjoy this next bit. He knew eventually he was going to have to do it, but the first time he wanted to do it alone. Get used to being a punter. Even though he sometimes pays when he's in other territories, he does it with a nod and a thumbs up. Most times they recognise him and the barrier is automatically raised. I doubt that will happen today.

Everyone groans and Matthew can feel their hatred. Without saying anything, he leans over to Philip, handing him a money bag full of coins. Philip takes one out ready to hand to

Andrew.

"Go to that one, there's no queue," says Jude.

"No, that one, on the right. It's always slow in that lane," says Nathaniel.

"This feels weird," says Alphie to Matthew, who nods.

Andrew picks a different lane altogether and Phil hands him a coin. He tosses it into the metal bin and the barrier rises up.

Matthew can't help looking at the offices, wondering who they got to replace him. He spent a lot of his money buying this toll area. He had to outbid some serious competition, all for it to be snatched away and handed to someone else. Wonder how much they paid? He notices that one of the booths on the other side isn't working and coming back into Galilee they are queuing; something he would never tolerate. He feels eyes burning into the back of his head, the awkward silence a reminder of who he is.

Once in Bethsaida, Nathaniel is picked up and then they go back through the booths to Peters.

When they finally get to James and John's house, their mother comes down the drive and over to the minibus as Andrew winds down the window.

"They won't be a minute," she says, "please look after them, the last time they went on a lads holiday their father had to bail them out of jail."

"What did they do?" asks Simon eagerly.

"Oh, you wouldn't believe me if I told you."

"Try us," says Jude.

Before she can say anything John comes out of the house carrying a small sports bag.

"Are you sure you have everything?"

"Mum, I'm fine," he climbs into the bus and sits next to

Thaddy.

"Alright boys!" shouts James as he strolls out of the house.

He is wearing shorts, a red and yellow Hawaiian shirt and is trying to squeeze a snorkel and goggles into his already bursting bag. He manages to zip it up and throws it towards the minibus. "Load that someone," he says before disappearing into the garage. When he reappears he's carrying a football, a couple of tennis rackets and a tennis ball.

"Er, a little help won't go amiss," he says as he drops the tennis ball and it rolls down the drive.

"James," says Philip from inside the bus, "I don't think this is a holiday, mate."

"'Course it is, the boss said he was tired, and we've just been on a solo mission. It has to be!"

He passes the football and rackets to Simon, who in turn sends them to the back with all the other luggage.

"Mustn't forget the essentials, he dashes back inside, only to reappear carrying two large packs of Goldstar lager, "a little something for the journey!"

"He's thought of everything," smiles Thaddy.

"Hey, do you think I could fix my surf board to the roof rack?"

"Just get in," Simon takes the beer off him, sliding it down the floor and pulls him into the bus.

Their mum comes over with a bag of goodies, handing it to Philip.

"Hey thanks," he says looking in the bag at all the chocolates, crisps and cans of coke.

"If I'd known you were leaving again I would have baked. Oh, I've included a few packets of paracetamols. I know what you lads are like if you've been drinking."

Andrew thanks her and they all wave as the minibus sets off.

By the time they get to Capernaum synagogue they have all polished off the bag of goodies. Large crowds mean there is no free space to park nearby. Andrew has to park in a Pay and Display a few minutes away. Walking back up towards the synagogue some people from Tiberius recognise the twelve.

"We've been looking for you, where's your boss?"

They follow and find Jesus is standing on the steps of the synagogue speaking to a large crowd, including a TV crew. Matthew notices the three Pharisees from the Old Fig Tree are also in the crowd.

The twelve push their way to the steps. Jesus is talking about the bread of heaven when he notices them arrive. He stops mid sentence, looking straight at James.

"What *are* you wearing James," who takes his sunglasses off and grins.

Jesus shakes his head and carries on addressing the crowd.

"Give us some breakfast," shouts one of those from Tiberius.

"Have you only come looking for me because I fed you for free. I am the bread of life, I offer more than what can fill your stomachs - food that will fill your souls. I am from the Father. I have come down from heaven to do the will of my Father who sent me. Not to do what I want. So that those who have seen the Son and believed in him should have eternal life and be raised up on the last day."

"He doesn't make any sense, talking about heaven and his father."

"I knew your father, he was Joseph from Nazareth," says

one man.

"Come on, give us another miracle," says the TV camera man.

"I am the living bread, anyone who eats this bread will live forever. This bread is my flesh, offered so that the world may live."

"Can't you get your teacher to do something, this is just preaching; it is the religious department's job." The cameraman stops filming.

Matthew watches, noticing that the Pharisees ask the cameraman for the film, or maybe a copy. He must remember to warn Jesus, they look like they're up to something.

Now the crowd, many of whom Matthew recognises from the day before on the hill, drift away unsatisfied. Jesus waves the twelve to follow him into the synagogue. Some followers who have been with Jesus from the very beginning walk out passed them, trying to avoid Jesus.

"Does what I say offend you?"

"It's too hard to understand, teacher," says a man.

"So you are just going to give up?" The man shrugs and walks away, others follow him out.

Andrew and Peter call Matthew over.

"We think it might be a good idea to bring the minibus to the back door and avoid the crowd. Keep an eye out will you."

A few minutes later Peter nods over to Matthew.

"Boss it's time to go, the minibus is here," says Matthew.

"This is becoming a habit," says James.

They all pile in, but as Jesus is climbing into the front passenger seat he stops and in a rather sombre tone asks, "What about you lot, are any of you going to leave me?"

They are all surprised and a little insulted that their boss would even ask them such a question.

"Boss, who would we follow?" says Peter, a little hurt, "we know your words bring eternal life!"

"I chose the twelve of you, but one is a devil!" Jesus says.

They all look at Matthew.

"Hey, don't look at me. Thanks a lot, I see nothing has changed, has it?"

Jesus gets in the bus and closes the door.

"Er boss, where exactly are we going?"Andrew says, setting off.

"On to the Tyre & Sidon highway."

The highway heads north, leaving behind the hot temperatures of Galilee and up into the cooler Syrian mountains. For the next hour no one speaks. The only sounds are the faint base tones that leak out of the headphones of both Simon's and Jude's phones. Jesus has closed his eyes, and though he may not be asleep, the mood in the bus has changed from excited holiday to subdued and contemplative.

Matthew sits staring out of the window, not wanting to look at anyone. He thought he was making progress, starting to fit in, becoming one of the group. Why did Jesus say such a thing? He is never wrong. It was so assertive, so... he searches for the right word in a vain attempt to explain Jesus' words. He loses his train of thought as Andrew catches the kerb whilst turning a corner.

"Oops, sorry, that was a little tighter than I thought."

As they head towards the snow topped mountains the warm air gives way to a more cooler feel.

"Andy, can you turn up the heating?" asks James.

"It's fine", says Thaddy, "someone throw him his bag."

"I have goose bumps."

"Just put some trousers or jeans on?"

"Er, I, er, anyone got any spare trousers?"

A collective laugh breaks out, immediately followed by a universal reluctance to share.

"I'll put the heating on for you," Jesus says, opening his eyes.

"Thank you."

Matthew wonders if it's a good time to ask why Jesus said one of them is a devil, but he is not that brave. Anyway he doubts he would be told, and what if the boss said it was him. Maybe it's better just to leave that unanswered.

"Boss, what's the plan?" asks Thaddy.

"Plans, someone mention plans. I think we should start to plan for lunch, I'm starving," says Peter.

Matthew checks his watch, it's 11.05am.

Up ahead is the border between Israel and Syria. As these countries are both now members of the Union, passports aren't required. A solitary border guard sitting in a small portacabin doesn't even look up from his paper as they drive passed.

"I've never been abroad before!" says Simon pulling out his earphones and looking up at the snow topped mountains.

"I wonder what the food will be like?" says Peter.

"Is that all you think about?" asks Thaddy.

"It is when I'm hungry."

"Don't worry, there will be something to eat when we get there," says Jesus.

"Good. So where are we going?"

"A holiday cottage, just north of Tyre and only a few miles from the coast. We can relax without all the crowds bothering us and you can start the next stage of your training. Plus, it should be warm enough for James to wear his shorts!"

"See, I told you it's a holiday!"

James reaches down to the beer on the floor and opens the pack. "might as well have a sneaky one before lunch."

"He never heard the training part did he?" Andrew says to Jesus.

When they arrive at the cottage it's bigger than Matthew had expected, six bedrooms and a huge garden, plus the fridge is full. Great, the mobile phone reception is good, forgetting for a moment that he doesn't have to keep in touch with the office anymore.

"Oh, there's only one bathroom!" sighs Thomas, "what's it gonna be like in the morning?"

For the rest, their first priority is acquiring a bed.

"I'm not sharing a double bed with anyone!" says Thaddy as he throws his bag on a single.

"The Boss should have the double room to himself, only fair," says Nathaniel.

"Why doesn't Peter take the other and I'll take the blow up mattress on the floor," says Andrew. The rest scramble for the twins.

Matthew sharing a room with Alphie had very little sleep and was quite happy to get up early. The previous evening they'd gone through all the beer and even polished off the bottles of wine found in the pantry. Peter, after talking to his missus and kids, had spent the rest of the evening working out a rota for the cooking and washing up. This morning he seems to have overlooked two rather large and annoying problems.

"Morning Matt, it's not exactly a holiday is it?" says James, as he burns the twentieth piece of toast.

"Thought you two said you could cook?"

199

"It's a lot more difficult than I thought," says John.

Matthew sees they have made drinks, he sniffs it, ughh, "What is this?"

"That's coffee."

"It smells and looks like tar."

"I don't understand? Mum makes it look so easy!" says John.

"It's not my fault, there must be something wrong with that toasting machine," adds James putting another burnt offering on top of the pile.

Sitting at a table with a drink is Alphie, "I made my own, they swore they didn't want my help."

"Maybe we should eat out for breakfast," says Philip when he comes in.

"At least Peter is on for this evening meal, I hear he's quite the chef," says Alphie.

"Only with fish," says John.

What a difference a few miles makes. Over the border there isn't the clamour for Jesus. Some of the lads, Jude, Simon and especially James have started to really enjoy being in the public eye. Matthew hates it, it's one of his biggest concerns. Also, when there are crowds the lads don't get as much quality time with their boss as they would like. So this is a nice break. They can learn from their teacher in private and not be embarrassed when they ask seemingly obvious questions.

Walking along the seafront, in the late afternoon sun, Thomas doesn't look happy and soon starts to complain, "look at my jeans."

All up the front are splashes of wet sand and mud, from walking closely behind Jesus.

"No offence Boss, I'll just move away from you. I don't have any more clean jeans."

"You should be pleased" says Matthew, who is walking at the back of the group.

"What do you mean?" asks Thomas.

"If a pupil of a Rabbi was seen to be covered in the dust of his Master, he was regarded as the favourite or the most keen student."

"Who told you that?" asks Simon.

"I read it somewhere."

Jesus doesn't say anything, he just keeps on walking, probably knowing that behind him there is a scramble to get in pole position, though Thomas has now decided to hold his ground.

Matthew doesn't get involved, preferring to stay at the back, for now anyway. As they walk up on to the main road a woman catches his eye, she is just getting into a parked car. He sees her look at him, quickly close the door and grasp at her handbag. As he walks past he hears a mechanical clunk as she locks herself in.

Oh that's just great, do I look like I'm going to nick your purse. He considers shouting at her, pointing out that he has changed from the violent collector he once was. Maybe not the best move, especially as the guys he is with are still pushing and shoving each other to the extent that they will probably need to be wrestled apart. His hand automatically goes to his gun in its holster. His thoughts drift back to a time when he would have revelled in the fact that people were scared of him.

"PROPHETIC! That was the word I was trying to think of yesterday, huh, funny how that happens isn't it" says Matthew.

The others all turn round, looking at him in bemusement.

"You talking to yourself again Matt?" asks Peter.

Matthew nods, and they all carry on walking.

As they continue to walk along the seafront someone recognises Jesus and starts running towards the group.

"Is that you, Son of David?" shouts a young woman.

Jesus ignores her and keeps on walking.

"What does that mean?" asks James.

"It means she knows who the Boss is," says Nathaniel.

"Oh great, if she keeps on shouting like that so will everybody else," says Thomas.

As the woman gets nearer, her voice becomes louder and more desperate. "Have mercy on me, Sir!" Jesus carries on walking and doesn't even turn to look at her.

"My daughter is in a terrible condition, please help."

To Matthew's surprise, Jesus still refuses to turn round.

"The boss isn't interested, shut up and go away," says James.

She ignores him and screams even louder. Jude tries to push her away, but with little effect.

"Boss!" says Peter, John and Andrew, "do something, this woman won't stop following us. Make her shut up and send her away. Soon everybody will know who you are."

Jesus stops, and slowly turns round to see the woman for the first time.

"I was only sent to the lost sheep of the house of Israel."

The woman approaches Jesus, kneels down and begs him, "Lord, help me!"

"It is not good to take the children's bread and throw it to the dogs," Jesus replies.

"Yes Lord, but even the dogs feed on the crumbs which fall from the masters table."

Jesus smiles at her. "You are a woman of great faith, get up, your daughter is now healed."

As the woman starts to get up, her mobile begins ringing. "Hello, she is what, completely better?" She runs off the way she came, shouting, "You healed her! Thank you Jesus, thank you."

"She's gonna tell everybody!" says Thomas.

"Does that mean we're packing up and moving on?" asks Alphie.

Jesus nods, "back to Israel, but at least we won't have to eat any more of James' cooking."

Chapter 21

"There you are, sir. What are you doing all the way down here?"

Annas is in the Temple basement where all the Temple post is sent to be sorted. He is sitting on a plastic chair watching a monitor. In his hand is a remote.

"Watch this," he says.

A recording of Jesus on the synagogue steps in Capernaum begins to play.

"I have come down from heaven to do the will of my Father who sent me. Not to do what I want. So that those who have seen the Son and believed in him should have eternal life and be raised up on the last day."

"Interesting, isn't it," says Annas, rewinding it and watching it again.

"Yes sir, very, but why down here. Are you OK?"

Annas starts the recording once more and only looks up at the end.

"Right, Jonathan, you're here, good, get the disc out of that thing will you," pointing to the DVD player. Jonathan ejects the disc and after he is unable to see the packing it came in, slides it safely into his jacket pocket and hurries to catch up to his boss as Annas is walking out of the room.

"Right, what about my two o'clock meeting?"

"Sir, it's gone three, I cancelled it when you were nowhere to be found."

"Well, you had better rearrange it, let's say by the time I get back to my office. Oh and watch that DVD yourself, see what you make of it."

Two guards appear, ready to escort Annas. Jonathan gives them a stern glare.

"I had the whole temple guard out looking for you sir, not to mention the palace guard and the police. Oh, this is going to get embarrassing. Protocol, protocol, please keep in touch at all times?" He takes out his phone as he hurries behind Annas and the two guards. "No signal, huh."

"No use trying to use that down here, the walls are so thick, nothing works," says one of the guards.

He points to his radio microphone, "not even these."

When they get up to the ground floor his phone rings.

"Hello, yes I've found him, false alarm, everything is now under control, thank you, yes, I'm sure, that's right, thank you."

"I'll see you back at the office, you've got meetings to arrange," Annas says to Jonathan.

Annas takes in the Temple floor, even managing to listen in at one of the scripture lessons, to the pleasure of the priests but much to the annoyance of his guards, all the time letting the recording of the Carpenter play over in his mind. After half an hour a guard whispers it's time for them to leave and he is ushered quickly back upstairs to the safety of his office chambers.

Annas marches straight into his office. "Well, is he here?"

"Yes Sir."

Standing in front of his desk is a Union soldier.

"I was wondering whom they might send."

"Captain Anthony Roberto, Centurion in the 31st Battalion of the Union Army, Sir," says the soldier.

"Career soldier I presume?"

"Yes sir, I was born in Italy and joined the Union Army straight from school, Sir."

Annas thought this might happen. He sits in his chair behind the desk and offers the Captain a seat.

So, the governor's office is wasting my time. Captain Roberto will have no knowledge of the minutiae of the security situation.

"What have you being told about this meeting?" asks Annas.

"Nothing Sir."

"We usually cover how well the Army and Temple guards deal with the mass influx of so many people in such a small amount of time during the many festivals of the Jewish calender."

"I am afraid that is above my remit Sir."

"Of course Captain, the Governor is playing with me, for as a Union Soldier you shouldn't even be in this part of the Temple. You wouldn't happen to be Jewish would you?"

"No Sir."

Annas knows all about the 31st Battalion, or as it's more familiar, *the notorious 31st* Their violent drunkenness is legendary and some say it's understandable. They kill thousands every year and they do it using the most painful method ever invented. The 31st are in Israel for one thing only: To crucify; capital punishment Union style. It has served the Union well and kept the troublemakers to a minimum during the festivals.

"I do apologise for your inconvenience, and it would be appreciated if you were to leave via a private exit. My assistant will show you the way."

Captain Roberto stands, nods and leaves the office.

For the Governor to send a soldier to the Temple, never mind one that has Jewish blood on his hands, sends a message Annas hears loud and clear. For years the Union has been trying to limit the number of festivals. They have used various methods, from health and safety to terrorist threats.

This must be their next play. He leans back in his chair. I am not going to be threatened, nor take offence. There must be a way I can use this to my advantage, but how?

Once Captain Roberto has been shown the private exit, Jonathan comes into the office, with the disc, plus a large pile of papers.

"You watched it?"

"Yes sir."

"And?"

Jonathan appears hesitant.

"Spit it out man."

"It's not the usual nonsense is it sir?"

Nodding, Annas waves "Go on."

"I've been working with you a long time now, and we've seen hundreds of would-be Messiahs. They range from egomaniacs, revolutionaries, and just plain psychos; most never last a month. This one is different."

"I prefer the word dangerous."

"Very, sir."

First the Carpenter and now the soldier. I will not be played by anyone.

"Get me my car, I must go to the palace."

* * *

Back at the palace, Annas has a large glass of whisky waiting for him - it's needed! He downs it in one and his servant hands him another; this he will savour a little more.

"Caiaphas would like a moment sir," says the servant.

Caiaphas enters, he is still in his ceremonial robes, having spent the day in the Temple.

"Thought you had run off to join Jesus of Nazareth," says Caiaphas laughing, "I was told you had disappeared, we were all very worried."

"Oh, I'm sure you were," says Annas before taking a sip of whisky.

"I believe the results from the opinion poll you have conducted have arrived."

Annas has another sip. "You're fine, if that's what you're worried about." He opens his briefcase and takes out a report, handing it to Caiaphas. Both men sit down. Caiaphas flicks through the report, reading out key results.

"Do you think Jesus of Nazareth is the Messiah? Yes 5%, No 58% Don't know 37%. Do you think that Jesus of Galilee is the Messiah? Yes 34%, No 29%, Wait and see 37%."

As Caiaphas reads out the results Annas can sense the frustration in his son-in-laws voice.

"This is contemptible, listen to this; Do you think breaking the Sabbath law is a punishable offence? 68% agree, but in another question: Is it right for a person to be punished for breaking a religious law? No 85%. It doesn't tell me anything that I didn't already know. People are cretinous, they believe only what we tell them to believe."

"Oh, give them a little more credit than that Caiaphas. Don't forget, your last approval rating was 35%. No, the results are very illuminating. All we have to do is ask the right questions. Whatever they may be."

Caiaphas, from his frown, doesn't appear to agree.

"Get your Pharisees and Sadducees to concentrate on catch-ing the Carpenter breaking the law. Healing on the Sabbath for example, and inform your priests they are to emphasise his Nazarene background. After all the Messiah can't possibly come from Nazareth can he?"

Caiaphas puts the papers on a desk and stands. "35%, is that all their High Priest is to them," he says shaking his head as he walks over to Annas' drinks cabinet and pours himself a large whisky.

"Oh, Caiaphas, have faith, next time we will re-word the question and I'm sure your numbers will rise. In the meantime we need to step things up, the Pharisees have done well, but I want more."

"What do you have in mind?"

"I think it prudent we set up a task force to look into the Carpenter and this group of his. I want to know everything about them, leave no stone unturned. If Jesus works on the Sabbath I want to know about it. The second he enters Jerusalem I am to be informed. If he enters the Temple I want to know by which gate."

Chapter 22

"We're all going on a countrywide tour, countrywide tour, countrywide tour."

"We're all going on a countrywide tour, countrywide tour, countrywide tour."

"Will you two shut up," says Jude pushing his earphones deeper into his ears.

"Oh 2 be a, Oh 2 be a Galilean."

"Oh 2 be a, Oh 2 be a Galilean."

Matthew has never been one for listening to music on headphones, but he's beginning to realise the benefits. James and John just never shut up. He looks over to Peter in the hope he will say something but Peter is in deep conversation with Jesus and doesn't seem bothered by it. Matthew stares at John, maybe a stare will be enough to silence the pair.

"You lot are boring," says James.

"We want our country back, we want our country back, Come on everyone, sing," pleads John.

"We want our country back," this they all can't help singing, a little anyway. Even Peter and Andrew join in. Matthew too sings along, though with less enthusiasm as the others. Having worked and done very well under the Union he's always been apathetic towards it, but knows first hand the

anger and hatred others feel. Simon, who was looking bored now stands up and takes the lead, *"we want our country back,"* he sings, his eyes burning with passion.

Matthew, feeling eyes on him, smiles and mouths the words. He knows they still think of him as a traitor to Israel. He doesn't want to give them any more ammunition.

Andrew, driving, begins to overtake a coach. As he pulls alongside Matthew notices James has gone quiet. Oh no he isn't, is he? Yes he is! James pulls down his jeans and pants and moons the coach.

Matthew hides his face from the horrified looks of the old people as the minibus slowly passes.

"James, grow up!" shouts Philip.

"Come on James, what if they recognise us?" says Thomas.

"Boss, tell him to behave," says Alphie.

Jesus has slunk down in his seat and has also covered his face. Though Matthew is sure he saw a smile. Peter appears totally oblivious to it all and continues his conversation, his arms waving as he talks.

"You lot are sooo boring, that will have made their day," says James laughing.

"Given them all heart attacks more like," adds Thaddy.

So it's another day on the road, another town, another step nearer to the promised land of God's kingdom being restored to Israel; though it's taking a lot longer than the lads expected, Matthew included. Surely Jerusalem is there for the taking. Who can stand against the man that has power over the wind, the waves, over everything. No one can that's who, not the High Priest, not the Governor, not the Union.

Andrew has turned off the main road and they look to be heading to a small village and not the city of Tiberius as

Matthew had assumed. He sighs a little too loudly for Simon and Nathaniel both look in his direction. Nathaniel nods back, giving the impression that he too isn't thrilled with the destination.

"This place is so small, I never even saw a sign?" Nathaniel sighs.

They all pile off the minibus and are shown into a house. Inside there is nowhere to sit, the place is packed. It looks like the whole village is crammed into the small house, including and to Matthews annoyance, some priests. Everywhere they go lately there are always priests present. Are they here to listen and learn or here to trap the boss into saying something blasphemous? He suspects the latter. Trying to find a seat is pointless; anyway they've been travelling constantly and a stretch will do him good. A place has been kept for Jesus in the centre of the open plan living area but not for the lads. This doesn't stop Peter, James and John who push their way in.

"Come on, make room, Jesus won't start until we're all seated," says Peter.

Philip, Nathaniel, Andrew, Thaddy, Jude, Alphie and Thomas all squeeze in and sit as close to Jesus as they can. Matthew and Simon stand by the door.

"I'm not sitting on the floor," says Simon.

"Me neither."

Matthew, still uncomfortable in crowds and confined spaces, finds it difficult to sit and listen to the boss without feeling vulnerable. He does after all still get those hateful stares and whispered curses from the Zealot.

As word spreads that the Miracle Man is here, more and more people turn up.

"Don't let anymore in. We are so squashed it's like Peter's family at a free buffet," shouts James through the mass of people to Matthew and Simon. He says something else, but is drowned out.

Matthew tries to shut the door, but people refuse to move, desperate to see and hear Jesus.

More and more are still arriving. Where on earth are they coming from? This wasn't even meant to be a publicised visit.

"It's too full, move along," says Simon to a bunch of young lads.

"Or what?" says one.

"Or he carves his initials on your forehead," says Matthew, waiting to see if the young man recognises the Zealot.

"You don't understand, we *have* to get in."

"Look, there's no room, maybe you could wait until Jesus leaves, he may have time for you later?" Simon suggests.

"That's no good, my friend needs to see Jesus now!"

Matthew looks round wondering which of them is in such need.

"He's in the car, he can't walk."

"Then he'd better stay where he is and wait," says Matthew.

"We'll let Jesus know, that's the best we can do," says Simon sympathetically.

Matthew waves in the direction of Jesus and the others in the hope of catching their attention and Simon even tries ringing the mobiles of Jude, then Nathaniel and finally Thaddy. He shakes his head.

"Now what are they up to?" asks Matthew.

The young men have gone back to the car and are helping their friend into a wheelchair. Matthew and Simon go to stop them.

"We are gonna see if there is another way in," says one of the young men.

"I have to say it, they're determined, I'll give them that," Simon says to Matthew.

Matthew nods. "Oh what the hell, we might as well help."

They follow the lads around the back of the house and find a single story extension with a back door. One of them checks the door.

"It's locked," he says.

Matthew shakes his head, health and safety doesn't seem to have been a concern does it? His company had hundreds of forms to fill out, and that was just to operate the kettle!

"Oh well, you gave it a try, come on back to the front,"he says.

What about that window?" asks one of the young men.

"Oh yeah" says another, climbing up a drain pipe and onto the flat roof of the extension. From there he climbs up the sloping house roof to an open window and peers in.

"What's he gonna do, climb in and go and unlock the back door?" asks Simon.

"Hopefully," says the young man in the wheelchair.

The lad on the roof puts his thumb up, but instead of climbing in, comes back down and studies the house, moving back for a better look.

"Well?" asks Matthew, getting impatient.

"That wasn't a bedroom, I saw everybody down there." He looks at the friend in the wheelchair, "I saw Jesus."

They all look up, searching for another way in. There doesn't appear to be any.

"Look, we are in Jesus' team, come wait with us, I'm sure he won't be that long. Peter is sure to be getting hungry by now anyway," says Simon.

A tear runs down the face of the lad in the wheelchair and a friend wipes it away for him.

"So, what is wrong with you?" Matthew asks.

"I don't know, nobody knows, I'm just getting slowly worse. I don't have any movement in my arms or legs."

"We want your Jesus to heal him."

"I'm scared that I will lose my voice soon too."

Matthew looks at Simon, not with suspicion but quizzically.

"You know we might be able to help, we've healed people before."

"Sure, we could do that."

Matthew bends down and is just about to speak when there is a intake of breath from the others.

"What is it?"

"You've got a gun!"

"You're the Collector? This won't work, I want to see Jesus."

Matthew's gun on his belt is showing. He stands, covering it with his shirt.

"Don't you do anything either," the lads tell Simon.

"Nice one Collector," says Simon.

"Hey, I need this for protection, from you and your kind."

"My kind? You mean true patriots. You, you're a traitor. The less of *your* kind the better."

"Er, hello, you helping or fighting? shouts the lad who has gone back up to the roof.

Matthew takes a deep breath, he can feel himself shaking and he never shakes. He puts his hands up stepping away. "Fine, now what do you suggest."

"The window is open and it's big enough for him and the

wheelchair to go through and to lower him down. We need to get him up here," says the young lad on the roof.

"What! That's impossible," says Simon.

"We do have rope in the bus," offers Matthew.

Simon stares at him.

Matthew too thinks it's useless, but he feels the lads desperation and urgency and he would rather be doing something than standing here with the Zealot.

"Great, we've got some too, maybe it could work," says a lad turning and running to the front of the house.

The bus was left unlocked as the side door is broken and Matthew quickly fetches a long line of tow rope.

"Why do we have that?" asks Simon.

"Andrew thinks it may be needed one day, especially if James and John get hold of the keys."

"Great, but that's only two ropes and we need four if you don't want him to fall out," says Simon

"Looks like we messed up the healing, I'll try anything now," replies Matthew.

"We messed up?...fine but, we had better make sure it works, or there is gonna be one hell of a mess."

The lads measure out both ropes, then secure one around both handles at the front. One rope, two anchor points, perfect. They do the same with the other rope this time fastening it to the front wheels.

"You will go down at an angle but it should work," says one lad to his friend.

Matthew and Simon insist on taking a line of rope each, being bigger and stronger than the young lads. They and two of the lads climb up onto the roof of the extension.

"First job is seeing if we can pull him up here," says

Matthew.

With one of the lads staying to help on the ground, Matthew and the other pull as hard as they can.

It's a lot easier than Matthew expected, or maybe he's just stronger than he thought.

"Now what," says Simon looking at the sloping roof.

"Now two pull and two push," say the lads, climbing up from the ground.

"Trust us to find the only sloping roof in the country?" says Simon as he and Matthew pull the wheelchair up the roof.

Once at the window they rest and get into position. Simon peers down into the room below.

"Yo Boss!" he shouts.

Everybody looks up in surprise and Simon waves, "Incoming," he says.

"Why are you up there Zealot?" shouts Nathaniel.

"What are you doing?" James shouts.

The weight puts a strain on Matthew's arms, "hurry up."

"Boss we are sending someone down to you," says Simon.

"Quickly," shouts one of the lads.

"There may not be enough rope, some of you may need to help this lad down the last bit."

With that Simon grabs his rope and braces himself on the window frame. The others all grip their ropes equally tight.

"Take the strain, now push him over the edge, gently," says Simon.

One of the lads not holding a rope inches the chair over. "Now," he yells.

Matthew shoulders jerk as the chair is now in the air. Quickly as they can they lower it down, his hands burning.

"Go, go, go," yells one of the lads wincing in pain.

Matthew is working so hard not to let go that he isn't looking down when the rope goes light.

"We got him, we got him," shouts Peter.

Breathing heavily Matthew, Simon and the lads all relax, their hands red raw.

"It was all their idea, we just gave then a bit of muscle," Simon shouts down in between breaths.

All five on the roof look down into the room, waiting to see what Jesus will do.

"You and your friends really do believe I can heal you, is that right?" Jesus asks.

"Yes, we do."

"And you also have guilt because of your sins?"

"Yes I do, Jesus."

"Well, son, I forgive your sins. Now get up and walk."

"You can't say that, only God can forgive sins," says a priest.

"This is blasphemy, he can't say that," screams another.

"Knob heads," says Simon.

"Just watch. Your friend has been healed," shouts Matthew.

Jesus turns to the priests, "why are you so sceptical? Which is simpler to say, I forgive sins or get up and start walking? Well I am the Son of Man and I am authorised to do both."

Jesus turns to the lad, "Come on, what are you waiting for, get up, you can go home now."

The young man, starts to move his arms. He feels his face and starts clapping his hands.

"Come on Johnny boy, you can do it," shouts the lad next to Matthew.

Matthew pats the lad on the back, ouch, his hand is still tender. Down below the friend stands up. The crowd are forced to make room and spill outside as the young lad walks towards the door, laughing as he does.

Chapter 23

"He's late."

"Patience my dear Caiaphas, patience."

"You still haven't told me his name? He is after all one of *my* priests."

Annas prefers it that way; he likes his little secrets. On this occasion however, he sees no reason to hide the identity of his agent. Just so long as Caiaphas can hold his tongue.

As the antique clock in the hall strikes quarter past midnight there is a faint knock at the back door. Annas turns the key and opens the door. A figure dressed in black enters. Annas leads the way into his office where an agitated Caiaphas is standing by a open fire.

"Did anyone see you arrive?" demands Caiaphas.

"No High Priest, I was very careful, as always."

"Did anyone suspect what you were up to?" asks Caiaphas.

"My sources are loyal to the office of the High Priest."

The priest takes an envelope from inside his long overcoat, handing it to Annas.

"Excellent," says Annas.

The priest bows his head to both men, turns and leaves.

Annas opens the brown envelope and takes out the report.

After switching on a lamp he reaches for his glasses and quickly flicks through the pages. For something that has taken months to research it is surprisingly short, only a few pages in total. But what it lacks in length it makes up for in value.

"Well?" asks Caiaphas.

"It's concise."

"Does it give us what we want?"

Annas smiles, it gives him all he had hoped for, and more.

"Have a look for yourself, you won't be disappointed."

Annas walks over to Caiaphas, hands him the report and puts his hands to the fire warming them.

Caiaphas nods with each recommendation.

"Read the conclusions."

Caiaphas skips a page, and smiles.

"So, we have enough to at least arrest him under the blasphemy laws."

Annas, unable to contain his pleasure, smiles and says "I couldn't have written it better myself."

He takes the report and locks it away in the palace safe, built into a wall in his office.

"So how do we proceed?"

"Oh, that is already under way."

Annas picks up a remote and turns the TV on. He flicks through the channels, searching for some adverts for the forthcoming festivals.

"Timing is everything." The adverts end and a programme about the Life of the Colossal Squid continues. Annas shakes his head, searching the channels once more, again stopping at more advertisements. "Might have better luck now." He doesn't, and has to turn the TV off.

"Alright, so timing isn't apparently everything."

"You don't appear to be making any sense."

"Let me put it this way, name three times in the year when a Jewish male should visit the city?"

"It's late, I'm not playing games!"

"Please Caiaphas, indulge me."

"Fine, I'll play, I just hope there is a point to all this. You are referring to the festivals, but the only ones that the law requires the journey to the Temple for are: Unleavened Bread, Harvest and," he smiles, "of course, the Feast of Booths. I'm guessing those commercials are playing night and day. You were most unfortunate not to stumble upon one of them."

The timing of the report could have been better, the Feast is only days away. If he can't set everything up in time the opportunity will be lost; for the time being anyway. While Caiaphas goes off to bed, Annas' mind races with all the details to arrange. Security won't be a problem, the Governor hates the holidays and always adds extra soldiers; those along with his Temple guards should be enough. This teacher and his team are only Galileans after all.

It does add some more excitement to one of his favourite times of the year. It commemorates God's deliverance, protection and provision during the Exodus out of Egypt. People erect booths or huts made from olive, myrtle or palm branches and leaves. They live in them for the length of the festival - seven days. It is very good for business. Maybe that's why it's become his favourite festival; there are just so many ways to make a profit. For not only do the Temple offerings increase, the Booths of Annas stock a very affordable line in easy to assemble huts for those too busy to go out and collect branches and wood themselves. This year will be the first time they offer a range of ready meals and his sons are particularly confident they will be big sellers.

* * *

Annas has been meticulous with the planning and has been unable to sleep the last few days. There is just too much to do, why waste time on sleep. Jonathan enters the temple control centre with Governor Pilate's defence adviser. They are going over the security plans; everything is in place. Annas stands watching the monitors.

"Everyone will expect him to be here," he says. "What are you doing to do about security?"

"The heaviest in years." replies Jonathan.

"Good."

"Only there is a fine line, we don't want him to get suspicious do we?"

"It would be better if we can arrest him quietly, without his team around."

"Agreed."

"The police are to control the streets of the city; we have in place extra units in case of any major incidents. The Governor has insisted that soldiers can be employed anywhere, at any time over the seven days of the feast. If necessary they will enter the Temple but only under extreme circumstances, you understand," says the defence adviser to Annas.

"The Temple Guard can handle any incident that is thrown at them. I cannot foresee any reason why the Union may need to get involved in Temple business. I have ordered all available guards to be on duty. Also, we have a state of the art surveillance system," says Annas.

This is really the perfect time to arrest Jesus. This is when the Governor wants peace at all costs. It is so much easier to arrest somebody for disturbing the peace now. They can bring fresh charges later. The Union does not take kindly to festivals that promote, as they call it *Anti-Union feelings*. The Governor demands a joyous, yet peaceful time. If he can't achieve peace somebody else will. The situation has just become even more explosive now that three high profile crucifixions have taken place. The Union likes to remind people just who controls Israel. Annas can use this Union anxiety for his own purposes.

A bank of eight monitors – in two rows of four, dominates the communications room. All the gates are covered by cameras, as are the gates to the courts. Much to Annas' annoyance the priests and Caiaphas have steadfastly refused to allow cameras into the main body of the Temple. Two guards are sitting at the monitors, scanning for any sign of trouble. Two more stand behind supervising. These teams of four will change every three hours. They will do this for the duration of the festival. There are several other trouble makers that the religious authorities have banned from the Temple. Annas will pay the guards extra if they are instrumental in the capture of Jesus.

Annas has been to the communications room several times already today. He is anxious and a little excited by the prospect of facing this Jesus. He has now returned to his office to read the latest business projections his sons have emailed to him. The ready meals are a big hit and their latest forecasts are that this will be a record-breaking year, though for a change his mind is not on money.

"Jonathan."

"Yes sir" Jonathan peers round the door, but does not enter.

"Any updates?"

"No sir, not since the last one."

When news does filter through, it is not what was hoped for. Reports of Jesus refusing to travel with his family have been broadcast on the internet. His followers too, seem to be spending the festival in Galilee. Members of his team have been spotted buying food at a local market in Capernaum. Others were seen collecting branches and leaves and loading up a pick-up truck in the hills around Bethsaida.

At the end of the first day of the Festival, the household of Annas start feasting. In the palace inner courtyard the staff have built three large huts. Annas, Caiaphas and their families gather round while the press take photographs. In the morning, as every year, the newspapers will have the House of Annas splashed across its front pages.

Before the press leaves, Annas has a quiet word with a few of his most reliable and supportive reporters.

"Why isn't this Jesus here celebrating. You would think a man of high learning and knowledge of the scriptures would want to show a good example to the people."

* * *

The morning newspapers all had the photograph on their front pages. This isn't a surprise, that is why they were allowed to work. Most papers had also questioned the where-abouts of Jesus, but not as prominently as Annas wanted. They made the point that it is too early to write him off just yet; it is a seven-day Festival after all.

Day two passes off quietly, although the guards did have a few things to deal with. One of the men banned from the

Temple tried to sneak in, but he was quickly arrested and taken to the city jail. Then there were the usual few who had drunk too much wine. They too ended up in the jail, if only to sleep it off.

Halfway through day three Annas is interrupted whilst eating lunch in his office.

"Excuse me sir," says Jonathan. "I just thought I'd update you. The internet is buzzing with rumours that Jesus has been spotted entering the outer limits of the city."

Annas picks up his napkin and wipes his mouth.

"Do we have anybody close to him?"

"Not at this time, as I say it's just rumours."

"Keep me informed."

A few minutes later Jonathan puts his head round the door again.

"Sorry sir, another false alarm."

There have been many over the last few days. With all the mobile devices people now have, he was sure someone would show up his location. Annas is puzzled, he thought he had started to understand this man, the need for attention, observing the law. He might have to think up another plan.

Annas hasn't even finished his hot green tea when Jonathan comes running in.

"Sir, he's here in the Temple."

Annas in his rush knocks over the drink.

"What!" How?"

"Look, someone is showing it live over the internet. It appears he is right here."

"Are you sure this isn't a recording?"

"Yes sir, positive."

"There are priests in the room, why haven't they notified

me?"

"They appear to be debating with him. Sir you can't go down there without a guard Sir!"

"Then you had better get me one," says Annas.

Annas, his heart racing, walks as fast as he can without running. He reaches the end of the corridor and is at the top of the steps when two guards come up behind him.

"Sir, please, it's extremely busy. Sir, I advise you not to go down there."

"I understand your concerns, but I insist."

A crackle comes over one of the guards' earpiece.

"He is in room three."

As they make their way to the meeting room another keeps Annas informed.

"Two guards have entered the room, they've spotted him. They have the door secure. No one is being allowed in or out."

Annas forgets his importance and runs. Finally he will get to confront this imposter. The guards push and shove people out of his way. They were right about the volume of people but as they arrive at room three it is emptying. Annas is recognised and many want to greet him.

"What has happened?"

"Update us," says a guard to the control room.

"He's vanished," comes the reply.

"He isn't here sir, it must have been a false alarm."

Annas pushes into the room ahead of his guards.

"You," he says to some men, "Who was here teaching?"

"Sir, I am honoured."

"Of course you are. Who was it?"

"Jesus, the Nazarene, sir."

"Where is he now?" asks a guard.

"He just vanished, the guards came in and the next minute he was gone."

"The last thing he said was *some were coming to arrest him*, then the guards entered."

Annas looks at the guards. One shakes his head, "if he was here, he's not now."

Chapter 24

"We're all going on a countrywide tour, countrywide tour, countrywide tour."

"Oh, will you give it a rest?" demands Peter.

"Do you have to sing that song every time we get back in the minibus?" adds Jude.

"We're only trying to have some fun," James and John grumble.

"Well maybe have a little bit of respect, Jesus is praying," says Matthew.

Jesus, having gone to Jerusalem alone, is back with his team and is sitting on a bench, several metres away from the minibus.

"We should never have let him go to Jerusalem by himself," says Peter.

"He shouldn't have gone at all!" says Thomas.

"You can't say that, it's Jerusalem. We should all have gone and I mean everybody, get all the crowds together, then let's see who's gonna stop us," says Simon.

All except Thomas agree.

The twelve found it hard to understand Jesus' reasoning. One minute he was resting in Galilee; the next, without telling them where he was going, he's shown up on the news down in

Jerusalem. To make matters worse, he'd come close to getting arrested. Why hadn't Jesus wanted them by his side? Jesus talked constantly about looking after one another; they're closer now than at any time. They spent the festival together at Peter's. Ruth and the kids had made them all feel very welcome. Even Matthew and Simon haven't tried killing each other lately, from what John can gather anyway. Andrew had pointed out that maybe Jesus leaving and the team still staying together was some kind of test. If it was, they have passed. Well, he still didn't like the fact that Jesus could have been arrested.

"Do you think our training's gone well?" No one responds so John continues, "I think it has. It helps not having to pass an exam though, right? Oh, you don't think there will be an exam at the end of this do you?"

"It's not about passing exams, you idiot. This is Jesus, it's more than that," says Peter.

"It's about the New Kingdom," says James.

"The power and the glory, baby," says Jude.

"Oh yeah......!" adds Simon.

Smiles spread on the faces of all twelve.

Jesus finishes praying and comes over to the bus. He sees them all smiling.

"What a scary sight."

Philip has the driving duties today so he starts up the bus and sets off. "Jericho here we come."

They are all looking forward to this trip.

"About time too, thought we'd never get to go," says Jude.

Thaddy is thinking out loud, "I heard the house is so big, we can all have a room each."

Simon nods in agreement, "I heard they have servants."

"Oh, if that's the case, I'll have breakfast in bed in the morning," says Peter.

As Philip drives along Kirenth promenade - a wide, straight road, lined with palm trees, he slows right down to read a road sign. "Am I on the right road? Do we need to take the next left, boss?"

Nathaniel notices a street sign. "Over there, we're on Kirenth promenade."

"I'm sure Herod has a palace round here somewhere, or he did at one time," says Nathaniel.

John looks out of the window at the huge mansions, so this is where all the top celebrities and sports stars live. We're so close, let's hope nothing else stops us now.

They had been invited to stay several weeks ago by the Tabinsteins, a very wealthy banking family. Unfortunately a sickness in Samaria, of all places, had meant that Jesus had changed his plans and gone there to do a Heal and Speak. John tries not to get too excited; with Jesus things can change in an instant.

"Phil, that's what you're looking for," says Jesus pointing to the next turn.

Philip indicates and turns left only to see a barrier a hundred metres further down the road and next to it a small office with two security guards.

"Look at all the signs: Private Residential Area, No Through Road, By Appointment Only, This is a surveillance district, Oh, No Stopping At Any Time," says Philip.

He drives up to the barrier and a guard comes over to the minibus. Philip winds the window down.

"Hi, er, hi, I'm looking for..." he fumbles for the address he has written down somewhere.

Peter leans over from the passenger seat. "We're here to stay with the Tabinsteins, they're friends of ours, you know."

"I know who you are," says the guard, "we've been expecting you." He waves over the other guard.

"Oh no, they're gonna arrest us," says Thomas.

John, sitting next to Thomas, thumps him.

The guard peers into the bus, "which one of you is Jesus?"

Jesus smiles to the guard and gets out of the bus. The three men then walk to the office talking.

"They're friends of ours, you know! Oh, la de da," says James.

"Oh S P, please speak with that accent all the time we are here" says Andrew.

"What are you talking about?" asks Peter.

"You were putting on a posh accent" says Nathaniel.

"It's how I always talk."

"Of course it is, darling. I was just saying to my friend Matthew, what a super chap that Simon Peter is," says James.

Peter shakes his head.

Jesus gets back into the bus and one of the guards lifts up the barrier.

"Follow the road to the right and then we are looking for a set of tall black gates."

As they approach, a set of ornate black gates begin to open, revealing a huge white mansion, three stories high with windows seemingly everywhere.

"Do any of you have a shirt and tie? 'cos, there is no way they're letting us in here, no way," says Philip.

The drive has a large turning circle. There is another minibus parked in front of the main door and a few cars behind it. To the left there is an entrance to what looks like garages.

It is all fenced in by tall green palm trees. Philip parks behind the cars.

"Didn't know there'd be others," says Jude a little disappointed.

John isn't that surprised at all, there is often a large following of family and friends. Sometimes it runs into hundreds.

"John, isn't that mum and dad's car?" asks James.

"Oh crap, it is!" answers John.

"First one in gets the biggest room," yells James.

The lads all pile out of the bus, collecting their own bags and racing each other inside. Naomi and Toby come running over to Peter, "Daddy, Daddy."

Peter drops his bag and scoops them up, kissing them.

"Mummy says we can stay here tonight."

He sees Ruth in the doorway.

"Surprise!" she says.

Pushing and shoving, the others make their way through big double doors, made from the finest oak and into a large hall. They all stop, staring in amazement at the white and grey marble floor and a showstopping staircase sweeping up to the floors above.

"Wow," says Thomas, open mouthed.

Welcoming everyone is the hostess, Leah Tabinstein; slim and beautifully dressed as always. Next to her, more casually dressed is her husband Tobias.

"Welcome, please come in. Good to see you again."

"I was only talking to her a few days ago. Never would have guessed she was this loaded," whispers Nathaniel.

"I want to cry, I think I'm home," says James.

"It is very nice to meet you, you have a lovely home," says Andrew to the hosts, as they all queue to be greeted by them.

"Champagne is being served in the lounge," says Tobias to everybody.

"Master," says Leah as Jesus enters.

One by one the guests are shown to their rooms in various parts of the mansion. James and John still haven't seen their parents when it's their turn.

"Oh yes, you are both staying in the annexe, please follow me," says a member of staff.

Excitedly they follow. They go out through the back, passed the swimming pool and tennis court towards some outbuildings.

"Can I go for a swim?" John asks the staff member, who nods. "So who else is staying here?" he asks.

"I believe just the two of you, sir."

"Hey, we've got our own house," says James as they approach.

The annexe is made up of a large games room, gymnasium, sauna, and steam room. There is also a changing room with showers that serve the swimming pool and tennis court. It also happens to be where the Tabinstein's two sons are hiding out, playing one of the latest games on a console.

"You've got Ghost Riders 4, awesome!" says James.

John is impressed, the games room has a big TV, soft comfy sofas, a pool table, even a dart board, as well as every games console on the market, all with the latest games. It looks like they have to sleep on camp beds, which have been made up at one end of the games room. Oh well, this is a lot better than some of the places we've stayed in.

"So you must be Samuel and Daniel."

The boys nod.

"Are you one of that man's friends?" Daniel asks John.

"Yeah, and part of his team,"answers John.

"You're young!"

"You're hogging the game! Now, move over and let us have a go," says James.

After they've played for over half an hour John is bored.

"I wish I'd brought mi shorts, I could just do with a swim."

"There are towels and swimming trunks in the changing area," says Samuel.

"Really! Great."

He's right, there are spare trunks, new, still in their packaging. John takes a pair and closes the door. White towels have been arranged along a bench; there are even goggles on the hooks. He quickly gets changed. I'll do a few laps before tea and work off some of this stiffness. It feels like we've been travelling forever.

Coming out of the annexe he notices Nathaniel and Philip walking towards him by the side of the pool.

"Incoming!" He shouts before jumping into the pool.

He surfaces and begins to swim to the shallow end.

"You idiot!"

"John, I'm soaked."

He stands up, oh, it's not as warm as he thought. Nathaniel and Philip do not look too happy. He does another length, but as he's turning for another, Philip shouts out.

"Hey, John, Mark Ruchenberg is here.

John stops and holding on to the side of the pool asks, "the actor?"

"Yes the actor!" says Nathaniel.

Wow, a real Hollywood star; John climbs out.

Philip and Nathaniel don't wait for him, they get James and dash off. By the time John has dried himself and got changed there is a large group around Mark and its difficult for John to get close. There also appears to be food out now plus a lot of people he's not seen before.

"What's happening?" he asks Peter, who is tucking into a lamb salad.

"It seems that all the neighbourhood want to meet the boss."

Looks like it's turned into a party since he arrived.

"So what is Mark Ruchenberg doing here?"

"Can you believe he lives next door? Just happens to be at home resting before he flies back to America to shoot his next movie," says Thaddy.

"News of the boss has even travelled half way around the world," says Jude all excited.

"What else have I missed?" asks John.

"That's Junior Johnson," another guest that John doesn't recognise. He is wearing the type of clothes Simon likes to wear, really baggy t-shirt, jeans and way too much gold. The girl he is with is hot though.

"Who's he."

"His dad built most of Tiberius city for Herod. Like built the whole city! Seriously loaded. He drives a Bugatti Chiron."

Junior is insisting that he be introduced to Jesus. John finds all this intriguing, they certainly mingle in different circles when they're around Jesus.

"Teacher, what good can I do to have eternal life?" asks Junior.

"Why are you asking me about what is good? There is only one who is good; if you want eternal life then keep the commandments," says Jesus.

"Which ones?" he asks.

"Do not commit murder: do not commit adultery, do not steal, do not accuse anyone wrongly, respect your father and mother and love your neighbour as yourself."

"Hey, I have kept all those commandments, teacher. Anything else?"

"The one thing *you* lack: go, sell all that you own and give your money to the poor, then come back and follow me."

Junior doesn't answer, but looks down at the floor, then at the girl. He changes from a cocky self assured young man, to a confused sad boy. He shakes his head and turns his back on Jesus. He walks away, putting down the champagne on a table as he leaves.

After he has left, Jesus says to everybody, "it will be so much harder for rich people to enter the Kingdom of Heaven."

John notices that there are quite a few people who are very uncomfortable. Wonder why Jesus said that here, today? All the lads hearing Jesus speak gather round.

"I'll say it again, it is much harder for a rich person to enter the Kingdom of Heaven, than for a camel to go through the eye of a needle."

"Who can be saved then?" asks Matthew.

"With people this is impossible, but with God everything is possible."

Peter, putting his arm around Ruth says, "we have left everything and followed you. What will we have?"

"You can be sure that when the Son of Man sits on his throne in the new age, then you twelve will also sit on thrones, to rule the twelve tribes of Israel," says Jesus.

They all look at each other, this is what they have been waiting for ever since they were chosen.

"For everyone who has left homes or brothers or sisters or

father or mother or children or lands for my sake, will receive a hundred times more and will be given eternal life. But many who are first will be last and many who are last will be first."

Jesus takes a drink, and goes into another room to talk to Leah and Tobias. He has left the lads open mouthed. They all try to digest what he has just said.

"Oh shit! Can you believe that?" asks Simon.

"Thrones, power and glory, at last it's finally going to happen," says Jude.

"This is the greatest day of my life," says Thaddy.

"Yes!" James pumps his fist. "I always knew I was special, I always knew."

They decide this is a special day and celebrate with a few more glasses of champagne. John wonders where their parents are, he knows they are around somewhere, but he hasn't spoken to them yet. He wonders if they've heard the news. He doesn't have to wait long.

"Oh, there are my boys, come here." his mother holds out her arms.

"I guess you heard!" says John.

"What's not to hear, everybody heard, my boys are going to rule Israel."

She hugs them both as their father looks on, shaking his head in disbelief.

"Rule Israel, those two? I don't get it, I really don't get it!" says Zebedee.

"Now, have you discussed which of these thrones you are going to sit on?" asks their mother. "I don't want you on the end, my boys should be next to Jesus."

"I bags the right," says James.

Before any of the others can say anything John quickly says

"lefties." They high five each other.

"Come on, let's find Jesus and make this official," says their mother.

They find Jesus still talking with Leah and Tobias. Their mother, not wanting to interrupt, but clearly impatient, stands waiting for a moment. Jesus turns to her and her boys.

"What do you want Salomé?" asks Jesus.

"Master, promise me that my boys will sit at your right and your left when you are King."

"You do not know what you are asking." Jesus looks at the lads and asks them. "Can you drink the cup of suffering that I am about to drink?"

"Course we can," they say.

"You will indeed drink from my cup, but I don't have the right to choose who will sit on my right or my left. Those places belong to the ones for whom my Father has prepared for them."

When they return to the living room, John can tell something is wrong, even Peter looks mad.

"I can't believe what you have just done!" says Peter.

"Nice going you two," says Simon.

"You want to be better than us, do you?" says Jude.

"I can't believe you had the nerve," says Alphie.

"You're only jealous 'cos we thought of it first," says James.

"You mean your mummy did," says Simon.

James pushes Simon, who pushes back.

"Yeah, you want a piece of me?"

"Any time, mummy's boy."

They square up to each other. John, defending his brother, pushes Simon away. Jude then pushes John. Andrew pulls Jude away, shoving him into Thaddy, who falls over. On

239

the floor, Thaddy, grabs John's foot, tripping him up. John stumbles backwards and grabs onto Nathaniel, ripping his shirt as he falls. All twelve have joined in what is quickly becoming a fight.

From the floor John notices Jesus watching from the doorway. He sees him sigh, the disappointment etched in his eyes.

"The boss is watching," he says. "Stop!" he says again, louder this time.

One by one they stop. James is the last to realise, aiming a swing at Simon, that luckily misses.

"JAMES!" John shouts, picking himself up and holding out a hand to Thaddy.

Jesus comes in and sits down on one of the sofas and beckons the lads over.

"Lads, come here and sit down."

Without speaking, and slightly embarrassed, they each find a seat.

"Kings and governments have great power and authority over their people. This is not how it is to be with you! If one of you wants to be great, he must first be your servant. If any one of you wants to be first, he must be your slave. Just like the Son of Man, who did not come to be served but to serve and to give his life for the ransom of many."

The quiet is interrupted by the ringing of Andrew's phone. He quickly stops it, only for it to start ringing immediately.

"Just answer it, will you," says James.

"Hello, hi Mary, Yes Jesus is here, everything alright? Oh dear, yes I will put him on."

Andrew hands Jesus the phone, who stands up and goes into hallway.

"Come on spill, which Mary was it?" asks James.

"And what's happened?" asks Philip.

"That was Lazarus' sister. He's sick."

"Aw, is that all."

"What!" You can't say that, it could be bad," Thomas says questioning James' lack of sympathy.

"Oh, please Thomas, come on, you think this is anything the boss can't handle, he's probably healed him already," says Nathaniel.

"Yeah, like the time in Tyre," Philip reminds him.

"Oh yeah, I forgot about that." Thomas cheers up.

Chapter 25

"I can't believe Lazarus is dead."

"Yeah well, death is real, get used to it."

"I can't believe Jesus didn't even go to see him."

The moment Jesus told them that Lazarus had died, the mood in the whole house changed. Everyone had assumed Jesus would save his friend. No one for a second expected Jesus to do...nothing.

They all knew Lazarus, he was a good man. Jesus has known him and his sisters for many years, well before the twelve were chosen. So why would he let him die? It wasn't even quick, he was ill for days. From what Andrew says after talking to the sisters Mary and Martha, he suffered a lot. When Matthew goes, he hopes it's quick and painless. He had always thought that one day his luck would run out and he'd be shot or stabbed.

He sips his morning coffee and stares at the Zealot, sitting opposite him, reading the paper. How things have changed. Never in a million lifetimes could he have foreseen what has now become reality. Thoughts of his previous life flooded back. The faces of his victims, his greed. There hasn't been much talk of death on the tour. So the news of Lazarus has hit them hard. He knows how much Jesus liked Lazarus, (he was a good friend) and by the look on his face he cared a great deal for him, so why didn't he do something? Maybe they could have been more persuasive? Peter and Andrew did ask him why he did nothing, only for Jesus to suggest it was for the best and that they will see God's Glory, if they believe. He'd gone up to his room seemingly wanting to be left alone. Strange! It's been four days and we're still here.

A member of staff comes into the kitchen and stops suddenly, he probably wasn't expecting anyone to be there.

"Oh, this is normally for staff, the dining room is laid for breakfast."

"Feel more comfortable here, thanks."

"I'll get you breakfast?"

"We're sorted thanks," says Thaddy.

"Not really hungry, a fresh pot of coffee would be good though," says Simon.

Matthew agrees - the stuff Simon made was far too strong.

"I hear you are moving on today, it will be a lot quieter around here when you're gone."

"I hope we can come back, under better circumstances," says Thaddy.

"Looks like we're really going then, better prepare," Matthew says to Simon, who nods. Yeah, he knows exactly what I mean. Matthew goes back up to the twin room he has been sharing with Alphie.

"What time is it," Alphie says half asleep.

"Gone seven."

"Oh is that all," he turns over, pulling the covers over his head.

Matthew has been up over an hour, he couldn't sleep. Lazarus' death, sad as is it, isn't the only reason he and the lads are concerned. Will the authorities try and arrest Jesus again? In Galilee, doubtful, here, highly unlikely. Where Lazarus' sisters live, in the small village of Bethany, on the east side of the Mount of Olives, only two miles from Jerusalem, highly possible! If the authorities know Lazarus was a close friend of the boss, could they be waiting? There is the real possibility that Jesus could be arrested - even worse, killed. Last night, Thomas fearing the twelve could suffer the same fate, asked the question, "do we go with Jesus?" Actually he had phrased it slightly differently, he had said "let's go with Jesus, so that we may die with him!" Matthew couldn't work out if he was being sarcastic or really meant it? Even so it was a question that needed to be asked. It was going to be a team decision. One for all, etc.

From the moment Matthew heard about the botched arrest, something changed and that bothered him. For this trip he had not only brought his own gun and extra clips, but he'd also popped his spare into his holdall. It had been months since he had even picked one up; now he's packing an arsenal. Old feelings resurfaced that he had long since hoped were gone, the feeling of death, the thrill of the chase and the intoxication of a kill. He can see the same thoughts going through Simon's head: The anguish, the memories, the do or die he hadn't seen in a while. He'd stopped obsessing about the Zealot's knife he occasionally noticed on Simon's belt. If he was going to use it he'd have done it by now. No, there is something else, and it feels all too familiar.

He takes out the spare, puts in a new clip and lays it on the bed.

"You may need that today."

"Mmm."

As Matthew and Simon both sense the danger and could quickly regress to old patterns, Alphie remains calm and cheerful. Matthew has always liked that about his young collector; a youthful innocence that the world could not destroy. He remembers how glad he was when Jesus had chosen the both of them. Alphie hadn't been in the business all that long. Matthew only took him on at the request of Alphie's parents and he doesn't have the deep scars, mental or physical, that Matthew himself has. That's why the others took to Alphie more easily than they did to him.

Alphie pops his head up. "We won't need them today."

"Just in case."

"Last night I saw Jesus praying in the garden. He had that look, you know, the one: The, he knows what he's doing look!"

"Just take it, I'm not so sure."

"It's gonna be a good day Matt, I can feel it."

By the time everyone got up and said their goodbyes to family and friends half the day had gone. It's hard for to Peter leave his wife and kids, especially now. Once again they are back on the road.

It's a difficult journey, Jesus is subdued and so no one really wants to speak. Headphones go on and all that can be heard is their annoying buzz. Even James and John sit in silence.

When they finally arrive in Bethany the funeral is coming to an end. Lazarus had been buried four days earlier but Jewish funerals can last up to seven days, and there are still many mourners in the village.

Andrew had rung to tell Mary and Martha they were on their way. As they approach the village of Bethany, Philip, again driving, spots a solitary figure wearing black, sitting alone on a bench.

"It's Martha," says Jesus.

Philip stops the bus and Jesus gets out and comforts her.

"I don't like the look of this," says Jude.

Matthew pats his gun. Jude and Nathaniel both nod.

"You think she is there to warn us?" says Thomas.

Philip puts the window down, doing his best to hear something.

"Martha just couldn't wait to see Jesus," he whispers.

She bursts into tears, asking over and over why he hadn't come sooner.

"Where is your sister?" asks Jesus.

She tells him that her sister Mary is in the house with some of the other mourners. With hands trembling she rings her sister, "the Teacher is here."

The house is close by, for within a minute, Mary along with many others arrive at the minibus. When she sees Jesus she falls at his feet crying, "Lord, if only you had been here my brother would not have died!"

Matthew thinks back to Dave Milo's death. No ceremony, no mourners, just death. He has some idea of what to expect at a traditional Jewish funeral, but even he is caught out by the theatricality of it all. Lazarus had been a good Jew all his life and obeyed the laws. Mary and Martha had stuck to Jewish custom and hired two flute players and even a wailing woman to help mourn their brother. This, along with the dozens of mourners, still crying four days after they had buried him, to Matthew seems over the top. With Jesus there is always hope, this morning Alphie was sure of that, though Matthew sees no difference here to Dave Milo's funeral. Mary and Martha seem desperate to believe Jesus could have helped, but the rest appear to be mourning out of despair.

Jesus asks to see the grave, which is outside the village, down a narrow track.

Philip decides to leave the bus where it is, rather than drive down. The twelve will have to walk, much to the annoyance of James.

Along the path on the way to the grave, Jesus, who is still comforting the sisters, sheds a tear. Some of the mourners see this.

"Look how much Jesus loved his friend."

Others are more cynical.

"He was supposed to have healed others. Why, if he was a true friend, couldn't he heal Lazarus?"

The grave surprises Matthew, for it isn't a hole in the ground, but a sepulchre, a small tomb. Lazarus must have been worth a bit. Built into a hill, it seems to be cut out of the rock. A plaque next to a steel door has the name of Lazarus on it.

"Weird huh, this is the family tomb, where Mary and Martha will be buried one day." says Nathaniel to Matthew.

"What!"

"There will be shelves for the whole family."

Matthew can't get his head round it, he'd rather not think about his own death and yet the sisters live five minutes from the place where they'll eventually be buried. Urgh!

The tomb door is small, near the ground and early versions would have had a stone in front. Now, for health and safety reasons it has to be made from steel and bolted onto the rock. It is so heavy that it takes four men just to open or close it. Most have strong locks to prevent grave robberies.

"Open it," says Jesus.

"What!" says Mary.

"Lord, it has been four days," says Martha.

"I can understand you want to say goodbye, but it's too late," says the local priest. "He will have started to decay. It was a traditional burial, we only used aromatic spices to neutralise the decomposition and wrapped him in linen."

"In others words it will stink," says James.

"Teacher, you must know that the spirit leaves the body on the fourth day. It's too late," the priest pleads.

Matthew looks around, would the sisters agree to having their brother's tomb opened? No one here wants to smell the rotting, decomposing corpse.

"It has been four days," says Mary, repeating her sister's words.

The twelve agree with the sisters, telling the boss it has been too long.

"Didn't I tell you, today you will see God's glory if you believe!" says Jesus.

Alphie nudges Matthew.

Mary and Martha reluctantly nod to the priest, who unlocks the heavy steel door. Peter, Andrew and James, with the help of one of the mourners, slide it open. Everyone steps back, bracing themselves for the putrid odour. Once the door is opened the smell explodes outwards, enveloping everybody in its path. Some quickly move away from the tomb, all cover their noses and mouths. Matthew's nostrils fill with a smell that knocks him backwards. He wants to vomit, that is the smell of death alright. It's far worse than any he smelled at the morgue. He wretches and is thankful he avoided breakfast this morning.

Jesus stands unaffected, next to the entrance.

"Father, I thank you that you have heard me. I know that you always hear me. I say this so the people here will believe that you sent me."

He then shouts, "Lazarus, come out!"

Some mourners jump in surprise; others gasp in shock at Jesus' words. "What did he just say? You don't think that..."

Everybody's eyes become transfixed on the entrance to the tomb. There is a sense of apprehension, what if Lazarus doesn't come out? What if he does?

Thomas turns his head, he can't bear to look. Matthew, his heart beating so fast he thinks his veins might burst, has goose bumps. Did he hear right? Did Jesus just ask a dead body to get up? What if it doesn't happen? How can it happen? Matthew is sure he hears something from inside the tomb. His brain must be fooling him. No, there it is again.

People stare at each other, did they hear it too?

"I swear I heard something," says James, bending down to peer in.

"James, give over," says Peter, edging closer to the tomb.

"Argh, something is moving, I'm positive," James jumps back, bumping into Peter.

First a glimpse of white cloth, something is definitely coming out. A body slowly emerges from the tomb. Everyone gasps! Mary and Martha scream. Matthew never liked zombie movies and this is why. Only this is real. Oh shit! This is actually happening. At least the smell has faded. He breathes in - it's completely gone.

"Someone untie him," says Jesus calmly.

James and Peter being the closest, clumsily, with shaking hands and in a state of shock, untie the cloth bandages, first from the head of this figure.

Mary faints as the face of her brother is revealed. Martha screams, this time with joy and begins to cry tears of happiness. Lazarus rubs his eyes, adjusting to the light. Mourners begin taking photo's of Lazarus and everyone wants to touch and feel him. Nathaniel looks in the tomb, checking to see if it is indeed empty. Lazarus hugs his sisters.

"He did it!" says Thomas, "I can't believe he did it! He brought a man back to life!"

Chapter 26

"The Sanhedrin are meeting, probably to discuss the boss," says Nathaniel, reading from a newspaper.

"Not surprised, I bet they're bricking it," says Thaddy.

"Yeah, it's an emergency meeting, they're going to issue a response later today."

Another day, another village - Jesus and the twelve have stayed overnight in a little place called Bethphage near Bethany. The day has started in beautiful sunshine, it matches the mood of the lads. They were up early wanting to see what the country thought of their boss' latest miracle. Nathaniel has been down to the local shop, to buy a newspaper and a bagel. He is now enjoying them both, sitting on a patio chair in the front garden of the house. A few others have joined him outside. Thaddy is lying on the grass, thinking and looking up at the near cloudless sky. Jude is finishing off his breakfast of coffee and toast. James and John have found a child's football. John is attempting to kick the ball over the house. James is round the back waiting for it to appear. John has a few unsuccessful tries before getting one to fly over. They can hear James cheer before it comes back over, hitting the minibus. John retrieves the ball, unfortunately on his next attempt he slices his kick and the ball disappears into a neighbours garden.

"Oops."

After a minute James appears.

"I kicked it over, you must have missed it," says John as convincingly as he can.

James shrugs, goes over to the minibus and starts fiddling around with the drivers seat, laughing to himself.

John sits down on the grass.

"Last night, Simon was wanting to march straight into Jerusalem," says Thaddy,

"He's right," adds Jude.

"I agree, we've been on the road too long," says Nathaniel, looking up from his paper.

"Jesus knows what he's doing," says John, "he's going to do something big, I can feel it."

"Well, now would be a good time," says Nathaniel.

James wanders back over.

"What were you doing?" asks John.

"Oh, nothing," says James, smiling.

Nathaniel turns a page of the paper and laughs aloud, "ha, it's Peter!"

The front page has the headline *Death defying* and shows an old photograph of Lazarus. In the middle pages are printed some of the photos sent in by the mourners at the funeral. They're not very good, but that may have been due to the shakiness of hands under the circumstances. The largest picture is of Lazarus, coming out of the tomb, all zombie-like. Peter is next to him, mouth wide open. There's another with Peter and James unwrapping Lazarus and a wide shot of the entire scene. Also a very good one of Mary and Martha hugging their brother.

"Is there one of me?" asks John, getting up to have a look.

Thaddy points to a blurred picture. John squints. "That's it, that's the only one I'm on! Peter's on loads, they even mention him by name."

"I'm on that one, that one...and that one," says James, rubbing it in.

"One crappy photo," complains John.

"Maybe the other papers have more pictures," says Nathaniel.

"Even Thomas is on more than me, and he spent most of the time throwing up."

John sits back down on the grass. "I can't believe loser boy gets on so many," he says.

"We should tell the others," says Thaddy.

"So, you know in the new Kingdom? I wonder what kind of cars we will have?" muses John changing the subject.

They ignore him.

"Yeah, we should tell Pete, he will love this," says James. He shouts, "Hey Pete, you need to see this."

"I think I'll have a Porsche."

"What does it say about the boss?" Jude asks Nathaniel.

Nathaniel turns back to the main story.

"It asks, is this more proof? Is Jesus the Christ?"

"Wow."

"I always liked that Dodge Viper, wonder if they still make them? Or a Lamborghini."

"It also asks, was that the ultimate miracle?"

"Waiting for Lazarus to come out, longest minute ever!" says James, laughing to himself.

"Could we have more than one? I mean we will be sitting on thrones. So we could have anything we want right? Oh, wait,

I'd also like a Ferrari."

"Aston Martin", says Thaddy. "That's what I'll have, always liked Astons."

"Oh, yeah, I'd forgotten about them. Just like James Bond. *Hello, Mish Moneypenny.*"

They all laugh.

There is a knock on the window, Peter has heard his name being mentioned.

"Hey big guy, it's you, look," says Nathaniel.

Peter waves for them to come in.

"No chance, you come here."

After a few minutes Alphie appears.

"Hey Jude, the boss has a job for us." He throws the minibus keys which Jude manages to catch one handed.

"Where are you going?" asks James.

"On a very important job for the boss," replies Alphie.

"Can we come?" asks John.

"Yeah, the boss said we may need extra help."

Jude gets in the minibus, and sits in the driver's seat. As he puts the key in the ignition... the seat collapses, "shit, oh...what the..."

Alphie, having first jumped from the shock, gives a snigger, before checking the front passenger seat and gingerly sitting down.

"James!" shouts Jude, "thanks a lot, you nearly gave me a heart attack."

"It was meant for Phil or Andy but you looked so funny."

"You'd better fix it."

James grabs a spanner from the buses toolbox and begins fiddling around.

"So, where are we going?" asks John.

"Why, what else has he done to the bus?" asks Jude, checking the tyres.

James fixes the seat but Jude doesn't trust him, it doesn't look very secure.

"John why don't you drive."

"Yes," says John and pumps his fist.

James puts the spanner away, and jumps in the back. Thaddy wanders over and he too gets in.

Jude knows that this is the first time John has driven the minibus, but there is no way he's being set up for another one of James' pranks. If anything happens let it be to somebody else. Anyway what could happen?

"I wonder how quick it is from nought to sixty - time me," John says to James.

The diesel engine takes an age even to get to forty-five. Jude points out an approaching left hand bend. John has been watching the speedometer, not the road. He stamps on the brake and turns. The bend appears to get tighter and tighter as he tries to keep the bus from tipping over. Alphie braces himself. In the back, Jude, James and Thaddy are thrown across the bus. They make the corner, just. Two wheels had briefly lifted off the ground.

"Wow," says John, trying be make it sound like it wasn't any big deal.

"You could have killed us, you idiot," says Thaddy.

"Everybody alright?" asks Jude.

"You got two wheels off the ground, nice one," says James.

"This is why Peter hasn't let you drive before," Alphie tells John.

Luckily they are only going a ten minute drive to Bethambry, another of the small villages scattered around the slopes of the Mount of Olives. A few dozen houses, a main street and one general store. There is no one about, just a few parked cars dotted here and there. John drives through the village and out the other side.

"Oh, turn round we must have missed it," says Alphie.

"Missed what?" asks John.

"A colt."

"The gun or the car?"

"I was guessing the car."

As John drives back slowly, Jude spots a side road he missed the first time. John stops at the junction, and all four peer down the road. It is narrow, with a solitary car parked next to a large house.

"That might be it," says Jude.

John parks the minibus just passed the junction and they all get out to look at the car.

"Mustang, could this be what we are looking for?" asks Jude.

"I forget, all I remember it was an animal's name, so it must be," says Alphie.

The Mustang is a black V8 convertible with its top down. It has a grey leather interior, chrome detailing and is fully loaded. The doors are locked so John climbs into the driver's seat.

"There is no way Peter will let you drive this bad boy," says Thaddy.

"I'll be driving it back, so don't get comfy," says Jude.

James jumps in the back seat.

"Oh sweet, there's a DVD player in the back too."

"Where are the keys?" John asks.

"Look under the sun visor. Jesus said the owner will let us

take it," says Alphie.

"Really, this thing's worth like a hundred grand," says Thaddy.

John looks under the visor but doesn't find any keys.

"This is the softest leather I have ever touched," says James.

A man bangs on the window of the house, shouting something inaudible.

"That'll be the owner, he must be coming out with the keys," says Thaddy.

"Yeah, he wouldn't have wanted to leave them in it, seeing as it's so valuable," says John.

The owner comes out shouting and screaming. "Get off my car or I'll call the police."

Jude steps towards him, "it's OK sir, the master needs it." He holds out his hand for the keys.

"Oh, you are from the master, and you think...ha ha," laughing he says, "follow me." He beckons the lads round the side of the house.

"These are what you're after," he points to two animals tied up next to a small stable.

The lads all stare at them.

"But, they're donkeys!" says John and Alphie together.

"I don't get it. Why do we need two donkeys?" asks James.

Thaddy laughs. "Because it's a colt. Well, the smaller one is!"

"That's right, that's what your master needs. Oh, by the way, it won't go anywhere without its mother," says the owner, who walks away shaking his head and laughing.

"What would the boss want with a donkey?" asks Jude.

"Maybe for the milk!" says James.

"So, how are we going to get them back?" asks John.

Jude unties the colt and pulls on the rope; the colt doesn't budge. He tugs at it again, but the animal refuses to move.

"Try untying the mother, maybe the young 'un will follow?"

"How come you know so much about donkeys anyway Thaddy?" asks Alphie as he unties the larger animal and leads it away - the colt automatically following.

"He's a genius, that's why. Now answer me this, do you think we can get them into the bus?" asks James.

"Worth a try," says John.

They walk the donkeys back to the minibus. James opens the side door, looks at the animals, and then at the gap. He decides the best bet would be to get them in via the back doors. He opens the doors, but one of the seats is in the way.

"This won't work," says Alphie.

"Quitter," says John.

"I'll get the spanner," says James, and he starts to unbolt the back seat from the floor, but Alphie is still not convinced that this will work.

"Once we've picked it up we had to let Jesus know," says Alphie.

"So, we may not need to take them anywhere," says Jude.

Jude rings only for it to go straight to voicemail.

"If we do this the boss will be so pleased with us, it's called taking the initiative," John says as James takes out the seat, but the gap between the rows looks too tight for the animals. They decide to see if they will fit in anyway. Thaddy gently coaxes the mother into position, it's a big step up into the bus. James pulls from inside as Thaddy and John push the backside of the donkey. It stands its ground.

"Push harder," shouts James.

"It's alright for you, we're at the wrong end, what if this

thing has a shit!" says John.

The donkey whinnies and both Thaddy and John jump back.

"It heard," says John.

James still pulling, asks "well, what else can we do?"

"What if we tie them to the back, and I drive slowly?" suggests John.

"NO!" says Alphie.

"Maybe it would climb in if we gave it a carrot?" says Thaddy.

James, having now given up too, jumps out of the bus. "You're gonna have to ride 'em, back."

"No way, I wouldn't be seen dead on a donkey," says Jude.

As he's speaking Jude's phone starts to ring. It's Peter, he wants to know where they all are, and why hasn't someone returned with the minibus.

"OK, apparently, we should only have been dropped off. Me and Alphie are to take the donkeys to a rendezvous point further round the Mount. You three need to take the minibus back and collect the others," Jude tells them.

"Did Pete say why the boss wanted these two?" asks Alphie, pointing to the donkeys.

"No, but he knew, I could tell! He did say that after we left, more followers arrived."

As the minibus speeds off with Thaddy driving, Jude, Alphie and the two donkeys set off along main street and round the side of the Mount. They still have no idea what Jesus is going to do with the animals, especially a colt which has never been ridden. Maybe they're going off the beaten track and need something to help carry things. Jude does know that farmers sometimes use them when the terrain is impassable for vehicles.

Soon they have travelled enough distance round the Mount to see Jerusalem. It is a spectacular sight from where they are. From this high up the mountain it is at eye level, the sun glinting off the white buildings. The Temple towers above everything else, surrounded by the old wall, a wall that seems to be cradling the city in its arms of stone. Jude thinks the eastern view of the city is the most spectacular. It has expanded to the north and west, the Kidron Valley protecting the east side from the developers, leaving the old wall to stand proud and resolute against the oncoming tide of modernisation.

Jude and Alphie stop to admire the view. From their vantage point they can see the main Jericho road and the east gate, which is pedestrian only, leading straight into the Temple. The area in front of the gate is busy with market stalls and swarms of worshippers and tourists. Further away is the car and coach park. Today is the first day of the Passover feast, thousands of pilgrims are already in the city. Smoke is rising into the blue sky from the sacrificial altar. Even from this distance, Jude and Alphie can smell the burnt offerings.

"We are so near, I can almost touch it."

"Yeah, it's nice," says Alphie.

"I mean the power."

They continue to walk to the rendezvous point, a car park, equal distance between the city and Bethany, along the Jericho road. A short cut down the mountain saved more than half an hour's walk, and to their surprise they are the first to arrive. Alphie sees a fruit and veg seller on the side of the road and pulls out his wallet; its empty.

"There's no cash machine around is there?"

Jude shakes his head.

"Give us a few cents for some fruit."

"You're becoming too attached to these two. Next you're going tell me you've named them." He gives him just enough to buy a carrot and an apple for each of the animals.

"Don't be stupid, I just think they may be hungry! You keep hold of that cash tighter than Peter keeps hold of a packed lunch!"

At the large car park, cars are constantly coming and going. Jude and Alphie stand waiting, holding on to the animals. They feel very conspicuous and nervous, for they are only a short distance from Jerusalem.

"Won't the authorities be looking out for us?" worries Alphie as they are recognised. "What if they are spotted by the police or a temple guard?"

"Hey aren't you Jesus' guys? Where's your boss? Were you there when he raised Lazarus? Why have you got a donkey?" They heard that many times. Jude tries to get hold of Peter on his phone, only to keep getting an *unable to connect* message. A minibus arrives – it's not theirs, but there are some familiar faces, including the Mary's, Jesus' Mother and Mary Mag, even Leah and her two boys. They all gather round Jude and Alphie, making a fuss of the donkeys. Jesus' mother gives Alphie a smile and a nod.

"There's that look, Jesus has the same one," Alphie says, "today is gonna be a good day."

More and more followers start to assemble. With a roar of their engines Mad Dan and the other bikers arrive. Jude and Alphie begin to feel less vulnerable and start to gain in confidence. They find out that Jesus has asked as many people as possible to meet him here, though he hasn't said why.

"There is only one reason why Jesus would get everybody

together here. We're going in," says Jude to Alphie and those close to him.

"You mean, this could be the day!"

"With our followers here, plus all those people in the city, how can they stop us?" replies Jude.

"With the army."

"They wouldn't dare!"

"We might be about to find out."

Finally the blue minibus enters the car park, followed by a procession of familiar cars and more motorbikes. The lads pile out of the bus, nodding in recognition to the many followers. With Jesus they make their way over to Jude, Alphie and the two animals. Simon points to the city and nods.

"I'll see you in the palace," says Jude to Alphie.

"So this is it."

"Yes Alphie, at last it's finally happening."

Peter has brought a blanket which he throws over the colt and everybody watches as Jesus leads it away from its mother before gently sitting on it.

"Let's go boys!" says Jesus to the twelve.

They start to walk towards the city, Jesus on the donkey in front, the rest following behind. As they walk, more and more people recognise Jesus and they too join in the procession.

"We should sing something," says Philip.

What should we sing? asks John.

James starts a chant. No one joins in with him.

"We can't sing *here we go, here we go!* This is Jesus, this is the Messiah," says Philip.

Andrew just starts singing.

"*Blessed be the name of the Lord, blessed be your name.*"

Peter joins in, he and others recognise the song as a psalm.

They also join in, until all the twelve and most of the followers are singing.

"*Blessed be the name of the Lord, blessed be your name.*"

"*Blessed be your glorious name.*"

Some start singing another song and lay down their coats in front of Jesus.

"*Blessed is the king, blessed is the coming Kingdom of our father David.*"

"*Peace in heaven and glory in the highest.*"

Jude can hear people as they pass asking, "Is this the man who raised Lazarus? Then, surely he is the chosen Messiah." He gets goose bumps.

Quickly, the crowd grows from hundreds to thousands, with more joining all the time. Word spreads that the Messiah is here and pilgrims rush out of the east gate to see Jesus. Reporters rush to the scene, camera crews scramble for good views. People line the street, waving as they pass. Some throw confetti in the air as Jesus goes by. Those without coats pull branches from the many palm trees, then line the roads and lay them in front of Jesus.

"Isn't that the Miracle Man, the healer from Galilee? Who else could perform miracles, but the Christ himself."

It has turned into a celebration, a dance, a party.

Peter has made his way to the head of the procession. He has to keep stopping to let Jesus and the rest catch up. He is singing his heart out. Andrew and Philip and Nathaniel are just behind, they are singing and occasionally waving to the crowd. James and John keep stopping for photographs on the side on the road and wave to the crowd. Thaddy takes out his phone and starts taking photos. Alphie and Thomas are further back with Matthew and the other followers.

263

Jude looks on – finally this is happening, oh how long he has waited for this moment.

"Put the TV on, tell everyone it's happening," he shouts down the phone to his mum and dad. Simon is doing his best to get the crowds involved, just like he used to. Only this time the words are praiseworthy, rather than angry and violent.

"*Come on everybody, 'Bless...ed*" shouts Simon.

The crowd shouts back "*Bless..ed*"

"*Jesus.*"

"*Jesus,*" they repeat.

"*King Jesus,*" shouts Simon.

"*King Jesus,*" the crowd shouts back.

Jude has never experienced anything like it, the nearer to the city they get the more people arrive. Everybody wants a view, everybody wants to be able to tell their children and grandchildren they were there when the Messiah came. Flashes from cameras light up the procession.

'Look, he's riding on a donkey,' shouts a voice from the crowd.

To some it just looks rather funny, a grown man riding a small donkey, but it is filled with symbolism. Jude hadn't realised, it's only now overhearing Nathaniel and Philip that he understands. Jesus has used the animal on purpose, it's from scripture. *Say to you the daughter of Zion, shout for joy you people of Jerusalem! Behold your King is coming to you, gentle and mounted on a donkey, a colt, the foal of a donkey.*

I bet the Pharisees get it, they must be bricking it by now. The raising of Lazarus proved beyond a shadow of doubt the power that Jesus possesses. Lazarus had been dead too long for it to have been a trick or a mere stage managed stunt. Too many eye witnesses – too many *reliable* eye witnesses, for it to be dismissed. The danger would come if the Galilean's power influences Jerusalem, and now it has and Jude is ready. Just look at the people's faces, how happy they are. He notices a Free Israel sign. That's why Jesus was quite subdued, he must have known the enormity of what raising Lazarus would do. The people seem ready to accept him and this Passover festival, so soon after the great miracle, was always going to be the key time.

One small step, he says as they enter Jerusalem, he can't believe how nervous he is. This is it. We're here.

Chapter 27

Annas has been helplessly watching the procession from his office window at the Temple ever since he first heard the disturbing news. He can't have the temple guards arrest Jesus, not now, not in front of so many. No, that would only inflame the situation. He can't get the Union soldiers to arrest him, they aren't prepared to heighten the risk of an uprising. Anyway, from his conversations with the Governor he was getting nowhere and Pilate watching it all unfold from the comfort of his headquarters at the barracks, was finding it all quite amusing. He and his soldiers see the irony in the parade. While Annas and the Jewish authorities only see trouble, the Union soldiers watching on can see the funny side. They have no intention of getting involved. At every Jewish festival there is potential for trouble. With so many people and such a small space, the city is a tinderbox, ready to explode at any moment. Provocation is not the best form of security in this environment, even Annas knows that. What disturbs him and something he didn't know was that Pilate believes if it does turn violent he hasn't enough soldiers stationed in the city. During the rest of the year the temple guards control the city. This wasn't part of the deal when the Union first took over. But after uprising after uprising, mainly aimed at the Union itself, the decision to allow the Temple authorities to guard the city was made. There are around eight thousand guards at festival times. Even they aren't enough to ensure the smooth running of a Passover festival, so extra soldiers are brought in, mainly as a reminder of the power at the Unions disposal.

Pilate is only thinking about himself, as usual. It is during the Passover festival that the Governor stays in the city, moving up from his main residence, on the Mediterranean coast at Caesarea. At festival times Governor Pilate comes to overcrowded Jerusalem Union style, with the pomp and ceremony even the Roman armies of ancient history would be proud of. Pilate travels by armoured car, emblazoned with the flag of the Union. At the gate to the City he leaves his car for a horse, surrounded by his own battalion of elite troops. Crowds gather to watch his spectacular arrival.

A phone rings and Jonathan picks it up.

"Sir, it's Pilate again."

"Governor," says Annas.

"Are you watching it Annas? Great fun, this is the threat you are worried about, it's the funniest thing I've seen in years. He rides a donkey, surrounded by boys, women and children, whilst I arrived on a white stallion surrounded by the finest infantry and tanks in the world. He has palm branches; I have fighter jets.

Annas has to listen to him go on and on, there's nothing he can do about it. He might have done very well financially out of the Union occupation but he hates certain events. The main one – one that he believes could be the Unions downfall, highlights the sheer bravado of Pilate. Every Passover he turns up with his army and when he gets to within several hundred yards he stops and a white stallion is brought forward. He enters the west gate of the city on his war horse, in his Union uniform, with a vast array of medals on his chest – even though he has never fought in a war – holding the Union banner, a golden eagle surrounded by stars. His vanity serves only to breed resentment, but what can anyone do about it?

Pilate ends the conversation, still laughing. One menace had arrived in the morning, another in the afternoon; both equally dangerous and all Annas can do is watch.

TV companies were quick with their coverage, every station showing the events live, helicopters in the sky and reporters at the scene. He and Caiaphas were both unsuccessful at having it stopped. By now the whole country will be watching. It serves only to increase the number of people rushing to the east gate.

"Jonathan," shouts Annas. When he doesn't appear, Annas goes to find him. He is watching it on his office computer.

One reporter, tears running down his face, is broadcasting live at the scene.

"I never thought, even in my wildest dreams, that I would witness the coming of the Messiah."

The camera pans to the crowd, before focusing on Jesus.

"Behold, behold your King is coming to you, gentle and mounted on a donkey, a colt, the foal of a donkey," says the reporter, quoting the prophet Zechariah.

"Turn that off and get me Caiaphas."

With all that is unfolding it would be impossible, even dangerous to try and get to the Palace. Caiaphas had been performing his ceremonial duties at the Temple all through the festival but left earlier and is now in the palace. Some priests are already there, worried about what is unfolding. As they start to assemble in the palace council chambers,

Caiaphas arranges an emergency meeting with Annas, via video conference. The priests want something done and quickly.

Jonathan connects up the call via his computer.

"Why hasn't he been arrested, or is it too late now? We had our chance. If this turns into an uprising then the Union will have the perfect excuse to take over completely. They want nothing more than to destroy us," say the priests.

"It is better for one man to die for the people than for a whole nation to be destroyed," says Caiaphas.

"It is too late!" says a priest.

Annas sits quietly in front of the screen, waiting for a moment. When Caiaphas turns to him for advice, he offers only a few words. "It is never too late."

He is just about to speak again when Theo and Benjamin turn up. They try to get his attention.

"You must excuse me, real men have arrived."

Jonathan apologises to the High Priest, ends the call and runs after his boss.

All afternoon and evening, Annas has had to watch, unable to do anything. Then a chance, the procession has come right up to the Temple itself.

Reluctantly Annas agrees to stay in his office and Jonathan puts the TV back on. He wishes he hadn't for again the Galilean has slipped out of his grasp.

"Where is Jesus? Where did he go?" ask reporters.

In all the confusion the crowd has lost sight of him.

"He just disappeared" says an onlooker.

"He is nowhere to be found," says another.

The camera crews, reporters and everyone in the massive crowds have lost him. The TV crews are suggesting that he must still be in the Temple; as they aren't allowed to film in there, they can only guess at his whereabouts.

Annas is equally bemused, where has he gone? One by one guards report back and say the same. "He has vanished."

"Not again!" yells Annas.

Theo and Benjamin are summoned back for a briefing.

"We had a visual of him standing on the Temple steps, I'm sure you know that from the TV pictures. We were all set, ready for the moment he stepped inside. He never did."

Annas waves them away, turning to look out of the window.

As both men start to leave Benjamin pauses. "Sir, I think I'd better tell you now, that I used to be mates with one of Jesus' team. He was one of my drinking friends when I worked up in Capernaum years ago."

"Thank you for your honesty," says Annas.

Benjamin leaves and Annas again looks out upon the City, as an idea begins taking shape. Interesting, this information could be useful.

"Get Benjamin back in here," he shouts to Jonathan. Maybe it's time Benjamin got reacquainted with this old friend.

Chapter 28

"We were there, we had the whole city on our side, I... I don't get it!"

To a man, the twelve were stunned by Jesus' actions once he'd entered Jerusalem. It had felt like the whole world was with them. They were on their way to the centre of power and no-one, not even the Union army would have been able to stop them. It was the best day of their lives, the cheering, the singing, the adulation. It was a history fulfilling prophecy - it was the taste of destiny. The one thing they weren't expecting, was to get to the Temple and then go home; if they can call living on the road home. Jesus had said that they would all understand soon enough, and that it is all God's plan. But the smell of success, the wealth, the riches, the new kingdom were all within touching distance. First, they were confused, why were they leaving the Temple as soon as they'd arrived? Was Jesus going to perform another miracle? Then came the realisation. He just wanted to leave - that was it!

The twelve handled disappointment in different ways. Simon, Thaddy and Jude were angry, they opened a case of beers, drank and shouted their feelings away. Andrew, Philip and Nathaniel, opened a couple of bottles of wine and talked it over, trying to figure out Jesus' reasons behind the sudden withdrawal. James and John sulked, they became annoy-ing, well, more than annoying. They put on a DVD and watched Star Wars, with the volume high, refusing to turn it down. Alphie and Thomas found quiet corners, popped on headphones and listened to music, both trying to hide their disappointment. Matthew borrowed the minibus and got away from everyone. And Peter went outside, away from the noise and rang Ruth – he wanted to hear her voice. He told her everything. Peter has known Jesus for, oh, it will be nearly two years now and it feels like they've been travelling around the country forever. Just when he thinks, yeah I understand, Jesus does something like... yesterday. Maybe the events of the previous week, Lazarus and talk of the new kingdom, has clouded their minds. Jesus had withdrawn and was staying on the other side of the village, at the hospitality of a couple he had once healed. He knew what the twelve were feeling, that was obvious. But sometimes it would be so much easier if he just came straight out and told them his plan, if he had one.

The next morning, the twelve are woken by the owner of a house where their makeshift beds are scattered around another temporary home. It was a good gesture of hers to let them all crash while she had stayed with friends. Now she has come to regain her property and let them know their presence is requested for lunch – at the home of Simon the healed leper, whom their boss has stayed with. So with their eyes bloodshot from too much drink and not enough sleep, they pack up their bags and slowly and reluctantly make their way through the village, leaving behind them the wreckage of a once spotless house.

Many people from the village are also invited to the meal,

which is going to be some kind of stew by the appetising smell greeting them. The night had been a long one and the morning was fast turning into the afternoon when the lads arrived.

"Morning boss," says Peter.

Peter hadn't hit the booze like some of them, and was the only one to wake up early. This morning when he woke, he turned to kiss Ruth, forgetting where he was for a second. Oh how he missed her. At the start of the tour it was fun, getting away from all the monotony of daily life – all he'd ever done was fish. He was a fisherman, then husband, then father in that order. He hadn't fished in months, and this morning he missed Ruth, the kids and fishing. When he got up, seeing all the others still asleep, he'd gone for a walk around the village. It was a nice place, great location, peaceful and quiet, yet only a few miles from the city. As he walked, he couldn't help but notice how large and exclusive the houses were. They've certainly met some well off people lately. He had talked over yesterday's events with Ruth. She wanted to visit but with the children at school it wasn't possible at the moment. Ruth had seen the events unfolding on the news and when Jesus had disappeared she had been worried. Once Peter rang, it had calmed her. They talked, but he wouldn't say exactly how he felt, explaining instead how the others were dealing with it all. He could tell she knew he was troubled because when she had asked if he'd eaten he'd responded, "he wasn't hungry."

On the walk to the house, Jude and Thaddy try and persuade Peter to ask Jesus about what happened yesterday. They wondered if Jesus had just got cold feet, if the enormity of it all had overwhelmed him.

"Does everyone feel the same?" Peter asks.

They nod. He too feels that way, but he also knows that

the boss does things differently. Peter decides they shouldn't question their boss's judgement and tells them that if they believed Jesus to be *The Christ* before yesterday, then surely he must be today.

"Put up or shut up! If you want to ask stupid questions, you can do it yourselves," he tells them.

No one asks!

They had become so focused on the events of yesterday that they'd lost sight of all the other things Jesus has done. They have become desperate for the new kingdom. He knew it and he guessed, deep down, so did they.

"There's nothing like a lamb stew to wipe away all those sad faces," says their host's wife, fetching out a large serving bowl of hot stew.

Peter, his appetite restored, is the first to help himself.

"Who let him go first? Save enough for everybody else," says James.

"Oh, there's plenty to go round," says the woman.

Peter takes another scoop.

Soon everybody is tucking into their lunch and slowly a more jovial atmosphere starts to emerge among the twelve.

"Hey, James!" says Matthew. "That driver's seat in the minibus is still not right, you gonna fix it before we move on?"

"Why don't you fix it, you're good with cars?" says James.

"Only expensive ones, like Mercedes." adds John.

"Which you bought with my taxes," says James, with a smile.

"Your taxes?" laughs Peter, "after all the damage you caused, you didn't earn enough to pay taxes!"

More guests arrive, one of whom is Mary, Lazarus' sister.

She is carrying a small gift box. Mary, seeing Jesus, heads straight over to where he is sitting, relaxing after the meal. She opens the box. Inside is a small but extremely rare bottle of perfume. The bottle is by Fabergé and the contents are made from the oil of nard, a herb found in the foothills of the Himalayas. The only way to open it is by breaking the top, and thereby rendering the bottle, with a potential value of thousands of Euro's, worthless.

Mary tries to crack open the bottle.

"Boss, don't let her, that thing must be worth thousands!" says Jude.

The twelve and the other guests all agree, some even hovering next to Mary in an attempt to take the bottle from her.

"This bottle could be sold and we could give the money to the poor," says Jude.

"Yeah," says Philip and John.

James agrees. "You could sell it on eBay."

"You don't sell antiques on eBay? It should go to Sotheby's in London," says another guest.

It's to no avail, Mary breaks the bottle and pours the perfumed oil over Jesus' head.

"Why are you bothering Mary. This is a good thing she has done. You will always have the poor, but you will not always have me," says Jesus.

"Phew, it stinks! I can smell it from over here," James waves his hand trying to get rid of the smell.

"Whenever this gospel is preached around the world, what she has done will be told in her memory," says Jesus.

James is about to say something else, but he sees Peter glare and for once he doesn't.

One of the people to arrive at the same time as Mary does not enter the house, preferring to stand by the door.

Peter notices how uncomfortable the man seems and has kept an eye on him as Mary anointed Jesus with the oil. He catches Andrew's eye, and gestures to to door. Andrew nods back in recognition. "Can we help you?" Peter asks the man.

"I have a message for your boss."

"Well, we are part of his team, you can tell us and we will decide if the boss needs troubling."

"I must speak to Jesus alone."

"Who sent you?" Peter snaps, a little indignant.

"Council member Nicodemus, one of the Chief Priests. I must speak with your teacher alone, you understand."

Reluctantly Peter agrees and has a quiet word in Jesus' ear about the messenger.

The house is too busy for a private conversation, so Jesus talks to the man outside, away from the house. Peter and Andrew stay by the door, watching, but are unable to hear any of the conversation. Both are convinced that the message is to warn Jesus that he is in danger. Here in a quiet village, with only a handful of followers, is the perfect place for an ambush. Simon wanders over, he has sensed something is wrong. He looks out at Jesus, who is showing no signs of stress and appears relaxed. When the conversation is over the man says goodbye and Jesus returns to the house and three very nervous men in its doorway.

"Well boss! Are we in danger?" asks Peter.

Jesus pats Peter on the shoulder, "We are fine, come, I believe there are cakes that need eating."

"Boss," says Peter. "Please tell us, what is happening! One minute we are being treated like kings, the next, here we are, afraid of being arrested."

"Are we safe here?" asks Simon.

Simon speaks rather too loudly, with the result that every-one in the room stops what they are doing and fixes their eyes on Jesus, waiting for his reply; even James and John, who are attempting to super glue the lid back on the Fabergé bottle.

Jesus looks around the room at the worried, confused and anxious faces. He sighs.

"Nicodemus has sent good news."

"Good news, as in we can pick out a room in the palace, or that there isn't an army coming for us today?" says Thaddy.

"People are asking for me in the Temple, so that is where I will be teaching for the next few days."

"That's not good news boss, that's a trap," worries Thomas.

"It is fine, Tom. Nicodemus is right when he says I will be safe for a while," Jesus replies.

Well, Peter didn't see that one coming, that's the last place he thought they would go. "So, when do we leave?" he asks.

"Actually, you all look tired, why don't you have a few days off, do what you want, it's up to you."

"What and leave you alone, no chance," says Peter.

"I promise you Peter, nothing will happen, I will be fine."

"This is another test, isn't it?"

"No John, it's not a test."

The twelve start to plan their free time. What should they do? Where could they go?

Chapter 29

The minibus stops at Jerusalem coach station and Peter and Jude get out. For Peter, there wasn't a decision to be made, he's going on the first coach to Galilee. A few days with the family is just what he needs. Jude too has decided to take a trip, though he is keeping the destination to himself. Matthew suspects he is going to meet a girl, Sarah maybe, but there have been so many others it could be any one of them!

Andrew turns round to the rest of them. "Anyone else getting out here?"

"No Andy, straight to Zeb's place now," says Nathaniel.

The rest of the twelve had talked about a trip to the coast but in the end they chose to stay together at James and Johns' family home in the city. Jesus had taken up Zeb's invitation to use the house whenever he is in the area. When the others find out, they want to go along too. James and John didn't mind, so long as they didn't have to cook, or take the blame for any breakages.

Matthew wonders why he doesn't want to go north and maybe check his house is still standing, it's a while since he last went home. He thinks about Rebecca, wonders if she's found someone new? His thoughts are interrupted by Simon.

"Yo, Matt," says Simon, "check out the view!"

This is a cue for all the lads to peer out of the windows. A group of five young girls, probably students, are standing at a bus stop.

James in the front passenger seat, winds his window down, "hey girls."

"Get lost," is the response of one of the girls.

They drive on, James winds the window back up, his ego a little bruised. "Huh, charming."

"You really, have no luck with girls do you?" says Philip.

James shrugs.

"James pulling a good looking girl, now that would be a miracle!" says John.

John whispers to Jesus, asking if that joke is OK. "Wasn't meant to be you know, bad taste, eh boss."

Jesus nearly smiles, so John's probably alright.

They arrive at the house and dump their bags. Jesus wants to go straight to the Temple. They are still not happy about it, but what can they do? Simon and Matthew, weapons at the ready just in case, insist they at least escort him. Philip, Nathaniel, and John are also here to help, although when John realises that because of the crowds they'd have to go on foot, is less keen. The others take the minibus and go shopping.

Crowds start to engulf Jesus and the lads as they make their way through the narrow streets and up into the old city. Some people just want to touch him, others to take photos.

"Peter would hate this," says Simon, as they push through the crowds.

"It's him, teacher, show us a miracle," someone cries.

A bead of sweat rolls down Matthew's face and he feels nervous. The last time they were here on the steps it could have been the greatest day of his life, today could be his last if he's not vigilant. He feels a thousand eyes burning into him as they push and shove just to get into the Temple. Once inside it is less intense, but is still very crowded. Straight away, the lads notice they have been spotted by the Temple guards. Jesus doesn't seem concerned and makes his way towards an outer court. Once Jesus begins teaching a calm comes over Matthew. He feels safe, comfortable; well for now anyway.

* * *

Later that evening, Matthew is sitting at a table in a bar near the Temple. He is drinking a pint of Goldstar and watching out for his old friend. He can understand why Benjamin wanted to meet here, it sells cheap beer, has live football on a big screen and the barmaids are young and pretty. He sees his friend walk in and beckons him over.

"Long time," says Benjamin before waving over a barmaid, "Evening sweetheart, my usual, and two large single malt whiskies, no ice."

He sits down opposite Matthew. "Thanks for meeting me here, we couldn't really catch up in the Temple, with it being so busy and my workplace. This is kinda my second home anyway, well away from the missus, if you know what I mean."

Matthew smiles, "Javan Benjamin, ex-marine, part-time bouncer, full-time drinker - now a Temple guard."

"Matthew Levi, The Collector, meanest son of a bitch on the planet - now a trainee Rabbi!"

The barmaid brings over the drinks, placing them on the table. Benjamin slides one of the whiskies over to Matthew.

"Cheers," says Matthew before taking a sip.

Benjamin downs his in one. "Cheers. I can't believe what I'm seeing, since when do you drink lager?"

"Times change."

"They do, I hear they took the business when you quit to follow your man Jesus."

Matthew nods in agreement.

"You still driving that Merc? oh beautiful car!"

Matthew shakes his head.

"Wow, I can't believe it. So the rumours are true, when you lost the business, you lost everything. Oh man, that sucks."

Matthew just shrugs.

"Oh, you must be desperate for your man to be the real deal!"

"Oh, he's the real deal alright!"

"Come on, Collector, your man's a fraud. If he was the real deal, wouldn't my bosses know about it?"

"The name Lazarus ring any bells? I was there, I could smell the rotting corpse, hey, I know death, right. I saw him come out of that tomb, alive. Is this why I'm here, your bosses sent you did they?" Matthew finishes off the whisky.

"Hey, dude, I only invited you here for a drink, calm down."

Benjamin leans back. "Remember the time when we all went on that booze up to Acco. Your mate Milo ended up in jail for punching a woman in the face. She pinched his bum and he thought one of the lads had done it, so without looking he turned round and BAM - blood everywhere. Good times. So, how is psycho Milo, you seen him lately?

"Not lately, he's dead!"

"Oh... well, I can't say I'm surprised."

Benjamin has quickly finished his pint. He catches the eye

of the barmaid and waves his empty glass.

"I still can't get over you. You never talked about religion. Shit, collectors aren't even allowed in the Temple. I honestly thought *you'd* be dead by now."

"I'm surprised they let you become a Temple Guard! Did you lie on your CV?"

"They have a more relaxed recruitment policy nowadays, they like the guards to have been around, if you know what I mean? Don't tell anyone but there are one or two guards who have done serious jail time."

Benjamin continues to talk about his job, about how he has become one of Annas' most trusted guards and all the things he has done for him; he always did like to brag. He even admits that he was one of the guards that had tried to arrest Jesus. Matthew tries not to take it to heart. He used to like this guy, they've done a lot of drinking together - right now it seems a lifetime ago.

"So there was this one time, I was just starting out as a guard, minimum pay, bottom of the ladder, and this guy comes into the Temple shouting, screaming saying he is the Christ, the Messiah, the whole false prophet shit. Anyway, me and this other guard, we are ordered to arrest this guy and take him deep inside the Temple, where no one can hear the screams. This guy cried like a baby. It was so funny."

"You trying to tell me something?"

Matthew realises Benjamin hasn't changed one bit and now he's starting to find him annoying.

"All I'm saying is, I've seen this all before, your man is no different. Look at you, hanging out with the Zealot, the Zealot for shit's sake. That team you are with, what a bunch of tossers. Fishermen and kids, that's all they are. I didn't want to tell you this, but, there's a rumour going round the Temple that your team don't trust you. How come somebody who has worked with money and numbers all his life and ran his own business, can't even be trusted with the petty cash for a bunch of losers and dreamers? That must really piss you off."

Matthew takes a long drink of his Goldstar. That did annoy him, he's right on that one.

"My boss could help," says Benjamin.

So he was right, Benjamin has an ulterior motive, "Go on."

"He's a very wealthy man, he would be willing to pay a decent price for some good information regarding your boss."

"As you said, I'm good with numbers, so give me some good numbers."

"For that you would have to talk to my boss. I'll have to arrange a meeting, privately of course."

"I'm not sure, what do you think?" Matthew says loudly, looking at the table next to them.

It is a few seconds before he gets a response.

"Yo, I heard." Simon slides into the seat next to Benjamin. "Man, you two can talk."

"Benjamin, this is the Zealot. Simon this is the old friend I told you about."

Simon takes out his knife. He waves it in front of Benjamin's face.

"This is my knife, you ever seen one of these?"

Benjamin shakes his head. Matthew wishes Simon would just put it away, he still hates that thing.

"You're lucky, 'cos they can be very dangerous, one little slip and..."

He slides the knife across Benjamin's face.

Matthew leans over the table and whispers.

"Listen."

Under the table Matthew has taken out his gun and flicks the trigger back.

Click.

"Did you hear that. That's my Jericho saying hello. Now, do you believe I've changed, 'cos if you don't, then prepare to take your last breath."

"Hey, Matt, come on, we go way back, this was all my boss's idea."

"Tell your boss he's wasting his time, he can't buy me or any of us off. Our boss *is* the real deal, got it? Now get the hell out of my sight."

Benjamin quickly gets up and heads for the door. Before leaving he pauses, turns to Matthew and shouts, "people don't change, you were a bastard then, you're a bastard now."

Feeling like the whole bar is staring at him, Matthew puts his gun away then downs the rest of his pint.

"People do change, and he knows it. Before the boss, I wouldn't have thought twice about firing the whole clip into my old friend."

"I need another drink, how much money you got?" says Simon.

Matthew looks in his wallet.

"Not enough."

Chapter 30

Jude slides open the door to the storage unit and smiles. Now here is a sight to please the eyes. "There was no way I was going to sell you," he says. His V-rod is just how he left it several months ago, along with his helmet and leathers. He wheels the bike outside and starts it up. It thunders into life, the sound reverberating around the yard and startling some sparrows perched on a nearby roof, sending them high into the sky.

He pops on the jacket and helmet and sits on the bike's perfectly sculptured seat. He still can't believe how close he came to selling it. It became clear very early on, that money for the team was going to be tight. There wasn't the big named backer with unlimited funds that some rabbis and teachers have. Funds were stretched right from the beginning. Yes, they have some wealthy followers, but it's not cheap looking after them all. Travel costs and food soon add up. There was never any reason for them all to have cars sitting doing nothing when the money could be put to better use. All the others moaned and complained at first but it made sense, especially when they were given the minibus to use. Jude was supposed to sell his beloved V-Rod, even though it was a present. He had all but given up on trying to keep it, until luck came his way and he was made the treasurer for the team. OK, so no one had wanted to do it, Peter had offered, but Peter offered to do everything. James and John, having worked with Peter, really weren't keen on him having control of the teams' money. No one asked Matthew, there was way too much resentment against him as it was. Jude was the compromise candidate so to speak, and he was more than happy to accept the job. It meant that he didn't have to hand over his bike to anyone. Instead he discreetly rented a storage unit in Capernaum. At first he covered the cost himself, but as no one ever questioned him about the team accounts he started paying for the rental out of petty cash.

A couple of days riding around, giving himself some precious time alone far away from the team and time to think is just what he needs. It can be quite claustrophobic, spending so much of your time with the same people. He gets on with them fine, but sometimes they do frustrate him. Like recently, they were as angry and disappointed as he was when Jesus decided to just leave the Temple; yet a day later, they were back to normal, passively standing by while the boss seemed unwilling and hesitant to use this amazing power to take on the Union. He had thought it would be different, he thought the team would have more high achievers in it, be full of the best people in the country. He thought he'd be more famous than he is. All the crowds want is to see Jesus, sometimes it's as if the rest of us don't exist. Maybe it's just frustration, he might feel better once he tastes the power of the V-Rod and the rush of speed. Jude has missed riding and really wants to ride it back to Jerusalem. It's no fun being squashed in the bus all the time.

He realises that if he turns up on his bike the others would know that he hasn't contributed any money to the team, and won't be too pleased. They may even demand he sell it. He could even lose control of the finances. Although he wants to ride into the city, it is not worth the risk, so after one last ride around the hills and valleys of Southern Galilee, he puts it back into storage and catches the coach back into Jerusalem.

Before he sets off he rings Andrew to find out if they are still in the city and then finds Peter is on the same coach. Andrew picks them up from the bus station in the minibus to take them to the house.

"It looks like we will all be staying here for the rest of the festival," he informs them.

Great, back to sleeping on a camp bed.

"Hey Andy, did you manage on the money I left for food? It's bound to be running low now?"

"Oh yeah, the boss wants to talk to you about that."

Jude's heart starts beating a little faster. Does Jesus know about his bike? Or that for the last few days he'd stayed at a very nice hotel, all paid for with the teams' money? Did someone recognise him? He thought he'd been discreet, well as discreet as he could. After all he was riding a V-rod. Trying to keep calm, he asks if Andrew knows the reason why.

"Something about the Passover meal."

Relief. For a second he thought he'd been caught.

Peter wants to catch up with all that's been happening, especially regarding Jesus, so Andrew brings them up to date.

"The boss's been in the Temple teaching most of the time. The city seems busier than usual. James and John have found their old pool table in the garage and have set it up and that's it."

That night Jude can't sleep. The air bed which he has been

given is uncomfortable and with the sound of snoring echoing around the house and a whispered conversation going on somewhere, he wishes he'd had a few more days in the hotel. There the bed was king size and the pillows soft. He fidgets until his frustration boils over and he throws off his quilt; a cigarette may calm him down. In the dark he fumbles through his bag for a pack and a lighter, then quietly goes outside to smoke. Pacing around the back garden unable to relax, he can hear the conversation more clearly. It's Simon and Matthew, what are they on about?

"Should we tell the others?"

"And say what exactly, would *you* believe me?"

"Your mate, will he do anything stupid?"

"He wouldn't call it stupid. No, he's tough, but he may be more afraid of us. Benjamin's no problem, it's Annas I'm worried about."

"He's getting desperate if he thinks he can buy us."

* * *

Jude was finding it difficult to get to sleep again the following night. They're pathetic fools, blind to the future. Don't they realise it is a win-win. In the end he didn't care. He had been away a few days and nothing had changed, back to the normal routine of just following the boss here and there and ultimately going nowhere. It was the same today, Jesus got up, went to the Temple, spent most of the day teaching about something trivial no doubt. Then in the evening Peter will have even more questions. Jude is not the only one who is a little bored. The twelve are itching for the boss to take control, do something. One of the thoughts he'd had while riding around, was that Jesus seemed to work best under pressure. In a crisis, there's no one better. If someone is sick he heals them: he meets a blind man, gives him sight, if there's a storm he controls the weather, everyone's hungry, he feeds them, when he was going to be arrested he escaped, a friend dies, no problem. The last two particularly interest Jude. Jesus should, by all accounts have been arrested, only he escaped through a guarded doorway and later, like he was really rubbing it in, he performs the greatest miracle ever. It can't be a coincidence. The only rational conclusion is that Jesus needs a push, someone to force the issue. Jude has already thought that if Jesus were to be backed into a corner, say in an arrest, successfully this time, it could be the catalyst for Jesus to use his awesome power and bring in the dawn of the new Kingdom. Then Israel will see the true Messiah, and finally the twelve will get to sit on their thrones. Only this time, *he* will get to sit on Jesus' right. The overheard conversation confirmed a few things - eventually the guards will arrest Jesus because it comes straight from Annas himself. The rest of the team are too cowardly and small-minded to plan such a thing and now he has an advantage. He has found out there is even money in it; money and power - the perfect win-win!

In the evening, when James, John, Simon and Thaddy were playing pool and the rest sitting around listening to Jesus, Jude sees an opportunity to slip out. He had hinted earlier that he needed some air, so he makes his escape in relative safety. He had thought about taking the minibus, but decided against it. Instead he walks to the nearest bus stop and rides in with the many pilgrims. Even this late in the evening there are hundreds heading up the hill into the main city centre and then going the short walk to the Temple.

He hadn't rung ahead, and he doesn't even know who he would see, but he does know the chief priests will still be there at this hour, if the news bulletins are to be believed.

On arriving at the Temple he wanders around in the hope that someone might recognise him. His chance comes when a chief priest, one of the Pharisees, stops and looks right at him.

"You, I recognise you, aren't you one of the Galilean's team?"

Jude smiled, at last someone knows who he is.

"That's right!" says Jude.

"Is your man here too?" It is said with a venomous hatred.

"No, I'm alone, but I am here to see your boss."

"Really," says the priest.

"Really," answers Jude.

He is in luck, the priest believes him and can introduce him to the right people. At first the priest wants to talk loudly, it is his chance to ridicule a member of Jesus' team in full public view, but Jude is having none of it.

"We need to speak in private, or I walk away."

"As you wish, follow me," Now the priest understands and leads Jude away from the main courts, upstairs and along a corridor. Between the arches he can see the main courts below. He wants to stop and take it in, but knows he needs to appear confident and not overawed.

"Please sit, I will inform the High Priest he has a visitor."

Jude sits down in the quiet anteroom. There are a few velvet upholstered chairs and a water cooler in one corner. Jude's throat is dry, probably from the meal - Andrew uses way too much salt when he cooks, so he helps himself to a drink.

He is left alone for what seems like an age. Finally a man calls him.

"Mr Iscariot."

Jude nods.

"I'm Jonathan Sethas, I work for Josephus Annas, would you please follow me."

They walk down another corridor, lined with cedar wood panelling and furnished with gilded benches. If it's meant to intimidate me it won't work, Jude thinks.

"Mr Iscariot," announces Jonathan as they both enter the office.

Immediately Jude recognises Annas and Caiaphas the High Priest who both stand on his arrival. He strides forward to meet them. As he was waiting, he'd kept telling himself, that even though he might meet the High Priest he shouldn't be overawed. He has what they need. They should be grateful to him, not the other way round.

"What can we do for you today Mr Iscariot?" says Annas.

"Well, you can call me Jude, Mr Iscariot is my father." He feels rather pleased with that reply, it tells them he's his own man, knows his own mind.

"Alright, Jude, would you like a drink?"

Annas and Caiaphas look relaxed and both look to be drinking whisky.

"Coffee, would be good, black, no sugar," he says. He doesn't want to smell of booze when he gets back.

Jonathan nods, "very good."

Annas sits back down, offering Jude the seat that Caiaphas had been sitting in. The high Priest stands behind the chair, making Jude feel a little uncomfortable.

"I do know who you are, I know all of the Galilean's team.

You are from Kerioth as I recall," says Annas.

Jude nods.

"Now, Jude, do tell us what it is you wish to discuss."

"My boss," says Jude.

"Naturally, we didn't think you were here to have a scripture lesson," says Caiaphas.

Jonathan comes back in with the coffee. Jude takes it, and holds the hot cup in his hands.

"It has come to my knowledge that you are in the market for information regarding my boss."

"Go on," says Annas.

"I might be willing to give you what you want, at the right price."

"What if I told you we had already purchased the information!" says Caiaphas.

"I would say you are a liar!" he says without turning to look at the High Priest.

"Bravo, there's fight in you, I like it, I really do. Ever considered becoming a priest?" says Annas.

"How can we be sure you are trustworthy, you are after all betraying your teacher?" asks Caiaphas, bending so close Jude can feel his breath on his neck.

"I'll give you a money back guarantee if you're not happy with what I deliver to you," he says looking Annas straight in the eye. Caiaphas huffs but Jude holds Annas' stare, after all it was his name he'd overheard between Matthew and Simon.

"Excellent, young Jude, excellent. Because what we require of you... Is your Jesus!" says Annas.

"Fine."

"It's imperative that this is done correctly, how can you be sure he will surrender to us? This must be done in secret," says Caiaphas.

"I'll deliver him to you personally," replies Jude.

Annas leans back in his chair. "Then you shall have your reward."

He shouts for Jonathan.

"Open my safe Jonathan, and give our friend Jude – oh what shall we pay?" He smiles, "what about thirty pieces of silver."

Caiaphs laughs, "most appropriate."

Thirty shekels, even at the current exchange rate wasn't what Jude was expecting. He'd been hoping for at least a few thousand euros, maybe he should haggle. Why only thirty? That isn't enough.

"It's from the scriptures, thirty shekels is the price paid in compensation if someone accidentally killed a slave," Jonathan whispers to him as he counts out thirty coins into a money bag and hands it over to Jude, who grabs it.

"Fine, play your little game, just don't get too comfy in that palace of yours. It will be mine soon enough."

The joke will be on them when Jesus refuses to be arrested and uses his power. Just wait, soon it will be me sitting in that chair.

"My assistant will help you with the details," says Annas laughing.

In Jonathan's office they go over what is expected. Jude needs to give them a time and place, preferably at night and away from the crowds. He can hear Annas and Caiaphas laughing as he makes his way back along the corridor and down into the Temple courts.

He is too angry to go back to the house straight away, so he hides the money bag in his jacket and walks the shadowy streets until he has calmed down. If only Jesus had told him the plans for Passover, then he would have been able to give precise details there and then and the money would have been a lot more. He knows there is to be a meal, but Jesus has given the job of arranging it to Peter and John; no surprises there, teacher's pets. All Jesus has needed him for is to sort out the cash. Rather than catch the bus back to the house, he decides to walk, calling in at a KFC on the way and getting himself a bargain bucket.

Chapter 31

"You know in some countries they have mint sauce with lamb."

"Really! Why would they have that?"

"I don't know, tradition I suppose."

John and Peter are at the Temple purchasing the Passover lamb. It's the first time John has been to the Temple during Passover and now he knows why his parents have never wanted to stay in the city at this time of year. It can be quite claustrophobic, with all the people and animals and the smell is awful. It's a lot easier at the Capernaum Temple, not as many people.

"It would not be the place to come if you're a veggie, would it?" says John as he pushes his way out, clutching the lamb that has been sacrificed, now wrapped in layers of brown paper.

"Don't drop it," Peter yells at him.

Why Jesus chose Peter to go with him, John will never know. Peter is the worst queuer in the world and he has never stopped complaining. People don't really care how *he* would have organised it. Especially when he'd been standing in the wrong queue for twenty minutes. They both had questioned whether they'd be safe. Just because Jesus had avoided being arrested didn't mean they'd be so lucky. That's why he questions the choice of Peter? He's not exactly suited for undercover work. His booming northern accent overpowers even the noisiest of animals; I mean the man stands out like a big hairy giant on a plate of figs. They are recognised by many people but thankfully the Temple guards leave them alone, although John saw many of them watching from a distance.

As the lamb is too big to be roasted in a conventional oven, Jesus has organised a venue that includes a roasting pit. John and Peter have instructions for after they have purchased the lamb.

They are to meet a man in the old part of the city. He will show them where to go. They don't understand the need for so much secrecy, but didn't argue. It has all the hallmarks of when Jude and Alphie had to pick up the colt, and they are a little apprehensive.

They walk down the street towards the High Priests palace. As they pass the gated building John stops and looks through the gates into the courtyard. He wonders if that will be his home once Jesus starts his new kingdom. A couple of narrow streets later, they are at the corner where they are to meet their mystery contact.

"This has got to be one of the strangest things we've ever done," says John.

They wait, Peter constantly checking his watch, until a man approaches.

"This could be the guy!" says Peter.

"It's like we're spies," adds John.

"Do you remember what we have to say?" asks Peter.

"No, do you?"

"Thought you were gonna write it down?"

"I couldn't find a pen! And I thought you'd remember it. It had something about my time or hour is come. Hang on while I ring Jesus," says John.

"Too late, I think this is the guy."

"If it isn't we're going to get arrested!"

"Hi, er...The teacher says *my hour has come...*" says Peter, hesitating.

"I must celebrate Passover with my team," says John, remembering the last line.

"Part of Jesus' team are you? Thought I recognised you both, my place is just across the road," says the man.

They are led to a large white house, with steps on the outside going up to another level. A sign on the wall reads Bed and Breakfast. Proprietor Z. E. Marith. In a window there is a NO VACANCIES sign. The man, scruffy and unshaven, with a cigarette glued to his lip, gestures for them to follow him up the stairs.

"Your boss has hired the upper room, you brought the cash?"

"Yeah," says John.

The steps lead to a large room where a long table dominates the centre. On the left is what looks like the kitchen area and at the far end is a bar. There are also a couple of sofas and recliners next to an open fireplace.

"This looks nice," says John a little surprised.

"You can put that over there in the kitchen," the man points to the lamb.

Peter takes out his wallet and the man produces an itemised bill.

"I've organised everything your boss requested, anything else, just ask. I'll be downstairs in the guest house all night.

My wife is the cook, so she will have told your boss what time to expect the lamb to be ready, but you can come any time, he's paying for it."

Peter looks at the bill and takes out the exact amount from his wallet, handing it to the man, who flicks through the notes before nodding and squeezing them into his top shirt

pocket. John peers over at the bill. Wow, Jesus has even ordered plenty of drinks. He smiles, this is gonna be a great Passover.

"Oh, yeah, one more thing. Could you do me a favour? The beer is downstairs round the back. You two look strong, do you think you could fetch them up for me?"

"No problem," says John.

They fetch the beer before heading back to where they had parked the minibus, in a car park near the old city wall.

* * *

Later in the evening Andrew takes the bus keys from the hook in the kitchen and heads outside. "Hey Andrew, why don't we order taxis so we can all have a drink," says John, leaning on the kitchen worktop.

"That's a good idea," says Thaddy entering the kitchen still towel drying his hair.

"I'll just have one glass with the meal, it's fine."

"Your call Andrew, but I'm gonna enjoy myself tonight," Thaddy says throwing the towel at John, who in turn throws it back at him.

All three go and get in the minibus and wait for the others. It's a long wait, Andrew has to hit the horn several times.

When everybody is finally ready, they drive back up into the old city. The roads around the palace have restricted access and Andrew, much to the annoyance of everyone, has to turn back and go to the upper room a different way. John and Peter had been on foot before and had only remembered the way they had gone. Eventually they arrive, find a parking space, and all climb the stairs to the upper room.

Even before Peter opened the door they can smell the aroma of roasting lamb. It is one of John's favourite smells equal only to that of the sea air on a spring day. While the others charge in heading straight to the bar he goes over to the kitchen area. Mrs Marith is pouring juices over the lamb.

"It smells fantastic."

Over at the bar Peter hands out the beer. James takes one, pulling the bottle cap off with his teeth.

"There is a bottle opener on the bar!" Mrs Marith points out.

"Doesn't that hurt?" Philip asks James.

James shakes his head while downing the bottle in one go and giving out a loud burp. Jesus thanks Mrs Marith as she leaves the room shaking her head.

"Boss, you having one?" asks Peter.

Jesus takes a couple of bottles of wine and begins to go round the table, filling each glass.

"Lads before you start on those, I want to say a few words. Gather round."

"There is a reason for all the secrecy. I have really wanted to eat this Passover meal with you twelve tonight, before I suffer! I shall never eat it again until it is fulfilled in the Kingdom of God."

Jesus raises up a glass and has a drink, the lads all do the same.

"Now follow me," Jesus goes over to a ceremonial washing bowl, placed on a small table by the kitchen area and washes his hands. While he is drying them on a towel he gestures for them to do the same. Before they sit down for the meal, James goes back to the bar and gets another beer. John notices that this time he uses the bottle opener.

The table has already been laid out with all the cutlery. Plates are piled high with unleavened bread, and several bowls of Charoseth - a paste/dipping sauce that is made with apples, dates, pomegranates and nuts. James is the last to sit down.

"Want to hear a joke? There was this guy, he could play the piano really well, and composed his own music. One day he goes to this audition and..."

Peter interrupts, "If this is the one you told at your Uncle Hagar's funeral, then this is not the time."

"Er, yeah it is!"

"Aw, come on Pete," says Simon.

"It's vulgar," says Peter.

"I'll tell you later," whispers James to Simon.

Once everybody is seated, Jesus brings over the lamb. He places it in the centre of the table and begins to carve.

"Oh, that looks so good," says James.

Jesus serves Jude first and John is a bit jealous. At Passover it is said to be an honour when the host serves you first. When Jesus serves James, he looks down at the small piece of meat, looks back at Jesus, "and?"

Jesus gives him another piece.

"Thank you boss."

The lamb is perfectly cooked and melts in John's mouth, oh heaven. He realises that for the first time today he can't hear Peter's voice. You can always tell good food, everybody goes quiet. For a while anyway.

"Miles better than Mum's," James says in between mouthfuls, breaking the silence.

John dips some bread into the sauce, umm, interesting, he's not sure about this? Mum's sauce is definitely better, this is more datey, than appley. Seeing James eyeing up more wine, he grabs it first. He knows that if it's left by his brother it will soon be empty. He pours out a big glass full and does the same for Peter and Philip until it is finished. His brother is not very impressed and has to get another from the bar.

Mrs Marith discreetly enters bringing in more bread and sauces. She places them on the table and takes away a couple of empty dishes. As she is leaving Thaddy stops her and asks if she will take a photo. They all gather round one side of the table as Thaddy shows her how to use the camera on his phone.

"Smile everyone," she says before taking the picture.

She hands the phone back and leaves the room as the lads all devour the sauce and bread she has brought in. James gets up again and fetches a few more beers. They continue to eat and drink, laugh and joke.

"Everything OK boss?" John notices that Jesus is looking sad.

"One of you here in this room will betray me," says Jesus.

"No we won't boss, don't say stuff like that," says Peter.

"We wouldn't betray you," says John.

Each one agrees, they are all upset at the suggestion.

Matthew looks Jesus in the eye, "boss, you don't mean me, do you?"

Simon says the same. The rest see this and all follow suit, asking Jesus personally whether they will be the one.

"The one who dips his bread in the bowl with me is the one who will betray me. The Son of Man will die as the Scriptures says he will, but how terrible for that man who betrays the Son of Man! It would have been better if that man had never been born!"

"Surely teacher, you don't mean me?" says Jude, dipping the bread into the bowl at the same time as Jesus.

"So you say," Jesus replies.

John, who was really enjoying the evening, is disappointed. That's a bit of a downer, Jesus sometimes makes no sense, they were having such a good time.

"Why would he say something like that?" John asks Andrew.

"I don't know," doesn't seem to have ruined the mood though," pointing to the others.

James has thrown a bit of bread, first at Matthew then Simon. They both respond by flicking sauce back at him.

"This is no time for a food fight," says Peter sternly, "this is far too good to waste," he adds, smiling.

When John turns back to Jesus and Jude he catches the end of a conversation.

"Go, do what you have to do quickly!" Jesus says to Jude.

Immediately Jude gets up from the table and without saying goodbye to the others, leaves the room.

Over the laughing and fooling around John watches Jude go over to the door, open it letting in the cool night air, and step out into the darkness.

When Jude doesn't return straight away, Philip, sitting next to John leans over.

"Where did Jude go?"

"No idea," John shakes his head.

"He may have gone downstairs for more dipping sauce, I like this better than Mum's," James suggests, "don't tell her I said anything, but she uses way too many apples."

While they all are still eating, Jesus picks up some bread before it's all gone and breaks it.

"Take, eat; this is my body," they pass it around the table, each taking a piece. Next he picks up a glass of wine.

"Drink this all of you, for this is my blood of the new covenant, which is poured out for many for the forgiveness of sins. I will not drink this wine again until the day when I drink it with you in my Father's Kingdom."

"What's happening?" Matthews asks as the bread, then wine are passed round. John doubts a collector would know this, having not been welcome in the synagogues. Simon and Alphie both lean closer to Nathaniel as he explains.

"It's a promise from God, like the ones he gave to Moses." Matthew still looks puzzled.

"It's like a modern contract."

"Deep," says Matthew.

At the end of the meal, the lads are all full and even James has to turn down more lamb, though he does manage another beer. Jesus, Peter and Andrew start to clear the table while the others go to rest on the sofas. Thaddy shouts to Philip and Andrew in the kitchen.

"A coffee wouldn't go amiss."

"Hey, why don't you give us a hand?"

"Yeah, in a minute."

All that food and drink has made them tired, John could just go to sleep. He closes his eyes for what feels like a second.

"Hey," says Andrew, "come on, we're off."

John opens his eyes, a little startled, "how long was I

303

asleep?"

"Only a minute" says Thomas, "Jesus wants to go somewhere quiet to pray."

"What about the washing up?" asks John.

"Like you care about that," says Andrew.

They all pile out, down the stairs and into the minibus.

"Where's Jude?" Matthew asks Philip.

"Not sure, I think Jesus has sent him on an errand."

Andrew drives out of the old city, following the outer wall until he gets to the east side. He stops in the car park of the Garden of Gethsemane. It is a quiet, serene place on the slopes of the Mount of Olives, high above Jerusalem, a place where people can escape the noise of the city. It's a place Jesus regularly visits when he needs peace.

Jesus, sitting in the front seat, opens the door. As he is about to step out, he hesitates, turning to the lads.

"Tonight you will all fall away from me, for it is written, 'I will strike down the shepherd and the sheep will be scattered.' But after I am raised I will go ahead of you to Galilee."

"What! Me, never! Even if all the others fall away from you I never will," says Peter.

"Oh, Peter," says Jesus, "this very night before the rooster crows, you will have denied me three times."

"Even if I have to die with you I will never deny you."

"We're a team, where you go we go," says Simon.

"Yeah, you taught us that boss, or me and Simon would have killed each other ages ago," says Matthew.

"We'll do whatever its takes" says Alphie.

"Count me in," "me too", "and me." Eleven voices one by one speak up in support of Jesus.

"Peter, James and John come with me, everybody else stay

here until I have prayed."

Jesus and the three lads go into the garden. At the entrance Jesus becomes distressed.

"My soul is so painful it almost crushes me, stay here and keep watch," Peter, James and John sit on a bench.

Jesus goes into the garden and kneels down beside a tree and begins to pray. The three can see how terribly he is suffering, they can hear parts of his prayers as he pleads with God to the point of crying. They feel helpless, just sitting there not knowing what to do.

John is woken suddenly; he looks up to see Jesus standing next to the bench looking exhausted, drops of blood are running down his face. John nudges Peter, who in turn wakes James.

"Are you asleep, could you not keep watch for one hour? Keep watching and praying that you do not come into temptation."

"Peter looks at his watch, "that was an hour, seems like five minutes."

"We'll stay awake this time."

"Maybe I shouldn't have drunk so much?"

Jesus goes away to pray, and again when he returns he has to wake them up. Once again he asks them to keep watch and pray, but their eyes are heavy and they don't know what to say.

Jesus goes away for a third time.

"Wake up..."

They all wake up at the same time.

"Huh, Oh, sorry, I'm so tired."

"What's happening?" asks Peter.

"I'm awake, I'm awake," says James, startled.

They stand up stretching, all rather embarrassed that they fell asleep three times.

"The hour has come when the Son of Man is to be handed over to sinners."

John looks around, he neither sees nor hears anything. Still half asleep, he is bewildered by Jesus' words.

Suddenly, there is the sound of a helicopter and a bright searchlight begins scanning the area. The helicopter hovers high above the garden, its beam misses them and instead focuses on the minibus. Now John can hear the sound of engines as several trucks and armoured cars come roaring towards them, their headlights piercing the dark car park.

The lads left in the bus are trying to escape the searchlight. They quickly come running over, Matthew and Simon both taking out their guns in readiness. Peter sees Simon's knife clipped to his belt and grabs it, Simon nods.

"What is happening?" shouts Thaddy.

Out of the trucks jump dozens of Union soldiers, all fully armed with rifles and wearing full combat gear. They surround the minibus and block all the exits to the garden. The lads all circle around Jesus, desperately trying to protect him. The searchlight finds them. They look at each other, what can they do? They are outnumbered and surrounded. John's heart is beating faster than ever before, he can barely think, the noise and lights are confusing his senses. More soldiers arrive on foot and with them more than a hundred Temple guards, all armed with batons. It is the Temple guards who move to the front and edge closer to the group. Following them are some priests who come forward.

"Which one is he?" says a priest.

Jesus steps forward, "who have you come for?" he asks.

"Jesus the Nazarene."

"I am he."

Peter tries to pull him back, as temple guards start surrounding them all.

"They're after us all, come on boss do something," shouts James.

"Who is it you want?" Jesus asks again.

"Jesus."

"Well, that's me, now let all these others go."

"Is that really him, the Miracle Man? How can we be sure?" says a Temple guard.

"I'll show you," says a familiar voice.

Jude steps out from the dark into the searchlight and comes right up to Jesus.

"Master," says Jude, kissing him on both cheeks.

"So, you betray the Son of Man with a kiss," says Jesus.

"Jude you bastard," says Peter.

Matthew and Simon both point their guns at Jude, but it is Peter with the knife who slashes at him. He misses, instead catching the ear of a man standing just behind, an assistant to one of the priests. He cuts his ear clean off. It falls to the ground and blood pours out of the gaping hole. The soldiers raise their weapons and are just about to open fire when...

"STOP!" shouts Jesus, the power of his voice knocking some of the guards to the floor. He puts his hand up to the man's ear and heals it instantly.

Turning to the lads he says, "put your weapons away, all those who take up the sword shall perish by the sword. Do you think I can't appeal to my Father, who would send down an army of angels...but how then will the Scriptures be fulfilled that says it must happen this way?"

He turns to the priests, "You come to arrest me like I am a bank robber or murderer. Yet you did nothing while I was in the Temple."

The guards, sensing their chance, seize hold of Jesus, handcuff him and drag him to a truck. They push him inside and it speeds away. Now they have their man, Jude, the soldiers and priests withdraw as swiftly and as suddenly as they appeared. The helicopter flies away, turning off its searchlight, plunging the garden into darkness once again.

The lads, fearing for their own lives all run; it's every man for himself as they scatter. Andrew heads for the minibus followed by Nathaniel, they don't wait for anyone else. Andrew sets off, driving as fast as he can. Alphie, Thomas and Thaddy head for the rear exit. James and Philip go out of the main entrance and along the side of the city wall.

Matthew and Simon stand, guns in hand, shocked and scared. Peter with a trembling hand gives Simon his knife back. Simon wipes the blood off on the grass before putting it away.

"Shit, shit," he says, kicking the ground.

Matthew goes and sits on the bench and puts his head in his hands.

"I wouldn't stay here if I were you, they might come back for us," says Simon as he starts to run to an exit of the garden.

"I don't know about you, but I want to know where they're taking him," says John.

Peter, doesn't say a word, he just nods and starts running. As John follows, he looks back at Matthew who is still sitting on the bench with his head in his hands.

Chapter 32

"Two minutes. Copy that."

"They're approaching the gates, get ready."

"One minute. Copy that."

"Open the gates."

"The gates are secure and the prisoner is in the palace," says Benjamin.

Theo puts his thumb up, "we got him."

Annas breathes a sigh of relief; that was most stressful, finally he has his man in custody. Never in all his life has he been so anxious, failure this time was not an option. Perspiration pours from his brow and he dabs it with his handkerchief.

"Well done gentlemen."

As Benjamin and Theo wait with Annas in his office the tension has given way to excitement. Theo opens the office door in readiness for their captive, before he and Benjamin stand either side of Annas. Theo takes out his gun and Benjamin picks up his Temple guards baton.

"Now let him try and get out of this one," says Benjamin.

Six armed Temple guards escort a handcuffed Jesus into the office. Annas holds his hand up and stops them.

"Thank you gentlemen, wait outside," says Benjamin.

Annas nods and the guards leave, closing the door behind them.

Theo and Benjamin move towards Jesus. Benjamin takes a practice swing with his baton, laughing. They stand either side of Jesus awaiting instructions.

"Finally, we meet Jesus of Galilee or should that be Nazareth? You have been quite the superstar haven't you? The great teacher who mesmerises and deceives. Well, one of your team has betrayed you and the rest deserted. So much for your power. I was expecting Superman - instead I get you."

Jesus stays silent. Annas is a little disappointed, this Galilean looks so much smaller in person and not at all special. Why would anyone want to follow him?

"Now is your chance to enlighten me with your clever words and false teaching. Come on, *Jesus*, speak, convince me you are *the one*! Or do you know I won't be as gullible as the rest of the country?"

"Why do you question me?" answers Jesus. "I have taught in synagogues and in the Temple. I spoke nothing in secret. Question those that have heard me, they know what I've said."

Benjamin strikes Jesus across his back with his baton.

"Is that the way you answer your superior?"

"If I am wrong, then testify so. If I am right why strike me?"

Annas stares at him... so underneath that plain exterior is the great blasphemer. Annas burns with hatred for this man but he knows he must remain calm. After all there is a plan in place and the first part has been a complete success.

"Take him away!" says Annas, "you know what we do to wannabe Messiahs."

* * *

Peter and John had sprinted after the convoy and when they finally arrive at the Palace gates Peter is surprised that a crowd is already beginning to gather.

"We have to get in," says John.

Peter can't respond, he bends double, gasping for breath. He'll need a minute or two to recover first.

More people arrive and begin taking photos and filming on their phones. Several cars had passed them as they ran from the garden and John had pointed out that each car carried a member of the council. Peter watches, catching his breath as another car arrives; cameras flash and people try to see who's inside. The gates open just wide enough for the car; a member of the public squeezes in at the same time. The guards are on him instantly; they beat him with batons and drag him away. Some soldiers look on, rifles at the ready in case of anything more serious than an over-eager sightseer.

Peter desperately wants to get in; he pushes his way to the front and grabs hold of the gates, but a guard standing on the other side pushes him back. "It's no good, we'll never get in," he says.

"Jesus kept using my phone, let's see who he called," says John.

"Well?"

"Hang on, people keep pushing me, I can't see properly."

Peter looks around desperately trying to think of a way in. John has to get hold of Nicodemus or Joseph, they're the only ones who could help. He looks at John, who shakes his head.

"Keep trying."

Just then a TV camera crew arrive; the gates open and the

van drives in. Once again the guards have trouble closing the gate. Soon it will be impossible to get near, let alone get in.

"No one is picking up, wait, I have the office of Joseph Arimathea. Oh crap, it's an answer machine."

"This is John, from Jesus' team, it's urgent, please ring me back.... please!"

He has almost given up when he receives a call from a withheld number. Peter listens, trying to work out what is happening.

"Thank you, thank you."

"It's Joanna, the wife of a Captain in the Union army."

"And..."

"And her husband has told her he was at the arrest and is now at the Palace. She wants to know if we are alright and if we know what is happening?"

John pushes through the crowd, at one point physically shoving someone out of the way.

"Come on, I asked if her husband could get us in," he shouts.

It's so squashed at the gate Peter has to stand behind John; he looks at the soldiers, wondering which one is Joanna's husband. After a few minutes one comes over and Peter recognising him, taps on Johns' shoulder and points.

"Are you Joanna's husband?" shouts John.

The Captain points his rifle at John, telling the guards "let that guy in."

One of the gates opens just wide enough for John to squeeze through. Before he is inside John grabs Peter. "He's with me."

The guard, without much thought, nods to Peter, allowing him to follow John.

They both thank the Captain, who points them to a smaller

gate which leads through a narrow passage into the inner courtyard. Peter quickly leads the way. They are now in the centre of the palace. The High Priest's wing is to the left side, Annas' to the right and the Council chambers take up the rest of the building. Peter didn't expect to see so many people, the courtyard is full. A camera crew films key areas and interviews of palace officials; reporters scramble around trying to get the latest information. At first glance there seems to be a lot of palace staff also hanging around. In one corner they have set up a table and are providing hot drinks. Patio heaters have also been brought out to keep people warm, and there are plenty of tables and chairs.

"We should let his mum know," John says.

"Good idea, you ring round everybody, I'll see if I can find out what's happening."

Peter sits near a heater in the hope of overhearing any news of Jesus. A woman, wearing a staff uniform is sitting nearby, sipping hot coffee. She stares at Peter.

"You look really familiar, are you from the press? No that's not it, but I'm sure I've seen you before."

She thinks for a minute.

"I know, you're one of *his* team!"

"I don't know what you are talking about, I've never met him."

"Huh, I never usually forget a face, I'm sure I've seen you with the teacher."

Peter just shrugs. Maybe I'd better get a hot drink, wonder why they aren't serving food.

"Coffee please."

As he is handed a coffee, a man next to him also recognises him.

"Are you one of Jesus team? You are aren't ya?"

"No, I am not!"

Oh great, now everyone has overheard, their accusing stares and pointing fingers convicting him right here, right now. I'm next, they're going to arrest me. I cannot be arrested, I just can't. He sees a camera crew coming towards him and tries to get out of the way.

"He's one of them."

"He's Galilean, just like Jesus."

"I've seen you with him."

"You're crazy! I don't know the man."

He turns to see the film crew focusing in on him. He stares into the camera at the exact moment he hears a rooster crow.

A shout, "quick he's here," there is a commotion as guards appear from everywhere. Peter's heart already pumping, fears the worst. He freezes with fear, unable to move, this is it, they are here to arrest me. When a guard pushes past him, Peter is confused, if not him who?

Jesus is being led out into the courtyard. He is handcuffed and surrounded by guards. Jesus turns in Peters direction and through the crowd fixes his eyes on him. Only now does Peter remember what Jesus had said: *This very night before the rooster crows, you will have denied me three times.*

The realisation of what is happening, what he's just said and done, is all too overwhelming. It feels like his chest is being crushed, those eyes are looking into his very soul. He has to get out of here.

Head down and hands up, he tries to hide from the camera's accusing stare and runs to the gates. As he approaches them one of the cars has dropped off another council member and is leaving. The gates are still open and he quickly slips through before they can close.

Now he runs, not caring where he's heading, just away from everybody. All he can see is the image of Jesus, the look on his face; it's all too much to take. He is angry and embarrassed at what he has done, but the longer he runs the more upset he becomes. He denied Jesus, he denied the Master. After all those promises of fighting and even dying for him, he couldn't even acknowledge he knew him. Tears pour down his face until he is so physically upset that he can't take another step. He stops in a dark corner and collapses in grief, crying uncontrollably.

Chapter 33

Theo and Benjamin, accompanied by Temple Guards, take Jesus through the courtyard and throw him into a small room adjacent to the council chambers and lock the door.

Jonathan enters Annas' office, goes over to a wall and slides open a cupboard. In it is a TV monitor. He turns it on, all it shows is static.

"Right gentleman, entertain me," says Annas.

A grainy black and white view of the room appears on the screen.

"Are we on, sir," says Theo waving to the camera.

"Yes, you are live," says Jonathan into a microphone.

Annas and Jonathan watch as Theo takes out a scarf and blindfolds Jesus. He punches him in the stomach, knocking him to the floor.

"Go on, gives us a prophecy, which one of us will hit you next?"

He punches him again, this time in the kidneys. Benjamin kicks him in the groin.

"Oh, that's gotta hurt," says Theo.

"I wish your team could see this, but they've all run away, not so tough now are they?"

He lashes out with a kick, knocking Jesus over. Benjamin

grabs Jesus by the hair pulling him back up and spitting in his face.

"You disgust me, all this talk about a New Kingdom. Yet you don't even fight for this one. I don't know why Matthew would ever follow you. You're just a little piece of shit, that's all."

"Try not to mark his face if he's going in front of the council," says Annas, laughing over the mic.

They carry out a frenzied attack, concentrating on Jesus' body. Jesus curls up in a ball and tries to protect himself, but blow after blow, kick after kick keep coming.

"That will do, for now," Annas' voice crackles over the speaker.

"That's enough, Annas needs you back here," Jonathan adds.

"We'll be back for you in the morning," says Theo to Jesus.

"Don't go anywhere, will you," mocks Benjamin.

* * *

In the morning Caiaphas is ready to start the trial. Under Jewish law, criminal trials are not legal if held at night, so the trial will not begin until first light; this gives Annas time to brief his most favoured council members and time for Caiaphas to prepare the prosecution. The Priests use the time to round up witnesses to testify against Jesus. Trials usually take place in the Temple chambers, which are larger, with each member having his own seat. But because of the nature and speed of Jesus' arrest, Annas had suggested the palace chamber be used.

Caiaphas sits on a raised platform at one end of the chamber.

317

Next to him are the chief priests and elders. Not all the seventy members could make the trial in time, but those that did are squashed inside and have very little room. The other priests stand wherever they can. Annas stands at the back, his two trusted guards next to him.

Jesus is brought into the chamber in handcuffs and placed in the centre of the room facing Caiaphas. A series of witnesses are brought in and each are asked what Jesus had said in the Temple that could be used against him. The priests hope they can make up stories, and tell lies that Jesus had broken the law, but each witness contradicts the others.

"Where did you find these people?" questions Caiaphas.

Annas shakes his head, this is not a good start. One by one the witnesses fail to find anything to use against Jesus. Annas has to turn to plan B.

"Fetch me better witnesses," he tells Theo.

Theo comes back with a chauffeur and a staff member from the household. Annas takes them into a quiet room and coaches them on what to say and how to come across. Their names are soon called and they are brought before the council.

"This man said: I am able to destroy this Temple of God and rebuild it in three days," says the chauffeur.

The servant agrees and repeats the line word for word. Annas knows he has something, for it was widely reported that the Galilean had said such a thing.

"Well, what do you say in your defence?" demands Caiaphas.

To Annas' annoyance Jesus doesn't answer the question.

"Is this accusation against you true? Have you no answer?" Again Jesus is silent.

"I remind you, you are under oath and must answer. Are

you the Christ?"

Some of the priests gasp.

"I am," says Jesus.

Now everyone in the room gasps. Annas can't believe what he has just heard.

Jesus continues, "You will see the Son of Man sitting at the right hand of Power and coming on clouds of heaven."

The priests gasp again. Annas watches on, proud as his son-in-law acts all horrified, even tearing his robes in disgust.

"Blasphemy," cries Caiaphas, "what further need do we have for other witnesses?"

Annas is waiting in Caiaphas' office when his son-in-law enters.

"Bravo, Bravo," Annas claps.

"Too much?"

"On the contrary, it was perfect, I honestly believed you were horrified at what you heard."

"Thank you, it was made rather easy for me."

Caiaphas begins to take off his robes.

"No, leave them on. I believe it will make for a very powerful image."

Now for the next part in Annas and Caiaphas' plan. This is more tricky and involves Governor Pilate playing his part. Annas has already briefed the Governor earlier when he asked for troops during the arrest. Pilate was hardly in a position to turn it down, for if a riot had occurred his job could be on the line. He is aware that the Jewish Authorities want a Union death penalty; what he isn't aware of is what crime has been committed. This has to be done right, so Annas selects five chief priests and elders to represent the Council and with an armed Temple guard, orders Jesus to be taken to the Union

Headquarters for an audience with Pilate.

Chapter 34

"This should be far enough. Thanks."

"Are you sure, I can take you further?"

"I'm good, the boss has friends here I can stay with."

"Keep safe, and I hope it works out for Jesus."

Simon gets out of the car and sets off walking, waving to the driver that may have just saved his life. What were the chances that someone sympathetic to Jesus would be driving along at the very moment he needed help. It was good to see a familiar face, even though he still can't remember the man's name.

His heart is racing, his thoughts are still in the garden. They came with so much force, what could we have done? It would have been a bloodbath. And Peter, Peter? The only one to stand up to them. Running from Gethsemane, Simon desperately tried to think of somewhere safe. But he couldn't, his brain was so scrambled. When the soldiers came he was sure it was for all of them and he still doesn't know why they were spared.

When the man asked where he wanted to go Simon hadn't a clue, home to Capernaum was what his head was telling him. It was only when he saw a road sign for Emmaus that he knew where to go; hopefully he'll be safe there.

Emmaus is seven miles west of Jerusalem, no one will think of looking for him there. Walking to Cleopas' home, Simon starts to feel safer, Lets hope Cleo *is* there.

Not having a phone number and only ever visiting Cleo and Sarah his wife once with Jesus, Simon isn't one hundred percent sure of the house number and he doesn't really want to bang on several doors trying to find out. He does remember that it is a red door. Looking around he realises that in the dark he can't tell colours apart. Good job he remembers the car. Parked in front of a house is a Golf Gti that James and John had once enviously admired.

Simon knocks on the door, gently at first so as not disturb the neighbours. When nobody answers he's forced to knock louder.

"Who is it?"

"Yo, Cleo, it's me, Simon, let me in."

Simon can hear the chain being removed and the lock turned. Before the door is fully opened Simon squeezes in, leaving Cleo checking to see if Simon has been followed.

"Don't worry, I was careful."

Cleopas closes the door and locks it.

"I'm glad you're okay, what about the others?"

Simon shakes his head, "I've not heard from anyone else, I daren't use my phone in case..."

"So, they finally got him."

Simon nods as he is shown into the living room. It's dark but Cleo only puts on a small table lamp.

"How? I don't understand, I thought you were going for Passover meal together. No one even knew where you were eating or where you were going afterwards."

"Jude!"

"What?"

"The bastard set us up."

Cleo puts his hand to his mouth. "I don't believe it, how could he?"

His wife Sarah is talking on the phone and pauses to ask who was at the door.

"It's Simon," he says. "who are you talking to?" Cleo whispers to her.

"Hang on Salomé," turning to her husband who now knows it's James and John's mother, nods back at her.

"I need a drink, will you join me Simon?" asks Cleo.

"Yeah, nice one."

"Don't have any of that Hennessey I hear you like, hope good old Israeli whisky is okay?"

"Sure," Simon nods.

As Cleo goes for the drinks, Simon sits down and listens in to Sarah's conversation. It appears that Salomé, up in Capernaum, knows more about what is happening than he does.

It seems so long ago that he was enjoying the evening. It's almost unreal. Like he might wake up any second. Who'd have thought he'd have ended up running for his life.

It has been a long time since Simon has felt this afraid or this helpless. As he ran, his mind had drifted back to the time he and Flatpack had escaped from the Caleb rally. Has anything really changed? He thought Jesus was the real deal. Why else would he give up his old life back in Capernaum and travel the country with collectors if he didn't. Surely he hadn't been wrong about Jesus. I mean the guy raised the dead. Who else could do that except the Messiah? No one that's who! Yet here I am, questioning everything that has happened over the last two years and wondering if I was wrong all along. Why, why did Jesus allow himself to be arrested?

Cleo comes in with two drinks, handing one to Simon. Good, the glass is full. He takes a sip, it's not bad either. He downs half in one go.

"I needed this, cheers."

When Sarah finishes on the phone she has tears running down her cheeks. "Salomé is coming straight down to Jerusalem, she is worried about John."

"Is he OK?" asks Cleo.

"He's in the palace courtyard with Peter. Well he was - Peter has disappeared."

"What are they doing there, are they mad?" Simon fears for them.

"Any word on the others?"

"Not yet."

As she speaks, there's a knock at the door and Simon jumps. Cleo puts his finger to his lips before going to see who it is.

"Hello?" he asks hesitantly.

"It's Andrew and Nathaniel."

Cleo quickly unlocks the door and lets them in.

"We weren't sure where to go, can we stay here awhile?"

"Of course, I'm glad you're both OK."

Andrew and Nathaniel enter the living room and smile when they see Simon.

"Zealot, good to see you," says Nathaniel.

"We've been driving round, not knowing where to go," says Andrew.

"You two look terrible, let me make you a drink," says Sarah as she switches on the TV. "Salomé told us the arrest is all over the news."

The ticker running along the bottom of the screen reads *Breaking News.* *The Teacher, Jesus of Nazareth, arrested in midnight raid.*

Pictures from the helicopter have been released to the press. They show the moment when the forces enter the garden.

The newsreader is giving the latest update....."At about midnight, Temple guards, with support from Union soldiers, began the plan to arrest Jesus of Nazareth, the one people are claiming is the Messiah. The arrest took place at the Garden of Gethsemane, just outside the city. This station believes it was one of Jesus' own team who led the Jewish Authorities right to him."

A picture of Jude is put on the screen.

"Why? Why did you do it Jude?" asks Cleo.

"We've been asking the same question," says Nathaniel.

"And we've no idea," adds Andrew.

"Why didn't the boss do something? We know he could have, there is always a reason."

"Only he was always here to explain it," Nathaniel points out.

The news is now showing footage from Gethsemane, "during the arrest one of the accompanying priest's assistants was seriously injured." says the news anchor.

"He was healed you stupid idiot," shouts Nathaniel to the TV, "they won't say that."

Now footage from the inner courtyard is being shown.

"Hey, Andy, isn't that Peter?" asks Cleo.

The camera zooms in on Peter.

"You're crazy! I don't know the man."

"Oh, brother, what have you just said?"

"Didn't the boss say he would deny him?" asks Simon.

"Yeah, you're right, but I never thought for a second he would."

"Peter... who'd have thought he'd be the one to crack?"

"First Jude then Peter. I wonder which one of us will be next?"

"They won't come after us will they? I mean what use are we?"

"They might, you saw the pictures of Peter, they were after him."

The pictures of Peter disturb Simon and now he fears for John's safety. This is turning into a nightmare, what else could go wrong?

"Any word from the others?" asks Nathaniel.

"John is at the palace, he went with Peter. He says he's gonna stay there and hopes to get inside and see for himself what is happening."

"Who'd have thought John would be the one to risk hanging around the palace?"

"John is tougher than you think. He can handle himself," says Andrew.

Simon has his doubts.

Chapter 35

The armoured escort, with priests and Temple guards, is readied and the transport truck starts up, waiting for its prisoner. With precision timing, Jesus is bundled into the back, the gates opened and the convoy sets off at high speed through the narrow streets.

John had anticipated this might happen and he knows where they are taking Jesus; the barracks. Nothing gets done in Jerusalem without Pilate's approval.

From overheard conversations and several phone calls, John has found out what happened to Peter. Although he is shocked that Peter, of all people could deny that he even knew Jesus, John isn't as surprised as the others will be. There is a tension in the air, a violent undercurrent that John has never felt before in his life. You would think a palace owned and run by priests would be a joyful place. This one has evil lurking in every corner. He can sense it and it gives him the shivers. Only he doesn't feel scared, actually he's too numb to be frightened by all this. It happened so fast, one minute they are having a great time, the next? He does wonder why he hasn't been called out? Part of him, only a tiny part, is disappointed that he hasn't been recognised. Should he have made a bigger impression?

It is one thing guessing what might happen next and another thing staying close to Jesus. Thank goodness for the boss's secret followers. As John stands away from the press and staff, pretending to be on his phone, a mysterious priest dressed all in black discreetly hands him an envelope. The contents give him everything he needs; not only is there a press pass Access All Areas but also a Union pass to enter the barracks. He clips his pass onto his jacket; now he just has to remember he is called Isaac Joshua Kelson.

As the transport truck leaves, the press scramble to their cars in hot pursuit. John, not really wanting to walk, figures he might as well blag a lift. If they guess who he is really is, what's the worst they can do? Write about it!

He confidently gets in a press car with three others. They all stare at him.

"Come on, they are getting away," he points and gets out his phone and pretends to be typing out an email.

"I haven't seen you around. Who are you with?" asks the man sitting next to him.

John looks down at his pass, "Galilee Gazette."

"Thought I recognised you" says the driver, looking in the mirror.

It's only a few minutes to the barracks and the driver isn't far behind the truck convoy when they arrive. They have to stop and show their passes. John waves his in the direction of the soldier while keeping his head low. They are allowed through, park up and all four run to the steps of the Governors quarters. Soldiers have pulled Jesus out of the truck and are just about to take him inside along with some temple guards.

"Wait," says a priest who is accompanying them.

"We are not allowed into an unclean Gentile building, and

especially not during a festival." says another.

A soldier reluctantly goes to inform his commanding officer.

The hairs on the back of John's neck stand on end as he recognises the priests. He hangs back, putting other reporters in his way and luckily he is close enough to hear what is being said.

After a few tense minutes Governor Pilate appears at the top of the steps.

"What do you accuse this man of?" he demands.

"We would not have brought him to you if he had not committed a crime," says a chief priest.

"Then you take him and try him according to your laws."

"We are not allowed to put anyone to death."

Pilate beckons Jesus towards him. "Are you the King of the Jews?"

"Does that question come from you, or have others told you about me?" says Jesus.

"Look, I am not a Jew, your nation and priests delivered you to me. So what is it that you have done?"

"My Kingdom does not belong to this world; if my Kingdom did, then my followers would fight to keep me from being handed over to the Jewish Authorities. No, my Kingdom does not belong here!"

"So, you are a King!"

"You say that I am a King. I was born and came into the world for this one purpose, to speak about the truth. Whoever belongs to the truth listens to me."

"Truth! What is truth?"

Pilate takes Jesus to the priests. "I can't find any reason to condemn this man."

"This man goes around the country teaching and starting a riot amongst the people," the priests insist. "He started in Galilee and now he has come to Judea."

"Not true," says John a bit too loud. Luckily only the reporter standing next to him overhears and smiles.

"Is this man a Galilean?" asks Pilate.

"Yes Governor."

"Then Herod can rule on this matter."

Suddenly there is movement again, the reporters all start to rush back to their cars. John follows, and as he's getting in the car asks, "why Herod?"

"Herod's in Jerusalem for the festival," says one of the reporters.

John has a really bad feeling about this. Herod is a nut-case, he kills people for fun. John thought Pilate hated Herod, or that's what the media says.

"Why is Herod down here anyway, your Galilee not sophisticated enough for him hey Isaac?"

John smiles, he doesn't know the answer, luckily one of the others replies.

"I heard that Herod likes to party at the festivals. Don't be surprised if he's too drunk to do anything."

John hopes that's the case, maybe Jesus has a chance after all.

The cars follow the convoy into Herod's palace. Again guards check their passes before showing the driver where to park. John starts to wish he'd run home from the garden, this is all too much. Here he is so vulnerable, this was a big mistake.

Whereas Pilate was courteous to the priests, meeting them outside, Herod is having none of it. His soldiers take hold of

Jesus and escort him into the palace.

"Well, do you lot refuse to enter a Gentile building like that lot," a soldier says to the group of reporters, pointing to the chief priests.

"Not a chance," says the reporters, accepting the invitation.

John follows, he can't believe he is actually setting foot in Herod's palace. Looking around he doesn't think he's ever seen so much gold, it's everywhere.

He, along with the other press are shown into a grand hall.

"Wow," says John, looking up at the painted ceiling and huge chandelier.

Herod is sitting on a gold throne at the far end of the hall. In front of him stands Jesus, between two soldiers.

"That's far enough," says a soldier, stopping the press from getting closer.

Herod seems to be in a good mood. He laughs as a captain whispers in his ear.

"It is him, oh I was so hoping Pilate had sent me the teacher or should I say King of the Jews?" Herod looks to Jesus, "I have heard much about you. If it had been someone else, I would have been so disappointed. Go on, entertain me. Perhaps you can perform a miracle for me, or say something wonderfully prophetic, like you said about the Temple."

John doesn't think Jesus will play along. He doesn't, he bows his head and stays silent.

"Oh, come now, don't be shy, give me just a small miracle, a glass of water into wine perhaps?"

John is relieved when Herod leans back in his chair and waves everybody away.

"I'm tired of this, send him back to Pilate. I find no evidence to convince me for an execution."

The soldiers take hold of Jesus and turn when Herod shouts, "on second thoughts..."

John's heart misses a beat. Jesus almost survived but by the glint in Herod's eye he's up to something.

"If Jesus thinks he's a ruler, maybe he should dress like a ruler."

The Captain moves forward and is given some instructions after which Jesus is led away through a side door.

"Please be patient, you will have your headlines soon enough," Herod says, addressing the press.

When Jesus returns, the soldiers have draped an old purple robe around him. All the press laugh, John closes his eyes, unable to look. Herod stands and bows.

"Your Majesty."

Chapter 36

"You know where I am if you need anything else."

"Cheers, you've been a big help."

"I'm sorry. He was a good man."

Matthew pulls the hood up on his borrowed coat and making sure he's not being followed, sets off to Zeb's house. Though he's sure this is a bad idea, he will at least check it out. Every passing car, every person he sees could be a potential threat. He puts his hand in a large pocket and finds the cold steel of his Jericho. Sliding the safety off, his old life appears to be starting over. He tries not to think about it, he's not that person anymore. He's seen so much, experienced life that he never thought possible. Yet here he is, walking down a different street in a different town with all too familiar old habits and the same old fears, hoping today is not his day to die. After all those denials, all those promises, it turns out to be true; once a collector always a collector.

Alone in the dark, he thinks about the boss, asking himself why he didn't fight to save him. He just wishes he could have done something, that's the worst part. Peter, of all people was the one to fight. He tries desperately not to think about what could be happening to Jesus. His collector friends suggested Jesus was taken to the palace. He hopes not, for if Annas

employs others like Benjamin then what is in store for Jesus?...
he can't think like this, it is too unbearable.

A car approaches slowly, the early morning sun dazzling
the windscreen, hiding the driver's face from view. His heart
quickens, his trigger finger twitches. There are no parked
cars to protect him this time, no wall to hide behind. He walks
faster and crouching down he takes out the gun. I'll make
myself as difficult to hit as possible. Now the car is right
opposite him, he lifts up his gun and...relaxes. The driver
isn't even looking at him, just fumbling around in the glove
box. The windows are fully up. Slipping the gun away, he
breathes a sigh of relief.

"Come on Matthew, keep it together." He checks to make
sure nobody else is watching. Better not turn up unannounced.
He takes out the burner phone he's been given and calls Alphie,
the one number he knows from memory. No answer, well
it is early. If he's okay, he'll probably be in bed anyway.
Continuing the walk towards Zeb's, he sees the houses are all
large detached, some with long driveways. Zeb bought well,
this is a very good neighbourhood. He wonders if Andrew will
come here in the minibus. If he does he'd have to park it out
of sight. As he gets nearer, he can see no sign of it, that's good.
Before going up the driveway he first walks past and looks
around, checking if the house is being watched. Only when
he's certain it's safe does he go up the driveway, taking out
his own phone and quickly searching for Zeb's home number.
He types it in the new phone and rings.

"It's me," he says after a few seconds silence.

"Me who?"

"James, it's Matt!"

"Oh, Matt, where are you?"

"Outside, let me in."

The door opens and James pulls him in, shutting the door immediately.

"You weren't followed?"

"No."

"Good."

"So where did you go?"

"Some..." Matthew hesitates – "...collectors I know, they helped me out. What about you?"

"I wanted to head straight home to Galilee where it would be safer, but we couldn't leave everybody else, so we came here."

"We?"

"Yeah, me, Phil and Tom."

Matthew goes into the living room to find Philip and Thomas watching the TV news.

"You came straight here, wasn't that a bit risky?"

"We've only just arrived. First we headed to Bethany but there were too many people there. It didn't feel safe," says Philip without taking his eyes off the TV.

"So we came here," adds Thomas.

"What's," he pauses, the words sticking in his throat, "happened to?" Matthew points at the TV, he wants to know what's happened to Jesus but part of him can't bear to hear.

"He is still in the palace, they're saying he is to be tried in the morning."

Matthew sighs.

"Hey, this is what the boss wants, just you wait until he does something big, you'll see," says James.

"He talked about dying, not performing an escape," says Thomas, "and we will be next."

335

That is what Matthew is afraid of. "So where is everyone else?"

"John's at the Palace, he was with Peter," says James.

"Was?"

"Yeah, you not heard? Peter was on the news, he denied knowing the boss."

"What? Peter, never!"

"He did, now nobody knows where he is."

"What about Alphie, he's not answering his phone?"

"With Thaddy at Mary and young Mark's place."

"Hey, Shhh, they are talking about us," Philip turns up the sound on the TV.

A reporter is asking where Jesus' team have gone and questioning whether they will be arrested too.

"John's there, should we warn him we are in danger?"

"It might be too late," says Thomas.

"Don't you think they would have arrested us at Gethsemane?"

"Listen, that's what the news guy is saying."

"The first place they'll look is here, maybe Mary's place is a better bet," Matthew now wishes he'd gone there.

"Let's hope they don't have that place surrounded," says Thomas having the same idea and grabbing his coat.

Chapter 37

"Why, in my own country can't I kill evildoers?"

When Annas finds out that even the insane Herod has dismissed the charges against their prisoner he erupts with rage, shouting and screaming that the whole world is against him.

"How could this be, the Union kill for fun; why now, when there is real danger do they sit on their hands?"

"Sir, Pilate has made his decision," says one of Caiaphas' staff, handing him a piece of paper.

"We've failed!" says Caiaphas, slumping down in his office chair.

Annas takes the paper from him and reads it. Both Governors have failed to find any reason for a conviction, they will agree to a public beating as a warning to others. It can be televised if the Jewish Authorities wish, but afterwards the prisoner will be released.

Jonathan, who has been in the palace all night, comes into the office. "Sir, Pilate's office will give a statement to the press shortly."

"Where is the prisoner now?" demands Annas.

"He is on his way back to Pilate. They will keep him locked up, for now anyway."

"That's it! That's all he gets, a public beating - it will only make him more popular."

"Sir, one more thing, the press are all over me, they want to know why Pilate and now Herod have rejected responsibility?"

"Tell them the truth, that this is all part of the negotiations when dealing with a danger to Jewish society."

Caiaphas, drained from the lack of sleep, looks to his father-in-law for inspiration. A furious Annas paces the floor, desperately trying to come up with a better solution. Another knock on the door....he can't think when he is constantly interrupted.

"Now what?"

"The priests have got back to the barracks and are waiting for your permission to hand Jesus over to Pilate," says a staff member.

Caiaphas nods, "they have my permission, and remind them not to speak to the press. All press questions must be directed through the High Priest's office."

Still pacing up and down, Annas tries to focus. He hates this arm's length politics, you can't read somebody via phone calls and emails. What is Pilate really thinking? An idea flickers in his head, he breathes slowly. Maybe? What if?

"That's it! Oh, I love my genius."

* * *

An unmarked car pulls up next to the staff entrance of the palace. Jonathan has a quick glance, checking to make sure there is nobody watching, before they both get into the back. At the gate the darkened windows hide them from the press and onlookers. People give little notice to a staff car leaving, they've been coming and going all morning. They are more concerned with finding out about the news conference Annas had arranged for Caiaphas, which has been timed to coincide with their departure.

It is the same at the barracks, the barrier swings open and the driver speeds into the base.

With Jesus now locked up inside, the priests have stayed, congregating by the steps to Pilate's quarters. They have been joined by some press and a solitary TV camera crew, plus a few people lucky enough to have been let in by the Union soldiers. The car goes unnoticed as it makes its way to an entrance on the other side of the main building.

As an ex-High Priest Annas knows he shouldn't set foot in the barracks and at no point must the priests out front find out about this. The meeting takes place in an oak-panelled, conference room that was once the dining hall for the first commanding officers of the barracks. Military campaign banners, photos, and crests of every company ever to be stationed here hang on the walls. In the middle of the room are a large oak table and chairs. Annas still doesn't know exactly what he is to say to Pilate. He hopes to persuade him to reconsider his verdict, but how?

Pilate arrives and Jonathan leaves the two alone, positioning himself outside the door.

"Shalom Annas," says Pilate.

"Shalom."

"I hear Caiaphas is to give a press conference, will it be to pre-empt my decision?"

"It will hopefully be to announce an execution."

"Only if you have another you want killing."

339

Annas does his best to convince Pilate of Jesus' crimes: the blasphemy, the danger of an uprising, the threat to the Governors power, all to no avail. Time is ticking and Caiaphas is going to speak shortly. He will appear to be positive but waffle on about how these things take time - but if Pilate can't be turned it will make them all look very foolish.

"Look, I'll be happy to give you a show-piece, just pick another offender."

Annas looks into Pilates eyes. The eyes can reveal a lot about a person, as can the body language. Being alongside his adversary gives his senses a boost, under pressure is when he works best. This time is no exception; looking into Pilate's eyes, the birth of an idea takes shape in Annas' mind. Another criminal of course! In all the furore, he had forgotten tradition, the one thing that he can use to his advantage. There is a knock at the door and a commanding officer enters. He has with him a photograph, "for your amusement Sir, from Herod."

He hands Pilate a picture of Jesus dressed in the Kingly robe.

"That Herod, mad and genius all rolled into one," Pilate laughs.

Annas looks at the photo.

"Not much of a King," observes Pilate.

The picture sends Annas' thoughts into overdrive, his idea becomes bigger and better all the time.

"Isn't it custom to release a prisoner during the festival," he says.

"Of course, do you want to make it look like the release is your idea?"

"Oh no, I still want my execution. There are crucifixions this morning, are there not?"

"Yes, as always at festival time."

"Well, what if we were to let the public decide who to kill this Passover. Say, if the people agree with you, that the teacher has done no wrong, then he will be released. On the other hand, if he loses the popular vote..."

Pilate leans back in his chair and considers it for a minute and Annas knows he's won. This was a battle of minds and face to face he wins every time. Annas remembers when Pilate took over, his main objective was to win the hearts and minds of the people. If this got out that he refused them a vote, it would take ages to get their trust back. It could even cost him his job.

"Fine, have your vote," Pilate shrugs.

Jonathan rings Caiaphas as he and Annas travel back to the palace.

"We will get our execution, after a public vote. The name of the other criminal is still to be confirmed."

Caiaphas was just about to face the cameras in the courtyard after stalling them as long as he could, when he heard the good news. A quick statement was written and a press officer sent out to give it. They have to act fast.

* * *

Once Annas and Jonathan arrive back Caiaphas calls his staff together for a briefing. There is a lot to do, but very little time. At 9.00 am the Passover crucifixions start as planned, with or without Jesus. Timing is crucial. He explains the plan that Annas has conceived. A vote, loaded in their favour, two contestants – one wins his freedom, the other is crucified. This isn't the first time the Temple has let the people vote, so all the technical framework is already in place. The phone numbers will be charged at premium rates, naturally. It would have been better if the lines could be open longer, giving more people the chance to vote; that would bring in more money. But the situation is unique, an hour is all they can afford, time-wise.

"On the Temple website there is currently a poll as to whether the teacher is a fraud. We can edit it to ask who they want to save?" says a member of staff.

"Good, get the phone lines up and running. As long as people hear the answerphone message telling them their vote has been counted, they will believe it has!" Annas is in a jubilant mood.

Speech writers scribble away on a statement for Caiaphas to read out to the press. He looks over their work.

"I am not saying that!"

He picks up the statement and rips the top off the sheet of paper.

"This is fine, someone else will have to explain the procedure. The Passover crucifixions start as usual at 9.00 am, so if we are to make this happen we need to act fast," says Caiaphas, before leaving to talk to the press.

"Pilate's office staff have just sent over the details of the other criminal, a Jesus Barabbas," says a staff member. "Ha, ha, and they've sent over a picture of the Nazarene to use, look."

Annas looks at the photo, Jesus looks a lot different to when he last saw him. The 31st have certainly been enjoying themselves. For not only is he wearing the old purple robe but also a crown made out of razor wire.

"Get that picture circulated to the press. That's the one I

want everybody to see."

"Sir, we also have this, I'm not sure if helps or hinders. A camera crew has recorded footage of the prisoners. Pilate thought it so amusing he had it uploaded to the internet."

The video shows the soldiers from the 31st battalion, who will be in charge of the crucifixions, heading down to the cells in the barracks. In command of the soldiers is Captain Roberto. It also shows the three men who are to be executed this Passover. Jesus Barabbas, the leader of a group of freedom fighters, one of his men and a thief. Captain Roberto orders the prison guards to open the cell of Barabbas and two of his men drag the handcuffed prisoner out. Barabbas snarls at the guards. He tries to fight the soldiers, shouting, "Israel forever" and "Death to the Union."

"A true patriot, who wouldn't vote for him?" says Annas.

The next clip shows Jesus, wearing the robe and crown, praying. He is dragged out of his cell and made to walk up and down, blood running down his face as the wire cuts into his flesh. The soldiers laugh and taunt him.

"Your Majesty."

"All hail, the King of the Jews."

While Annas finds it amusing and is pleased with how well this is going, he is also repulsed at the thought that this man claims to be the Christ.

"What are you waiting for, this is gold. Get it to the press, quickly."

Chapter 38

The phone lines are now open. Special Passover crucifixion. Have your say on who lives and who dies. Vote now.

Film of Barabbas and Jesus is shown. Reporters explain what has gone on during the night. On every channel experts do their best to clarify the situation. The priests queue up to speak to the media, giving their reasons why it should be the teacher who is crucified. They now have only one hour to convince as many people to vote for Barabbas.

"Come on, keep dialling," says James, frantically voting for Jesus.

Mary's house has become the focal point for a large number of Jesus' followers. The twelve, with the exceptions of Jude and John are all here. All over the country, Jesus' followers are desperately voting, in the hope of saving him.

"You do know how much this is costing don't you?" Thomas doesn't share James' enthusiasm.

"What's money when we can help free the boss."

"It's all pointless, the boss talked about dying, he didn't talk about us voting to save him!"

"What else can we do?" asks Thaddy.

"Oh no! I've run out of credit," says James.

"The hour is almost up anyway, what does the news say

about it?" asks Philip.

"It says it's too close to call," replies Matthew.

"Oh, surprise, surprise, more money for the priests," moans Thomas.

Peter, though back with friends, is alone in his thoughts. He had walked around for hours then rung Ruth and they had talked. How he wished he could be with her. She begged him to leave the city, drive, do anything to get back to her side, but he couldn't, he wouldn't leave the others, even after what he's done. "Then go to them, they will understand" she had said. Ruth was right, of course, for they were all scared and afraid. If any of them had been accused, each would have done the same, well that's what they all told him when he eventually found them. It's probably what they thought he needed to hear, only they didn't do it, he did and he knows it was the worst thing he's done in his whole life. The look on Jesus' face will haunt him forever. While the others spend their time watching the news, he can't bear seeing the images of Jesus. What they are doing to him makes his heart bleed. Why does it have to be like this?

As Peter is making his fifth cup of coffee since he arrived, John slips in through the back door.

"You're not exactly hard to find?" he says, surprising Peter.

Peter tries to smile, but he can't. John gives him a pat on his shoulder.

"We need to prepare for the worst," he says going into the living room and beckoning Peter to follow.

Mary, Mark's mother spots him first and gives him a half smile, "it's not over yet, he can still win."

John shakes his head, "no, he can't."

She bursts into tears and has to be comforted by a friend,

who glares at John for being so insensitive. Peter stands in the doorway as John goes over to Jesus' mother. She puts her arms out and he hugs her. Peter can't hear what John says to her, but does hear her response, "it's all Gods' plan, my boy won't disappoint you," tears pour down her face.

Peter has to turn away, he can't bear to look her in the eye. John is just about to speak when Thaddy turns up the TV.

"Shhh, everybody, the results are about to be announced."

The ticker is now showing *polls have closed, the results are being counted.*

A hush fills the house as all of them are glued to every TV, even the one in the kitchen. John squeezes past Peter and goes to put the kettle on. Peter agrees with John and Thomas that the result is a forgone conclusion, though he dare not say so. There is a part of him that still hopes Jesus will win.

"We now go live to the steps of the Governor's House at the Union barracks," says the TV anchor.

Standing on the steps are Pilate, three chief priests and several soldiers. The parade ground is full, with TV crews, Press and over a thousand people. A camera pans the crowd; in the background soldiers can be seen guarding its perimeter.

Pilate steps towards a microphone and is handed a white envelope.

"The result of the people's vote is as follows." He opens the envelope, shaking his head when he sees the result for himself.

"Jesus of Nazareth...33%. Jesus Barabbas 67%, I declare the winner is...Barabbas."

The crowd cheers. Streamers shoot into the air. The camera cuts to Annas and Caiaphas at the palace. Annas, aware that the cameras are on him, looks gracious and merely claps.

Pilate announces: "By the power vested in me by the Union of Nations, I declare that Jesus Barabbas is a free man. And to you, people of Israel, I hand over the King of the Jews, whom I believe to be innocent, to do with as you wish."

The crowd cheer. Pilate heads back inside shaking his head, clearly unhappy. The Priests shake hands, congratulating each other.

"No."

"It was fixed."

"Shit, shit, shit."

The hush now descends into cries of despair. John makes himself a coffee. Jesus' mother cries, sobbing on the shoulders of her friends.

The TV company, knowing that the crucifixions take place in only a few hours, are already showing adverts moments after the result. Pictures of Jesus, dressed as the King are shown, with a deep voice saying...

"*Live crucifixions, the nastiest death ever invented. Watch the self-proclaimed Son of God die.*

He saved others, can he save himself? Tickets are still available."

"Someone turn that off," shouts Peter.

John starts to speak, but hesitates, "What is it John? What's wrong?" asks Andrew.

"It's about Jude."

"Oh, is that all? Thought it was important," says Simon, turning away.

"Don't speak to me about him," says Thaddy.

Peter stays quiet, thinking about his own failings.

"He can go and jump off the city wall as far as I'm concerned," says James.

"He might have done!" says John.

"Good," says Thomas.

"Look, he is still one of us, at least we should see where he is, for his parents' sake at least," says John.

"How do you know this?" asks Matthew.

"Nicodemus told me. When Jesus was taken to Pilate, you know, when the authorities were trying to get Pilate to sentence him. Jude went into the Temple and threw down the money they'd given him."

"Bastard."

"Traitor."

"Tosser."

"Why should we do anything? He's not our problem now," says Simon.

"I'd rather go looking for him, than sit cooped up here, maybe give him some of our justice, if you know what I mean," says Matthew.

"I agree," says Alphie.

"Me too, I need to get out, do something, anything, take my frustration out on that traitor," says Thaddy.

"At least if we find him we can tell him how we feel," says Philip.

Andrew doesn't look convinced.

"We're not going to kill him, just hurt him a little," says James, all for the idea.

"And who's next, me maybe."

"Come on Pete, that's different?" says Nathaniel.

"How, aren't I a traitor as much as Jude?"

They all try to assure him that what he did was different. Peter isn't convinced, the guilt he feels is too strong.

In the end all the lads agree to go and after some persuasion even young Mark is allowed to join them. They all pile into the minibus.

"Nicodemus told me Jude was seen heading south of the city and a policeman later reported someone tall and broad shouldered, wearing a blue top was seen acting strangely," says John.

"That could be anyone?" Philip stares at John.

John shrugs. "It fits Jude's description and he was wearing blue, I think."

Andrew drives into the Hinnom Valley. The area is a small business enterprise district and quiet during festival time. He drives up and down and they all look out for Jude.

"This is stupid," says Philip, "why would he be round here?"

They all agree, so Andrew drives further out of the city, pulls up and they all pile out of the minibus and search on foot. After a fruitless search they are just about to give up and go back...

"Try him," says Alphie, pointing to a man walking by on the other side of the road.

"Really?" asks John.

"Yeah, he crossed over when he saw us."

"I'm not surprised, look at us!" Simon points out.

"Excuse me," Nathaniel runs over, "Have you seen this man?" Nathaniel shows him a picture of Jude from his phone. The man shakes his head and continues walking. Nathaniel shrugs.

"You were too nice," shouts Alphie. Turning to the others he says, "the man clearly knows something, he looks scared. Matt would have gotten to know everything, from what he had for breakfast, his greatest failing and even his bank PIN number."

They all look at Matthew, who doesn't seem too thrilled at Alphie for pointing that out.

"Well," says Simon.

"Well what?" answers Matthew.

"Well go on, we need to know if he's seen Jude!" says an impatient James.

Matthew strolls across the road. This should be interesting, thinks Peter following. Everyone has the same idea, they all join him.

"Old man," says Matthew, "I don't want to be messed about with, you gonna tell me what you know?"

Matthew puts his hand around the back of the man's neck, forcing him to look at his gun.

"I don't need to use this do I?"

The man shakes his head.

"Good, now take a look at the picture again." Nathaniel holds up his camera.

Matthew stares into the man's eyes.

"Yeah, he's seen him."

Trembling the man points towards the end of the road.

"It could be the man I saw earlier, sat on a wall, down by the fields."

"Wasn't so hard was it grandad?" Matthew pats him on the side of his face.

They all pile back into the minibus and head down towards the fields.

"He'll have long gone by now, this is pointless," moans Thomas.

As Andrew approaches the fields Peter is the first to spot a police car.

"Oh great, please tell me that man hasn't set us up," says Thaddy.

"Should I keep driving?"

"Look at that van, it's a crime scene van," says young Mark.

"Well spotted," says Thaddy, ruffling the young lad's hair.

Andrew stops and they all get out and slowly walk over. The solitary police officer puts his hand up to stop them coming near. He has taped off the area where a crime scene officer is taking photos of a body hung from a tree.

"Jude!"

"It can't be?" says Thaddy.

"It looks like him," says Simon.

Andrew covers his mouth and turns away. He also tries in vain to stop young Mark from seeing the body.

"Come on lads, this is a crime scene, please don't come any closer," says the officer.

"We are looking for somebody, do you know who that is yet?" asks Matthew.

"It's Jude, I can tell," says Philip.

"It is."

"Oh no," says John.

The crime scene officer overhears and comes over.

"You say you recognise the body, who do *you* think it is?"

"Jude Iscariot," says Simon.

"And how do you know the victim."

"He was in our team," says James.

"Oh, right, I recognise you lot, shouldn't you be watching your boss die?"

Simon goes for his gun only for John to stop him.

"It's OK," says John to Simon and the officers.

"You gonna cut him down, or just leave him hanging?" asks

Nathaniel.

The crime scene officer goes back to Jude's body. The police officer takes out his notepad, and asks for details of Jude's last known whereabouts and any information as to how this might have happened.

"Maybe you should try asking at the Temple and charge them with assisting his death," James suggests.

"Have you informed his family yet?" asks Nathaniel.

"How do you tell them something like this?" James says looking at Matthew.

"The police have people trained for it."

On the way back to Mary's, the lads question whether they should grieve for Jude. He was their friend, but in betraying Jesus he had betrayed them also.

"It's a selfish way to go. What about his family?" says James.

"Maybe he realised what he did was wrong," says Andrew.

"I bet he thought that the boss would do something! I know I did. If the boss wanted to, he could have easily stopped them," says Alphie.

"Then why didn't he?" asks Simon.

No one has an answer.

Chapter 39

The Rolls Royce Phantom slowly makes its way through the expectant crowd and pulls up at the players and VIPs entrance of Calvary Stadium, home to Jerusalem FC. Temple guards including Theo and Benjamin jump out of accompanying cars and form a protective barrier for Annas and Jonathan.

"Morning sir, Looks like its gonna be a big crowd today," says a steward.

Annas has no time for chit chat, though he does hear Jonathan behind him mention something about football attendance.

"Sorry sir, but the lift isn't working, we'll have to take the stairs," says Theo.

"It's time they tore this place down," says Annas.

"Maybe Jesus could rebuild it in three days," says Benjamin.

The VIP entrance to the executive boxes is neglected with worn carpets and peeling paint. Pictures of former players are on the walls, some in black and white. Annas doesn't recognise any of them, he doesn't care for football or any sport come to think of it - it's a waste of passion. If everybody spent as much time and effort visiting the Temple, they would be a lot happier and he a lot richer.

At the top of the stairs another steward eagerly awaits. He

smiles and bows as Annas approaches.

"Good morning sir, your presence is a great honour."

Annas nods his head.

"Please allow me to show you to your box, we have provided a fine selection of food and drink for your enjoyment."

"I thought this place was going to be knocked down," remarks Theo.

"There are plans for a new sixty thousand seat stadium."

"I've heard that before," says Benjamin.

They are shown into their box where some priests are already waiting.

"Sir," they bow.

"A great day, gentleman."

The stadium, on Calvary Hill, is horseshoe shaped, with the open end overlooking the new city below. A stage has been erected and technicians are at work lighting three steel poles used for the crucifixions. Annas looks down on the field, covered in rows of seats. The smell of hot dogs and onions permeates the box. It seems the old stadium has a new purpose; instead of celebrating goals it now celebrates death.

To one side of the stage a large screen has been erected and camera crews hurriedly set up. Music plays from the stadium loudspeakers and drowns out a TV presenter doing a piece to camera. Annoyed he stops, looks around, then composes himself ready for another take. The seats are starting to fill up, whole families are here for the day out. A sign with Barabbas' name on is being taken down.

Annas smiles to himself, this excitement, this anticipation must be how others feel when their team is playing on cup final day. Only he knows in advance what the result will be.

"Sir," says Jonathan, "would you care for champagne?"

"Of course," he turns to the priests, "to our success."

While they wait for the start, priests from other boxes come and make their presence known. All are in a joyful mood.

"May I ask when the High Priest will join us this glorious morning?" says one.

"Caiaphas has duties to attend, but I'm assured he will find time to watch a little on TV."

Annas sips his champagne and tastes some exquisite caviar. He notices the priest and council member Joseph Arimathea passing by along the corridor between boxes. He is surprised Joseph is in attendance, being such a keen fan of the Nazarene.

"Jonathan, wasn't that council member Arimathea, I saw pass."

"Yes sir."

"He wouldn't insult me by not stopping to offer congratulations this morning would he?"

"No sir, an oversight, surely."

Jonathan disappears and returns with Joseph.

"Council member Arimathea, welcome."

"Annas."

The usual smile and cheerful persona of Joseph is lacking this morning, he looks subdued and thoughtful. He quite clearly wants no part of this, yet here he is. Maybe expecting a miracle from his man.

"Please watch with me. Jonathan, champagne for our guest."

Joseph waves the champagne away but does stay in the box, at the back. Annas leaves him be, as his attention is taken by a presenter appearing on stage.

"I think it's about to begin," says a priest excitedly.

A hush descends on the now full stadium. Children in the

crowd cheer him and he waves back at them. He has a hand held microphone and addresses the crowd.

"Welcome everybody."

There is loud applause; he smiles and moves around the stage waiting for silence.

"We go live to the nation in five minutes, so when we do, I want you to make as much noise as possible."

Everyone claps and cheers, and he gives a thumbs up. There is some last minute scurrying around by stage hands as the time counts down to nine o'clock. The presenter fidgets a little, waiting for his cue.

5,4,3,2,1...

"Welcome to the crucifixion special, live from Cal..va..ry Stadium, Jerusalem."

On cue the crowd bursts into cheering and clapping.

"What a line up we have for you this Passover. We have music from the sensational Elizabeth, runner-up on Israeli pop factor and a juggling act that is truly amazing. But I know most of you are here today for one reason only..." he pauses, looking down away from the camera, before turning back with a smile on his face. "He saved others, can he save himself? Yes, today watch the crucifixion of Je...sus, of Nazareth."

Music starts, the presenter moves off stage, and the first act appears. Five performers, who juggle, do acrobatics and their show-stopping finale, juggling burning crosses.

When they finish and have received generous applause the presenter reappears.

"Wasn't that amazing, what a dangerous finale, wouldn't want anyone to get hurt though."

"Come on, we aren't here to see this," says Theo from the back of the room.

"Patience my guard, patience, why don't you listen to the lovely Elizabeth."

"Yeah, I know you have all her albums," says Benjamin.

Elizabeth belts out a medley of sentimental love songs. including *stand by your man*, *angels* and *love changes everything*. When she has finished the crowd gives her a sympathetic round of applause and the presenter comes back on stage. He stands by, waiting for his cue.

Annas takes a deep breath. He turns to Joseph. "Please, join us for a better view."

Joseph hesitantly comes forward as the presenter walks back on stage.

"Ladies and Gentlemen, are you ready for the main event?" he says over lots of shouting and clapping.

Next to the stage are a few rows of reserved seats. These are for family and friends of the criminals.

"First we have two of the most violent men in the country, so dangerous it took the whole of the Union army to catch them." Boos ring out at the mention of the Union.

The family and friends of the two men are shown to their seats.

"Please welcome on stage David Sychar and Samuel Ben Ammi."

Music starts playing and the crowd cheers as the men are led out by soldiers of the 31st. They are carrying their own cross beams and struggle with the weight, dropping them once on stage. A soldier pushes first Sychar and then Ben Ammi to the floor. The whole stadium falls silent. Another soldier aligns them into position and then nails their hands to the wooden cross beams, using a heavy duty nail gun. The sound echo's around the stadium. Sychar cries out in pain and the crowd wince. Then they are put into a crane, which rises high, stopping near the top of each steel pole. The wooden beams are then fixed to the poles. The last thing is their feet. They are perched on a detachable piece of wood, which is itself fixed onto the poles. The feet are then nailed to the wood. Both men cry out in pain.

"Finally, the one some say is the Son of God, while others claim he is the promised Messiah. But you and I know him as... the magician. He saved others, can he save himself? Jesus... of... Nazareth."

Again the music starts.

Some of the crowd stand for a better look. Jesus appears, surrounded by soldiers.

Next to Annas, Joseph recoils when he sees Jesus. His body is red with blood from the lacerations caused by the whip and the beatings. He is still wearing the razor wire crown. Blood runs down his face, he can't wipe it off because he is carrying the heavy wooden cross beam. He stumbles, weak from the punishment he has taken. Unable to carry the beam he drops to the ground. A soldier goes to the crowd and chooses someone to help. The man lifts the wooden beam and carries it onto the stage. Once on the stage he puts it down and waves to the crowd. The presenter comes over to him, asks him his name and where he is from.

"Give a big hand to Simon from Cyrene."

Everybody claps, Simon waves again, before going back to his seat.

While Jesus is being nailed onto the beam, his family and friends are shown to their seats.

"Recognise anyone?"

Joseph doesn't answer.

"Looks like his team have deserted him," says Benjamin.

"Of course they did," sneers Annas.

Jesus is hoisted up on to the middle steel pole, but before the crane is lowered the soldier sticks a sign above Jesus' head.

The cameras zoom in, it reads: Jesus of Nazareth, King of the Jews.

The priests in the boxes turn to their TV's for a better view and are the first in the stadium to be able to see the sign. They don't like it, objecting to the reference King of the Jews. Annas shouts to Jonathan.

"Get me the Governor!"

Jonathan is already on it, and brings his phone over.

"Pilate sir."

"What is this? King of the Jews is blasphemous."

Pilate tells him the sign stays and Annas, who is not in a position to argue, doesn't take it further, though it's not an image he likes. "He is no King of mine."

"Sir, listen to the crowd, on the TV it's much clearer," Jonathan says.

Theo turns the sound up on the TV at the back of the box. Some of the crowd have started shouting at Jesus.

"I thought you were the one, the Messiah, you made me look stupid."

"If you are the Christ come down from there and I will believe you."

"You healed others, heal yourself." That gets some laughs.

"You're a fraud, you deserve to rot."

Even Sychar and Ben Ammi hurl insults towards Jesus.

"You came in peace, yet look what it got you," says Samuel Ben Ammi.

"I tried to destroy the Union, what did you do? Nothing,"

says Sychar.

The mood in the box is joviality, the priests clink their glasses. "He trusts in God, well let God save him now," says a priest.

"Today gentlemen, even sons of God, hang dying at our feet," says Annas, to laughter.

Killing by crucifixion takes a long time, it's one of the reasons the Union likes it so much, but it does make for a rather boring spectacle after a while. Once they've seen the nails go in and watched the agony, people get up, stretch their legs, get something to eat. They are allowed to approach the stage and see close up the brutal savagery of a crucifixion.

"So what do you think of your Christ now?" Annas asks Joseph.

Some of the priests leave, going back to their work in the Temple. For Annas, this is his first live event and he has arranged meetings to take place in the middle hours. Jonathan also has papers for him to sign and reports to read. He looks down at the stage from time to time to see if there is anything happening.

"We must do something about the Unions interference at our festivals," says a priest.

"I am fully aware of the problems we face and I assure you I am working hard on the country's behalf," says Annas.

As they talk all the lights go out and they are plunged into darkness.

"Oh, this useless stadium," says one priest.

Emergency lighting flickers on in the executive boxes, but down below the crowd is left in complete darkness.

"This isn't the stadium! We still have power, it's the sky, it's gone dark," says Theo rushing into the box.

"What is happening?"

"It appears to be nationwide sir," Jonathan says.

"An eclipse!" suggests a guard.

"Nonsense, there are no such events due.

"Then what has just happened?"

People in the crowd take out lighters or mobile phones.

The presenter is quickly escorted on stage.

"Please, don't panic, everything is OK. It appears the whole country is suffering an eclipse, please stay calm," he says.

A quick thinking lighting technician sets up more spotlights pointing towards the stage. In all the darkness the only thing shining out across all TV networks is the picture of the three crosses.

"Sir, would you like me to arrange transport back to the Temple?" says Jonathan.

"Why the rush Jonathan, afraid of the dark?"

"I thought you..."

"Sir," says Theo stopping Jonathan in mid-sentence, a hand covering his ear as he listens to reports coming from his earpiece. "I advise that we stay here. There is panic on the streets."

Benjamin stands at the door and checks the corridor. "Status update," he says into his mic. After a few seconds he puts his thumb up. "The stadium is secure, Sir."

"Then we all stay." says Annas, "Though I do wish to have better lighting," he says pointing up at the ceiling.

"I'm on it Sir." Jonathan scurries off.

* * *

After three hours of darkness and the light-bulb that Jonathan had procured starting to flicker Annas has had enough. Theo and Benjamin are now confident of a safe journey back to the Palace so there is no need to stay here any longer.

They are just about to leave when a priest points to the TV. "Listen, Jesus is talking. He's asked for a drink."

A soldier sticks a sponge soaked in cheap sour wine onto a long pole, and holds it up to Jesus' lips.

"My God, My God, why have you abandoned me," cries Jesus in a loud voice.

"He does not look like he'll last much longer," says a priest.

"Father into your hands I commit my spirit." Jesus bows his head. "It is finished."

At that moment lightning flashes across the sky followed by loud thunder. The whole stadium begins to shake like the earth is opening up. The spotlights pointing at the stage smash into pieces. Annas is knocked to the floor, unable to get up as the box shakes and pieces of ceiling and plasterboard fall on top of him. People scream in terror as the earthquake shakes the whole place. Bits of the stadium crash down. The window of the box cracks and smashes onto the floor. Theo helps Annas to his feet and ushers him to the door.

"We have to get out of here, now."

They have only reached the corridor when the shaking stops. Annas pulls away from Theo.

"Everybody alright?" shouts Benjamin, looking at Annas and Jonathan.

"We appear to be unharmed," says Annas dusting himself off.

"What about the criminals?" asks a priest.

Yes what about them? Annas also wants to know. Are they still upright, have the beams held? He climbs over debris from the ceiling and back into the box looking out at the stage. He is relieved to see all three crosses standing and the stadium is once again in full sunshine. An eerie calm descends, the only sound is the voice of Captain Roberto, standing at the foot of Jesus' cross.

"You really were the Son of God," his words reverberate around the stadium.

"They're checking to see if Jesus is dead," a priest points out soldiers at the cross; one stabs a spear into Jesus' side - blood and water seep out of the body. The soldier nods back to his officer.

They begin checking the two criminals.

Annas checks himself for any cuts from the broken glass. He is surprised to find himself without a scratch.

"I told you this place should be torn down, it's unsafe," he says.

"Sir, Captain Roberto reports that Jesus has died," says Jonathan on his phone.

"Good," snaps Annas.

Annas can feel the presence of Joseph Arimathea before he appears at the door.

"Your friend is dead, what do you want?" he says without turning around.

"Pilate has granted my appeal to release the body to me, once his Commanding Officer has signed the death certificate. I am to place it in my family tomb, that has so far remained empty, thanks be to God."

Annas remains silent.

"You are quite welcome to view the body before it is buried."

Annas waves him away.

As Joseph leaves, another priest hurries into the box. "Sir,

363

I have the most distressing news."

Chapter 40

Simon knew when Jesus died; his world went dark. Way before he received a text from John he knew it was all over, the darkness, the earthquake. Part of him has died too.

It may have been by Union soldiers, but it is Israeli hands that are covered in blood.

As he sits in a dark corner of a dark bar all he can see is the bottle of Hennessey in front of him. How will he recover? He gave up everything to be one of the twelve. He knows how much he has changed, the things he has seen and done; people he now hangs out with all because of one man and now that man has died in front of a watching world and he could do nothing about it.

* * *

Thaddy gets up from the sofa to make a drink. He had been trying not to watch the news, but in the darkness he put the TV on to see what was happening. He hoped that maybe the boss had done something, come down from the cross, anything! While he's sure the 'quake wasn't a coincidence, there is still no miracle, the boss is still dead and the journey is all but finished. All he can think about is the events of the last few years. All he saw, the fun they'd had; the words the boss spoke so convincingly of the new Kingdom. Thinking back on it, he does remember the sadness, the warnings that the boss gave. He mentioned death often. Thaddy wonders what he'll do next, how he'll get over it all, start something new. He can't help thinking that Jude died because he couldn't bear to be a nobody. He wanted the Kingdom, the power and the glory. He couldn't have it and it killed him. What does *he* want? He wants the boss to return, that's all he wants.

* * *

Andrew, after seeing his brother so desperately sad, and Ruth unable to get away from Capernaum until they'd arranged Jesus' burial, had promised her that he would look after **Peter**. If that meant not going with John and the others to the stadium, fine. He didn't really want to go, he couldn't bear to see Jesus die. The best way for them to get through it was to do what they always did - fish. Not so easy in the city, so Andrew drove the bus to Joppa on the coast to hire a boat and fishing tackle. They sailed out into the vast Mediterranean sea, and cast off. They didn't talk much, couldn't put their feelings into words; if they did speak it was about the catch, the boat, the wind. Occasionally Peter would remember something Jesus did, or said and they would both smile. This is what they've always done when things got bad: the day their parents died, the loss of the business, however and wherever they were, the thing the boys did was fish. They can't remember why when the going gets tough they go fishing. Peter thinks their dad used to do it when they were young, then as they grew up, he'd take them with him, giving mum some much needed time alone.

* * *

Matthew walked up the Mount of Olives. Andrew had offered a lift to anyone who wanted to go to the coast, but only Peter had gone along. Matthew reckoned he could be out all day, returning when it was all over. Hopefully not meeting nor seeing anyone, just being alone. He bought a bottle of whisky with the last of his money and set off, only to find many people walking up the mount. The views over the city were incredible and there were lots of families and pilgrims making the journey. There are cafés along the road and they were all busy. He sat in one, ordered a coffee and put a drop of whisky in it. The waitress saw him do it, but the look on his face told her to leave him alone. He sat listening to people's conversations; they were all talking about the same thing, the crucifixion. Though opinions were mixed as to who Jesus was, most had thought he shouldn't have lost the vote, but from the sound of it nobody actually voted. By the time the darkness came he had left the café and gone to sit alone on the hillside contemplating. He had been staring at the only bit of the stadium he could see from his vantage point when the sun vanished. He looked at his watch, thinking he must have lost track of time. It showed midday, yet it was dark. He stayed on the hill, watching the lights flicker on as if it was night time, drinking his whisky straight from the bottle. Where he was on the mountain it was complete darkness, there were no street lights, with only the occasional car headlights glinting from the nearby road. He thought it would last only a short while, so he didn't move, but after two hours he began to feel the cold and so carefully found his way back to the warm café. There he met **Philip**, who had stayed at Mary and Mark's house, but had found it too difficult to watch it all unfold on the TV so he'd left during the darkness to look at the view. He was sitting drinking coffee when the earthquake started and thought the mountain was going to split open and erupt.

* * *

James had gone back to his parents' city house, calling first at the supermarket and buying a pack of lager. At nine am he opened his first can. He played pool, played on his old playstation and drank. He did anything but think about what was happening to Jesus. If he started to, he got all emotional and he couldn't bear it. He wasn't like his brother, who could cry easily or talk things over. He needed to keep things bottled up. If he were to cry, it would be only after drinking his inhibitions away.

* * *

Thomas went and hid from the world. They had been up most of the night and he was so tired. He went back to the house with James and had gone straight to bed. He tried to sleep, hoping that when he awoke the boss would have saved himself, that everything would be alright again.

* * *

Alphie stayed at Mary and Mark's with some other followers. He watched the news, only getting up to make a drink or go to the toilet. He sat thinking, sometimes shouting at the TV. He, out of all the lads was the most angry, the others seemed sad, disappointed. He was mad, mad at the world and mad at Jesus for allowing it to happen. Once the anger had all drained away he needed comforting and Mary and the others were there for support.

* * *

Nathaniel argued with himself and anyone in Marys and Mark's home who would listen. How could it all end like this? Why after all they have done and seen, would Jesus just let it happen? He searched some scriptures but he could barely see the words for his tears. In the end he went outside and sat in the garden – alone. His memories of the last two years tormenting his mind.

* * *

John was the only one of the lads to go to Calvary. He saw the brutality and the pain that Jesus endured. He listened to the derision and the jeers. He watched his boss, his friend, his Christ, die. He held Mary, Jesus' mum and he stayed until the very end. When it was all over he sent all the lads a text. It read: *It is finished.*

Maybe he was holding out, hoping for something, but he couldn't let him go. When Jesus was taken down from the cross and the Governor released the body to Joseph, he asked to go along. It was only a short journey away from the stadium and round the old wall to Joseph's tomb. As a council member and very rich man, Joseph had no ordinary burial place. It is an exclusive area, the rich and famous all want to be buried here and it is where the High Priests and other council members are laid to rest. The price of a tomb here makes it one of the most expensive addresses in the city. They are cut out of the side of the hill, and the stone slabs the bodies lie on are carved by the best in the business. The door, the same design as bank vaults, is twelve inches of reinforced concrete, covered in high-grade steel.

While Joseph took care of the body and made arrangements with Jesus' mother for the burial, Nicodemus had bought the spices and linen for the embalming. The cemetery has a small morgue, where bodies can be prepared, before being placed in the tombs. Joseph and Nicodemus, these two prominent highly respected men, embalm Jesus' body themselves. They place the mixture of aloe, spices and myrrh along the lengths of the linen and carefully wrap it around Jesus' body. His mother, John, Mary Mag and some others watch as the two council members then move the body to the tomb. When they arrive, four Temple guards are waiting. It was getting late and the Sabbath was about to start so Joseph and Nicodemus tenderly lay the body on a stone slab and watch as the guards close the heavy door and lock it - steel bolts sliding into place with satisfying clunks.

The Sabbath starts at sundown on Friday and finishes at sundown on Saturday, so once the tomb is sealed nothing can be done to arrange the funeral until Sunday morning at the earliest. John takes Jesus' mother to Mary and Mark's home, and seeing that she will be well cared for, leaves to go to his parents' city home. He walks all the way, tears pouring down his face. Once home he takes a beer out of the fridge and sits in the living room. James is lying on the floor, a DVD playing, but he isn't really watching, just staring, a glazed look in his eyes, born out of beer and grief.

Chapter 41

John wakes up with a jolt, in the living room! He must have fallen asleep. Around him lie several empty beer cans.

"Sorry, did I wake you?" says Andrew.

John rubs his eyes and looks at his watch; it shows 8:30 am.

"It's fine."

"You hungry? I'm cooking some fish."

John thinks for a moment, trying to remember the last time he ate. His stomach makes a growling noise.

"Yeah, that would be great, thanks."

"How are you today?" asks Andrew.

"Numb and a bit hungover. When did you and Peter get in? I don't remember seeing you last night."

"Got back an hour ago, we drank too much to drive back so we crashed down in the bus."

John nods.

Andrew cooks enough fish for the whole team, in case any of the others get up. Peter is the only one to smell the food and come down stairs, having showered; the three eat the lot.

"Thanks for the text," says Peter.

"We didn't get it 'till we were back on land, but thanks anyway. We kinda guessed when he died, owing to the darkness and the earthquake," says Andrew.

"Thanks for looking after Jesus' mum," says Peter.

"It's fine, she's a mess, but then again aren't we all."

One by one, throughout the day the lads appear, until they are all together. By mid afternoon they start to talk about yesterday's events. They wonder if the darkness was a sign, then try to make out that the 'quake didn't frighten them. They apprehensively talk about the future, what next, where to go, what to do?

"I guess it's back to fishing," says James.

Peter, Andrew and John all look at each other.

"It's okay for you lot, just go back to your old life. What am I to do? It shouldn't be like this, something is not right. The boss was never wrong about anything, yet now it's as if nothing happened," says Matthew beginning to get angry.

"Hey, it's not our fault, Peter has a wife and family to think of," says James.

"Yeah well, maybe he should have been thinking about them instead of denying he ever knew the boss," says Simon.

"That's it, rub it in, don't you think he feels bad enough. You're just asking for a beating," says James.

"Who from, your mummy, she's not here to fight for you now."

"I can take you any time Zealot boy, bring it on."

They stand up and are in each others face. Peter pulls them apart.

"Look, stop this now!" His voice trembles, "everyone knows I made a mistake, alright? If you lot want to keep reminding me, fine. I have to deal with the fact that the boss was there just at the very moment I fell. I saw the look in his eyes. So what any of you say is nothing, nothing compared to how I felt at that moment. How I'll feel for the rest of my life."

"Didn't we start like this? Fighting," says Thaddy.

"Makes sense, we've just come full circle," says Philip.

"No! we haven't" says John. "We are not the same, Jesus taught us different."

"Yeah but John, everything he taught us didn't point to this did it?" says Nathaniel.

Thaddy flicks on the TV.

"Oh, come on, Thaddy, you watched that all day yesterday," says James. "Give it a rest."

"Better than arguing."

Peter, not wanting to watch it, leaves the room. The news is showing highlights of the crucifixion. The others try not to look, but they are drawn to it.

"This is stupid, at least put on a movie, something other than this." says Matthew.

They watch Jesus' body being taken away. There is a close-up of Jesus' mother, John and the others.

"Hey John there's you," points Thaddy, adding, "Is it me or does Mary Mag look good in black."

"It's you," says Simon.

"What do you think about her? If you squint she looks quite hot," says James, leaning forward for a better look.

"You know she used to be a model," says Simon.

Thaddy mutes the TV. "No! Go on."

"She did all the men's magazines. If I remember, she was once voted Playbunny of the year."

"How come no-one told me this? It's something I should have known," says James a little annoyed.

"So what happened? Looking at her now you would never have guessed," asks Thaddy.

Simon gestures with his hand. "Drink and drugs. She ended up stripping at the Angels. I used to see her sitting alone, only she wasn't; she had too many demons for that. She never told you her story?"

They all shake their heads.

Simon is hesitant, almost not wanting to relive the past. John suspects it's because of his mate, the one he never talks about.

"The boss came in the bar one time. Me and..." he stops, glancing away. "Well a couple of us had invited Jesus to the Angels, you know, to see what he was all about. Well, you know the boss, first he healed everyone that asked."

"including Mary," says Alphie.

Simon nods, "including Mary."

"I thought she looked vaguely familiar. Wonder if I still have one of them mags she was in. I might ask her if she remembers which ones."

"James you'd better not," shouts Peter from another room.

Thaddy turns the TV sound back on as James' attention has now turned to Matthew's ex, Rebecca.

"What I really can't understand Matt, is why you didn't keep seeing Rebecca. I would have done anything to keep her. Even sold one of Johns' kidneys."

Matthew smiles. "Haven't thought about Rebecca in a while."

"You don't know if she's still single do ya Matt? I mean if you're not seeing her, maybe she would prefer a real man," says James.

"You couldn't afford her, she prefers her men to have money."

John thinks about Jude's girlfriend. "Jude's girl, now she

was fine."

"Sarah, yes, very nice, " says Andrew.

John looks at James. "When we first met her you told me her name was Sonia."

James laughs. "Ha! Did I?"

"Yeah. I kept calling her Sonia all that night!"

"Sonia, Sarah, whatever, she was way too good for Jude," says James getting up and leaving the room.

"Can we not talk about that bastard," says Simon.

James comes back in with a beer in his hand. He sits down and slurps the froth from the top of the can. They all stare at him.

"Where did you get that from?" says Simon.

"From the fridge!" James looks at Simon like he's an idiot.

"There isn't any beer in the fridge."

"There is now! I opened a new case, it's a bit warm though."

"I thought we'd run out," says John.

"We had!"

"So where did it come from?" they all ask.

James still looks at them like they are imbeciles. "Oh, right, you weren't here. By the way lads, the guy from the upper room came by. He heard about the boss, so he brought us the booze we never drank. Plus, out of condolences, he's thrown in some extras."

"Thanks for telling us," says John.

"I'm telling you now, what's the big deal."

"I'm thirsty, that's the big deal."

When they go to investigate it seems that Mr Marith has been very generous, for not only has he left the beer and wine they never finished, he's given some extras, including two bottles of Israeli whisky.

Andrew and Peter open a bottle of wine, the rest raid the fridge. Beer is beer, even when it's warm.

Chapter 42

"Wake up, Wake up. Everyone, wake up."

John bursts into one of the bedrooms and is confronted by Matthew, his gun pointing straight at him.

"Don't shoot."

"What the...?" says Matthew lowering the gun.

John is too excited to explain. He points and waves.

"It's...It..."

From another room, Simon appears, he too is holding his gun.

"What's happening"

"It's Jesus, his body is gone! Mary Mag says the boss is alive!"

"Oh," he sighs, "So they've stolen the body, they'd better not blame us," Simon lowers his gun.

"No, you don't understand. Mary Mag's seen the boss alive," says John.

"Yeah, right," says Simon, slamming his door shut.

"Look John, just admit it, the boss is dead." Matthew too goes back to bed.

If they don't believe it, tough, he's off back downstairs, where Peter is scrambling about trying to put on his boots, a piece of toast in his mouth.

"Who else is coming...?" John is already out the door as he shouts.

Standing on the step of the house are Mary, Jesus' mother, Mary Mag and Joanna. They came straight away to tell them the tomb is empty and Mary Mag saw and spoke to Jesus. John rushes passed them yelling, "Thank you, thank you, I knew it, I knew it."

John is in the bus and has started the engine by the time Peter jumps in. With a screech of tyres and crunching of gears John sets off.

"So, why were they at the tomb this morning exactly?" asks Peter holding on to the door as John takes a corner a little fast.

"Finishing off the embalming, it was late Friday, so they had to wait until today."

"And you know where you're going?"

"Sort of."

John, desperately trying to remember where to go, doesn't slow down at a set of lights, this is gonna be close...

"Slow down, you're going to kill us," shouts Peter.

"It was fine," you wanna get there quick don't you?"

"Yes, but, where are you going? You need to turn right, RIGHT!"

John stamps on the brakes and turns hard right. The bus jerks and skids, only just making the entrance to the burial grounds; it screeches to a halt, stopping in the middle of the car park. John flings open his door and jumps out.

"This way," he shouts back at Peter.

Realising he's left the engine running and keys in the ignition he hesitates, oh, it will be fine, won't it? Yeah. Now which tomb is it? Hoping he's going in the right direction, he recognises a statue. Yes it's just round the hill. When he sees it he points it out to Peter, who is struggling to catch up. At the tomb the big steel door is wide open. John stops, they were right. Hesitantly he peers inside. He can see a pile of linen wrapped and neatly placed on the stone slab. Wow, what has happened?

Peter, gasping for air, finally catches up. He pushes John out of the way and enters the dark tomb. John follows him. Peter stands on the spices that have fallen to the floor and points at the neatly folded linen.

"What do you think?" asks John.

"If you stole a body, you wouldn't unwrap it first would you!"

"So does that mean it's true, he's alive?"

Chapter 43

The veil, a high curtain separating the Most Holy place from the rest of the temple, has been torn in two from top to bottom.

"I know what I saw."

"Coincidence is the only explanation."

"I agree, shocking as it is, but people are starting to ask questions."

The earthquake not only shook Jerusalem, it has shaken the hearts of the people. The veil in the Temple, a curtain that separated the holy of holies from them, was ripped in two from top to bottom. News has quickly spread that the most holy place in Israel is on show and many people have rushed to see it for themselves. The queue stretches all the way through the Temple and out around the whole building. To make matters worse Annas has now something more pressing to deal with.

In Annas' office are four guards, standing in a line facing his desk. They are wearing body armour and are carrying rifles and handguns. Annas himself is looking out of the window.

Caiaphas enters, having come straight from his Temple duties and is still wearing his robe, the bells on the hem ringing as he walks in. An assistant follows behind. The guards turn round.

"Please, heads forward," says the assistant, who now helps Caiaphas de-robe.

Annas turns and offers his chair to Caiaphas.

"Right, tell me exactly what happened," says Caiaphas sitting down.

The guards are reluctant to speak. Annas points to one of the men, indicating he should speak first.

"Sir, it was supernatural, there was nothing we could do."

"There was this bright light. Then the whole place started shaking. We saw a figure dressed in pure white, glowing," says another.

"There was nothing we could do, sir," says the third. "The next thing we knew, everything was normal, except the tomb door was open and the body had gone."

"We couldn't fire our weapons, move or anything, sir."

Caiaphas addresses the fourth guard. "What about you, have you anything to add?"

"No, sir. It was just as they described, if it had been Jesus' team we would have fired, sir."

A priest knocks on the door, and enters with Benjamin and Theo.

"Hand over your weapons to these men," says Annas to the guards.

"Yes sir." they reply.

Annas and Caiaphas leave the office to go and talk to some of the chief priests.

"Is it true?" asks one priest.

"It appears so," says Caiaphas.

"This has to stay between us, if this gets out that Jesus is…"

"And if it gets out?"

"We will tell the truth, that his team came while the guards were sleeping and stole the body," says Annas.

"Excellent idea," says Caiaphas.

"What shall we do with the guards?" asks one of the priests.

"No more killing, surely we've had enough of that," says another.

"What about money? Could they be bought?" asks one.

"Everybody can be bought, especially when they are expecting punishment," says Caiaphas.

Annas and Caiaphas go back into the office.

"I *should* hand you over to Pilate to be crucified!" says Annas entering his office. "I can't even look you in the eyes. You're an embarrassment to God and to the Temple. Your very presence in my office makes it unclean." He walks up and down behind the men. "We may need you later but if it wasn't for that, I would have no trouble sending you to your deaths, understand?"

The men nod their heads, "yes sir."

"Your High Priest will give you your orders. If you disobey them I will find you. And I won't be so accommodating next time."

Annas steps aside and once again goes over to the window and looks out, watching the crowds swarm all round the side of the Temple.

Caiaphas sits back down in Annas' chair. His assistant follows and hands him some papers.

"Right gentleman, this is the statement we require you to sign. It states that you were negligent, that you were asleep on the job, and that Jesus' team came and stole the body. This is the official version of events. If the press find out the body is missing, you will recite this statement. This is what the Governor will be told, if necessary. Memorise it, make sure you know it by heart. Failure will not be tolerated."

He takes a pen from the desk, handing it to the first guard.

"Oh, to help your conscience, if you have any, there will be a little, lets say, signing bonus."

Caiaphas' assistant hands him four thick brown envelopes. The men all look at each other and smile.

Caiaphas opens an envelope, it is crammed with hundreds of ten Euro notes. The men can't sign fast enough.

Chapter 44

"We've been set up."

"They didn't have anything on us before, so they hid the body and say we stole it, giving them enough reason to arrest us."

"Oh, stop it Simon, he's alive. I can feel it. Mary Mag says she's even seen him."

"Oh great John, that's the defence at your trial. Mary Mag saw Jesus alive, but he looked different and no one else has seen him since."

"Shhh Thaddy, what was that, did you hear something?" says Alphie, sneaking a look out of the window.

"We're safe in here, everything's locked up and tighter than Jude's wallet," says Nathaniel. "What? Too soon to make fun of the traitor?"

"No, but it's probably Thomas anyway, he shouldn't be much longer. I thought he was only going out for some bread?"

"He'd better remember to park the bus away from the house," says James.

"They always come in the dark - should we fight?" suggests Thaddy.

"I am, they aren't arresting me," says Simon, patting his

gun.

"We should get more weapons, remember what the boss asked in the garden car park? He asked how many guns we had. Maybe it was for now," says Thaddy.

"I have a spare upstairs in my bag. Alphie, you got yours today?" asks Matthew.

"No, sorry."

"You lot are so negative, the boss is alive," says John.

"Yeah, Yeah, if he's really come back from the dead, don't you think he'd have shown himself to us by now?" says Philip.

"That's what you would assume, isn't it Philip?" says Jesus.

Standing right in the middle of the living room is Jesus. The lads are terrified. They can see the boss, he's here. No one dare speak, they are so frightened. Can their eyes be deceiving them?

"Relax, everything is alright."

"Boss, is it you, really you?" asks Andrew.

"It's a ghost, do you think it can hear us?" whispers James.

"You think I'm a ghost. Oh James, do ghosts have real bodies like mine?"

"But...you died. You're dead!" says Nathaniel.

"You're alive, I knew it! I knew you were alive," says John. He turns to Matthew, "See, Mary was right."

They all gather round Jesus. He shows them his hands and feet. They prod him, touch the scars where the nails went through. He shows them the point where the spear entered his side.

"Have you got anything to eat?" he asks.

"We've fish," says Andrew.

"Fish, is that all you eat?" asks Jesus.

Andrew shrugs. "It's all I know how to cook."

"Then fish it is."

Andrew fries up some fish and Jesus sits and eats it in front of them.

"Would you like a beer? Water?"

"You think he's still a ghost, that the water will pour out of his side don't you James?" says Andrew.

"Well excuse me for never seeing a dead person alive before!" he thinks for a second, well you know, apart from Lazarus!"

Jesus drinks a glass of water. James seems a little disappointed.

After Jesus has eaten he disappears.

"Hey, where did he go?" asks Philip, who'd turned his back for a second.

"Ghosts can walk through walls."

"Oh, shut up James," says John.

They are all amazed, happy, but also confused.

"Was he real?"

"Did that just happen?"

"Were we all dreaming?"

A key is heard in the lock and Thomas enters.

"Hey guys, so there was only whole grain bread, not white, but I did get us some more chocs, I notic...ed. What's wrong, you all look like you've seen a ghost?"

"Jesus was here, right in this room, standing right where you are," says John.

"He even ate some fish Andrew made," says Philip.

"Yeah right. Come on you guys, this isn't funny."

They all try to convince him.

"So did anyone video it for me?"

"No, but would you believe it even if we did?"

"Er, maybe not. Unless I can see him, put my hands on his scars, touch where he was nailed, then I won't believe it."

"It kinda makes sense. Remember when we went up the mountain and met Moses and Elijah. Jesus went really bright and then God spoke."

"What are you talking about?" asks Nathaniel.

"John...shh," says James as he and Peter both stare at him.

"Come on spill, what do you three know?" insists Simon.

"Moses and Elijah are long gone, you're making no sense," says Philip.

"Jesus said we couldn't tell anyone." says James.

"Oops!" John thinks for a moment. "ah... but: *not until you see the Son of Man raised*, that's what he said wasn't it? I think it's alright now."

James and Peter don't seem too convinced.

"There may have been low oxygen up the mountain, you were all hallucinating," says Simon. The others all agree.

"This is why Jesus didn't want you to know, you're all negative."

"And you're Teacher's pets," says Thaddy.

"So what else have you hidden from me. How come I miss everything?"

"Well, if I'd have seen Moses and Elijah I wouldn't have denied the boss. Eh Pete," Simon says getting agitated. "Some Rock you turned out to be."

"Don't start on Peter, you weren't there in that courtyard. Anyway I didn't see you defend the boss in Gethsemane, you were hiding behind the big man, that's what you were doing."

Peter doesn't argue. He gets up and leaves the room without saying a word.

As the lads are still trying to make sense of all that has just happened, Andrew gets a call.

"Alright Cleo; we're at Zeb's place. Yeah, come on over."

Ten minutes later, Andrew is waiting at the door when Cleo swings his car into the drive, parking at an acute angle. He has a friend with him, Samuel.

"Are the others here, we've got amazing news?"

Andrew points inside. Cleo and Samuel rush into the house and the living room where the lads are all hanging out including a subdued Peter.

"Lads, guess what?" says Cleo.

"We've just seen Jesus!" says James.

Cleo is surprised, "oh, that's our news, so have we!"

"Oh, *great!* More people have seen him. Am I the only one who hasn't?" says Thomas.

Cleo is bursting to tell the lads what just happened, but James is just as eager and the guests have to sit and wait until James has finished. While James is recounting Jesus' visit, Andrew and Philip brew up some tea and coffee, it's going to be a long night. Finally Cleo and Samuel recount what happened to them earlier.

"We were in the city, so we thought it would be a good idea to give Mary our sympathies. On the way home we needed petrol, so Cleo stopped at a garage a couple of miles from home. As we were leaving we saw a man standing by a bus stop. Feeling generous, we offered him a lift. He listened to our conversation and asked us why we were sad. So we told him about Jesus and all that had happened to him and what he had taught and done," says Samuel. "We said we were sad because we thought he was the Christ who had come to free Israel from the Union."

"He said we were foolish and slow of heart to believe." I

389

know, can you believe it? "He went on to say it was necessary for the Christ to suffer these things and enter into his glory. As we drove, he started to explain some of the scriptures regarding the Messiah."

"Why didn't you know it was Jesus?" asks Nathaniel.

"He looked different. We didn't realise it was him, but what he said was really amazing, so I rang the missus, and I asked him round for supper. Samuel rang his wife and we all ate together. This man just kept telling us more and more things. Samuel started to write some of it down. It was amazing. It was only when he was eating we all recognised who he was."

"Then what?" asks John.

"He vanished, just disappeared into thin air."

"He did that to us too," says Alphie.

"One minute he's there, the next, gone," says James.

"I wouldn't know!" moans Thomas.

"Anyway, we got straight back into the car and came here, we wanted to tell you face to face," says Cleo.

"Do you remember what scriptures he mentioned?" asks Nathaniel.

Samuel takes out a note-pad and hands it to him.

"You'll find the scriptures on the bookcase in the hallway," says John, not making any attempt to fetch them himself.

Nathaniel goes and digs the book out. He blows dust off it. "When was the last time you opened this?"

Nathaniel flicks through the pages until he finds one of the verses that Samuel had written down. It was from the prophet Isaiah. He reads a few lines that stand out.

"But he was pierced for our transgressions, crushed for our iniquities: The punishment that brought us peace was upon him, and by his wounds we are healed. He was arrested, sentenced and led off to die and no one cared about his fate. He was put to death for the sins of the people. He was assigned a grave with evil men, but was buried with the rich, though he had never committed a crime or ever told a lie."

"You're making that up, it's exactly what happened! Come here, let's have a look," says James.

He reads it for himself.

"Wow, he's right."

Chapter 45

"I'm telling you, they're watching us."

"Come away from the window Thomas."

"I have a bad feeling Matthew."

"You always have a bad feeling."

Thomas comes away from the window and slumps on the sofa.

The phone rings for the hundredth time today.

"Don't answer it, it will be the press again," shouts Philip from another room.

"Hello," says Thomas, picking up the phone. "No news, sorry. Yeah we'll let you know if we see him."

"I thought I said don't answer it."

"It was Mary, Jesus' mum, you call screening her now are you?"

Matthew smiles. Thomas isn't the most positive lad at the best of times and now over a week since he missed Jesus he's gotten far worse. He's even more negative and morose than usual and it's affecting everybody. Matthew finds him funny. In everything the group does, there is always his little voice, warning what might happen. He looks across at him, his arms folded and a big frown across his forehead. Thomas wants desperately to see the boss, well, we all do.

Simon comes into the room and carefully peers out of the window. Thomas looks up.

"Simon, don't you start," says Matthew.

"They're watching us aren't they?" asks Thomas.

"Someone's there," replies Simon.

"If we were in trouble wouldn't they have done something by now?" Matthew is getting a little fed up.

"Maybe they're waiting for backup?" suggests Thomas.

Friends and followers of Jesus have been coming and going all week. Ever since he appeared it's been busier than the Temple at festival time. There is never anywhere to sit. They have nothing to do apart from eat and drink and now when they have a bit of peace the night comes and these two start to get nervous. Matthew takes out his gun and decides to face this threat head on.

"Right, come on. Simon, tool up."

"What?" says Simon.

"Let's go see what this is all about."

"I'll stay here," says Thomas.

"You will not, you're coming with us."

With a nervous Thomas following behind, Matthew and Simon go outside in the dark to investigate the suspicious car.

"Close the door, don't let any light out," Simon whispers to Thomas.

Matthew and Simon carefully edge around the house and down the drive past the minibus. Bending down they both run to the garden wall, and squat down behind the gateposts. Matthew points his gun and looks, first one way then the other. He signals to Simon to do the same. Matthew knows this is all a bit of an exaggeration but it will prove to Thomas that they are taking it seriously and there is nothing to be frightened of. It may also go some way to help convince himself.

Only trouble is, he isn't happy with what he sees. Simon has spotted the same thing. Bending as low as they can, so as not to be seen, they head back to Thomas, pushing him into the house and quietly closing the door.

"Problem," says Simon.

"Oh, no," says Thomas.

"James, John, is there a back way out of this place?"

"What are you talking about?" asks John.

"There is a car with two men in, parked just down the road," says Matthew.

"What should we do?"

Matthew has an idea.

"Me and Simon are going to get a better look, close up."

"From behind," Simon works out what Matthew is thinking.

"I'll give the house phone two rings, then I want some of you to go outside and make a noise, laugh, shout, anything."

"Oh a distraction, like it," says John. "Will do."

"We will be safe, right?"

"Maybe," Matthew winks.

He and Simon head out the back and over a fence. It's not the easiest route, having to negotiate their way through other peoples' gardens, trying not to be seen. Once on the street, they casually walk towards the rear of the parked car.

"What's the betting they are Temple guards," says Simon.

That is what Matthew himself was thinking. If it's his old mate Benjamin he's not sure what he will do. Is there any reason they won't shoot first? After all, the Temple authorities are trying to blame the lads for stealing Jesus' body.

"Who would have thought we'd be walking down a street to do a job on someone?"

"I always wondered, have you swapped sides or have I?" asks Matthew.

"You, definitely."

"Then why does this feel like I'm back in the old routine?"

They stop thirty yards away from the back of the car and hide in a driveway. Matthew dials the house.

"Oh, come on. It's engaged!"

"What!"

"The home phone's engaged."

Simon grabs the phone off him and rings John's mobile.

"Yo, like now would be a good time to..."

"They're idiots," he says giving Matthew back his phone.

Matthew's not going to argue with that one.

"What if these guys are only here to spy on us, see if we have the body," Simon wonders.

"That's possible. Maybe we go about this slightly differently."

"Go on."

"Remember the first test? What John and Thomas did by accident."

Matthew nods, "I'm with you."

A door bangs and there are shouts and singing.

"*We're all going on a countrywide tour, countrywide tour.*"

Banging on the minibus and shouts of "Galilee" ring out.

"Go, Go, Go."

Simon and Matthew run up behind the car and get in the back seat. The two men in the front don't realise until its too late.

"Glad we caught you, Bethany please," says Simon.

"Been busy?" asks Matthew.

Matthew can't see any weapons, but the men were definitely watching the house, of that he is certain.

"Get out," shouts the driver.

"What are you doing, this isn't a taxi," says the other.

"Then why are you parked here?" asks Simon.

"Look, you gonna get out or are we gonna have to kick you out."

Matthew and Simon look at each other and nod. They both point their guns at the backs of the men's heads.

"Keep your hands on the steering wheel and you," he says pointing at the man in the passenger seat, "hands on the dashboard, where I can see them. No sudden moves OK!" says Matthew.

"Now why are you watching MY house?" asks Simon.

"We have been ordered to watch you."

"See where you've hidden the body."

"What! That's stupid," says Simon, pushing his gun hard into the man's skull.

"No, it's the truth, we aren't even armed, honest."

"We haven't got the body, haven't you heard, he's alive. We've seen him."

"*We're all going on a countrywide tour,*" James and John are still singing and are heading down to the car waving.

"Do you honestly think those two could steal a body?"

Matthew can see that the men are petrified, it's a look he's seen many times before. James and John are only frightening them even more.

"Come on, let's go," says Matthew, getting out of the car. "That means you two. You must be hungry, sitting here for so long watching us. Andrew and Peter must have dinner ready by now, there's always plenty to go round."

With James and John still singing, Matthew and Simon lead the men to the house. Inside, Philip and Nathaniel show them around the house and gardens, everywhere they care to look. Afterwards they share the fish supper Andrew and Peter have made.

When the two guards leave, the lads sit in the living room.

"If the boss doesn't come back soon, I think we should go home," says Nathaniel.

It is what everyone of them has been thinking.

"No, I want to see the boss, we wait here."

"We've been waiting for over a week, I want to go home," says Nathaniel.

Everyday they all get up thinking, today Jesus could come. When it doesn't happen they become more and more disillusioned and fearful of the authorities. Matthew knows that the fishermen will all go back to their lives pre-Jesus and the rest will eventually find other things to occupy them. As for himself, who would employ him? An ex-collector and now an ex-follower of a dead Christ.

He isn't the only one who feels like that.

"We need to accept that he may not show up again," says Philip.

"I need to get home, see Ruth and the kids."

James puts on the TV to check the news and see if anyone is reporting a new sighting of the boss before he commits to his decision to leave the city.

"Oh, do you mind, I can't see the screen," says James.

"James!"

"What? Do I stand in front when you're watching it?"

"James!"

James looks to see who's blocking his way.

"Oh, hi boss, do you mind shifting out of the way a touch."

Everybody waits for him to realise who's blocking his view.

"Oh, Ohhh it's you! Boss you're here again."

"Thomas," says Jesus, "come here, look at my scars, put your hand in my side and don't be so unbelieving."

Thomas with the biggest grin on his face, carefully reaches out and touches Jesus' scars on his hands and in his side.

"You're alive, really alive."

His face then goes all serious, as he begins to realise what this must mean.

"But you died, like really died. Now you're alive. How? No one can do that unless you are... God, you're God," he says.

Jesus looks at him "Oh Thomas, you believe because you have seen me with your own eyes, but one day people will believe in me without the benefit of seeing me."

Chapter 46

"Hey, you've managed a whole night on a boat without being sick!"

A small fishing boat makes its way slowly into the harbour after a nights fishing. At the helm is Peter. Also on board are Thomas, Nathaniel, James, John, Andrew and Philip. There are more people on board than fish, it hasn't been a good trip. After Jesus' last appearance, the lads all came back to Galilee. Jesus had hinted that he would see them here, but he was vague about the where and when.

All four fishermen decided to go out in a boat together, get their sea-legs back and take a more leisurely trip. James had promised Philip and Nathaniel that he would give them a trip around the lake if they did his turn at washing up, so they are tagging along. Thomas, not known for his sea-legs, but not wanting to be left out of anything again, decided that he'd go everywhere the rest of them went – even if that meant going in a boat.

What none of them were expecting was a long hard night going up and down the lake chasing invisible fish.

"How can you call yourself fishermen, if you don't catch anything?" says Nathaniel.

"You should really just be called sailors, for that's all you're doing," adds Philip.

The boat they have borrowed only has a small net. The lads have to throw it over the side and trawl across the lake, but the fish seem to see them coming and swim out of the way. Peter and Andrew caught more out on the Mediterranean with fishing rods.

It hadn't been that bad, they have at least done something rather than been stuck inside waiting for the boss to turn up again and Thomas has coped with the soft rolling motion of the boat, only being a little ill.

Peter decides they've been out long enough, and they head back into the harbour but when they are a hundred yards from the entrance, with the sun starting to come up, John spots a solitary figure standing on the harbour wall.

"Morning lads, caught anything?" shouts the man.

"Not a thing, it was terrible," says Nathaniel.

"Try looking on the right side of your boat," calls the man.

What does he know? Peter keeps a path straight to the harbour, but the others look over. They can see lots of fish swimming alongside them. James and John scramble for the net.

"Wow, I've never seen so many fish," says Thomas carefully looking over the side.

The net sweeps up the fish. James starts to pull it on board, but is worried that the weight of the huge catch will tear the net. Peter gives Thomas the helm and the rest quickly help haul the fish into the boat. Thomas concentrates hard on keeping the boat straight so much that he steers away from the harbour, heading along the coast a little. He can't take his eyes off the man who is now walking on the shore.

"That man, he looks like the boss," says Philip.

They all look closer.

"Oh, yeah, he does."

"It is the boss," says Nathaniel.

"Just think, if the boss were a fisherman, we'd be rich!" says James.

"It'll take this boat ages to get to the shore, the little engine is struggling to cope with the weight." says Peter, "I don't want to wait that long."

He slips off his boots and fishing gear and in only his t-shirt and shorts dives into the sea and swims to the shore.

"He's mad, it's freezing," shivers Thomas.

"Well at least the boats a bit lighter now," says Philip.

Jesus shouts to the lads. "Bring some fish, I'll cook us all some breakfast."

Andrew takes over and carefully nurses the boat back to the harbour.

When Peter gets out of the water Jesus has started to build a fire. He looks slightly different in a way Peter can't quite figure out.

Now standing alone with the man he denied, Peter can't find the words. He feels so guilty for what he'd said and done. "Sorry," is all he can say and to his surprise Jesus doesn't answer. He half expects Jesus to turn him away, telling him he is no longer one of the team. As a result he can't look Jesus in the eye for fear of breaking down in tears again. In the boat all he wanted to do was be near Jesus, back to how it was before the trial and crucifixion. When he'd jumped into the water he hadn't cared how cold it was, now as his t-shirt clings to his freezing body he shivers, the small fire doing little to warm him. He is relieved when the others arrive from the harbour with the fish, even more so when Andrew throws him a towel.

In no time Jesus and Andrew have gutted the fish and placed them on the fire to cook and during their breakfast, Jesus speaks of the scriptures; how they have been fulfilled, how good it is that they can see him alive and that soon more things will be revealed to them. He even teases Thomas about his steering skills.

"Call that steering in a straight line!"

"It was my first time and at least I didn't hit the harbour wall!" he says, looking at James and John.

After the breakfast, during which Peter had sat quietly eating and not joining in any of the conversations. Jesus asked Peter a question.

"Simon Peter, do you love me more than fishing?"

"What! Boss, of course I do."

"Then I need you to tend my lambs."

Peter tries to look Jesus in the eye, but he can't quite bring himself to do it.

Jesus asks again.

"Simon Peter, do you love me?"

"Yes Lord you know that I care for you."

"Then take care of my sheep."

The others are all looking on, not daring to say a word.

"Simon Peter do you care for me?"

Why is he doing this to me, surely Jesus can know my heart, "Lord, you know all things, I can't hide anything from you, so you must know that I love you."

"Then tend my sheep."

Peter realises he has been asked three times. Three times he had denied Jesus, so three times Jesus had questioned his loyalty.

"I am going to tell you something," says Jesus, "when you were young you could go anywhere you wanted, but when you are old your hands will be tied and you will be taken where you don't want to go."

Peter, his heart restored with the knowledge that he still has an important part to play, is more than happy to suffer for Jesus, whenever that time may be.

Chapter 47

"We've only been home a couple of weeks and we have to go back to Jerusalem."

"You heard the boss, he wants us down there."

"Yeah, but how come *you* get to drive?"

"'Cos, I'm the one with the keys."

James climbs into the driver's seat of the minibus and turns the key in the ignition. After a couple of attempts the diesel engine splutters and rattles into life. There haven't been many occasions when he's been allowed to drive it. The lads feel a lot safer with Andrew or Philip behind the wheel. Matthew throws his bag onto a seat and climbs in. He is joined by Thaddy and Nathaniel.

"Come on John," shouts James, revving the engine.

John jumps in the front passenger seat and turns round nodding to the lads in the back.

He hasn't had chance to put his seat belt on before James floors the accelerator.

"It's going to be a long journey," Nathaniel says to Matthew and Thaddy.

Matthew still misses his Merc. He never did buy a new car and hasn't got used to begging lifts everywhere he goes. Today may be the worst one yet.

"Those two have been using the bus to tow boats this week," says Thaddy.

"So that's why I can smell burning oil?" says Nathaniel.

As they travel towards the motorway heading south, they are trailing a cloud of smoke and it is definitely getting thicker and blacker. Matthew, Nathaniel and Thaddy take it in turns to point it out to James.

"It's been like that all week, it's fine."

"It's burning a bit of oil, that's all. We've had loads of boats do that," John shouts over the engine noise.

A car sounds it's horn as James overtakes, covering it in a blanket of oily smoke. Matthew sinks into the seat, embarrassed that anyone should see him.

Suddenly there is a loud BANG as the engine blows up, scattering bits of metal and oil all over the place. Other cars have to swerve out of the way as James fights with the bus, eventually stopping it at the side of the road. They all jump out as quickly as they can, coughing from the smoke.

"Huh," says James.

"Now what we going to do?" says Thaddy.

* * *

The lads had to beg for lifts with the other followers all heading south. Matthew has spent the last two hours squashed in between two elderly women who constantly talked about what they'd just eaten, were going to eat and what it does to their bodies. It's put him off puddings for life. Every time they passed a car dealers he'd looked longingly. He makes a promise never to rely on James and John for lifts ever again.

When he is dropped off, the ladies are delighted they could

help him and even pay for his bed and breakfast, thrusting a handful of notes into his hand when he says goodbye. They thank *him* for his company. They know who he is, they will have known what he used to do to people who couldn't pay him, yet they don't bear any ill will towards him, even giving him money.

He feels guilty at the nasty thoughts he'd had. He'd wanted to shoot them or at least tape their mouths shut. There was a time, before Jesus, when he would have done just that, no question. It's a strange feeling he has these days, the knowledge that people are not afraid of him anymore. Weird!

Walking up to the Mariths B&B where he'll be staying over the next few days, he finds the city buzzing with news of more confirmed sightings of Jesus. People are recognising him, smiling and saying hello. The danger he felt the last time he was here has gone. There is an excitement and anticipation that something is up, something is about to happen. There have been too many reports of Jesus alive for the lads to be under suspicion of stealing the body. Hundreds of people have now seen and talked with the boss.

When he arrives at the B&B, Peter and his family are unpacking their truck. Peter organises the family like he does the lads. Ruth, Naomi and Toby are all given bags to carry and he shepherds them inside. He sees Matthew and waves. It's good to see Peter so happy again.

"We are meeting in the upper room later," says Peter as Matthew comes inside and goes over to a small reception desk.

Matthew puts the money he was given down on the counter, looking in his wallet for the rest. The gift will come in handy and he might be able to stay here a little longer than he could otherwise.

"I don't need that, it's all been taken care of," says Mrs Marith, handing him a room key.

"Really?" he wonders who would have done it.

"Don't ask me who paid it, you know I won't tell."

Matthew picks up the money, leaving one of the notes on the counter and winks.

Once he's been up to his room and freshened up a little, he decides to see who else is around and wanders outside. He climbs the stairs to the upper room. Inside he finds Alphie talking to one of the bikers along with Thomas, Simon and around thirty other followers.

"Yo, Matt! So you finally made it."

"Get the man a drink, he deserves one," says Alphie to a young couple at the bar making drinks for everyone.

They already know about the exploding minibus and the disrupted journey. Alphie and Simon had come down with Thomas and his twin.

"Where's the boss?" asks Matthew.

"He keeps appearing occasionally," says Simon.

Over the next few hours all the team arrive including James and John who were driven down by their parents. They don't look too pleased. Many more arrive and call in, they are staying all over the city in a range of places, from B&Bs and hotels to friends and acquaintances - anywhere they can.

Philip arrives with four lads Matthew has never seen before and once they are all fixed up with drinks Philip comes over to introduce them.

"This is James, Joe, Jude and Simon," Philip says.

They all say their hellos.

"We are Jesus' half brothers," says James.

That surprises Matthew. For all the time spent with the

boss and his mum for that matter, Jesus never really talked about his family much. Mary did, on many occasion, but from what Matthew could gather they weren't that keen on their older brother being the proclaimed Christ and Son of God. He could understand their scepticism. It must be a difficult thing to take in. Yet here they are talking happily about him.

"He was always the favourite," says Joe.

"We never believed who he is until..."

"...we saw him after he had died," says Simon finishing Jude's sentence.

Peter enters holding a clipboard.

"Can I have everyone's attention." The noise level quietens. "Thank you for coming, I hope everybody has been allocated a room, or at least a bed. Please see me if there are any problems. As for meal times, Mrs Marith will be serving a running buffet here in the upper room at lunchtime and for the evening meal."

James raises his hand, "How come some of you are staying in a hotel, while me and John are stuck at mum and dad's place."

"James, I thought you liked my cooking," says Salomé.

"Because you destroyed the minibus that's why," says Simon, to laughter.

"Apart from James and John, anyone else need anything, see me. Mrs Marith says the evening meal is now ready, so please enjoy."

Matthew had only just begun to eat when Jesus appeared.

"How come he always turns up at meal times?" whispers Alphie.

After they had eaten Philip asks, "Boss, we're all wondering if this is the time you're going to restore the Kingdom of

Israel?"

"It's not for you to know the times that the Father has set, " says Jesus, "but...you'll receive power when the Holy Spirit comes to you; and you'll be my witnesses here in Jerusalem, Judea, Samaria and even to the ends of the earth."

"OK, I think we can settle for that," says James, laughing.

Matthew is having such a good time, laughing and joking that he didn't notice when Jesus disappeared. It was dark when he realised that Jesus had left them. They all have a good time eating and drinking together before heading back to their various lodgings.

Later that night, unable to sleep, Matthew opens the complimentary bottle of water from the mini-fridge and sits by the window, looking out at the city. Even at this time of night there is an energy, a buzz unique to Jerusalem. Sipping the water, he goes over in his head the days events, trying to make sense of it all. The sounds of the city recede and he becomes still, focusing on Jesus. He wasn't sure at what time that night the boss had disappeared, but now as lights from passing cars sends strips of light across the room, he can see in his mind Jesus talking, encouraging. It feels significant. He smiles, thinking back to the time he was in his office and Jesus appeared. From that day Matthew's life changed. It wasn't always easy, there were a few times when the others wanted him gone... or dead. Hard to believe he now considers them friends. Who would believe what he saw, who could raise a dead man to life, who could calm a storm, with words alone. No-one but God himself. Ever since Jesus appeared, was resurrected, there has being this clarity of thought, not just for him, Matthew but the for whole group, even James! Now when Jesus teaches and talks it all makes sense. The scriptures about the Messiah telling of his miracles, his death, his res... Matthew shakes his head unable to finish the word, it seems too unbelievable even now.

He looks at his watch, half past three. "Better try and sleep," he says, standing up and heading over to the way too soft mattress.

* * *

Surprisingly, he slept well, and once up he heads to the upper room, expecting there to be a few dozen up by this time. He is surprised to see only Nathaniel, Alphie and Thaddy.

"Eight o'clock, you slept in!" says Thaddy piling up a plate of Mrs Marith's eggs, toast and morning pastries.

Matthew nods and goes over to the pot of coffee, and pours himself a large one.

"Wonder what's in store for us today" says Alphie, looking around the room. Matthew suspects that because it's meal time, Alphie is looking for Jesus to appear. "Is it me or could you listen to the boss like forever, and how come it's taken this long for it all to sink in. I mean, water into wine, calming that storm, you and the Zealot not killing each other."

"Maybe we'll get this power today, the one the boss mentioned yesterday," Thaddy says through a mouthful of toast.

As more and more of the followers arrive, and the room is filling up, it's Alphie who notices Jesus standing at the table filling up a plate of food. Alphie nudges Matthew, "Whenever he comes, Mrs Marith serves better food."

Matthew just shakes his head, but watches Jesus. Just as last night the boss is able to talk on a one-to one with people. Matthew wonders what is being said. Each time the person nods and smiles.

"...and then on our way home last night we met these girls and they recognised us and wanted to know about the boss, if he was alive. Are you listening Matt?"

Matthew, turns to find John has sat down at the table with them and seems to be in mid conversation with Alphie and Thaddy. Matthew smiles, not really sure what John is getting at.

"And then what?" asks Thaddy.

"Nothing, but don't you get it, girls talked to James... it's another miracle!" John laughs, but when the lads just shrug, he gets up and goes over to another group and repeats the same story.

"Everyone, can we have some quiet, people, PEOPLE." Peter tries to get the groups attention.

Eventually the room quietens down, the last voice to be heard is James. "don't you get it, it was a miracle, girls talked to John. HA, HA, HA."

"James shush," says Salomè.

Jesus stands up, and pats Peter on the shoulder. "Thank you Peter." Jesus takes a deep breath and looks around the room. "Over the last few days I've had a few words with each of you." He turns to Matthew, "don't worry Matt, Simon, I'll speak to you later."

Matthew smiles.

"Remember the things I've said to you, in private as well as in the Temple. James, where's James?"

"I'm here," James waves his hand.

"Use this," Jesus points to his head. James nods.

"That goes for all of you, as I've said, you won't be alone, you'll receive help." There is a pause as Jesus again looks around at the group and wipes away a tear.

"Good, good. Right, let's go, follow me."

"Boss where are we going?" asks Peter.

"The mount of Olives."

"I need a lift then, who can fit me in?" asks James.

"No James, we'll all walk. So everyone grab gear, or whatever you may need, we'll set off in five minutes.

"Walking, I don't wanna walk, why are we walking?"

"James, shut up!" say a dozen voices, including Matthew.

It takes more than five minutes for the whole group to get ready, the queue for the toilet being the main reason for the delay, but when they finally set off there is joy, an excitement in the group. Gone is the fear they had experienced just after the resurrection. As they walk through the streets, Matthew looks around for Jesus; he's leading the group. With him is Simon. Matthew waits for his turn, and takes in the city. They have walked around the Temple and are heading towards the east gate at the city wall. Matthew can't help thinking about the last time they went though this gate. It was all so different that day. The crowds, the singing. They all thought that was it, the City was theirs. Yes, he now understands the reasons why it had to happen the way it did, but then it was euphoria to disbelief and to anger.

A large hand thuds on Matthew's shoulder. "The boss wants to talk to you now," says Peter.

Before Matthew has even caught up, Jesus calls out. "What did I tell you Matt, right at the beginning?"

It all seems so long ago, things have changed so much. He thinks back to those early days, when every day was a struggle, when all the followers apart from Alphie hated him and wanted him to quit. It helped that he was used to being hated and could cope. As long as Jesus was there he had a reason to stay and stick it out.

Jesus has begun heading up the Mount of Olives when Matthew gets to the front of the group and to a laughing Jesus.

"Didn't I tell you it would all be worth it!" Jesus aims a playful punch at Matthews shoulder, thankfully it's not as hard as Peter's. "I'm happy with you Matthew. You stuck in there, when others would have fallen away."

As they walk, it's as if he is all alone with Jesus. He only hears Jesus' words, they filter though his whole being. Jesus reminds him of the things he has done, how the scriptures have been fulfilled. It feels so final, like a football manager is giving the team last minute instructions before they go out onto the pitch – alone.

Once at the top of the Mount, overlooking the city, Jesus stops.

"Gather round."

Matthew takes a deep breath, looking at the others. No-one speaks, not even James. Matthew starts to tremble.

"Remember what I taught you. Stay in Jerusalem until the time you receive my spirit." He holds out his arms, blessing them. "Peace, comfort, joy and power be on you all."

This is it, Matthew knows... Jesus is leaving them. It feels so final. Yet he feels no sadness. It's a good feeling, he's happy.

Suddenly he sees a low cloud swirling around his feet. It flows inbetween everybody until it settles at Jesus' feet, raising him up. They all watch in disbelief as the cloud takes Jesus higher and higher. "I will be with you always, to the ends of the earth."

The cloud, that's right, the cloud is carrying Jesus away, up towards the heavens. Still no-one speaks. They are all transfixed, even when Jesus is out of sight, nobody stops looking, staring.

The silence is broken only when two men, dressed in pure white ask. "Why are you staring up into heaven?"

"Er dude, did you just see what happened?" James answers.

"This Jesus who has been taken into heaven will come back in just the same way as you have watched him go."

Before James can reply the men leave. John puts his arm across his brothers chest to stop him following them. For once James lets it go, instead laughing. It should be a sad time, Jesus has just left them. Then why are they all happy. Everybody laughs, and starts hugging each other. They all feel the same, that this isn't a bad thing but something good.

They all start to head back down the mount.

"Wonder if anyone else saw what just happened?" says Thaddy.

He doesn't have to wait long to find out. Even before they arrive back there are people hanging around outside the B&B expecting to see Jesus.

"He's not here," Peter tells a reporter.

"Can you tell us when he will return?"

The group start to laugh.

"Your guess is as good as ours," says Philip.

"Well at least can you confirm he is alive."

Peter points to the whole group of people.

"We all can."

* * *

Every day they all meet in the upper room. From every part of the city they travel there in the morning and don't leave until the night. One hundred and twenty people, mostly from Galilee, gather and wait for the next stage. They don't know when that will be or even when it will occur. Some of the group are quite keen to pray for an answer. Peter encourages everybody and that includes the team, to pray to God and even the boss, for the knowledge, the wisdom and the answer as to what is going to happen next.

One of the things they start to agree on, is the need for someone to take Jude's place in the team. Peter gets out his clipboard and writes down the criteria that the person must possess.

- Knew the boss personally.
- Must have been a follower from the beginning.
- Travelled with them throughout the time Jesus was with them.
- Someone who was a witness to the resurrection.

Matthew, sitting next to James, notices he's added one more, while Peter isn't looking.

- Get the first round in.

Peter reads out the list "...and get the first round in. Hey I didn't write this!"

He looks at James.

"What, why look at me?"

"Who else could it be?"

From the criteria Matthew reckons it's between two people, Joseph Barsabbas and Matthias. Peter prays, asking for the right man to be chosen before handing out papers and pens and asks everyone to vote, not for their own preference, but God's.

When the results are in and counted Matthias wins.

"So, it must be my round then," says Matthias.

He is immediately welcomed into the team.

* * *

The next morning Matthew is woken by loud voices. Looking out of his window he sees some reporters and a group of curiosity seekers congregating around the outside of the B&B and the upper room. Some have been there every morning since they'd arrived. Not as many today, thank goodness. He watches as some priests are being interviewed by a TV crew - right under his window.

Matthew now fully awake, gets showered and dressed and heads to the upper room.

"Why is there a TV crew outside?" he asks Mrs Marith at reception.

"The priests have been on the news demanding Jesus show himself."

He doesn't make it to the steps of the upper room before he is confronted with shouts from a group of youngsters.

"Bunch of losers." says one.

"Religious freaks."

"Come and worship me," shouts another.

Over the years Matthew has gotten accustomed to name calling. It was a downside of his old profession. He would show his gun and they would run. It has always gone on, even when he joined the team he could hear their whispers and feel their stares. He pats his side, where is gun used to be and smiles at the young lads. They run away. Mmm... still need to work on my smile.

He climbs the stairs happy in the knowledge that the team mates who he didn't get along with, he now considers his good friends. Once inside he finds Peter.

"Why are the priests and press outside, why today."

"It's Pentecost, fifty days after Passover – the harvest festival. They think it would be a good day for us to give up on our delusions and go home, or they want proof," says Peter.

"What more proof do they want, five hundred people saw Jesus in one day alone," says Nathaniel.

"The priests are trying to use the press to discredit Jesus and us," says Philip.

Matthew grabs a black coffee and rubs his head. He looks at the bread rolls and buttered scones laid out for them but decides to pass on them this morning, he is eating way too much lately. Once everyone has arrived Peter tells them as it is Pentecost they should all start the day in prayer.

They all sit in silence and pray, only after a few minutes Matthew can't concentrate, he is sure he can hear things, noises, probably from outside.

"What's that noise?" asks John.

Apparently he's not the only one to hear things.

"I hear it too, what is it?" asks Nathaniel.

The noise sounds like a violent rushing wind. As it gets closer and louder Matthew suddenly feels overwhelmed by the sound. It's as if a hurricane is right outside, well, not for long; it bursts through the walls and windows without breaking them. It seems violent in its sound, yet it is as gentle as breath. It has form, like fire, but there is no heat. It spreads out over the whole room and all at once tongue-shaped flames

417

fork out from it and rest upon every person in the room.

It is a good feeling. He has this great sense of peace, like when Jesus did miracles. He looks around expecting to see him. Everyone else is happy too, they smile and laugh. Matthew wants to know if those outside heard the noise and experienced what he feels. He heads for the door and is followed by the others who in their excitement push him out of the way. All one hundred and twenty of them go bursting through the door and rush down the stairs. As they do, they all start to speak, only it's in many different languages. The noise they make is as loud as the hurricane itself. Matthew notices there are many more people outside than earlier. Hundreds more. With more and more coming all the time.

"What's happening," ask the TV crew. "What was that noise? What is going on?"

The noise was so loud people come out of their houses. Some are frightened – all are confused.

"How great is our God," says Matthew, he wants to laugh, to sing and he never sings. He speaks again, only it's in a foreign language! What? How? He speaks again "Who is like you O Lord... doing wonderful works."

The whole group are now down the stairs, all praising God. "Glory to God for all the wonderful things he has done." They are being surrounded by the crowd, Jews here for the festival from all over the world.

"Aren't those people Galileans? Then how can I understand them in my own language?" says one after another.

Matthew hears so many countries mentioned he is aston-ished: Iran, Turkey and Egypt; Libya and Italy; Crete and Greece.

The priests mock them. "They've been drinking, typical of

them, they are all drunk."

Peter goes over to his truck parked next to the doorway, now surrounded by reporters. He jumps in the back to gain a higher platform and addresses the crowd.

"These people are not drunk, it's only nine in the morning, not nine at night."

Everyone laughs.

"When do *we* ever get drunk?" asks James.

The camera crew scramble to get shots of Peter.

"Let me quote to you the prophet Joel; *And it shall be in the last days, God says. I shall pour out my spirit on all mankind. Your young men shall see visions and your old men shall dream dreams.* You were here, you saw the miracles, wonders and signs. Then you crucified Jesus on a cross. By the hands of Godless men he was put to death, but God raised him up, putting an end to the agony of death since it was impossible for him to be held in its power."

As he speaks, the crowd gets bigger and bigger. Everyone wants to hear what Peter has to say.

Matthew is once again pushed out of the way, this time by some other camera crew rushing to film Peter as he continues speaking. Matthew rubs his shoulder, don't you know who I was? He smiles to himself.

"Many saw him alive after death, including some of you right here. For as David said of the Christ...*I saw the Lord always in my presence; for he is at my right hand, so that I will not be shaken. Therefore my heart was glad and my tongue exulted; moreover my flesh will live in hope; you will not abandon my soul to hell, nor allow your holy one to undergo decay. You have made known to me the ways of life; you will make me full of gladness with your presence.* It was David who looked ahead to the resurrection of the Christ when he wrote *He was neither abandoned to hell nor his flesh decayed.* This Jesus, God raised up again, we are all here as witnesses..."

Peter turns, looking for the camera, staring straight at it, knowing this is going out live to the whole country, he finishes...

"Therefore, let all the house of Israel know for certain that God has made him both Lord and Christ, this Jesus whom *you* crucified."

I hoped you liked getting to know the twelve.
If you want to read more, there are deleted scenes,
authors notes and interviews with some of the characters on
my website.
thetwelve.co.uk